The Stonemason's Tale

MORE BY THIS AUTHOR

Historical Fiction

The Testament of Mariam
This Rough Ocean

The Chronicles of Christoval Alvarez

The Secret World of Christoval Alvarez
The Enterprise of England
The Portuguese Affair
Bartholomew Fair
Suffer the Little Children
Voyage to Muscovy
The Play's the Thing
That Time May Cease
The Lopez Affair

Oxford Medieval Mysteries

The Bookseller's Tale
The Novice's Tale
The Huntsman's Tale
The Merchant's Tale
The Troubadour's Tale

The Fenland Series

Flood
Betrayal

Contemporary Fiction

The Anniversary
The Travellers
A Running Tide

The Stonemason's Tale

Ann Swinfen

Shakenoak Press

for

Nikki & Pascal
With Much Love

Chapter One

Oxford, Spring 1354

The strange series of events which was to overwhelm the Queen's College began innocently enough, if noisily, shortly after dawn on the first day of March. I had stayed up late the previous evening, for Emma Thorgold had that afternoon brought me the first three gatherings of the book she was scribing and illuminating, consisting of the old stories I had persuaded my scrivener Walter Blunt to write down. I found myself so caught up in the tales, and so delighted by Emma's clever and witty drawings – which demanded careful scrutiny – that I let my candle burn out, and needs must grope about in the dark to light another. By then my sister Margaret and the children were long abed, and the dull gleam from the damped down kitchen fire was barely enough to enable me to find a fresh candle and a strike-a-light. By the time I was eventually settled in my bed chamber, the bell of St Peter-in-the-East had already tolled midnight.

Now I awoke with a start and a pounding heart to the sound of shouting from the street. Although my bed chamber overlooks the garden at the back of the house – it is my sister's room which faces on to the High – the clamour was so loud that it reached even to where I was burrowed under my feather quilt, still in need of more sleep.

The men's shouts were augmented by a shrill and

angry horse's neigh, and then a crash, with the accompanying sound of splintering timber.

I groaned and pulled my pillow over my head, but it was not enough to shut out the noise of a growing quarrel in the street. As my wits slowly began to return, I realised the source of the trouble. Today was marked down for the start of fresh building work at the neighbouring college. Queen's College had been founded nearly thirteen years before, when Queen Philippa's chaplain, Robert de Eglesfield, had begun to buy up a scattering of small properties near us on the High, and also along Hammer Hall Lane, both those opposite to St Peter's church and to the north of it. Perhaps the founder had not been able to persuade enough patrons to invest in the venture, for the handful of Fellows had been obliged to live and work in just a few of the buildings on this nearside of the lane, while most of the property on the far side had remained derelict.

I had arrived in Oxford as a student soon after that first tentative founding of Queen's, so that I had watched the college growing slowly ever since. It seemed that the cluster of hovels north of the church were in so perilous a state that Queen's had not the funds to develop them, but the main site, two doors away from my shop on the High, was beginning to grow into something resembling a college, though it would be a long time before it matched the grander establishments, like Merton.

Strictly speaking, the correct term for the group of buildings was a 'hall', even at Merton or Exeter, while it was the body of Fellows who formed the 'collegium' or 'college', but of late people had begun to speak of the larger establishment – buildings and people together – as a college. These more permanent establishments were governed by a Provost or Warden, together with a body of Fellows, who were guided by a book of rules laid down by the Founder. The smaller halls, like my friend Jordain's Hart Hall, were run by more junior academics, Regent Masters, and provided lodgings for the undergraduate students. Both their incomes and their permanence were more chancy than the colleges', which possessed endowments of land and other properties. Queen's had aspirations to rival the larger colleges one day, but rumour whispered that despite some benefactions from the king's family, its future was not quite secure.

However, the new building work suggested that, for the moment at least, the college had the confidence to build in stone.

The two small cottages next to my shop belonged to Queen's, but were leased out for the moment, one to an alewife and one to a ribbon weaver. Fortunately, many years ago my father-in-law had purchased our shop and house (a double messuage and burgage plot) outright, so there was no danger that we would be gobbled up, should the college ever have coin enough.

Work on the college buildings had stalled during the Great Pestilence, and the Founder, Robert de Eglesfield, had himself perished in that same catastrophe, five years ago now. He had been replaced as Provost by William de Muskham for no more than a year, for he had soon moved on to more distinguished positions, although he remained a generous benefactor of the college, as he had been from the outset. The present Provost, John de Hotham, had taken matters in hand. The cost of labour was high, now that so many had died in the plague, and it was hard to come by the skilled stonemasons who could construct buildings of the quality every Oxford college aspired to. Surely de Hotham must have persuaded some rich patron to support Queen's with a grant of coin or the gift of a property which would provide a permanent income for the college. De Hotham himself had told me that his first task was to build the college chapel.

'Ever since our Founder's time, Master Elyot,' he said, poised elegantly just inside the door of my shop. 'we have been obliged to make use of one of the old houses on the site as a chapel, a building hardly better than the cottages we have allocated to the cook and the porter. It was never meant to serve for more than a year or two. The disasters which overtook us all in the years of the plague meant that we have not been able to replace it until now. I plan to build a short nave in addition to the chancel and choir, with north and south transepts. It will be a cruciform chapel, though not of great size.'

'I believe your Fellows have little room for themselves or for their teaching,' I commented, recalling some complaints I had heard from those same Fellows, who were regular customers at my shop.

'Our college is dedicated above all to the study of theology,' he said sternly. 'It is most fitting that we should have a chapel worthy for the worship of our Lord God. In time we shall build a dining hall which can also be used for teaching. And at present our collection of books is housed in another of the old cottages, but I am planning, eventually, to build a library.'

His eyes gleamed in anticipation. I knew that Philip Olney was fretting over the delayed plans for Merton's library. Which college would win the race? Almost certainly Merton. But Provost de Hotham had the right of it: the chapel for Queen's must be built first.

I bowed in acknowledgement of the Provost's words, wondering whether the rest of the Fellows had had any voice in the choice of the new work, or whether this strong-willed man made all the decisions first, and informed his colleagues afterwards.

To do him justice, de Hotham had warned me of the date when the work would start, and apologised for the unpleasantness we should be obliged to endure. Then he bowed stiffly and left the shop. I groaned again when I thought of it now. 'Unpleasantness' hardly did justice to what we must suffer while the building work was carried on. Every time my shop door on to the High Street was opened, clouds of stone dust and sawdust would billow in, clinging to my scriveners' wet ink and infiltrating even the pages of the books.

The alewife next door would have her goods

contaminated. Probably even the ribbon weaver would be affected. Moreover, if the wind blew from the east or north-east, the grit would be carried across the street and into the bread ovens of John Baker and the milk churns and cheese presses of Mary Coomber.

As a man of God and a theologian, perhaps John de Hotham had a mind above such considerations, but the rest of us must get our living however we might.

I could see that I had no chance of further sleep now, so I threw on my old house gown over my night shift and padded on bare feet out of my chamber. The door of my sister Margaret's room stood open and I could see that she was already gone down to the kitchen. I crossed to the window, flung open the shutters and leaned out.

The source of the noise was plain to see. Beyond the ribbon weaver's house, a passageway had been made through to the main grounds of the college by knocking down a small unoccupied cottage, which had been trembling on the verge of collapse for months. It was one of the many properties which Queen's had been able to buy up cheaply after the plague. The purpose of this passage, I assumed, was to create an easier way to carry in the building materials from the High, instead of trundling them up the lane and in through the gatehouse, one of the few substantial college buildings so far constructed.

Outside this opening I could see a group of men standing and arguing around a team of horses, who were harnessed to the kind of sled used to drag stone down the hill from Headington quarry, then across the Cherwell by the East Bridge and along the High. It is a precarious business at the best of times, for the rough hewn stone is fearsomely heavy and awkwardly balanced. Besides, after the deep snows of the previous winter, which had only just thawed, the low lying ground near the Cherwell had been flooded for the last fortnight, leaving a layer of slippery mud everywhere.

Clearly this first load of stone had reached its destination safely, but perhaps a sudden stop, or some carelessness on the part of the driver and his mate, had caused the load to shift. It had crashed to the ground, frightening the horses and smashing part of the sled. The argument – as far as I could judge from the gestures – was about who was responsible for the problem, and who was going to move the stone into the grounds of the college.

I sighed. This beginning did not augur well for what we must endure for the following weeks.

Once I had dressed, I made my way down to the kitchen, where Margaret, grim faced, was sliding her loaves into the bread oven.

'So it has begun,' I said.

'Aye.' She pushed a loose strand of hair out of her face and tucked it under her wimple. 'Good weather at last, yet I dare not open the door for air. Even here at the back we shall find the dust blowing in.'

'Take advantage while you may,' I said. 'They are but bringing in the stone. No cutting or chiselling yet. That is when the real trouble will begin.'

'You probably have the right of it,' she said. 'Do you open the door, then. But what will it be like in the heat of summer?'

'Unpleasant.'

I opened the kitchen door and took a step outside. The air was cool and fresh, a balm after the heat of the bread oven. There were still snowdrops clustered about the base of the trees in our small orchard, and patches of purple crocuses showed along the wall of my new stable.

'Better?' I said, turning back to the kitchen.

'Aye.' She slipped her arm through mine and breathed deeply. 'How long do you suppose this work at the college will last?'

I shrugged. 'The Provost did not say. Till the building of the chapel is complete, I suppose. Or at least until the money runs out.'

'Weeks,' she said bitterly.

'It will hit Mary hard,' I said, 'over at the dairy. And John Baker.'

'Well, I suppose we small folk must simply endure. The grand scholars must have their fine stone buildings.'

'Not very grand at Queen's, I think. And I daresay the ordinary Fellows might have been rather more pleased about better rooms for themselves, and a large hall for teaching, instead of being crowded hugger-mugger, no better than in one of the student halls. Most of them are lodged in those ancient cottages that lie up behind the houses along the High and beyond the gatehouse on the lane. They barely have more room than Jordain has at Hart Hall.'

'Perhaps the Fellows of Queen's have minds above such things.'

I laughed. 'I doubt it.'

I crossed the kitchen to the passage which led through to my shop.

'Do you not want to break your fast?' she said.

'I shall be back by the time the bread is baked,' I said. 'I am going to remove all the best books from the shop and put them in the coffer in my chamber. I cannot risk the damage they will suffer from the stone dust. And I must warn Walter and Roger to keep their ink bottles covered at all times, or we shall have grit in the ink. I wish there was some way I could keep the dust out of the shop, but with the door opening straight on to the street, I cannot see how.'

'You could pin an old blanket over the door,' she said. 'Your customers must needs push their way through, but surely they would understand. It would provide some protection.'

'Aye, an excellent idea. After breakfast, let us see what we can contrive.'

Alysoun and Rafe were excited about the activities beginning at the college. Alysoun must always investigate anything new in Oxford, and where Alysoun went, Rafe would follow. She would also draw John Baker's son Jonathan into any mischief she planned. From long experience, I knew I must take a firm stand from the outset.

'You are to stay well away from the building works,' I said, in my sternest voice at breakfast time. 'They are dangerous places even for grown men, and they are not a playground for children.'

'But I have never seen how a chapel is built,' she said, in a tone of sweet reason. 'And the carving in the Oxford colleges and churches is so beautiful. I want to see how it is made. You always want me to learn about new things.'

'Certainly,' I said, 'but not by getting under the feet of the stonemasons and carpenters. Once the work is begun, I will speak to the master mason, or the college Fellow who is in charge of the work, and ask if I may bring you both, *with me*, to watch a little of the carving. But that will not be for some time yet. First they will be putting up scaffolding and building the rough work on the walls, before they continue with the finer work. You must wait awhile.'

'What is scaffolding?' Rafe asked, through a mouthful of bread and honey.

'Manners,' Margaret said automatically, although I could see that her mind was on other things.

'When you are making a tall building,' I said, 'you can use ladders for some of it, but mostly you need something sturdier to stand on while you are moving heavy stones about, and buckets of mortar. Scaffolding is a wooden framework holding wicker hurdles laid flat, for the men to walk on. You know the kind of hurdles, Rafe. Like the ones Cousin Edmond's shepherd Godfrid uses to pen the sheep. But laid flat instead of standing upright.'

He frowned. 'I don't see how it would stay up.'

'I think they build some of the timbers of the wooden framework into the walls as they go. Then the wall holds everything steady.'

I hoped I had this right. Why do children never stop asking questions?

'But–' he was still frowning, 'but then the . . . the scaffolding would still be there when they finish the building. And it isn't.'

'Oh, I think they just pull it out of the holes in the wall when they finish,' I said carelessly, as if I knew what I was talking about. 'Or else they saw off the timbers close to the stone of the walls. I've seen the scaffolding holes in the walls of Oxford castle. I will show them to you some day.'

Rafe opened his mouth again. He was getting as bad as Alysoun.

'In any case,' I said hastily, 'we can watch what they do at Queen's. Or ask one of the stonemasons. Now I am going to fix this blanket your aunt has found over the door of the shop, to keep the stone dust out. I promise you, it will not be a great deal of fun for us once they do start cutting the stone.'

I nailed the blanket to the lintel above the shop door, to the surprise of my two scriveners, who arrived when I was perched on a stool, hammering in the last nail.

'Ah,' Walter said, enlightened, 'the stone dust.'

'Do you reckon it will be very bad?' Roger asked.

'I do.' I replaced the stool behind my desk. 'And be sure to keep your ink stoppered all the time you are not using it. I fear we will we be having a difficult time.'

'That blanket should help,' Walter said, 'if it does not deter our customers.'

'I shall put a notice in the window,' I said. 'Explaining.'

I sat at my desk at once, to write the notice while I remembered.

The blanket was long enough to reach to the bottom of the door, but it was much too wide, so I had been obliged to double part of it over, which made it even more awkward for customers trying to push their way through. However, Margaret was unwilling for me to cut the blanket down to size, so they must just grow accustomed to it.

My first few customers were students arriving soon after the earliest lectures of the morning to buy quills and to rent *peciae* of the texts recommended by their tutors. They regarded the draped blanket as a source of crude raillery, but I was prepared to endure that if it helped to protect my stock. Hard on their heels, Jordain Brinkylsworth pushed his way into the shop.

'Are you under siege?' He looked around at the empty shelves, which now held nothing but the cheaper sort of greyish paper used by the students, a stock of quills, and the usual *peciae*. As most of the latter had passed through the hands of several students, they could come to little harm from stone dust.

'As you see,' I said. 'I have stored my valuable stock out of danger.'

I had left a few of the cheaper books on display on the shelves inside the window where I placed my secondhand stock. There needed something to show that I was a bookseller.

'If you are hoping to keep the stone dust out of the shop, you had best cover that as well.'

He nodded towards the open window, where I had lowered the horizontal shutter which formed a counter used by some shopkeepers, though not by me.

'I know,' I said, 'but I must be able to show that the shop is open. Besides, we need the light. I cannot afford to burn candles all day long. Whenever anyone comes through the door, it creates a draught, which will bring in the dust. I hope there will be less trouble from the window, except perhaps on very windy days.'

He smiled sympathetically. 'Trying times. Although it will be good for Queen's to have a fine stone-built chapel. It must enhance Oxford's prestige, over the Other Place.'

I grinned. Ever since a group of Fellows and students had decamped to the swamps of Cambridgeshire after one of the battles with the townsfolk many years ago, there had been rivalry between England's two universities. We knew we were the oldest and best, but it was as well to remind Cambridge from time to time.

'I was hoping to look at the parts of that new book of tales,' he said. 'The one Emma is working on. Or must it be kept hidden away?'

'I will fetch it. At least they have not begun cutting the stone yet, so it can come to no harm.'

When I laid the first gatherings of the new book on my desk, we sat down together to look at it, and I beckoned to Walter to come over and see for the first time what Emma had drawn to illustrate his tales. He grinned shyly as we turned over the pages.

'Aye, the lady has the sense of it, does she not?' he said.

Out of the corner of my eye, I saw that Roger was pretending to hide his annoyance under the guise of indifference. Until I had obtained the book of hours Emma had made while still a novice at Godstow Abbey, Roger had considered himself a master of illumination. Confronted by Emma's art, he had been forced to recognise a greater skill. He kept his thoughts mostly to himself, but he needed to be given demanding work, lest he sulk.

'When will this book be finished, do you know?' Jordain said.

'I have told Emma to take as long as she needs,' I said. 'Her next task will be the book of troubadour songs, and I am still working on my poor attempts to render the Occitan words into something better than clumsy English. I have even taken some instruction in Occitan from a Fellow of Exeter. I should be glad if you would cast your eye over my efforts. Then, after Emma has finished the complete troubadour book that we plan, I shall have Roger prepare the shorter one for Lady Amilia. He is quite a favourite of hers.'

I had not turned to Roger, but I could tell he was listening. There was a palpable relaxation of the tension in the air.

'And do you not plan copies of Walter's book as well?' Jordain said.

'Aye, certainly. We will keep this full collection for customers to see, so they may choose to order a complete copy, or only part.'

'And you will do the same with the song book? As well as making copies of that compilation Roger put together last year from those old hero stories?'

I laughed. 'All of those, and selling secondhand books, *and* the usual work of providing *peciae* for the students. Perhaps I may need to hire another scrivener.'

'As long as I do not spend every day copying the student texts,' Walter said mournfully. 'After all these years, I think I might write them with my eyes closed.'

'Perhaps you and Roger might work together on the copies,' I said. 'With you scribing and drawing the borders, Roger painting the large illuminations.'

Walter had a fine copyist's hand, better than Roger's, but no pretensions as an illuminator. However, he could draw a delicate border of flowers, leaves, and tendrils. Indeed, I could myself.

'You are becoming quite a merchant, with all your plans,' Jordain said, amused.

'Never that. The production of books is too slow ever to rival a rich trade like Peter Winchingham's, buying and selling bolts of cloth woven by other men's hands. Come, I will put these parts of the new book safely away and you may look over my poor efforts at words for the songs. We will leave Roger and Walter in peace.'

I turned to Walter, who had resumed the tedious work of copying *peciae*.

'You may call me if the shop becomes too busy.'

I put my note of explanation about the blanket just inside the window which opened on to the High Street, propping it up in front of the display of secondhand books, and took Jordain up to my chamber to examine my work on the troubadour songs.

The Queen's College was not alone in having building work undertaken, now that the last of the winter weather had passed, although March can be a chancy month, often very cold and damp in Oxford. Our two rivers, the very reason for the town's existence, have their disadvantages.

And our low-lying position means we are often beset with mists and fogs as well as floods. However, this year the first week in March seemed to promise a brief period of fine weather, so I had sent for the thatcher to roof the new stable I had put up three months before. He arrived just as Jordain was leaving.

'Aye, Maister Elyot,' Eddi Thatcher said, 'we'll soon have that done for you, me and the lad. We'll leave them wooden shingles in place and lay the thatch over. Give you a good warm roof. Yon horse will be snug as an alderman, you'll see.'

We were inside the stable, so that Eddi could check that the temporary wooden roof met with his approval, and my horse Rufus had paused with a mouthful of hay half chewed, watching us with interest. The work on the roof would prove somewhat noisy, but he was a placid fellow and unlikely to be disturbed.

Eddi led me outside and scrutinised the roof from all angles.

'It will do fine. We'll lay a good layer of thatch over. I can start this afternoon, if you will,' he said. 'I'll bring a load of straw along now, and we'll be back after dinner.'

I nodded. 'Best if you can get to it quickly,' I said. 'They are building the new chapel at Queen's. For now they are just bringing in the stone, but once they start cutting, you will be breathing in their dust, up there on the roof.'

He made a face. 'Cannot see why these colleges must build with stone and roof with slate. Timber and plaster walls, with a roof of fine warm thatch, has been good enough for all men save kings, centuries past. Why not be satisfied with that?'

I hoped that he was not condemning my own shop and house. My father-in-law had built them of the same materials as the colleges, mindful of the danger of fire, since his stock was books.

I supposed, now that the university had begun to acquire so much of the land in Oxford, it must mean less work for the thatchers, although there were private houses enough still to be thatched, and their thatch renewed every few years to keep it in good heart. However, every craftsman must make his complaint about hard times.

Eddi duly delivered the straw, and now Margaret had bits of straw and fragments of chaff blowing in the back door, so that I found it wise to keep well out of her way, spending the afternoon while the thatchers got to work seated at my desk, making the improvements Jordain had suggested to my translations of the troubadours' songs. As if summoned up by the words of one of the songs we had heard during the Christmas festivities at Leighton-under-Wychwood, Emma came into the shop halfway through the afternoon.

'Good day to you, Walter,' she said, laying down a sheaf of parchment on his desk. 'Tell me whether you care for these illuminations. Some of the creatures in your tales have called for much thought on my part. You will see that I have just sketched several in lightly, until I have your nod of approval.'

She turned to Roger. 'Are you near finished your newest book of the Arthur tales? I think I have a customer for you.'

'Good day, Emma,' I said, trying to keep any hurt from my voice. Then spoiled it by saying, 'Do I not merit a greeting?'

She eyed me coolly.

'I had hoped I might hear from you what you thought of the pages I left with you yesterday.'

'I sat up till midnight reading them,' I protested. 'They are wonderful. I was coming to St Mildred Street this evening to see you, but it has been a difficult day.'

'I did observe the notice in the window,' she said, sounding somewhat mollified, 'and the blanket over the door. They have started work at Queen's, I see. There is a cart coming along behind me from Carfax, loaded with stone. I thought they would use the Headington quarry.'

'That is for the rough work,' Roger said, 'the

Headington stone. For the ashlar dressings and all the fine work, they will use Taynton stone. That is what you have seen coming from Carfax.'

'Taynton?'

'It is a village near Burford,' I said. 'Taynton stone is finer than Headington.'

'So they are bringing both sorts of stone in already,' Walter said. 'Seems they mean to press ahead. Someone must have given them a tidy sum for the work. Several of the stonemasons were in Tackley's Inn at dinner time.'

'Aye.' Roger sounded grumpy. 'They may not be cutting the stone yet, but they shed the dust from their very clothes and hair, wherever they go. I've no wish to have my pottage sprinkled with their droppings.'

'It might add a fine new flavour.' Emma grinned at him. She seemed to have recovered her good humour. 'I do not suppose they can help the detritus of their craft, any more than we can.'

She spread out her fingers in front of her for us to inspect. As well as the stains of black and red ink we all bore, there was a rainbow of coloured paints, and even, here and there, a glint of gold leaf.

'At least we do not shed our materials into Roger's pottage,' I said.

I turned to Walter. 'Did you speak to the stonemasons? Did they say when they will begin the cutting?'

'From the way they were talking, it will be within the next day or two. They want to make the best of the good weather. I had a few words with the master mason. Robert Hanbury, he is hight. Seems there are two kinds of masons working for him. That I didn't know before.'

'Two kinds?' Emma said, pulling up a stool and sitting down. 'Three, surely. Masters, journeymen, and apprentices.'

'That too, I suppose. But it seems they're paid different.'

Walter assumed a knowledgeable air. 'The ones that

do the skilled work – carved window jambs, tracery, gargoyles and such – they are paid a regular daily wage and take what time they please over the work. Then there are what they called the "banker masons". They are paid by the number of stones they cut and dress. Mark them with their sign, and get their money according. So they are anxious for good weather. Poor weather – no work – no pay.'

''Tis an odd name,' Emma said. 'Banker. As if they were in charge of the royal finances.'

'Nothing so grand. Their workbenches are called banks.' He thought for a moment. 'Then he said something about "setters" as well. I suppose they would be the men who set the stones in place for the walls, but I don't know how they are paid.'

'It seems we shall all be learning a great deal,' she said. 'Perhaps I shall make a pictures of the masons in one of my initial letters.'

'Alysoun is determined to worm her way in amongst the building work,' I said, gloomily. 'I needs must keep a sharp eye on her. We all must. Else she will be tripping them up or taking a tumble over the heaps of stone or slicing off a finger with one of their chisels.'

Emma laughed. 'You should be glad she has such an enquiring mind.'

'Aye. If it did not so often land her in trouble.'

'We shall all watch out for her,' Walter said seriously. 'At the moment they have put up no barrier across that opening they have knocked through to the High. Anyone may wander in and out of the college as easily as they please. Including the children.'

'I am surprised the Provost is not worried about thieves,' I said.

Roger grinned. 'Everyone in Oxford knows that Queen's is a poor college. Why should any thief waste his time on them? And no one living there but a handful of tedious old scholars, no one for the town lads to pick a fight with.'

'I am not sure the Fellows are all of them old,' I said.

'Will the stonemasons and carpenters be living in the college during the work?' Emma asked. 'No one would venture in there with so many men about.'

Walter shook his head. 'According to the master mason, there is only one partly derelict cottage a few of them will use. He stays at Tackley's, along with the master carpenter. Others have found what lodgings they can in the town. They have already put up a shelter where they can do the fine work. A "lodge", he called it. While the weather holds, the apprentices will sleep there, on the ground. Seems there will be a fair crowd of them.'

'That is some relief,' I said. 'The more hands to the work, the sooner we shall be quit of their noise and dust. Let us hope they are quick workers. Or else that the money runs out.'

'For shame!' Emma said. 'Shall you not be pleased to have a fine new chapel almost next door?'

'We have St Peter's,' I said. 'Queen's could have worshipped there, for it is no more than a step across the lane from their gatehouse, but it seems every college must have its own chapel, each one trying to outdo the others.'

'Are you not busy about some building work yourself?' she said, with a mischievous glint in her eye.

'Aye.' I got up. 'Come. Let us see how the thatching progresses.'

Eddi had made a good start. The bottom course of thatch already reached about a third of the way along the nearside of the stable roof. Not altogether to my surprise, I found Alysoun, Rafe, and Jonathan Baker watching – and possibly hindering – the work.

'Look!' Alysoun held up a flexible wooden peg. 'This is a *spar*,' she said, importantly. 'It holds down a bundle of the thatching straw. See, there.' She pointed. 'Then the next course hides the spars, all the way up to the top.'

'To the ridge,' Eddi called over his shoulder from the top of a ladder, where he was banging the next bundle of straw into place.

'The *ridge*,' Alysoun amended.

'I hope they are not being a trouble to you, Eddi,' I called.

'Nay, maister. As long as they keep away from the ladders.'

Eddi's lad heaved a bundle of straw on to his shoulder and scampered up the second ladder, with a certain show of bravado for the children, I thought. I grinned. Perhaps it was also for Emma's benefit.

'You'd best shut them hens away, though,' Eddi called. 'Came near to treading on one of them.'

'They'll be looking for any stray bits of grain. Come,' I said to the children. 'Help me round them up and shut them in the hen house.'

The hens were in a skittish mood, so that it took some time for us to herd them into the hen house and out of danger, where they could be heard protesting at thus being shut up early. By then the children had lost interest and taken our dog Rowan and Jonathan's dog Digger off to the Bakers' house, no doubt in the hope that Jonathan's father might have a leftover ill-shaped bun or two for them.

Back in the shop, Emma sat down with Walter to discuss the drawings she had brought for him to see, and since Roger was working hard to finish the latest copy of the hero tales, it was left to me to deal with the customers. There is always something of a rush in the late afternoon, when both students and Fellows suddenly realise that they may find themselves short of paper or ink or quills before the shop opened again in the morning.

I know almost all my customers by sight, and most by name, too, as well as their colleges and halls, what stage the students have reached in the *trivium* or *quadrivium*, and what particular branch of knowledge the older scholars are pursuing. Sometimes a new face will appear. That was how I had come to meet the merchant Peter Winchingham the previous year. While he was attending St Frideswide's Fair, he had come looking for my father-in-law, whom he had known in the past.

The new faces were most likely to appear at the beginning of the Michaelmas term when the latest young students arrived in Oxford, or else at times like the fair, when the town was full of strangers, some of whom were book lovers. I was surprised, therefore, to see a strange young man fingering the secondhand books on a day like this, in mid-term, when there was no occasion for visitors to be in town.

I suppose he was about eighteen or nineteen, of an age to have taken his Master of Arts, although I was sure I would have seen him before now if he had been a student. He was difficult to place. Well dressed. Better dressed than most of the students. From the look on his face, he clearly had a poor opinion of the secondhand books.

'May I be of service?' I asked politely.

'You are Master Elyot? I understood that you dealt in books of quality, not just such as these . . .' he flicked a finger toward the display shelf. He had good reason. The stock was much picked over at the moment.

'We are expecting problems from the building work at the neighbouring college,' I said, trying to hide a small surge of annoyance. 'It has been necessary to move the books of quality to a safe place. What would interest you?'

'Oh, for the moment . . . do not trouble yourself. You will be closing soon. I will come back.' He looked around vaguely. 'Perhaps a book of hours. Or I am told you have secular books? Tales of Arthur and Robin Hood?'

'We do. My scrivener, Master Pigot, is completing one at the moment.'

'I shall come back.'

He was suddenly decisive. He bowed briskly, and left, pushing the hanging blanket aside impatiently.

'What an odd fellow,' I said.

'Doubt he'll be back,' Walter said.

'Aye,' I said. 'I cannot think what he wanted. I am sure he will not be back.'

But I was wrong.

Chapter Two

Three days later, I woke to the unpleasant sensation of grit crunching between my teeth. It had been unseasonably warm the previous night and I had left the shutters on my bed chamber window open. As I sat up, a gossamer veil of dust floated up from the bedclothes, billowed in a soft cloud and settled again. I sneezed. I must have slept with my mouth open, for the same dust lay on my tongue like a foul taste, as well as the coarser grit lodged in my teeth. Already, barely past dawn, the stonemasons had begun their cutting and a brisk east wind had carried the fine stone dust into the room.

Muttering curses, I fastened the shutters and dressed in the half light which filtered around them. Down in the kitchen, I found Margaret laying out our breakfast, even more grim faced than on the day the first stone had arrived. There was no need for either of us to comment. She had kept the door into the garden closed, but I carried a cup of small ale outside – shutting the door behind me – where I swilled out my mouth and spat out as much of the grit as I could dislodge from my teeth. Eddi had finished thatching the near side of the stable roof and made a start on the far side, which entailed taking his ladders and straw through the ale wife's cottage next door. By way of apology I had purchased some of Aldusa Tranter's ale, although its quality did not match Margaret's. Good enough to rinse out my mouth, though I would not tell her so! I could hear Eddi talking to his lad now, and the creak of the ladder as he climbed up to start work. He would have an unpleasant time of it, up there, in the direct line of the wind-borne dust.

Sometimes it is the trivial annoyances which cause the worst tempers. Although the insinuating dust could not be compared to a disaster like fire or flood, it was a constant irritation, both to Margaret in her kitchen and to my scriveners and me in the shop. Fortunately, Roger had completed the book of hero tales, for he found it impossible to work on the large areas of colour in his illuminations when at any moment a scattering of dust could ruin hours of work. To put an end to his complaints, I sent him off with his finished pages to the workshop of the bookbinder, Henry Stalbroke, with an additional commission to buy a supply of fresh parchment from Dafydd Hewlyn while he was on Bookbinders Island. Walter and I worked grimly on, in no mood for friendly chat.

We had hardly any customers, for the shop was not very welcoming, stripped down as it was, and those who came did not linger. I knew that Jordain had a full day's teaching, and Emma would be working on the next part of Walter's book. Both showed the good sense to keep their distance from the Queen's building works. Our only diversion was the arrival of the alewife Aldusa from next door.

Flushed and angry, she came surging through the shop, on her way to unburden herself of her grievances to Margaret. Her voice carried through even to the shop.

'Bits of straw I was prepared for, Margaret, but Eddi is as careful as any thatcher may be, and he will be quick and neat with his work. No more than a few days, surely. But these masons! No warning! Could they not have told us when they would begin their pestilential sawing? I had a fresh brew in my two gallon pot, for Tackley's had bespoken two gallons for tomorrow, and, before I know what is afoot, filth and dust are coating the surface of the ale like grease on cold gravy.'

'Could you not skim it off?' Margaret did not sound

very convinced.

Aldusa gave a snort. 'Huh! With the coarser bits already sunk to the bottom? The whole batch is ruined. If I still kept a pig . . . pigs will devour anything. I once had one that seized a pair of hose drying on my lavender bush and ate them before I could seize them back.'

'I remember.' Margaret paused. 'Edric Crowmer keeps a pig behind his wine shop.'

Both women burst into laughter.

'Perhaps he will give me a few farthings for it,' Aldusa said. ''Twould make a change for the porker from drinking the lees of the wine.'

Walter looked at me and grinned. Edric's pigs were always cup-shotten. This early in the year, the vintner's pig would be a youngling, the last one having been slaughtered at Michaelmas.

'Perhaps Aldusa's small ale will be kinder to the piglet than the wine lees,' I said. 'That is more suited to a pig of greater age and discretion.'

'I am glad she does not plan to pass the spoiled ale off to Tackley's,' Walter said. 'Else Roger and I would be obliged to dine elsewhere.'

Aldusa seemed to have grown calmer, having shared her grievances. Her voice was milder, though she had always had a good carrying cry.

'Poor little Aelyth Walker,' she said. 'She is half blind at the best of times, leaning over with her nose almost in that ribbon loom of hers. She came weeping to me, not able to see her threads or her shuttle, the dust in her eyes turning them red as raspberries. I helped her wash out the dust, but I doubt she'll be able to weave until this building work is over with. She's the nearest to it. Even worse than for us.'

That could be serious, I knew. The ribbon weaver always trembled on the edge of poverty, for, although her work was beautiful, it was slow, and it sold for no more than a few pennies, poor recompense for the hours she worked on it.

Aldusa and Margaret spent some time commiserating with each other, the alewife eventually leaving, to attempt another brewing behind sealed doors and windows, just as Roger returned.

As the two scriveners set off for their dinner, Walter told Roger of their near miss with polluted ale.

'She should have brought some over to the inn,' Roger said, 'and served it to those masons. Let them see the trouble they are causing.'

'You could explain to them,' I said. 'Ask, could they warn the cottagers when they will be cutting. And could they do their cutting under cover, so less of the dust would trouble the neighbours.'

Walter shrugged. 'I went and had a look at the work yesterday,' he said. 'Invitation of the master mason, who's a polite enough fellow. This "lodge" they talk about is not even a shed. 'Tis nobbut a canvas nailed over a timber frame, open on all sides. It keeps off the rain, but I suppose they don't want to work in an enclosed workshop. They'd do nothing but eat and drink stone dust all day long.'

'True enough.' I was curious. 'Have they begun building yet?'

'Nay,' Walter said. 'They have laid down the outline on the ground, marking it out with powdered lime. Very simple tools they use – knotted string for the lengths of the walls, pegs and strings for their corners.'

'The magical three, four, five?' I said.

Sire Raymond had taught me that triangle when I was about four years old. He had made a game of it.

'Aye. And the carpenters are making patterns in wood, to hold up the arches, they said. And cutting the timbers for the scaffolding. Oh, aye, and they have dug a pit for making the lime mortar.'

It sounded as though the work was proceeding quite briskly. Perhaps we would not have to endure too many weeks of misery.

They went off to Tackley's Inn, and I sat down with Margaret and the children to a somewhat bland vegetable pottage.

'I could not add herbs,' Margaret said defensively, before we could complain. 'Everything in the garden will be smothered.'

'I hope the hens will not come to harm,' I said.

'I have kept them shut away, but they will not care for it. We'll soon see a drop in the eggs they lay.'

'Rafe and me are going over to Jonathan's garden this afternoon,' Alysoun said. 'It isn't so bad there, though Master Baker has to keep his window on the High closed and he fears there will be grit in his bread.'

I saw Margaret open her mouth to make some comment on John Baker's bread, but I gave her a warning look. John's bread might not be as good as hers, for he must bake in large batches, and not always with the finest flour, but any criticism she made might be carried by the children to the baker's ears, and he was a good friend.

When Walter and Roger returned after their dinner, they were accompanied by another man. It took no great effort to recognise him as the master mason, Robert Hanbury, of whom they had spoken. All masons, even the masters, carry about with them the imprint of their trade, as easy to read as a book. Every crease on face or knuckles becomes permanently engrained with the very finest stone dust. It roots itself in their hair, so that even the younger men seem grey pelted. However much they wash, and I am sure they wash as often as any man, they cannot rid themselves of this tracery of stone. Perhaps the dust itself becomes a kind of mortar, clinging to every crevice in the human form.

Robert Hanbury was maybe forty years of age, or a little older, a square, thick-set man, quiet and confident of demeanour.

'Master Elyot,' he said, bowing, 'I apologise for the trouble we are causing you. I understand your work is affected and you have had to take steps to protect your stock.'

He looked around at the bare shelves and the blanket

over the door.

I shrugged. 'I understand that there is little you can do about it. We will manage as best we can, but others are suffering worse than we. The ribbon weaver, whose cottage is next to that opening you have made through to the High, and the alewife next door to us.'

He grinned. 'I have met Goodwife Tranter. She stormed in late this morning and told me exactly what she thought of me, my men, and my ancestors for several generations back.'

'Your dust ruined two gallons of her new ale,' I said mildly. 'It will be difficult for her to sustain the loss. And the little ribbon weaver – she is elderly and frail, and cannot work for the dust affecting her sight.'

'I will speak to the Fellow who is overseeing the building,' he said. 'Perhaps he will be willing to pay her some compensation.'

Walter gave a snort. 'Take care to make sure it is compensation and not an insult. You remember that slater, Nicholas?'

'The one who fell from the roof at Queen's, about two years ago? Aye, I remember. Four pence, was it, they gave him?'

'Aye. Not much for a broken leg which kept him from work for weeks, and 'twas the fault of the college. He wanted to put up scaffolding. They said a ladder would be good enough, but it wasn't.'

'Well, I shall do my best for the weaver,' Hanbury said.

He turned to go, then paused.

'You have not had any thefts of late, Master Elyot?'

'Thefts? Nay. Except for the occasional student who tries to pocket a handful of quills, or slip a *pecia* under his cotte when he thinks we are not looking. We soon get to know the ones who are light fingered.'

'A *pecia*? I never heard of such a thing.'

I picked up the portion of Aristotle's *Ethics* which Walter had been copying that morning.

'Short sections of the student texts, which they borrow and copy for themselves,' I said. 'Since few of them can afford to buy whole books. It is the backbone of my business. But why do you ask about thefts?'

He shrugged. 'It may be nothing, but a few things have gone missing – a couple of chisels, one very fine one, its owner's pride and joy. Three mallets – not valuable, but leaving us short, so that the carpenters must make new ones when they should be working on the centrings.'

I frowned. 'Centrings?'

It seemed that we spoke two different languages.

'The wooden patterns, with a curved top, on which we build the arches. They hold all in place till the mortar dries. I have no need of them yet, but I like to have everything well in hand before it is required. These thefts are no more than petty pilfering, but it will cause us delays. I thought perhaps some local thief might have been visiting our neighbours as well as us.'

'It is very easy to enter the college now,' Roger said. 'It used to be – before you knocked down that cottage for a passage through – that the only entrance was by way of the gatehouse in Hammer Hall Lane, where they have a porter, and a locked gate at night. Now anyone who wishes can walk in from the High.'

'Ah, well, the college told me Oxford was an honest place nowadays and no one would steal from us. For the last few years I have been working elsewhere, though I am an Oxford man, recently returned. I was going to block the passageway at night, but they said there was no need. I shall do so now.'

'Aye,' I said. 'Best do so. Oxford is no better and no worse than any other town for crime, although we have our own particular form in the warfare which breaks out from time to time between the students and the lads of the town. You'll know about that, though it is not likely to trouble you. But,' I added, with some feeling, 'anything which may delay your work should be prevented.'

He laughed. 'I promise you we shall do our best,

Master Elyot. At least the weather is set fine for the moment. I had not thought Provost de Hotham would want us to begin the work in Lent, but he was most insistent. It seems some wealthy patron from the north country has made them a gift to finance part of the building, and he will be coming to Oxford in a month's time or thereabouts. The provost hopes that we will be far enough ahead with the work that he may make a show of it.'

'Queen's does have a connection with the north,' I said. 'The Founder came from Cumberland, and, although admission of Fellows – and the poor boys who are supported by the college – is supposed to be open to all, preference is always given to those from Cumberland or Westmorland.'

'These thefts of yours,' Walter said slowly, 'you should report them to our deputy sheriff, Cedric Walden. He maintains that thieves who start small will always go on to worse crimes.'

Hanbury smiled. 'I promise you, if more goes missing – and my men's tools are their livelihood – I will indeed report it. For the moment . . . it is possible that things have simply been mislaid, save that my most skilled carver, him that lost the fine chisel, looks after his tools as carefully as 'twere a newborn babe. He swears that chisel was taken from his tool belt, which was left hanging up in the lodge when we went to supper at the inn yesterday evening.'

'Well, I hope you may recover it,' I said. 'And Roger has the right of it. Block up that entrance from the High at night, and perhaps even set a watchman there.'

When he was gone, Walter, Roger, and I looked at each other.

'Who would steal the men's chisels?' Roger said.

'Another mason?' I said. 'Or some petty thief who thought he might sell them on?'

'But mallets?' Walter said. 'Just rough wooden mallets? Why bother to steal three wooden mallets?'

'Some thieves are like magpies,' I said. 'It is the stealing that gives delight, never mind what is stolen.'

Walter shrugged. 'Perhaps. It still seems odd to me.'

A few days later, I was invited to an evening dinner at the castle with Cedric Walden and his captain, Thomas Beverley, with whom I had travelled most of the way to Burford the previous December. As it was Lent, I hardly expected a feast, but I suppose soldiers must eat well to stay strong, whatever the season. Or such will be their excuse. The meal kept within the restrictions of Lent, but those restrictions can occasionally be somewhat loosely interpreted.

We dined in the deputy sheriff's own quarters, just the three of us, and were served with a magnificent pike, elaborately garnished and with a sauce of cream, chopped dill, and pickled nasturtium seed pods.

'The pike,' I asked, 'caught locally?'

'Aye,' Cedric said. 'We are conveniently placed here beside the Thames. Our cook is also a keen fisher and keeps us well supplied. He has been pursuing this pike for weeks. It was after he caught it that I sent you the invitation to dine.'

'Certainly it is a fish I have rarely tasted. And your cook seems a mite talented to be catering for a castle full of rough soldiers.'

Thomas laughed. 'High Sheriff de Alveton poached him from some nobleman's household, in the hopes of making the man his personal cook. And since de Alveton rarely honours us with his presence here in Oxford, but prefers his Berkshire lands, it would have meant the cook following him about.'

'And he does not?' I said.

'He does not.' Cedric grinned. 'The cook has found a woman here, in a cottage off St Giles, and will not leave. He is a free man, and may do as he chooses. So we benefit and de Alveton must look elsewhere for a cook.'

After the pike, we had chicken. Now some may say

that chicken is meat and should not be eaten during Lent, but since the flesh is white, the Church has ruled that it counts as a kind of fish, so we could consume it with a good conscience. This capon had been seethed in red wine – which, to be frank, gave it more the appearance of meat than of fish – along with shallots and thyme, and was served with a purée of white beans and onions, together with braised cabbage. We finished with a confection of preserved chestnuts in honey, a little sweet for my taste, but a dish which would not disgrace the king's table.

Afterwards we sat beside a small fire (for it had turned somewhat cold in the evening), cracking walnuts and sipping a fine French wine.

'You do yourselves very well,' I said, 'here in the castle. I had not realised that you dine like princes.'

Cedric grinned. 'Ah, this is not everyday fare, Nicholas. I was moved to pity by the thought of your diet of Headington limestone, with just a dash of Taynton. I met your scrivener Walter at Carfax the day before yesterday, and he told me how you have all been suffering. Unremitting noise and filth, he said.'

'It is certainly very trying.'

'So Provost de Hotham has managed to secure the coin he needs to build his chapel,' Thomas said. 'He has been talking of it ever since he took charge of the college.'

'According to the master mason,' I said, 'some benefactor from the Founder's north country has made them a gift. The provost is anxious for as much of the building to be complete before this man visits Oxford. As a result, the builders start each day before it is barely light, even if it is raining, and carry on till dusk. And we must endure all the while.'

'If you would enjoy a diversion, you may accompany us when we leave Oxford tomorrow,' Cedric said. The two men exchanged grins. 'Although I cannot promise you a quiet time.'

'Oh? And where do you go?'

'Banbury. There is a band of rogues haunting the

town and the farms round about, stealing, burning, and sometimes killing. I am taking a good part of the garrison with me to put a stop to them and their activities, though I will leave enough men here for the usual duties. It is a quiet time just now in the town.'

'Though there are thieves about, even so.'

I told them of the missing items from the stonemason's equipment. More had disappeared since those first thefts, despite the erection of a barrier across the High Street entrance at night.

'Nothing serious as yet,' I said, 'but we have heard of no other thefts nearby.'

'Nor have I,' Thomas said. 'These thefts do not seem very serious.'

'Serious enough for men who get their living with their tools,' I said. 'And it is strange that it is only the builders who have suffered.'

'Perhaps it is some desperate heretic,' Cedric said lightly, 'who objects to the building of a chapel. Though in that case, he must be ill at ease here in Oxford, for one trips over a church or chapel every few yards.'

I laughed. It was true, though I felt a faint quiver of unease at the word 'heretic'. Some of the university's philosophers, like John Wycliffe, maintained opinions which the more hardened members of the Church might regard as heretical.

'Well,' Thomas said. 'If there is more trouble at Queen's, tell the master mason to report it here at the castle. William Gurdin will be in charge.'

I nodded, but refrained from comment. I knew William Gurdin. Had done ever since he insolently barred my entrance to the castle a year ago. I could not imagine him being of much help to Master Hanbury.

Our talk turned to other matters.

The following day, the deputy sheriff, with Captain Beverley and their troop of soldiers, left Oxford in a fine flurry of polished armour and brightly coloured pennants snapping in the March breeze from the tips of their spears. Clearly Cedric hoped that this display of strength would intimidate the outlaws around Banbury, so that they might be rounded up without daring to offer too much resistance. He was uncertain how long they would be absent from Oxford.

'At least a week, I expect,' he said, 'but surely no more than three. If we take longer than that I shall believe myself a poor fellow, not fit to hold office.'

He said it in jest, for he was an able soldier and an able administrator, far more so than the High Sheriff. And unlike High Sheriff de Alveton, he had never been suspected of fraud and malpractice or, like de Alveton, found guilty. The youth of Oxford lined Northgate Street to cheer the soldiers on their way, including my own scamps, who had to be fetched back, protesting, when they took a fancy – along with a number of Oxford's youngsters – to follow the contingent all the way up St Giles.

The deputy sheriff was barely out of sight before William Gurdin appeared, patrolling the streets of the town with an attendant group of soldiers, all of whom bore the marks of past fist fights (and worse). It was understandable that Cedric would take his best men with him to Banbury, but it was a little hard on Oxford that he had left us the dregs of the garrison. I foresaw trouble before he returned, and said as much to my family and my scriveners.

Emma had brought more of the finished gatherings of Walter's book and was cooling herself after a hot walk with a cup of Margaret's raspberry cordial, when I warned Walter and Roger of the trouble I expected to erupt under William Gurdin's term of command.

'Let him but try to bully decent folk,' Roger said angrily, 'and he will soon see that Oxford men will not tolerate it.'

Walter shook his head. 'Have a care. With no officer above him, William Gurdin may do as he will. If you defy him, you may regret it. You do not want to find yourself clapped into a castle prison cell. Or even worse. Will he have power to put offenders on trial and carry out executions, think you, Nicholas?'

I realised that Walter was trying to scare Roger into caution, so I shook my head dolefully. 'Perhaps. Who can say? Best not to run the risk. There is no appeal once you have been hanged.'

Roger subsided, muttering, and Walter and I exchanged a glance. I hoped it would be enough to keep Roger out of trouble, but there would be other young men who would resent the high-handed behaviour of William Gurdin.

Emma was smiling into her cup.

'Perhaps you should tell the master mason to take the story of the stolen tools to this acting captain,' she said. 'It might divert him from chasing shadows.'

'I doubt it,' I said. 'I think he would dismiss such trivial matters out of hand. I suspect he dreams of some great crime that he may solve before Cedric returns. Murder, at the very least. Or a full-scale battle between town and gown.'

Walter shuddered. 'Do not even think it.'

'He shall have one if he will,' Roger muttered.

Emma perched on the edge of his desk. 'Now, you have heard what Walter and Nicholas have said, Roger. Keep well away from trouble. And besides, even punching an adversary in the jaw would ruin your hand for scribing, days together. Even weeks. Besides, on which side would you fight? Town or gown?'

Roger shrugged. ''Tis difficult. When I was younger, I was town through and through, before I came here. But now . . . well, we work under licence from the university and most of our customers are students and Fellows.'

'But of course there are townspeople, too,' she said. 'Like the lovely Lady Amilia. I understand your difficulty. Divided loyalties.'

Roger shrugged at the mention of our demanding and excessively arrogant customer, Lady Amilia. He grunted. 'Very well, I will take part in no trouble-making for

William Gurdin. But there *will* be trouble.'

Our discussion was interrupted by the arrival of a customer, a rare sight since the beginning of the building work. I could not place him at first, then I remembered that he was the young man who had come into the shop the first day I had pinned the blanket over the door and looked about him in that disparaging manner. I had dismissed him from my mind, thinking that he must be some passing traveller who had stayed in Oxford overnight, perhaps at the Mitre, and been gone the next day on the way to London. He had merely wandered into my shop to pass an idle hour and found nothing of interest. Why should he return?

I left the others talking quietly, but also eying the stranger curiously. We see few strangers in town except at the time of festivals.

I bowed. 'May I be of service to you, Master . . .?'

'De Musgrave. Sir Thomas de Musgrave. You are?'

'Nicholas Elyot, seller and maker of books.'

We both bowed.

He glanced about him, vaguely. 'I have been thinking of buying a new book of hours. My own is old and rather worn, and was never of much quality. Have you any in stock? I remember that you said you had been obliged to store your better books away from the dirt from the college.'

He jerked his head in the direction of Queen's.

'I have none available at the moment,' I said. 'It is our practice to make them to each man or woman's personal tastes. I can show you an example.'

I moved toward the passage through to the house. Emma's first book of hours was in my bed chamber. I allowed my wealthier customers to examine it and make their choices. Sir Thomas de Musgrave was clearly, from his clothes and his demeanour, a young man of considerable means.

'I will fetch it, Nicholas,' Emma said, slipping off Roger's desk.

I nodded. She knew that I kept it beside my bed and said my daily devotions with its guidance. And she had guessed that I was reluctant to leave de Musgrave in the shop. Why I felt this, and how she had divined my feelings, I did not know.

In a few minutes she returned and handed the book to de Musgrave. To do him justice, he handled it carefully.

'I thank you, goodwife,' he said.

I felt myself flushing at his impertinence. Emma was dressed quietly, but could hardly be mistaken for a servant.

'This is the Lady Emma Thorgold,' I said sharply.

'My mistake,' he said, inclining his head, but not quite far enough. 'My lady.'

Impudent dog! I thought.

Emma smiled with acid sweetness and dropped an excessively low curtsey. 'Sir Thomas,' she murmured demurely, but her eyes glinted.

Roger and Walter had their heads bent low over their parchment, but I caught the edge of Roger's grin.

'Aye, something like this will do,' de Musgrave said carelessly.

I clenched my teeth. It was the finest book of hours which had ever passed through my hands – except, perhaps, others Emma had made. I had a particular affection for this one.

I sat down at my desk and drew a sheet of paper toward me.

'If you would like to tell me your requirements, I can set the work in hand,' I said. Not for anything would I reveal that Emma was the scrivener and illuminator.

'Let me ponder the matter for a while,' he said, 'now that I have seen this.'

He laid the book of hours on my desk.

'I am staying in Oxford for the moment, at the Mitre. Tell me, do these properties along the High Street have grounds behind them? I understand that the next cottages . . .' he waved in the direction of Aldusa's house, 'are not private messuages, but part of a cluster of buildings belonging to that college.'

'That is correct,' I said. 'This property and the rest in the other direction along this side of the street towards the Mitre are full-sized burgage plots. This is a double one.'

'Were you thinking of buying a property here in Oxford, sir?' Walter said, raising innocent eyes.

'Nay . . . I merely wondered.' His tone was vague and offhand. 'I might, perhaps. I understand that renting out a property to be used as a student hall can be a useful investment.'

With that the fellow departed. We looked at one another. I shrugged.

'What do you suppose he really wanted?' Emma asked.

'Who can tell?' I said. 'Not, I suspect, a book of hours. And why did he want to know about these burgage plots? None along this part of the street is large enough to serve as a student hall.'

It seemed that Master Hanbury had been able to persuade Queen's to provide at least some small compensation for Aelyth. It was impossible for her to continue to work at home, so she decided to stay for a time with a niece who lived south of Oxford, at the far end of Grandpont. She set off the next morning with a carter travelling to Wallingford, carrying with her the materials of her trade – the narrow loom for weaving ribbons, her bobbins and shuttles, and a bag of silks and the finest woollen thread.

'I doubt I shall be able to accomplish much,' I heard her telling Margaret, who had stepped out into the High Street with Aldusa and Mary to see her on her way. 'My niece has four children, all under seven years of age, and there are only two rooms and an attic in their house. But I cannot be without my little toys.'

She ran a caressing finger over the loom.

'This belonged to my mother, and my grand-dam before her. How many miles of ribbon has it woven, I wonder?'

She smiled sweetly, if a little sadly.

'I do not know how much longer I shall have the sight to go on weaving. And no daughter to pass it down to.'

'Your niece?' Margaret said.

'Nay, she scorns my little treasures. Says I labour like Hercules to make trimmings for maidens' hair, who will lose them heedless, and never care for the work that went to make them. Her husband is a wheelwright, and she helps with the carving of the spokes. Sits astride spoke-shaver's bench like any man, wielding one of those two-handled knives.'

She shuddered. 'What if one of the little ones should light upon it? It could take your hand off at the wrist.'

When the women had waved her off, Margaret and Mary came back inside, pushing their way through the blanket.

'Poor little woman. I wonder whether she will come back,' Margaret said. 'One day soon, the college will be wanting her cottage. And no one to pass on her skills to.'

'She should take on an apprentice,' I said.

'Do you think any girl has the patience to learn such slow work these days? Ever since the Pestilence, the young are so restless.'

'Well, there is a task for you and your friends,' I said. 'Find a girl to apprentice to Aelyth. Some worthy orphan,' I said.

'Are you mocking me, Nicholas?'

'Indeed,' I said. truthfully, 'I am not.'

Several days passed with no lessening of the nuisance from the college. The clouds of sawdust and stone dust began to form a paste in every cranny and window ledge along our portion of the High, and the constant noise of sawing, hammering, and graving left us all sore of head and short of temper.

I had done the best I could with my rendering of the troubadours' songs into English, taking into account the improvements suggested by Jordain, Emma, and Philip Olney. Philip, *librarius* of Merton College, with his extensive knowledge of books and the languages of other nations, was able to correct a few mistakes I had made. At his invitation, I spent two afternoons in his rooms at Merton writing out my final versions of the verses.

'It is a relief to be able to breathe freely,' I said, stretching and walking over to his window.

It looked south over the meadowland leading down to the Thames, which glimmered silver in the spring sunlight. I leaned out and drew in deep breaths of the clean air, like a wanderer in the desert come to a cool oasis.

'I swear, I feel as though my very lungs are clogged up with the dust,' I said, turning and leaned my shoulders against the window jamb.

'It cannot bode well for your health,' he said, pouring me a cup of ale and pushing it across his desk to me. ''Tis a wonder all stonemasons do not die before they reach the age of thirty.'

'I have noticed that some of them, the older ones, tie cloths over their noses and mouths.' I took a grateful drink of the ale. 'Though the younger men do not.'

He laughed. 'Probably afraid of looking foolish. They will learn. Have you been to see the work yourself?'

'Not yet. Walter has made quite a friend of the master mason, Robert Hanbury, and he has kept us abreast of how they fare. The foundations of the walls are laid, and they are beginning to rise. I have promised to take the children to see how the scaffolding is erected, which should be soon.'

'And have there been more thefts? Did you not say they had delayed the work?'

'Aye. Master Hanbury is both angry and perplexed. There has been no thieving in our part of Oxford for weeks, yet every day or two, something goes missing – tools, mostly, which comes hard on the masons and carpenters, for each man's set of tools is his means of livelihood. Sometimes, too, a chisel will be found, not stolen but deliberately damaged, its cutting edge chipped and broken. They have a smith working with them on the site, for it seems stone-working tools need constant sharpening, but he has spent far too many hours trying to restore those which have been deliberately damaged. Sometimes they are beyond repair.'

'A cruel mischief, that sounds. Spiteful.'

'Aye.' I looked at him thoughtfully. 'What do you make of it? And if the culprit is caught, could he be punished in law?'

Philip was a lawyer by training, and taught in the law schools of the university, but he shook his head now.

'I am not sure. I have never come across such a case. Theft, certainly, can come to trial. Where malicious damage deprives a man of his living, that too may be punishable.'

'You had building work here at Merton last year. Had you any trouble like this?'

'Not at all. Like you, we had the disagreeable noise and dust, but I was well away from it here, and my window, as you can see, faces in the opposite direction. There was certainly no trouble with thefts or damage to tools, not that I heard. And I am sure I would have done. It was a different master mason, of course, though perhaps some of the men may have been the same. Could it be that someone has a grudge against your Master Hanbury? A rival stonemason? Someone who hoped to get the work and is jealous that it has gone to Hanbury?'

'It is possible, I suppose,' I said slowly. 'But he is a quiet, pleasant fellow. Not a man to make enemies in the normal course of things. I wonder whether he has considered that possibility. Certainly it seems that someone wants to delay or prevent the building of the chapel. The provost is anxious for much of the work to be finished before this patron from the north comes to Oxford. The more trouble there is, the less of the work will be completed.'

'It does sound like the work of a jealous rival,' Philip

said. 'If he can compromise the work he will damage Hanbury's reputation.'

The next time I saw Robert Hanbury, I tried out this theory with him – hesitantly – for I was not sure that I knew him well enough to tread on such delicate ground.

He shook his head.

'Nay,' he said, seemingly not offended by my interference in his affairs. 'There are two other master masons working in Oxford at the moment. There were more before the plague, but now there are but the three of us left with the skills the colleges require. Of course, they may always hire in masters from elsewhere, but for the most part they place the work with Oxford men, who know the local stone and the needs of the colleges.'

'And neither of these other two master stonemasons might resent your work at Queen's?'

He shook his head again. 'Both are good friends of mine, these many years. One I trained with when we were boys, the other is a little older, a journeyman when we were apprentices. Besides, they all have work of their own. These days there is so much a-building in Oxford, and so few of us, that we never lack work. Indeed, I think none of us will be without employment for the rest of this year and next. Nay, it was a timely thought, but I do not suspect my fellow masons.'

'So it remains a mystery,' I said.

'It does. I wish I might catch but a glimpse of the fellow. I should shake him till his teeth rattle, and demand to know what he means by it. There can be no profit in it for him. Although some of the stolen tools might be sold for coin, I have spoken to all the smiths and tool-makers in Oxford, asking them to watch for anyone selling what we have lost, and they have seen nothing. And who would buy our mallets? And as for the tools not stolen but damaged – how can he benefit from that?'

'That is an argument for the whole business arising out of malice,' I said.

'I agree. Malice, perhaps, but I think not against me or my men. The carpenters have also lost tools, and their master is an old friend of mine. We have worked together often. He is as baffled as I.'

'Malice against the college, then, do you suppose?' I said.

He shrugged. 'It could be. But I know little about the Fellows here. I have had dealings with but one or two.'

'Nor have I. They are regular customers of mine, but beyond that I know none of them well.'

'I have only had brief meetings with the provost,' he said, 'who set out his original requirements and occasionally gets under our feet, urging us to swiftness and preventing it at the same time. Otherwise I answer to one of the Fellows, Master Brandon. He has copies of my plans, sometimes tries to persuade me to introduce a more elaborate window design, and holds the purse strings. As far as I can tell, they have the coin to complete the building, although I am not privy to their accounts.'

'The only reason for haste is this visit from the patron?'

'As far as I know. Of course, the quicker the work is finished the less it will cost. My banker-masons will shape the required number of stones, and that cost will not alter, but my carvers are paid day-rates, so fewer days, less cost.'

'But does it not take a certain time to carve – well, say – a trifoliate window? It cannot be made to take less time, any more than my scriveners can write a page any faster without making mistakes or blotting the ink.'

'There you have it exactly, but I cannot make them understand that.'

'So,' I said, 'the building can hardly be finished any faster. But with all this interference, it could be slower.'

'Indeed.'

'You will not be penalised, if you take longer than was promised? Could that be the motive behind this trouble?'

He gave me a shrewd look. 'I will never allow such

penalties in any agreement I make. Bad weather can slow down the building, sickness amongst the men, accidents. I take good care that I will not be penalised.'

'Well, it is a bafflement,' I said, getting up.

Master Hanbury had invited me to join him for a drink at Tackley's Inn after the day's labour, and it had seemed a good opportunity to put Philip's theory to him. It appeared unlikely, from what he said, that professional jealousy lay behind the attacks.

Nay, attacks was too strong a word. A series of malicious pranks.

It was a constant irritation to the stonemasons, as their dust was a constant irritation to us. Certainly a loss to those men whose tools were stolen or damaged, but nothing so vicious as an attack.

That night I lay abed, waiting for sleep to come. The weather continued fine and indeed almost hot, with only the occasional brief shower, so that keeping the window shuttered made for an unpleasant atmosphere in my bed chamber. To have left the shutters open would have made it worse. I had just reached that blurred point when one seems to swim between waking and sleeping, never quite certain which is which, when I was brought sharply awake.

From the direction of Queen's College there had come an almighty crash, so great that the floor trembled and my bed shook. The shutters, the catch having worked loose, flew open on the startled night. An attack, after all, had taken place.

Chapter Three

For a moment I thought I was dreaming. Had I really heard the noise? A tremendous crash? I thought the house had trembled, but all now seemed quiet and still. I turned over in annoyance. It was surely a dream, like those alarming nightmares when one seems to fall suddenly, or tries to shout and no sound emerges from a strangled throat.

Then two things happened.

There was a wail from the children's room. If I had dreamt the crash, so had Rafe.

And as the loosened shutters swung lazily in, a cloud of . . . something . . . obscured the frail light filtering in from a small moon.

I sat up, then climbed out of bed and went to the window. At once I began to choke and cough. It was more stone dust, but in a sudden mass, thick as fog, which drifted into the room, then settled, and grew quiet, almost like a live thing.

I wiped my streaming eyes on the sleeve of my night shift and leaned over the sill. In the fitful light I could make out the shape of my stable, now neatly capped with its thatched roof. Nothing amiss there. Beyond, there was the small yard behind Aldusa Tranter's cottage. It reached only to the end of my stable, not the full length of our garden, and was very narrow. The far end of the neighbouring two gardens had been cut off to make room for building, when Queen's College had first acquired the land. In her small garden, the alewife grew some vegetables, and the herbs she used in her brewing. She did not even have room for a few hens, but traded ale for eggs with Mary Coomber at the dairy, whose work at milking, and her butter and cheese making, left her no time to brew ale.

I could not really see properly as far as Aelyth's cottage, and hoped that no harm had come to it while the ribbon weaver was away. Yet there seemed to be no disturbance there. Beyond the cottages lay the college, and as I watched, a dull light flickered and grew, where I thought Walter had told us the stonemasons had their lodge. I remembered that the apprentices, who could not afford better rooms, were sleeping there under the canvas shelter. One of them must have lit a rush dip. Then I saw other lights beginning to move about.

Before I could make out anything further, I heard the slap of bare feet on the boards, and Rafe came in, sobbing, followed by Alysoun, who looked frightened but was doing her best not to show it. I picked Rafe up and carried him to the window.

'See, my little man? Nothing to be afraid of. I think some stones have fallen over at the building in the college.'

It was now clear that a number of candle lanterns were moving about the college grounds. The noise must have woken all the Fellows, since it was loud enough to wake us, two doors away. Alysoun stood on tiptoe, the better to see out of the window.

'I thought the house was falling down,' she confided. 'And so did Rafe. But I soon knew it was all right. He is silly to be afraid. You can see that everything is safe here.'

'Aye,' I said. 'Everything is safe here. It must have been a pile of stones over at the college. Someone didn't stack them properly. I expect Master Hanbury will give them a proper scolding tomorrow. Come now, back to bed.'

Margaret was standing at the door of her room as I carried Rafe to the children's bed chamber, Alysoun trailing reluctantly behind, clearly hoping for more excitement. Rowan was curled up on her bed, oblivious.

'You see,' I said, as I tucked Rafe into the truckle

bed. 'Rowan hasn't even woken up.'

'But she did,' Alysoun said, slipping in beside the dog and trying to pull up her share of the covers. 'She woke up and barked once. Then she whined. And then she went to sleep again.'

'Sensible dog,' I said, kissing them briskly and slipping out.

I hadn't heard the dog bark, but perhaps my ears had been ringing still with the noise of the crash.

'Something at Queen's?' Margaret said.

'It must be,' I said. 'I cannot see to be sure, but there were lanterns, and people moving about. Falling stone, surely.'

'I am surprised it was so loud,' she said. 'If a pile of stones merely began to topple, they would slide, wouldn't they? Not make such a loud noise. And I would be surprised if any man working under such a well-known master mason would be so careless as to pile stones badly. They might fall on someone and cause an injury.'

I nodded. It was the way my own thoughts were running, despite my reassuring words to the children. I bade Margaret goodnight, and went back to my bed chamber, the fresh dusting of fine grit on the floor unpleasant under my bare feet.

Leaning once again out of the window, I could see more movement of lights over at Queen's, and could catch a faint murmur of voices, but they were too far away to make out. There was a light also in Aldusa Tranter's cottage, but as I watched, it went out.

Should I close the window, lest more dust be blown this way? Or hope that we might be spared for a few hours, while the stonemasons set all to rights? I decided to leave the shutters open, but just as I began to turn back to my disturbed bed, I thought I caught sight of a movement at the far end of the garden. I peered out again, but the moon was no more than a thin crescent, while skimming clouds, though little to speak of, caused the starlight to flicker like a badly trimmed candle. It was probably nothing, or else some night creature – a squirrel, or a night prowling tom cat, or a bird roused from its perch by the disturbance, or even something as small as a mouse, rustling amongst last autumn's fallen leaves. I had noticed no more than a quiver in the air.

I crunched my way back to bed, and tried to make myself comfortable under the rumpled bedclothes. Why is it, if we are roused when just on the threshold of sleeping, we find it so much more difficult to go to sleep again? Finally I found myself relaxing and drifting off, but at that very moment a voice in my head said decisively: *That was more than the simple tumble of a pile of stones.*

It was the next attack.

I had arranged with Robert Hanbury to take the children to see the building work the next day, because the first level of the scaffolding was to be erected, and I had explained Rafe's interest.

'Aye,' bring the lad,' Hanbury said, 'and the little maid too, if such things interest her.'

I did not explain that Alysoun was every bit as eager as Rafe. Those who do not know my daughter sometimes find her alarming.

Now, over breakfast, I considered what was best to do.

'I think,' I said, wiping my mouth and getting up from my stool, 'that it will be better if I go first to the college alone. If they have had some mishap during the night, they may not start to build the scaffolding today and Master Hanbury may wish us to put off our visit.'

Rafe's mouth turned down, and Alysoun looked rebellious.

'Your father has the right of it,' Margaret said firmly. 'Best if he sees what is afoot. No use in your going to the college this morning if they are not ready to build the scaffolding. However, I would like you to help me decide which of our hens looks broody. I want to set a clutch of eggs to hatch, so that we may raise more pullets. We can never have too many eggs. And while the stonemasons are not making their fearful dust, we may let the hens out for a while to run about.'

I smiled my thanks. I knew that she had already chosen her broody hen, but she would let the children think they had chosen her. Once the hens were outside, she would have their help in cleaning out the hen house, but it was probably better not to mention that in advance.

There was a small crowd lingering in the High Street outside the opening into the college. Clearly we were not the only ones to have been disturbed last night.

'What's afoot?' I asked Aldusa Tranter who, not unexpectedly, had pushed to the front.

'More trouble,' she said, with a certain note of satisfaction in her voice. 'Part of a wall come down, they are saying. Poor builders they must be, seems to me, if a wall tumbles down as soon as they build it.'

Odd, I thought. I was sure that Robert Hanbury was a skilled mason, and that Queen's would not have hired some slipshod workman, even if their money was tight. Yet Margaret had pointed out (and I agreed with her) that the noise had not sounded like the slithering of a pile of stones.

'I have need to speak to Master Hanbury,' I said to the people standing about, as I worked my way through them to the gap where the old cottage had stood.

Within the college grounds Robert Hanbury was standing close to the foundations of the chapel, his arms folded, and glowering. In front of him, the first courses of the south wall should have stood to a height of about five feet, extending the full length of the outline, which had been marked out on the ground and the foundations laid. Here the whole central portion of the stonework had tumbled down in a broken mass, as if some gigantic monster had bitten a piece out of the wall, as a man might take a bite from a slice of bread.

The fallen stones lay in a disordered heap at the master mason's feet. Some appeared to be intact, but others were chipped or cracked.

'What happened?' I asked.

Robert Hanbury started and looked at me for a moment as though he had no idea who I was, then his face cleared and he gave a tight-lipped smile.

'As you see. The wall to build again.'

'An accident?' I said. 'Surely not. And would it not have required a good deal of force to be pushed over?'

'It would. Though not as much as would have been needed if the mortar had set. We laid the top two courses yesterday, so the mortar was not yet set firm. Those were prised away easily, and they dragged down the lower stones with them.'

'Prised away? It *was* deliberate, then?'

'Oh, aye.' He grimaced. 'It was deliberate. You can even see the marks where a crowbar was used.'

He stepped over the nearest of the fallen stones and pointed. There, clear to see, were the deep and ugly scratches made by some tool. I could well believe that they had not been made by the masons.

'You think this has been done by the same person who has been stealing and damaging your tools?'

He shrugged. 'How many enemies do you suppose we have in Oxford?'

'Could one man have overset your wall? It would surely need some strength.'

I stepped closer to look. The scratches Hanbury had pointed out were on two large stones which would have been in the centre of the broken portion of the wall. It seemed that if those could be loosened, it might not have been too difficult to tumble the rest.

'One man could have done it,' he said, 'if he knew what he was about. Levering those central stones – it would take some strength, but nothing out of the ordinary.'

He pounded his fist against his thigh. 'God's bones! We have blocked the entrance to the High. I have a guard set there at night. I even have those lads sleeping on the site.'

He gestured toward the canvas shelter where a group

of apprentices crouched miserably, looking as though the damage was their fault.

'They must have heard the noise,' I said. 'It woke us, along the street.'

'Oh, they heard the noise. Clung to each other like a pack of milk-faced maidens. By the time they had the courage to venture out, the deed was done and the villain gone.'

'I cannot see how he broke in,' I said. 'Could it have been someone already in the college? A rogue workman? A college servant? Surely not one of the Fellows, when it is their money paying for the work.'

He looked at me thoughtfully, then gestured at me to follow him. He led me past the building work and the orderly stacks of stone and timber, then around behind a group of half derelict buildings on the west side of the college grounds. Here there was a wooden fence, a temporary barrier separating the college from the ribbon weaver's cottage. It reached about as high as my chin. Over it I could see Aldusa Tranter, returned to the further cottage, spreading out her washing in the sun. And beyond her I could hear, faintly, the sound of my children's voices.

'I think he came in this way,' Hanbury said.

At the base of the fence, where the sun had not yet reached to dry out the ground, there were two clear footprints, quite deep, as though someone had jumped down from the fence. The top of the fence itself was slightly splintered.

'Do you think he could have come in through the empty cottage?' I said. 'Aelyth has gone to live with her niece in Grandpont until the building work is finished.'

'I am about to go and see,' he said. 'There is no way down the side of that cottage, is there?'

I shook my head. 'The only way through to the back of either of those two properties is through the cottages themselves. Land is valuable along the High Street, or it was before the pestilence. Now, as Queen's has discovered, houses are sold cheaply. But when those were built, every advantage was taken of the whole width of the burgage plot.'

'And your property? It is double the size, is it not?'

'It is. My father-in-law bought two adjacent plots, and left a narrow alley along this side of the property. It provides the way into my garden and stable, but I have a stout gate on to the street, which I keep locked at night. It is higher and sturdier than this.'

I laid my hand on the wooden fence and shook it. It yielded a few inches in my hand.

'And beyond you?'

'There are one or two empty properties. Let us look at Aelyth's cottage. It would be the nearest way in, to come over the fence. I think you have the right of it. He must have come this way, along the back. He could not have come past your watchman on the High, nor could he have easily broken in from the east, from Hammer Hall Lane. The big college gatehouse is there, with a gatekeeper, and the main Fellows' houses, and a substantial wall.'

Back at the building work, Hanbury gestured to one of the older masons, who were standing about, looking as gloomy as the apprentices.

'Set another batch of mortar a-making, John,' he said. 'And tell the lads to clear the fallen stones. We must chip away the mortar before they can be reused.'

'Aye, maister.' The man nodded grimly. 'That'll put us back, two-three days at the very least.'

'It will. The setters can start to rebuild that section of the wall with fresh stones, and the bankers had best put their backs into it. We will need more dressed stone before these will be cleaned fit to use again.' He pointed to the heap of stones with the toe of his boot.

'And some damaged past use,' the man said.

'They must needs be cut down. Once they are sorted we will see what can be salvaged.'

Leaving the men to their work, we made our way out to the High Street. Most of the gawpers had gone about their day's work, apart from two young lads who stared as we headed toward Aelyth's cottage, then lost interest in us.

Hanbury seized the latch of the cottage door and shook it firmly.

'Securely locked, it seems,' he said.

'No sign of any break-in.' I pointed.

There were two small windows on the ground floor, one on either side of the door. The upper storey was hardly more than an attic, but it had a single window in the gable end. All three windows were securely shuttered and showed no sign of interference.

'Not here, then,' I said. 'And he could not have gone through Goodwife Tranter's, or she would have woken the street with her shrieks before ever he reached your fence.'

Hanbury gave a small smile. 'Aye. I think we may forget Goodwife Tranter's cottage.'

The next opening to the street was my own. I unlocked the gate and led Hanbury through, along the alleyway to my stable. The children and Margaret were still cleaning out the hen house, but came over at once to see what we were about. I made the introductions and Alysoun stared up at the master mason with interest.

'Has your chapel fallen down?' she asked. 'It woke us up, and Rafe thought our house was going to fall down, too.'

'So did you,' Rafe protested.

'I might have, for a minute, but I soon saw that we were quite safe.'

'Part of a wall has come down,' Robert Hanbury said, regarding them both quite seriously. 'I am sorry it woke you. Someone broke it. Your father and I are trying to discover how he got into the college.'

Margaret turned quite pale.

'You think he came this way, Nicholas?'

'He came over the fence next to Aelyth's cottage, Meg. Before that, he must have come across the gardens, but it isn't clear where he broke in from the street.'

A substantial stone wall marked the line between my property and Goodwife Tranter's cottage. There was nothing to be seen on the section running between the stable and the street. I showed Hanbury the way round behind the stable. Here there was an old shed where I kept a garden spade, hoe, and rake, and Margaret had stored a few of her own possessions, not currently in use, like the churn she had used to make butter when she was married. Her husband Elias Makepeace had been too miserly to pay for butter from Mary Coomber's dairy when he had a wife to do the work for him, unpaid.

'Here,' Hanbury said.

The section of wall beyond the shed rarely caught the sun except in midsummer and was cushioned with a growth of moss and lichen. We could clearly see the deep gouges where someone had clambered over the wall, probably making some use of the shed to gain a foothold. Margaret and the children had followed us, and Alysoun stared at the damage, open mouthed more with excitement than fear.

'Did the thief do that?' she asked.

'He wasn't a thief,' Rafe pointed out. 'He broke the wall.'

'I expect he was a thief as well.' Alysoun was somewhat put out at being corrected by her little brother.

'As far as we know,' I said, 'he did not steal anything, but it is a *kind* of theft, to steal men's labour. The building of the wall is all to do again, and some of the dressed stone ruined.'

I led the way across the garden, through our small orchard, to where another stone wall marked my western boundary. Here again there were the signs where someone had climbed over.

'He took no care to cover his tracks,' Hanbury said.

'It was dark,' I pointed out. 'Perhaps he did not realise he had left any tracks. Or he was in too much of a hurry. We had best look further along the street for the place where he broke in.'

Once we were out of earshot of the children, I said quietly, 'I thought I saw movement in our garden, after the noise of the falling stones. It might have been your intruder, but I hardly saw enough to be sure. It could as easily have been some animal he disturbed – 'twas no more than a stirring of the dark.'

'No one you could identify?'

I shook my head. 'Nay. Impossible.'

Walking up the High toward the church of St Mary the Virgin, we found what we were looking for. Since the pestilence, several of the smaller houses here had been abandoned. One by one, the colleges were buying up the empty property in the town, but this stretch of the street was not convenient for any college building, so the derelict houses remained undemolished. Gradually such houses would be rented out to shopkeepers, for the High was a busy thoroughfare. At present, however, due to Oxford's diminished population, even these remained empty.

Four houses along from my shop, just before the premises belonging to Edric Crowmer, the vintner, we found an empty house with window shutters newly broken and hanging askew.

'I am sure I would have noticed this,' I said, 'last time I passed. It can only just have been done.'

Hanbury swung the shutters fully open and we both peered through the window.

'That looks to me like footprints in the dust,' he said, pointing.

'And to me,' I said. 'This must be where he climbed through, then went from garden to garden until he reached the college. He went to a great deal of trouble.'

'Aye.'

Hanbury straightened up and leaned his shoulders against the wall of the house.

'To tell truth, Master Elyot, I do not know what to make of it. Who would want to go to such trouble? I know of no enemy who would have so determined a desire to damage my work.'

'Can we be sure it is an enemy of yours?' I said. 'Just as likely an enemy of the college. Or else some troublemaker, simply out to cause mischief.'

I knew I sounded unconvincing. I wasn't convinced myself.

'Will this be an end to it?' he said. 'I fear not. First the missing and damaged tools, now this. But we cannot keep watch on the works day and night, my men need their rest. It is hard work we do.'

We began to walk slowly down the street again.

'It is unfortunate that our deputy sheriff, Cedric Walden, is away from Oxford at present,' I said. 'He has gone to Banbury to deal with some trouble there, and taken much of the garrison with him. The man left in charge, William Gurdin, is a pompous fool, but he is all we have in charge at the castle. I think you should report this to him, though I fear you may get little satisfaction from him.'

'I will do so,' he said, 'once I have set the work in hand again. And I must take conference with Master Brandon. He is the college Fellow who is overseeing the work. Doles out our wages with a grudging hand, and questions every bucket of mortar we make and every handful of nails used by the carpenters. He will not be happy at this latest trouble. Before, he accused us of losing our own tools. Now I suspect he will think we pulled down our own wall, out of some scheme to be paid for extra work. Mark my words, we shall receive nothing for the labour of rebuilding that wall.'

I made a sympathetic noise, but feared that he had the right of it.

It was about halfway through the afternoon that Jordain burst into the shop, his gown more than usually awry and the hair that ringed his tonsure sticking up in spikes where he had been running his fingers through it.

'What's amiss?' I said. 'You look as though you have lost the cost of a month's boiled cabbage.'

Usually he laughed when teased about the poor fare served by the cook at Hart Hall, but now he seemed distracted, as though he had barely heard my feeble jest.

'Have you seen Piers Dykman?' he demanded,

looking about as though he expected to find the boy hiding under one of the desks.

'Not for a week or two,' I said. 'Have you lost him?'

The boy in question was the youngest of the students under Jordain's care at Hart Hall, no more than twelve, with the small stature and gaunt features that mark out the children of paupers. He might be penniless, but Jordain had found him a bright, hard-working student. Having come from a poor family himself, he felt a particular interest in the lad.

'He never came home last night,' Jordain said. 'Nor this morning. The other lads say that he attended lectures yesterday morning, but no one seems to have seen him since around midday. We have all been looking for him today, whenever we were free of lectures. Within Oxford, and beyond the walls.'

I could tell, from the pain in his eyes, that he was thinking of that other student of his, William Farringdon, whom I had found just a year ago, floating in the Cherwell. Murdered.

It was not unknown for a student to stay out all night, but that would normally be one of the older boys, and they could generally be traced to one of the taverns, sleeping off a bellyful of ale, or to a whorehouse in Magpie Lane. They faced a fine, and, from some wardens of halls, a beating. Repeated misbehaviour might mean being sent down from the university. But this was a young boy. Neither a tavern nor a whorehouse was likely to be to blame for his absence.

For a moment I wondered whether Piers Dykman could be Robert Hanbury's mischief maker, but dismissed the notion as absurd. Not only was the boy a docile and serious student, he was far too weak to have overturned that wall.

'He is very young, Jordain,' I said, taking him by the elbow and leading him through to the house. By the signs, I could tell that he had not eaten all day and unless someone took him in hand he would continue to search the streets of Oxford until he collapsed. I sat him down at the kitchen table and looked about for suitable sustenance.

Margaret was out somewhere with the children, but I found a slice of cold rabbit pie in the larder and put it down in front of Jordain, together with a cup of ale and a dried apple turnover. He hardly seemed to notice them, but began to eat automatically. I sat down opposite him.

'He's very young,' I repeated. 'You know how hard it can be. Even for us, at fourteen. Leaving home for the first time, away from family. Perhaps he has just run home.'

Jordain shook his head and took a long draught of his ale. I topped up his cup.

'If that happens at all, it happens in the first few weeks. You know that, Nicholas. He came up in October, and now it is March. I think he pined a little for home at first, but he soon got over it. And he loves his studies. He's going to be a true scholar.'

I felt sick, remembering that William Farringdon, Emma's cousin, had also been a promising scholar.

'Could he have had bad news from home?' I was trying to think of anything to ease Jordain's mind, but I was becoming infected with his worry.

'Nay, he has had no letter. Besides, I am sure he would have spoken to me if he wanted to go home. He is not thoughtless, like some of these lads. He would have come to me, or at least left a letter. I am sure of it.'

'Where is he from? Somewhere in Oxfordshire or Berkshire?'

'Not at all. He is one of our furthest flung. He comes from Westmorland, hundreds of miles away. All the more reason why he would not have run off willy-nilly.'

'A long way indeed,' I said.

Why did the thought of Westmorland seem significant to me? Then I realised.

'Is he one of Queen's poor boys?' I asked.

'Aye, he is. And deserves every penny, though there are not many of those.'

'They are spending out a large sum on this new chapel of theirs,' I said.

When Robert de Eglesfield founded Queen's College, he had large ambitions. The plan was for a substantial institution, dedicated above all to the study of theology, with a Provost, a body of Fellows, and a fund to support a number of poor boys whose families could not find the means to send their sons to the university. As a chaplain to Queen Philippa, he named the college in her honour, and also, no doubt, in the hope of royal patronage. The college had received some of the latter, though not a great deal. Had de Eglesfield not died of the plague, in the same year as my wife, he might have been able to secure a greater endowment for the college. As it was, they were constantly short of funds, and supported very few of the poor boys.

Robert de Eglesfield came from Cumberland, as did his original lord and patron, Sir Anthony de Luce, Lord of Cockermouth, which was why he had laid down that the poor boys were, if possible, to come from Cumberland and the neighbouring county of Westmorland. It was a fact that most students and Fellows of the university came from the wealthier southern counties of England, and it had been an excellent plan to try to redress the balance a little by offering the chance of a university education to poor but gifted boys from the north. In theory the places at Queen's for both poor boys and Fellows were to be open to all, merely with preference being given to those from the north, but I understood that all the present boys were northerners.

The college still being young, the scheme itself was also in its infancy. Time would show whether these boys made their way in the world. I had heard that they were sometimes mocked by the other students for their manner of speech, which was sometimes almost incomprehensible to our southern ears. However, they soon learned to change it, as the young will do, to fit in with their fellow students. I had noticed Piers Dykman's altered speech over the months he had been coming to my shop.

'I agree, then,' I said, 'that he is unlikely to have run off home. It would be hard for such a young boy, without means, to reach Westmorland, even should he be able to beg a ride with carters. I wonder . . . might he have gone to the college for some reason, and stayed overnight? But surely he would be back at Hart Hall by now. Or they would have sent you word.'

Like all students before they reached the rank of Master of Arts, the poor boys of Queen's did not live in college. They 'lived out', in one of the many halls scattered about Oxford and governed by a Regent Master as warden, like Jordain at Hart Hall.

Jordain shook his head.

'The first place I asked was at Queen's, although they seemed very distracted by some accident and took little interest in a missing student.'

'Part of the new chapel wall deliberately pulled down last night,' I explained. 'They have reason to be distracted. But surely they would know if he had come to the college and would tell you.'

'No one seems to have seen him. And if he had gone to Queen's, he would go in through the gatehouse on Hammer Hall Lane. The porter swears he has not seen him.'

'Do you have any more of the Queen's boys?'

'Nay,' Jordain said. 'They are all in different halls.'

'And had he any particular friend amongst your students, who might know where he would go?'

'He is much younger than most of them. They are friendly enough, but I think they regard him as a child. And indeed he keeps to himself, being so young, and having little money. Queen's allows little coin to their boys, except for necessities.'

I drummed my fingers on the table. Jordain, I was glad to see, had eaten all the food, apparently without noticing.

'Have you heard about all the troubles at Queen's?' I said.

'I know *you* have been very troubled.' He gave me a wan smile. 'All the dust and noise of the building works.'

'Nay, it is more than that.'

I gave him a brief account of the missing and damaged tools, and the latest disturbance, the breaking down of the newly constructed wall during the night, by some intruder who seemed to have come across our garden.

He looked shocked.

'I suppose the missing tools *might* have been nothing but chance or accident,' he said, 'but from the way you describe it, this latest act was deliberate and malicious.'

'Oh, it was certainly that,' I said, 'and the culprit went to a great deal of trouble, as Master Hanbury and I ascertained.'

I explained what we had discovered about the way the man had broken into an empty house some distance up the High Street, then climbed through an entire row of gardens to reach the grounds of the college, in order to avoid the watchman at the opening to the High Street.

'And he must have come equipped with a crowbar,' I said, 'for it was clear none of the workmen's own tools were disturbed last night. Everything was planned carefully beforehand.'

'Then I can see why they could not give their full minds to what has become of Piers Dykman.' He ran his fingers up through his dishevelled hair again. 'You do not think he had some part in what happened last night?'

I hesitated, then shook my head.

'Nay, how could he? Why should he wish to do any harm to the college which is supporting him? Besides, it would have taken a strong man to break down that wall, even though the mortar was not yet set. A somewhat undersized young boy could never have done it. For a moment I thought it seemed strange – all this mischief afoot at Queen's, and one of their boys missing – but surely it must be no more than an unhappy coincidence.'

I volunteered to join in the search for Piers Dykman, and told Walter and Roger that they might leave their work to hunt for him. Despite my doubts, we checked all the taverns, and searched the land beyond the Cherwell, where the students sometimes went to snare rabbits. There was nothing to be seen there, nor in the meadows which stretched south all the way down to the Thames from the town wall along the back of Merton College and St Frideswide's Priory. Nothing, that is, but a few courting couples, nestled like hares in the long damp grass under willow trees beside the river.

Although it was still too cold for students to swim in the Cherwell, under the wall of St John's Hospital near the East Bridge, we searched there as well. And I could not drive from my mind the memory of William Farringdon floating lifeless in the river, as I had looked down from the bridge.

All the rest of that day we searched every corner of Oxford, but of Piers Dykman there was no sign.

As I was closing the shutters in the shop front that the evening, Robert Hanbury came along the street from the direction of Carfax, his face set and grim.

'Well, I have done as you suggested,' he said, stopping beside my door. 'I have reported the thefts and the breaking down of our wall to your Captain William Gurdin, and little good it did me.'

'I do not claim him as mine,' I said mildly. 'I have never known him as anything other than a puffed up popinjay. So, he did not take you seriously?'

Hanbury shrugged. 'Listened with a supercilious sneer on his face, then said it was no concern of his if careless workmen lost their tools or could not build a wall strong enough to stand until the mortar dried. Said he was concerned with *real* crime and I should take care to watch my men more carefully, or else dismiss them and hire new ones. Fool!'

He kicked the wall of the shop, which must have hurt, even though he wore the sort of thick boots favoured by masons to protect their toes.

'Well, I feared it would be so,' I said, as I finished fastening the shutter. 'Let us hope that Sheriff Walden will return soon. He will treat the matter seriously.'

'The tools and the broken wall are serious enough, Jesu knows, but what else does he plan, this devil by night? That is what worries me.'

'And why does he do it?' I said. 'Is he some madman? Or some idle fellow with nothing on his mind but making trouble? Or is there some real purpose behind it?'

'The real purpose seems to be stopping us building the college chapel,' he said frankly, 'though why that should be, or who would want to do it, I cannot guess. You do not harbour a nest of heretics in Oxford, do you? Sometimes one hears odd rumours.'

I shook my head. 'Nay, we do not.'

Some might whisper the word 'heretic' behind their hands when they spoke of John Wycliffe's strange ideas, but they were not quite serious. Besides, Wycliffe was a devout man. He would never lay hands on a building dedicated to Christian worship.

'Come you in-by,' I said. 'You have had a trying day of it. Take supper with us. That is, unless you are still at work in the college.'

He shook his head. 'Nay, I gave my chief journeyman instructions for the rest of the day, not knowing how long I should be delayed at the castle. I might have saved myself the trouble and the long walk, as it has turned out. The men will be finishing work for today.'

'I do not think you have wasted your time,' I said, opening the door of the shop for him. 'Should there be more trouble, at least you will have reported to the castle all that has happened so far. When Cedric Walden returns, I am sure he will take note and find the culprit for you.

'Let us hope so.'

He followed me through the shop, casting an apologetic look at its bare shelves and Spartan appearance. In the kitchen we found Margaret bent over a pan resting on a trivet in front of the fire. She straightened up, flushed from the heat.

'Meg, I have invited Master Hanbury to sup with us, instead of taking himself off to Tackley's Inn. He has had a poor reception at the castle and is in need of good friends and good cheer.'

Margaret bowed, still with a roasting fork in her hand. If she was taken aback at having to provide supper for one more, she made no sign of it. Hanbury, however, began apologising for his intrusion.

'Nay, it is no trouble.' She smiled at him. 'And we have another guest for supper as well. Please – sit, sit. Nicholas, fetch a flagon of my new brewing of ale. It was a kindness of you to buy some from Aldusa, but it is fit for nothing but adding to a pottage.'

'And what have we for supper?' I peered at the pan, from which an enticing smell arose. 'Collops?'

'Aye, with onions and last autumn's dried mushrooms.'

I raised my eyebrows. We did not normally eat so well in the evening. Was she expecting Peter Winchingham? His praise of her cooking had put her on her mettle whenever he visited, but I had not heard that he was in town. I fetched the ale, and as I set the flagon down on the table, I heard a light step on the stairs which I knew well.

'Emma!' I beamed at her. 'I did not know you were coming to sup with us.'

She smiled and held out a bundle of parchment pages.

'I have finished Walter's book, so Margaret said we must celebrate.'

'But why . . .?' I nodded toward the stairs.

'Oh, I have been reading one of the stories to Alysoun and Rafe, by way of a bribe. Margaret wanted them to eat before us, so I promised them a story if they took their supper and went up to bed.'

'They will not be sleeping yet,' I said, for the evenings were beginning to stay light later, now that spring was come.

'I suggested that they should make up a story to follow on from the one I read to them. I left them arguing over it. They are to tell it to me tomorrow.'

Emma was glancing enquiringly at Robert Hanbury, so I remembered my manners and performed the introduction.

'You say that you have finished a book, mistress?' Hanbury was clearly puzzled.

Emma glanced at me, and I gave a slight nod. We made no public announcement of the fact that she worked for me as a scrivener, but I did not try to hide it. It was her decision to say what she would. I had only indicated, by my nod, that I did not think Robert Hanbury was either a blabbermouth or a man to scorn a woman doing a man's work.

She held out the pages for him to see.

'Walter Blunt is one of Nicholas's scriveners,' she said, 'as you may know, who has a great fund of old stories passed down from his mother. She could neither read nor write, but she came from a long line of storytellers. Nicholas persuaded Walter to write them down – and it was not easy, for he is a modest man. I have been making the book of them.'

Robert took the pages from her and sat down at the table, turning them over with wonder in his face. Although he had the square, strong hands of a mason, he handled the loose pages with great care.

'But these are beautiful,' he said, looking up at last. 'You made the illuminations also? I have never seen such work.'

The cup of ale I had poured for him stood untouched.

Emma coloured a little. 'I thank you.'

'Emma has mostly worked on religious books until now,' I said, 'but many of my customers are seeking secular work as well. Collections of tales are very popular. I will keep this in the shop and they may choose what they will have made for them – the whole collection or only a few of the tales. My scrivener Roger Pigot has put together another volume, made up from many small books of hero tales. He has prepared several copies already for different customers. Of course, much of our business is still books of hours, or lives of saints, or – for those who can read Latin – the Gospels and the Church fathers. That is in addition to the *peciae* for the students, so I keep copies of all the standard student texts.'

'Yours is a more complex business than I supposed, Master Elyot,' Hanbury said, passing the pages of Walter's book back to Emma, who set them carefully aside on a coffer.

'We have no formality in this family,' I said. 'I am Nicholas to my friends.'

'I am honoured to be considered so,' he said, rising from his stool and bowing. 'It seems I am in need of friends. And to them I am Robert.'

That called for explanation to Emma, who had not heard of the latest troubles at Queen's. By the time we had finished, Margaret was dishing out our supper.

'Not Lenten food, Meg,' I said.

She shrugged. 'When I was shopping in Northgate Street this afternoon, I saw a servant from Exeter College buying a great basket of these collops from the butcher there. When I enquired, he told me they were for the Fellows at the college, all of them in holy orders. If they may break the Lenten fast, then so may mere seculars like us. As Emma says, it is a celebration for the completion of Walter's book.'

'It is a pity he is not here to celebrate with us,' Emma said.

'I sent them both home when we ceased hunting for Piers Dykman,' I said. 'Walter did not come back to the shop.'

The two women looked at me blankly, so I explained about Jordain's missing student. They stared at each other in concern.

'And you found no sign of him?' Emma said.

I shook my head. 'No sign, good or bad. In some ways, that is a comfort. The hunt will continue tomorrow.'

'Perhaps he has simply quarrelled with the other boys,' Margaret said slowly, 'and has hidden himself away.

He will come back when he is hungry.'

'Aye, that is probably what happened.' From what I knew of Piers Dykman, it was unlikely, but I had no wish to spoil our meal, so I changed the subject.

'And now, Emma, are you ready to make a start on the book of troubadour songs?'

'I am. I have the copies I made of the music. Are you satisfied at last with your elegant rendering of the words?' She smiled at me, mischief in her eyes.

'As satisfied as I will ever be.'

There was need then to explain to Robert the whole story of the troubadour book, and what lay behind it, which occupied most of the evening until I saw him out of the shop on the short walk to Tackley's. Soon afterwards I accompanied Emma to her aunt's house in St Mildred Street.

'I will come tomorrow,' she said, 'and we can put together all that we need for the troubadour book.'

'Aye,' I said, somewhat absently.

'You are worried about this boy, are you not, Nicholas?' she said softly.

'I am.'

We were both thinking of her cousin William Farringdon, but neither of us spoke his name.

Chapter four

The following morning I rose before dawn, for I had asked Margaret to wake me when she went down to the kitchen to heat the bread oven for the day's baking. Despite the dark, just beginning to soften in the east, the birds in the garden were already full-throated in song when I opened the shutters and leaned out. I drew in deep breaths of the clean air, not yet tainted with the day's burden of stone dust. It was colder than the previous days had been, and the faint outlines of the stable and the orchard trees were blurred by more than darkness. A mist was rising. After closing the shutters again, I dressed and slipped quietly past the children's room, and although Rowan whined briefly, Alysoun and Rafe did not stir.

'Does not Jordain lecture in the Schools this morning?' Margaret said. 'Sit down. There is a heel of yesterday's bread left. No need to go forth on an empty stomach.'

I did as I was told, and she poured me a cup of ale, setting down a pot of honey and a piece of cheese beside the bread. Her tone had implied that the bread was only fit to give to the hens, but (like all my sister's bread) was still soft and delicious, even on the second day.

'I am honoured,' I said, pointing with my knife at the honey pot.

She shrugged. ''Tis a cold damp morning. Best fortify yourself.'

'Jordain does not lecture until eight o'the clock

today,' I said. 'That is why we decided to make an early start. Although I cannot think there is anywhere we did not search for the boy yesterday.'

I spooned some of the honey on to my bread as Margaret sat down opposite me.

'What do you think can have become of the child, Nicholas?'

Piers Dykman might be a university student, but in Margaret's eyes a boy of twelve was still a child. I shook my head and hesitated before replying.

'What is so worrying is that he is a serious boy,' I said, 'not given to madcap capers. Jordain says that he is almost pathetically grateful to be taken on by Queen's as one of their poor boys. His father is a small tenant farmer, holding his land from a lord in Westmorland, but he suffers from some lingering illness. The mother is dead and the eldest girl keeps house for the family. She is but fourteen and there are five more children. Piers caught the eye of their parish priest several years ago when he sang in the church choir. It seems he devoured learning like a starving dog, and the priest, who knew of de Eglesfield's foundation, sent a plea to the college that this was a boy who deserved the chance to study at Oxford. Ever since he arrived, his nose has barely been out of his books, never missed a lecture, and though he is so young he can debate with the best of them. Jordain has very high hopes of him.'

'So he is not the sort to run away for no reason,' she said.

'Not at all.'

'And there has been no trouble at Hart Hall? The older boys have not been unkind? If a youngster shows himself more apt than they . . . it could cause problems.'

'Nay, Jordain says they have made rather a pet of him. He is no threat to the more . . . worldly activities of the older boys. And there are no difficult students at Hart Hall this year.'

Sometimes, I knew, Jordain had had problems in the past. Although most of the students at Oxford were preparing for a career in the Church or in law, perhaps to serve in one of the king's new arms of government, there were also quite a few sons of the nobility and gentry, even of London merchants, who came to the university for other reasons. They would not take holy orders, might not even complete the full course of *trivium* and *quadrivium*. They came to learn the rudiments of the law and legal Latin, for most would serve, in time, as local Justices of the Peace. Some skill in figuring would be useful, so that they might keep a watchful eye on their stewards' accounts. Indeed, a younger son of the lesser gentry might in turn become a steward to some great lord.

It was these secular students who were the most likely to cause trouble. And for the most part it was they who drank too much, found their way to the whorehouses, and brawled with the youths of the town. Not that the students preparing for the Church were always blameless.

Although many of these secular students continued to study the traditional courses, in recent years new provision had been made for their less scholarly needs. Master Thomas Sampson and certain others now taught the rudiments of business in a course which was finding favour with sons of the gentry, who needed such knowledge for the running of their estates, and with rich merchants' sons, who would one day step into their fathers' shoes.

Conducting a court of law, acting as a coroner, managing household and business accounts, understanding legal language, writing formal letters, preparing wills and conveyancing – these were the subjects which were gaining in popularity amongst those who had no taste for Oxford's scholarly curriculum. It was a development which appalled the university's more entrenched Fellows and heads of colleges, but it seemed to me a natural outcome of King Edward's fresh approach to governing England. Slowly the power in the land was shifting from the Church and the great landowners to the wealthy merchants and the king's network of paid officials. It had begun before the Death, but since that great catastrophe any man of sense could see that the world was changing.

'Jordain has no secular students at the moment,' I said to Margaret. 'At least, there are two who do not plan to take holy orders, but they are studying the full university curriculum, and they are well behaved. He is certain none of his own lads could have aught to do with the disappearance of Piers. They seem as worried as he is.'

I finished my breakfast quickly and made my way out through the shop and along the High toward Hammer Hall Lane. The opening into Queen's was blocked with a makeshift gate, and from behind it came the growl of a large dog as I walked past.

Jordain was standing on the corner beside St Edmund Hall, looking as though he had slept in his clothes, if he had slept at all.

'Where shall we start?' I said, as I came up to him.

He gave me a despairing look. 'I cannot think where to search that we have not searched already.'

'Will any of your students be joining us?'

He shook his head. 'I cannot take them away from their studies any more. Most of them have lectures this morning, and those who do not should be making up for the time they spent hunting for Piers yesterday.'

'I think we searched the town very thoroughly,' I said, 'and spread the word about generally, that the boy was missing.'

'Perhaps he is not in town, but somewhere round about. He must have sought shelter *somewhere*. It was quite cold last night. One of those nights when the weather forgets that it is spring.'

'Aye,' I said, 'and not a spring-like day this morning.'

I gestured toward the East Bridge, where a thick mist hung over the course of the Cherwell, rising even to curl about the roofs of St John's Hospital. I did not like to think of the boy outside overnight in this cold and damp.

'I remembered that derelict mill,' he said. 'The one where you were attacked last year, over beyond the meadows on the far side of the Cherwell. He could be hiding there, and no one the wiser.'

I pulled a face. I had no wish to revisit the place where we were sure William Farringdon had been killed, before his body was dropped into one of the streams which flowed into the Cherwell.

'Do you think he could have gone so far? And there is no reason he should know of the old mill. I was unaware of its existence myself until I stumbled upon it.'

'I do not know what to think,' he said. 'I might reason better if I but knew *why* he has disappeared.'

'Nothing has happened out of the ordinary? I know you said he has had no letter from home, but has there been anything strange in his behaviour in recent days?'

He shook his head. 'Nothing to speak of. He was interested in the new building work at Queen's. So were all the lads, since they often pass the college on the way to the Schools. And I suppose, since he is one of the college boys, he was curious about the new chapel, but I noticed nothing particular about his interest.'

'And none of your other students can throw any light on it, even now they have had time to think?'

'There was but one small thing, though I cannot believe it has any importance.'

'Aye?'

'It seems that after morning lectures, the day before yesterday, he was seen talking to a gentleman in the High. The man stopped him, and they spoke briefly, but Giles Wetherby – you remember Giles? – Giles said they only spoke for a moment, as though the gentleman asked for directions.'

He paused.

'Giles is no great scholar, but he is no fool either. He says he got the impression they knew each other, but that the man was a stranger in Oxford.'

I blew out my breath, which I realised I had been holding.

'When did Giles tell you this?'

'Not until late last night. He had quite forgotten it, for he barely noticed the encounter, hurrying back to the hall for dinner. He only remembered when I sat them all down before we retired to bed and asked them to remember exactly when and where they had last seen Piers. That was the last time any of them had seen him.'

'But Piers did not come back for dinner with the others that day?'

'Nay.' He smiled ruefully. ''Tis not a dinner worth hurrying for, as you know, and sometimes they will buy a pie in the street instead, and make do with that. No one minds, for it means a little more of the scant provision for the rest of us.'

'But did you not tell me that Piers was very short of coin?' I said. 'Would he have spent it on a pie?'

'Probably not. But sometimes he missed meals because he was studying, or had gone to consult one of the Fellows who had given a lecture that morning. He was used to small rations and seemed not to care if he missed a meal.'

It seemed to me that a poor boy who had probably been hungry all his life, would be less likely than the others to skip even the dreary and skimpy meals produced by Hart Hall's cook, but Jordain knew Piers far better then I did, so I did not argue.

'If he was last seen with this man.' I said, 'that seems a fair starting point. Did Giles describe him?'

'Barely. He was not really heeding him. Young, he said, and well-dressed. Certainly a gentleman. That was all he noticed. Besides, the man walked away, up the High, leaving Piers standing there, outside the Schools. They were not together when Giles last saw them.'

'I still think it has some importance,' I said stubbornly. 'Piers behaves as normal up to the morning of the day before yesterday. He attends his lectures as usual. As he comes out of the Schools, he is accosted by this man, and then he disappears. Although they spoke only briefly, you say that Giles had the impression they knew one another? This must mean something.'

'I do not see how it can help us,' he said. 'We cannot go about accosting every young gentleman in Oxford, in the hope that he may have spoken to Piers. Giles could not give an accurate description. And not all the students wear their gowns, as they should, particularly the wealthy ones. He might merely have been a student Piers had met somewhere, passing the time of day.'

'Giles thought he was a stranger to Oxford, perhaps asking the way.'

'Aye, but when I asked him why he thought that, he could not tell me, and said he was probably mistaken.'

All this while we had been standing on the corner at the end of the lane, which was contributing nothing to the search for Piers.

'I have thought of one more place we might look,' I said.

'The old mill?' Jordain took a step in the direction of the fog bound East Bridge.

'Nay. In town. Come with me.'

I took him by the elbow and turned him to head up the High Street.

'There is somewhere along here that I want to search.'

We walked back past Queen's, past my shop, and stopped four doors further on.

'This house, you see?' I said. 'The shutters on this window have been forced open. The master mason, Robert Hanbury, and I found it when we were trying to discover where their intruder had broken in, to climb through the gardens into the college. Perhaps we were mistaken, and it was Piers who broke in here.'

'But why? It seems unlike him.'

I shrugged. 'I do not suppose we will know that until we find him, but, as you said, he must have found somewhere to take shelter.'

'Are you proposing to climb in?'

He glanced uncomfortably over his shoulder. He was

wearing his academic gown and it would not look well for a Regent Master to be seen climbing into a derelict house in full view of the High Street.

'No need,' I said. 'Edric Crowmer will be opening his shop soon. He is likely to know who holds the keys. We will enter like two respectable citizens, anxious to apprehend the miscreant who has been causing wilful damage to the new chapel at Queen's college. Should we find Piers instead, then that will simply be our good fortune.'

I had been a little too optimistic about Edric's opening of his shop. After we had stood outside in the dank cold air for some time, we went off to the nearest tavern and warmed ourselves, inside and out, beside a good fire with a flagon of hot spiced ale between us.

'Jesu!' said the pot boy who served us. 'I reckoned spring had come, but now 'tis nearer November weather.'

''Twould not be so bad,' the tavern keeper said, resting his ample belly on the counter, 'if 'twere not so damp. These Oxford fogs get into my bones. I come from the high Cotswold sheep country, and we never had such fogs there.'

I agreed with them, and commiserated with the tavern keeper about his aching joints, but Jordain's mind was elsewhere. When I felt sure Edric must be finally at work, we paid for our ale and crossed the street, where we saw, with relief, that the shutter was down from the window of the vintner's shop, and his apprentice was idly sweeping the doorstep.

'Is you master in?' I asked.

'Aye, Maister Elyot. In the back shop. Go you through.'

We found Edric drawing a sample from a wine barrel and sipping it thoughtfully. I explained about the empty house and the keys.

'Aye,' he said, laying aside his sampling rod. 'I saw the shutters had been broken open. I hold the keys myself and meant to take a look, but never had the time. Duty, you know. Duty.'

I hid my smile. Edric had been elected constable for a second year, and regarded it as a mark of personal honour, though to tell truth most of us were happy to avoid the duties he so enjoyed. They might give him standing, but they were very irksome and interfered with business.

'Master Hanbury and I thought that it might have been Queen's intruder who broke in,' I said, 'but now we are wondering whether the missing student might be there.'

'Aye, I heard tell of it yesterday,' Edric said, 'though I cannot say I have seen or heard anything of either the student or the wall breaker. Wait you a minute and I will fetch the keys.'

He went off with pompous dignity and we could hear him climbing the stairs to the living quarters above the shop. He returned with a cluster of keys strung on a thin chain.

'It is one of these,' he said. 'I hold the keys for several empty properties. Best take the lot and see which one fits. Bring them back when you have done.'

There was a momentary gleam of interest in his eyes. 'And tell me what you find. If a crime has been committed – and breaking in is certainly a crime – then it is my duty to deal with it.'

'I thank you, Edric,' I said. 'We will do so. Although if it is the fellow who has been making mischief at Queen's, then I suspect he will be long gone.'

'And if it is my student,' Jordain said, suddenly determined, 'then it will be the business of the university to deal with him.'

Edric opened his mouth to argue, then seemed to think the better of it.

Back at the empty house, the third key we tried proved to be the right one. At first the door would not move, swollen, perhaps, with the snows of several winters since the cottage was last occupied, and with the rains of as many springs and autumns, even with today's insidious fog, which had now crept into the town from all sides – from the Cherwell in the east and the Thames in the west and south. The grey fingers met and intertwined here in the middle of Oxford. I thrust my shoulder against the warped planks of the door and heaved, then with a groaning of rusted hinges it scraped its way over the earthen floor.

I shivered as I stepped over the threshold. These sorrowful empty houses, once the home of some small family, are haunted still with such an atmosphere of horror and tragedy that they bring back all too vividly those terrible years of the plague. This cottage, I remembered, had been the home of a jobbing carpenter, a man who took work wherever it offered, mostly for the colleges, but also in the homes and shops of his fellow townsmen. I had never employed him myself, but I had known him well enough to give him a nod and a 'Good morrow' when we passed in the street. He had died, together with his young wife and their three children, in the space of less than a week.

A few poor remnants of furniture were left in the room we entered. The empty house in St Mildred Street which had been granted to Emma's aunt to live in, rent free, had been stripped of every scrap of furniture, every cup, pot, and fire iron, but it was tucked away in a narrow side street. Here all was open to view on the busy High Street, and the house must have been secured soon after the family had perished. There was no musty smell as one might have expected, however, for the broken shutters had let in the air.

We paused just inside the door.

'Master Hanbury reckons those are the footprints of his intruder,' I said, pointing to a clear trail through the dust, which led from the window across to the door opening into the back room, which stood ajar.

Jordain leaned forward, the better to make them out.

'Those are a man's footprints,' he said, 'not a boy's.'

'Aye,' I said slowly, following his glance. 'But–'

I took another step into the room.

'I think there are two sets of footprints. See here.'

Not so noticeable, being smaller and less disturbing of the dust, was another trail. Hanbury and I had not seen it before because, curiously, it did not start at the window, but halfway across the floor. Both trails converged at the other door.

Suddenly I was reluctant to go further into the house, sickened at the thought of what might lie beyond that door. Could Piers have seen the intruder climbing into the house? Perhaps called out to him? And been silenced?'

I did not know whether Jordain had been seized by the same fearful thoughts as I had, but he went forward resolutely, the long sleeve of his gown sweeping something off a low stool on to the floor. I stooped to examine it. It was part of an embroidered purse, unfinished, the rusty needle still thrust through the fabric where it had been left when it was set aside. Through the thick dust I could make out the bright crimsons and azures of some exotic bird, and I remembered that the carpenter's wife had made these pretty purses to sell at the market and eke out their small income. Unaccountably, this fragment of needlework, bravely begun, brought tears to my eyes as the empty house had not.

Jordain was pushing the further door wider.

'We had best look everywhere,' he said grimly, and I realised that he had had the same terrible thoughts as I.

I crossed the front room and we went together into the one at the back of the cottage. This house was built on the same plan as the house Mistress Farringdon now lived in – a room at the front for daily living which would also serve as a work place and even a shop, a room at the rear which was the kitchen and storehouse, with access to the upper floor. The Farringdons' house had a rickety staircase, but here there was nothing but a rough ladder reaching up to a hatch in the ceiling.

Jordain laid his hand on the ladder, but I shook my head.

'Let us look in the garden at the back first,' I said.

'Very well,' he said, though with reluctance.

The back door of the house was not locked, but like the front door it was warped. However, it yielded fairly easily, as though it had been opened not long since. As we could have expected, the land beyond was a wilderness, thick with nettles and bindweed, but we were not the first to fight our way through it in recent days. There was a clear furrow through the tangled growth, leading from the back door of the house diagonally across to the partially broken fence which divided this property from the next. Certainly the intruder had been here, and just as certainly he had not needed to climb the fence. There was a gap wide enough for a man to squeeze through. He must then have crossed the next three gardens before climbing the wall into my own.

'Aye,' I said. 'No doubt of it. He came through here. And must have made his way so silently that he did not disturb the other householders.'

'Therefore,' Jordain said, 'we have certainly established what you suspected. That the fellow who overthrew Master Hanbury's wall broke into this cottage and made his way across all the gardens between here and the college, including yours, in order to wreak havoc on the building works. He must then have made his retreat the same way.'

'Aye,' I said, 'So it seems. Did I tell you that I noticed a movement in our garden a few minutes after the noise of the crash? I wasn't sure at the time that it was a man, but now I am convinced it was the intruder. I am surprised that he managed to both go and return without anyone noticing.'

'It was late and dark, you said. Folk would be in their beds, and no one about in the High, save the Watch. All he needed to do was to go softly and choose his moment when the Watch was further along the street, so that he could enter and leave the cottage unseen.'

'We have made certain of one thing,' I said, 'although it brings us no nearer discovering who the man might be, unless he has thoughtfully left behind some fragment of his clothing on one of the fences. For sure, there was nothing to be seen at the college or in our garden.'

'It seems to me,' Jordain said, 'that this is a careful fellow. I doubt he would leave any clear trace behind, though you could ask Master Crowmer to investigate.'

'He would enjoy that.' I grinned. 'Or should it more properly be the duty of William Gurdin, in the absence of Sheriff Walden?'

'From what you have told me, Gurdin takes no interest in the matter.'

'He does not.'

'Now.' Jordain turned and walked purposefully back to the cottage. 'Now we must search the upstairs, whatever may be there.'

The ladder was in a poor state, several of the rungs worm eaten, others loose. I frowned.

'I am not sure that will bear our weight, Jordain.'

'I will try it,' he said. 'I am lighter than you.'

It was true. I am not a large man, but Jordain has always been small and undernourished, even after reaching manhood.

'Very well. I will stand here at the bottom and catch you when you fall.'

'Then I shall try not to crush you.'

He began to climb the ladder gingerly, testing each rung before putting his weight on it. Even so, one cracked as he stood on it, so that he scrambled up the last yard in a flurry of splinters and sawdust.

As he disappeared through the hatch into the upper floor, I called up to him.

'You'll not be able to see much. Shall I try to find a candle or a rush light, if there are any left after the rats have feasted on them?'

'Nay, I can see well enough.' His voice came down to me muffled. 'There are some holes in the thatch.'

I could hear him moving about, but he said nothing further until he reappeared, leaning out of the opening, his face streaked with dust and with cobwebs in his hair.

'Take care coming down,' I said. 'More of those rungs may break.'

'I shall.'

He began to feel his way down, sometimes awkwardly feeling ahead with his foot two rungs at a time. He was carrying something bundled under his arm. When he was safely on the floor again, he shook it out. It was an old and worn academic gown.

'Why–' I began, and then I realised.

'That is Piers's gown?'

He nodded, and turned back the neckband, which was faced with a strip of plain undyed cloth, inside the black fabric of the gown.

'I make sure all the students mark their gowns with their names, so there can be no squabbling over ownership, though I would know this one anywhere. Jesu alone knows how many hands it has passed through since it was new.'

There, clearly to be seen, inked in on the plain cloth, was the word 'Dykman'.

'So he has been here,' I said. 'Are there any other signs?'

I did not specify what signs, but he understood me well enough.

He shook his head.

'Nothing else. The place is bare. Of course, the beds and bedding would have been taken away and burnt when they removed the bodies.'

'They would indeed. Nothing at all?'

'There was a tin flagon with some water in it. That cannot have been there long, else it would have dried up.'

'No sign of . . . of a struggle?'

'Nothing,' he said again, firmly. 'If he came with your intruder, or chasing after him, then there is no sign that he was harmed.'

'Do you think he might have come *before* the intruder,' I said, 'and hidden out of sight?'

'I think not. That would mean that he broke into the

house first. For one thing, I do not think he would have the strength to lever open the shutters. You have said the intruder had a crowbar. For another, I do not believe he would break into a house, even an empty one. He is an honest boy. If he found an open barn or stable, he might hide there, but I do not think he would damage another man's property.'

'You probably have the right of it,' I said. 'But I wonder why he left his gown behind.'

Before he could respond, I realised the answer.

'Of course! He did not want to be known as a student,' I said. 'Without his gown he could easily pass for a lad of the town.'

'Aye. I think that must be the case.'

'Well,' I said, giving him a reassuring smile, 'I think we may deduce that he had not come to any harm when he left here. Whether or not he was here at the same time as the Queen's intruder, I can see no way of telling. That was two nights ago, the overthrowing of the wall, and the first night Piers was missing. It could be that he only came here last night, seeing the shutters open on an empty house. He would have been glad of somewhere out of the cold. It could be that the two were never here together.'

Jordain nodded.

'There is nothing more for us here, I think,' he said. 'Let us return the keys to Edric Crowmer. You may tell Master Hanbury that you have investigated further, and it seems certain that what you supposed was indeed the case. The intruder broke in here and made his way from here to the college. As for Piers, he probably hid here for one night at least, but is now gone forth without his gown, dressed like any town boy, so we need to spread the word that folk should look out for such a boy, and not a student.'

'It still does not explain *why* he has run off,' I said, as we went out into the street and I locked the door. 'Perhaps when you return to Hart Hall, you will find him there.'

I tried to sound cheerful, but Jordain continued to look bleak. The boy's gown, folded over his arm, was evidence enough to suggest that Piers had not intended to return when he left the cottage.

''Tis nearly time for you to lecture,' I said. 'Do you make your way to the Schools. I will return the keys to Edric and advise him to have the shutters repaired, else every beggar in Oxford will be sleeping there. Later, we will discuss what else we may do to hunt for Piers.'

He nodded and set off down the High. Before I returned to Edric's shop, I leaned through the open window and studied the footprints in the dust. They were now overlaid with those that Jordain and I had left, but I could still make out the faint trail of smaller feet.

Why did they not start at the window, but halfway into the room?

On my way back to my shop I overtook Emma, and I remembered that she had said the day before that she would bring her notes on the troubadour songs so that we might begin fitting words and music together this morning.

'You are early abroad,' I said, as I caught up with her.

She turned to me and smiled.

'Aunt Maud and I have plans for a vegetable plot, now that the land behind the house has been cleared. We intended to make a start with the planting today, before I came with the troubadour papers, but it is so cold and damp, we decided the seeds would not take kindly to being thrust into a cold bed. We will wait until the weather brightens a little, so I am come earlier than I meant.'

She was wearing a thick cloak, more suited to winter than a spring day, and her hair, worn loose like all unmarried girls, was sprinkled with droplets of mist. She slipped her arm through mine.

'I should rather ask what you are doing so early abroad,' she said.

I explained how Jordain and I had set out to look again for Piers, and what we had found at the abandoned cottage.

'Strange,' she said, 'that he should leave his gown

behind. Even if he wished to conceal the fact that he is a student. It was very cold last night and again today. Surely he would be glad of the warmth. From what Jordain says of the boy's poverty, I cannot suppose that the cotte and hose he wears under his gown would give much warmth. He could have carried his gown rolled up in a bundle.'

'Perhaps he is not so shrewd at planning an escape as a certain novice I might name,' I said.

She laughed. 'Aye, a novice who came near to drowning through her carelessness. Poor lad! I cannot imagine that he *was* escaping, not from Hart Hall with Jordain in charge. There must be some other reason that we have not fathomed.'

'I am inclined to find the cause of his uncharacteristic behaviour in this stranger he was seen talking to.'

'What stranger was that?'

So I told her what Giles had seen, and his impression that the gentleman was someone known to Piers.

'Yet Giles said the man walked away?' she said. 'And Piers was left standing in front of the Schools. How could that be the cause of his running away?'

I shrugged.

'I do not know, but everything Piers did up till then was normal. After that, he disappeared.'

She nodded. 'Perhaps you have the right of it, though what the explanation can be, I cannot imagine.'

'There is one other thing which troubles me,' I said.

I told her of the odd way the small footprints did not start below the window, but halfway across the floor.

'Perhaps the draught from the open window swept the dust across them,' she said. 'Or else he stepped in the larger footprints part of the way. There must be some explanation.'

I did not pursue it, but it troubled me.

Walter and Roger had not yet arrived when we reached the shop, but I lowered the front shutter to give us the benefit of what little light the gloomy day afforded us. While Emma laid out her papers on my desk, I fetched my own final English versions of the songs, then we drew up two stools and began the task of fitting words and music together. This was not always easy.

'We may need to make further changes in my words,' I said, after we had struggled with the first song. 'In the English, the most important words do not always fall on the most important notes.'

'Hmm,' she said, scribbling on a scrap of my cheapest paper. 'We could try this.'

She had made a small change, but it did seem to fit the music better.

'I wonder–' She ran her finger along the line of verse.

'Aye?' I said.

'It would occupy more space, and that would mean more parchment and a larger book, but what do you say to including both the Occitan and English words? Occitan because that it how the songs were first written in Provence, English for most of us who do not speak Occitan?'

'How would you set it out on the page?'

She turned over the paper, and took her straight edge out of her scrip. With a few swift strokes, she scored the lines for the musical stave on the paper with the lead tool she used for ruling the lines for a written text.

'Ink?' she said. 'Quill?'

I fetched them for her and she quickly transcribed the first line of music in the song we had been studying.

'Now, the Occitan like this.'

She took the page containing the Occitan words for the song, which I had copied from the troubadour's song sheets when we were at Leighton-under-Wychwood in January, and set them out below the notes, with long dashes to show where a word must be sung over several notes.

'And your English words below, like this.'

She picked up my slightly amended translation and set it out below the Occitan, again showing how the words were to be fitted to the music.

'Aye,' I said, smiling. 'That is excellent. Without the

original words, these might be any songs, not true songs of the troubadours. Now, this way it is clear what they are, even for any who understand not a word of that language.'

'Even without the original words,' she said, 'I am sure that anyone with an ear for music could guess at once that these are not English.'

Once we had made this decision, the work went ahead more easily. Somehow, seeing the Occitan words in place enabled us to fit the English words successfully, although we must needs make a few adjustments. By the time my two scriveners arrived for work, we had laid out the first three songs, ready for Emma to make a fair copy on parchment for the finished book. There were a great many more still to transcribe, but we had made an excellent start to the work, which compensated in some sort for the failure to find Piers.

For the next two days all seemed to be quiet at Queen's College, as though the culprit, having demolished a large portion of wall – thereby delaying the building of the chapel and forcing the stonemasons to repair the damage over two (mostly unpaid) days – had done all the harm he intended to do. Robert Hanbury began to look less worried and his men (although they grumbled) appeared relieved that nothing worse had happened.

There had been no further trace found of Piers or where he had been, but Giles was prowling the streets of Oxford whenever he was free of his studies, hoping to recognise the stranger he had seen with Piers, although he was uncertain whether he would recognise him again.

Emma had carried off to St Mildred Street all the papers containing the words and music for the song book, and was setting them out at the desk I had had made for her. In the meantime we worked as best we could in the shop, despite the annoyance of the noisy building at the college. Roger collected the newest bound volume of the hero stories from the bookbinder, then he and Walter began to copy out two collections from the tales which had been bespoken by two of our customers. Mercifully, Lady Amilia was still away from Oxford, at her husband's country manor, awaiting her latest lying-in, but she sent me a querulous letter, demanding to know how much longer she must wait for her book of troubadour songs, ordered so many months before. I replied in soothing tones, and (privately) hoped that her new confinement might distract her for a time.

The weather turned spring-like again, so that the work at Queen's continued briskly. It meant more disturbance now, but perhaps an earlier completion.

On the fourth day after the overthrowing of the wall the children were personally invited by Robert Hanbury to watch the construction of the first stage of the scaffolding. We went round to the college immediately after breaking our fast and found a spot well out of the way of the carpenters who were erecting the structure. The various timbers were already cut to the right lengths, the joints marked with a series of scored lines so that they could be fitted together in the correct order, and the framework went up surprisingly quickly. The first vertical supports were driven into the ground to a depth of about two feet. The horizontal supports were placed at regular distances along the latest completed course of stonework, jutting out at around shoulder height, and as the carpenters fitted these timbers into the notches cut by the masons in the upper surfaces of the stones, the men building the wall, the setters, laid and mortared the next course on top, to secure the supports in place.

Rafe frowned thoughtfully.

'It is a sort of shelf, isn't it? A shelf for people?'

'More than a shelf,' Alysoun said. 'They have to walk about on it. And carry heavy stones.'

We watched as the thick hurdles of woven wattles were laid across the timber framework and I must admit I should not like to risk my neck climbing about on what looked a somewhat fragile structure, with a hod of stones on my back, or a heavy bucket of mortar in my hand. The hurdles flexed as the carpenters walked across them, securing them to the framework with thick leather thongs, but the men seemed unworried by the rippling under their feet.

'But,' Alysoun said, frowning and trying to work it out, 'now they can only reach as high again as the first bit of wall, so I don't think that will be any good.'

She gave Robert a reproving look.

He smiled down at her.

'You are quite right, my maid. Once it is as high as we can reach from this stage of the scaffolding, then we build another layer. Another shelf, as Rafe says. And up and up until we reach the roof. Then the carpenters take over and build the trusses to hold the slates for the roof. That will be after we have constructed the stone arches inside the chapel.'

'How will you climb up there?' Rafe asked, pointing to the walkway of hurdles.

'We lean ladders against the sides, or climb up the timber frame like a ladder.'

'I should not like to carry one of your great stones up several layers of scaffolding,' I said, suppressing a shudder.

'Oh, for the higher courses and the heaviest blocks we use a hoist.'

Robert jerked his thumb at a pile of machinery lying beside the canvas lodge. I could make out a large wheel, a cluster of pulleys, and coils of rope.

'Not needed yet,' he said, 'but necessary higher up. And for the lintels. They are our largest blocks. I will not risk my men carrying dangerous loads, as some masters will.'

We walked round the whole base of the chapel, as Robert pointed out the shorter east and west walls and how they were joined to the south wall by alternating long and short stones at the corners, so that the two walls were tied to each other.

'Like this,' he said to the children, clasping his hands together, the fingers threaded through each other.

The north wall was also begun, though only two courses high so far.

'Here at the east end we shall leave an opening for a fine window,' he said. 'You have seen the opening for the south door. That will have ornamental jambs and an arched top. And there will be a door on the north side as well. The carving for the east window is the most beautiful, and I shall take a hand at it myself.'

'So you don't just tell the men what to do?' Alysoun said. 'You can carve yourself?'

He laughed. 'Aye. I was not born a master mason. I was an apprentice like those boys over there, then a journeyman, and I learned every skill a stonemason must have, not only working as a banker mason and setting the stones for a wall and doing fine carved work. You must know how to plan a building in every detail, whether an ornamental window or a spiral staircase. You must be able to set your hand to anything – a curtain wall for a castle or a grand chamber for king's palace, a London merchant's fine townhouse or a sturdy village pound. In the end, if you work very hard, you may become a master mason.'

'Are you very old?' Rafe asked.

Robert grinned at me. 'Older than your father, but not so *very* old.'

'I thought the plan was to have north and south transepts,' I said. 'At least, so Provost de Hotham told me.'

'When I explained to him just how much it would cost to have the transepts as well as the main structure, he had to give up the idea. They can be added later, should they find another generous benefactor.'

'He is still coming to see the work?' I asked. 'The benefactor? So you must make haste?'

'We heard that he has been ill, not able for the moment to travel, so I hoped for a little extra time, but now we are told that if he does not come himself, his son will come in his stead, so aye, we must make haste and hope we have no more "accidents" to delay the work.'

'Amen to that,' I said. 'I have never heard who this

generous benefactor is.'

'Ah,' Robert said, ''tis Sir Thomas de Luce, son of that Sir Anthony who was the Founder's patron, when Robert de Eglesfield was a mere man-at-arms, before he came late to the Church and royal service.'

'Indeed? I had not known that he began life in a secular calling.'

I was surprised. Most men who enter the church come to it early, as boys. Some of our students now at the university would become parish priests, some would have higher ambitions, aiming for an abbacy or a bishop's mitre, or even a cardinal's hat. Many men in the royal service were in holy orders, finding their vocation as clerks or accountants. Under our present king, however, places were beginning to be found in his administration for seculars as well. I wondered whether Robert de Eglesfield had entered the Church due to a religious vocation, or through worldly ambition. He must have risen quickly, if he had begun life as a man-at-arms in the service of Sir Anthony de Luce, and only taken holy orders late.

'The de Luce family continues to take an interest in the college?' I said.

'So it seems. They are a powerful family in the north country, I understand.'

'Not to be offended, then. Do you know when he comes, the benefactor? Or the son?'

'Not of a certainty,' he said, 'but in about four weeks, I believe. We cannot have completed the building by then, impossible, but if the outer walls are up, and the carpenters at work on the roof, the bases of the inner pillars in place in the nave, and some of the ornamental carving complete, then I think he should be content.'

'I wish you every success,' I said. 'Surely your trouble-maker has done his worst.'

He laughed. 'Amen to that.'

But I was grievously mistaken.

Chapter Five

The construction of the scaffolding at Queen's College and the setting of more stones in the chapel's outer wall without further disturbance lulled us all into a belief that whoever had played his unpleasant pranks on Master Hanbury's works had grown bored or was satisfied with the trouble he had already caused. As well as the outer walls of the chapel, the stonemasons were also building a double rank of pillars within, to divide the side aisles from the central portion of the nave. I could not but admire the skill of their work in shaping the square blocks of stone into the cylinders from which the pillars were constructed. Although they had a wooden pattern for guidance, almost all the shaping was done by eye, merely checked occasionally against the pattern. The arches which would leap from pillar to pillar, and support the roof, had yet to be made.

At home and in the shop we continued to endure the constant irritation of the dust, the maddening noise of stone being sawed and chiselled, the hammering of the carpenters, and the shouts of the men. I suspected that I was losing customers to the two rival bookshops in the town. Not being licensed by the university, they could not rent out *peciae* to the students, but they could supply ink, quills, paper, and parchment. I hoped that I should not lose my customers for good.

Philip Olney called in one day to invite my family to a quiet supper at Beatrice Metford's house, out beyond the

East Gate.

'There you may breathe clean air and eat without grinding away your teeth on chips of Headington stone,' he said.

We accepted gladly, I all the more readily when I learned that Emma too had been invited. Despite the vast gulf which lay between them, of birth, rank, and riches, Emma and Beatrice had become good friends ever since they had worked together at St Frideswide's Fair.

It was a happy, unpretentious evening. As we were still in the period of the Lenten fast, Beatrice served us no meat, but instead fresh trout dressed with a sauce of cream and chopped dill, preceded by a white onion soup, and followed by a salad composed of the early thinnings from her lettuce plot mixed with wild rocket and the first young dandelion leaves, picked before they turned bitter, the whole sprinkled with herbs steeped in *verjus*. We finished with a confection of figs, honey, and hazelnuts.

'This is no simple supper, Beatrice,' Margaret said, smiling. ''Tis fit for a lord's table.'

Beatrice blushed, for she was well aware of my sister's reputation as one of the best cooks in Oxford.

'Nay, you flatter me,' she said.

'And already you have food from your garden,' Emma said. 'My aunt and I have but planted our seeds this last week.'

'Ah, but I have a long start of you,' Beatrice said. 'I have lived here for eight years now, and my garden is well grown. Besides, I have had time to stock my larder with preserves and dried herbs. I made the *verjus* from last year's crab apples. We have a small orchard behind the house. And the hazelnuts are some left over from when we all went a-gathering on Headington Hill in the autumn.'

''Twould not be so peaceful there at present,' I said. 'Although we went to a part of the hill well away from the quarry, they have been cutting so much stone for the building work at Queen's, and dragging it down into the town, that I fear even our quiet little copse would fare little better than the racket we must endure at home.'

'Are the stonemasons at the college still troubled by that malicious intruder?' Philip asked. 'The last I heard was that much of a wall had been thrown down.'

I assured him that all was now forging ahead unhindered. 'Nothing more since then,' I said. 'Master Hanbury hopes that is an end to it. The site is well guarded, and the way the fellow made his way in, through the deserted cottage along the street from my shop, is now barred to him, for the cottage has been secured.'

'Let us hope he does not choose to break open the shutters again,' Philip said. 'Although since it is close by Constable Crowmer's premises, no doubt he would consider himself personally affronted if that happened.'

'There remains our worry over Jordain's missing student,' I said. 'Nothing has been seen or heard of him since Jordain and I came upon his academic gown in that deserted cottage, although whether he was there at the same time as the intruder, it is impossible to tell. If he has not been found within this next week, Jordain must write to his family, or more likely to their parish priest, since none but the boy in his family can read.'

'It is dreadful to think of,' Beatrice said, 'that young boy wandering alone in the streets of Oxford.'

She glanced aside at her son Stephen. Now that our meal was finished the children were sitting on the floor playing a game of knucklebones, at which Stephen was proving to be very skilled.

'But surely if anything serious had happened to the boy,' Philip said, choosing his words carefully, in the hearing of the children, 'then he would have been found.'

He did not say 'his body', though we all took his meaning.

'It seems likely,' I said. 'But why he has run off and why he has stayed away, no one can understand. Giles Wetherby has not been able to find the stranger he saw talking to Piers. He too seems to have disappeared.'

Philip and Beatrice had not heard of this encounter,

so I explained.

'Perhaps, as Giles thought,' Margaret said, 'the man was nothing but a stranger passing through Oxford and has now gone on his way.'

'It seems to me,' Emma said slowly, 'that a boy like this, a boy everyone says is a serious student, courteous and thoughtful, would only have behaved in such a way for one of two reasons.'

We all turned to look at her.

'He might have been ashamed or guilty about something he had done,' she said. 'Such children are often hard on themselves. Perhaps he thought he had performed badly in a disputation or been thoughtless, and seen it as a sort of wickedness. Yet both seem unlikely, from all we know of his character. Or else,' she paused, and glanced at Beatrice, as the mother of another young boy, 'or else he was afraid. Terribly afraid. Of someone or something.'

Beatrice nodded. 'I think you have the right of it.'

'That also is what I believe,' I said. 'That he was afraid. But what could have so frightened the child that he does not come back to Jordain, who has been a second father to him?'

Emma shook her head. 'Until we know, or guess, what frightened Piers, I think we shall not find him.'

The following morning I had a few customers in my shop early – students on their way to lectures, and one of the Fellows of St Edmund Hall wanting a jar of ink. When they were gone, all was quiet except for the scratching of Walter's quill, and the clink as Roger stirred a pot of viridian for the illuminated letter he was working on. He had erected a sort of tent-like structure over his desk from an old pillow bere Margaret had given him. Crouched under this he could work without the danger of dust marring his painting. I was adding up the figures of last month's spending and earning – several times over, I must confess – and trying to set them out in two columns according to the new Italian fashion in book-keeping that

Peter Winchingham had been urging on me with enthusiasm.

It was all the more shocking, therefore, when this peaceful scene was torn apart by sudden terrible screams. All three of us leapt to our feet, Roger cursing as his paint pot tipped and he only just managed to catch it in time.

'Jesu save us!' Walter cried. 'Is someone being murdered in the street?'

'Another fight, town and gown?' Roger said, pushing the cork into his paint pot and laying down his brush carefully on its holder.

'Nay.' I shook my head. 'We would have heard shouts and running footsteps if that were the case. That was one man only. One man badly hurt.'

We pushed aside the blanket and half fell out of the door in our haste. The screams, I was sure, had come from the direction of Queen's, and now we could hear more, a high pitched keening, the sound of someone in great pain.

I ran toward the opening into the college, the other two close behind.

Within the college grounds, all was confusion. Stonemasons and carpenters alike were crowded together over near the area where I had seen the orderly piles of timber and undressed stone. Several of the Fellows were hurrying across from their quarters on the far side of the college. The howls of pain were rising from somewhere in the midst of the crowd of workmen.

Suddenly two of the apprentices broke out of the crowd and dashed toward the college well. By the time I reached Robert Hanbury they came staggering back, each carrying two buckets of water. The crowd parted to let them through.

'Dear God, Hanbury,' I said, 'what is afoot?'

He ignored me, but shouted to the apprentices, 'Pour it over him, all of it, then fetch more.'

Peering past him, I could see one of the other apprentices lying on the ground, writhing in agony. His hose were nothing but tattered rags, and his legs were as red as raw flesh, already bursting into blisters. Just beyond him was the pit dug in the ground for slaking the lime for mortar.

The water was poured over those horribly disfigured legs, and the injured lad stopped howling so loudly. His gasps of pain were almost worse, great shuddering gulps, as though he could barely draw in enough air to breathe.

'More,' Hanbury snapped to the apprentices standing holding the empty buckets and staring helplessly down at their fellow. 'Another dowsing.'

They ran off again and he turned to me.

'Burned with slaked lime,' he said grimly. 'Such an accident should never happen. They know how dangerous it is, until it cools.'

He turned to one of the other apprentices, whose face was as white as the lime mortar, and who had just been quietly sick behind the piles of timber.

'How did this happen?'

I had never seen him afire with such anger, not even when the wall was broken down.

'It wasn't Wat's fault, Master Hanbury.' The apprentice was beginning to sob. He could not be more than fifteen, and the other boy's legs were a sight to sicken any stomach.

'Of course it was his fault,' Hanbury snapped.

'Nay.' Despite his horror and his master's anger, the apprentice was determined to defend his friend. 'The setters were yelling for mortar and telling us to hurry about it. The lime was still smoking, but Wat dipped the mixing bucket at the pit, same as usual, and lifted it out to add the sand, he was being careful, and then it just, it just . . . fell apart, and all the lime poured down over his legs.'

He gulped, and looked as though he might vomit again.

'See!' He moved to one side and pointed. Behind him and just beyond Wat's ruined legs, the remains of a large bucket lay scattered on the ground. It was perhaps twice the size of the water buckets that were now being emptied again over those terrible burns. Its staves should have been held together by a round metal hoop near the rim and another near the base, like those used by coopers in making barrels. The remains of the hoops lay amongst the shattered ribs and the strewn lime.

'Will it have cooled enough now?' I asked Hanbury.

'Aye, 'tis only dangerous for a short time. Why?'

I did not answer at once, but picked up the pieces of the two hoops and examined them carefully.

Most of the workmen were drifting away now.

'You, lad,' I said to the apprentice still standing miserably beside us. 'Run as fast as you can to the hospital of St John, just by the East Bridge. Do you know it? Ask them to send a physician as quickly as may be.'

'I know it,' he said, and set off at a run.

It seemed to take a long time, though it was probably no more than minutes, before the physician came bustling in, his face full of concern.

'Lime burns?' he said. 'Nasty. Very nasty, but I will do what I can. Carry him to our infirmary and I will salve the burns, but I fear the skin will never recover.'

The boy Wat was shivering now, and moaning, as though he was trying to hold back his cries of pain, but when they started to move him, it must have been more than he could bear. In the end they managed to lift him on to one of the scaffolding hurdles, despite his screams of pain.

'A blanket,' the physician ordered. 'Lay a blanket over his upper body. He is cold, in a state of shock. But keep it well clear of his injuries.'

One of the apprentices brought Wat's own blanket from the pile folded in the corner of the lodge, and tucked it carefully around his chest and shoulders, though it seemed to do little to assuage the shivering.

Two of the masons picked up the hurdle and carried him off to the infirmary at St John's, Robert Hanbury and the physician walking beside them. The master mason returned at last, tight mouthed, and gave his orders for the men to continue with their work. Finally he came back to me, where I stood still holding the broken hoops. I had already sent Walter and Roger back to the shop, remembering that we had left it standing open.

'Not for anything would I have had that happen,' Hanbury said. 'He is usually a sensible fellow, Wat. I would never have expected him to be so careless. Even if his legs can be saved, the physician says he will be crippled for life.'

'As the other lad explained,' I said, 'it was not Wat's fault.'

'What do you mean? How could the bucket have fallen apart? It was perfectly sound, we have been using it every day. It must have broken when Wat dropped it.'

I shook my head. 'Look at this.'

I held the pieces of the hoops out to him.

'These have been sawed through, or almost through. It would have needed a very fine saw which could slip between the staves of the bucket. See?'

I pointed to the bright edges of the metal, which bore the scratches left by the saw. On each hoop, just below the cut edges, the metal was broken off raggedly.

'When they were cut through, just enough of each hoop was left intact,' I said, 'so that the bucket held together and looked whole enough. Then when it was filled, the weight of the lime burst the last fragment of the two hoops and the staves fanned out, spilling the burning lime all over that unhappy boy. I don't suppose it was meant for him in particular, merely for whoever next lifted a bucket of slaked lime. Would the lime normally still be hot when you lift it from the pit?'

He shook his head. 'Nay. It does not take long to cool. Once it has done so, we lift it out and mix in the sand to strengthen it.'

He pointed to heap of coarse sand lying on the ground behind me.

'Then, had it already cooled,' I said, 'it would have done no great damage, merely caused you a nuisance.'

Robert Hanbury examined the severed metal, then raised appalled eyes to me.

'It is clear enough. That is how it was done, you have the right of it. Nevertheless, it is monstrous. Wat could have been killed. As it is, I do not suppose he will ever work again.'

'It is indeed monstrous,' I said quietly. 'Your intruder is becoming more dangerous.'

'You think it is the same man?'

'Do not you?'

He had no answer for that.

I returned to the shop in sober mood. Above all, I wished heartily for the return of Cedric Walden to Oxford. The stolen and damaged tools, even the broken wall, were annoyances, but had caused no injury. This latest occurrence was very different. It could no longer be regarded as a prank. Even if the intruder had not intended serious harm, there would always have been a risk, for the slaking of lime can be dangerous, if not treated with respect. Now the boy Wat had been grossly disfigured. Even should he live, his future as a stonemason must surely be ended, for a mason, almost more than any other craftsman, depends on strength.

My two scriveners were working when I entered the shop, both of them looking pale and shocked.

'How is it with the lad?' Walter asked.

I shook my head. 'Bad. He is taken to St John's, and they will do what they can for him, but the injuries are serious. His legs will never recover, even if he does not lose them. And besides . . .' I hesitated. 'So severe an injury can sometimes cause hidden damage within, even stop the heart, or start the body burning up with a raging fever. It will be days, I would guess, before we can be sure he will even live.'

I paused. 'There are signs that the bucket was tampered with.'

Walter looked horrified, seeming to find no words to respond to this, but Roger stood up, clenching his fists angrily.

'It must be stopped!' he cried. 'These are no accidents! Why does that fool William Gurdin do nothing? That boy could have been killed, and you say he may still die. We must put an end to it.'

I shook my head at him.

'There is nothing we can do to stop this wickedness at present, Roger,' I said. 'Robert Hanbury has made all as safe from intruders as he can. Let us hope that Cedric Walden returns soon. He has the powers to investigate, which we have not.'

'Do you think the fellow has broken in again?' Walter said. 'Is not that cottage made secure?'

'It is,' I said. 'But I suppose that this latest trick may have been prepared before now, perhaps even on the same night when he was in the college grounds and threw down the wall.'

I explained how the metal hoops had been sawed almost through.

'I thought at first that they would break as soon as the bucket was filled, but perhaps not. It might be some days before the last bit of metal gave way. They might have been tampered with several days ago, and only collapsed today. Mayhap the fact that the lime was burning hot caused it to happen now. Wat cannot have been singled out as the victim, it was just his misfortune.'

A dreadful misfortune indeed. I do not think I shall ever forget the sight of the injured youth writhing in almost unspeakable pain on the ground.

We worked for the rest of the day in gloomy silence. Even Roger had little to say. I sent him round to Queen's halfway through the afternoon to ask for news of Wat.

'Master Hanbury has heard nothing, good or bad,' he said when he returned. 'Save that the apprentice has a high fever and is out of his wits.'

'Little to wonder about in that,' Walter said.

I sent them both home early, for none of us had the heart for working.

Although Emma had completed the collection of Walter's tales some days before, it had not yet been bound. She insisted that the choice of binding should be Walter's, while he insisted that he could not make such a decision on his own, so that in the end I agreed to go with him to Henry Stalbroke's workshop, and we set off together the next morning to walk across Oxford to Bookbinder's Island, leaving Roger in charge of the shop – no very arduous task, given our lack of customers.

'I'll continue with my illuminations,' he said, 'though I am running short of crimson.'

'I shall stop at the paint seller's on the way back,' I said. 'Are you in need of aught else?'

'There is not much blue left,' he said. 'Not the costly lapis blue for holy figures, but the periwinkle that I use for the lesser things.'

'I'll buy a supply of both, then.'

It was warm spring weather again as we set out, the golden Cotswold stone of the colleges glowing in the shafts of low-lying morning sun. When the light catches it, the stone seems almost as precious as some of those rarities imported from eastern lands for garnishing the crowns of kings, or the amber come from the Baltic countries, possessed of magical properties. In certain evening lights, the stone turns the colour of honey.

I know that I am not much travelled, but can there be any more beautiful stone in the world? And with skilled stonemasons like Robert Hanbury, it may be carved into most exquisite forms. Only the day before yesterday, while all was still tranquil at Queen's, I had watched the master mason begin the carving of the trifoliate framework for the chapel's east window, which would hold stained glass. When it was in place, the beauty of the multicoloured glass would draw the eye, but the framing stone was every bit as fine. I had watched how, with nothing more than a handful of chisels and a wooden mallet he had begun the delicate work.

'The carving lies within the stone, Nicholas,' he said. 'I am but God's instrument. My task is to coax the intricate shapes which are hiding inside this piece of seemingly rough Taynolt stone, to coax them out into the light, to bring them forth.'

He smiled shyly.

'We may think that our skill lies in creating something out of nothing, but it is not so. God is the Creator of all things. Our years of training serve only to teach us how to recognise what lies beneath the surface.'

He ran a caressing hand over his block of stone, as a father might caress the cheek of his child, and smiled again, secretly, to himself.

As Walter and I now headed west toward Carfax, I thought that this is one of the loveliest times of year in Oxford. Most of the winter mud was gone, and many of the timber-framed town houses were newly lime-washed. In the first years after the pestilence, people were too shocked, too worn down by grief and fear, to give any heed to their surroundings. We crawled about like ants scattered from a broken nest, scarcely aware that we still lived, but slowly we were beginning to recover, like a patient emerging half dazed from weeks of fever. The fresh lime wash gleaming here and there along the High seemed like a smile on the face of the town.

Walter's thoughts must have been running the same way as mine.

'Fruit blossom coming out,' he said, nodding toward the cloud of pale blossom which could be seen rising above the roof of a cordwainer's shop. 'Looks to be a good crop. Pears, likely.'

'Aye.' I grinned, remembering youthful wickedness scrumping apples and pears from the orchard of Leighton Manor. John, Margaret, and I had no need to steal, for there were trees a-plenty on the farm, but does not the stolen fruit always taste the sweeter?

'Margaret complains that we had a poor crop of quinces last year,' I said. 'I hope we may do better this autumn.'

It was good to be walking carefree through the town with an old friend, talking of naught but fruit and leaving behind the distresses of the previous day. The sun had grown warmer by the time we reached Bookbinders Island, and unfortunately the wind was southerly, bringing with it a certain powerful odour from Dafydd Hewlyn's parchment workshop further along, so we were glad to enter Henry Stalbroke's bindery, with its warm scents of dressed leather, polish, and glue.

I lifted the pages of Walter's book carefully out of the stiffened satchel I use for carrying manuscripts, and laid them on Henry's table. I saw that Henry had taken to wearing eye-glasses, very like those I had bought Walter at St Frideswide's Fair. They were hanging from loops of tape over his ears, but he tied them on firmly now, and examined the pages carefully.

'Ah,' Henry said, 'do I observe the hand of your newest scrivener here?'

'You do,' I said. It had not been possible to hide Emma's occupation from Henry, who could probably recognise the hand of every scholar and every scrivener in Oxford.

'But this,' I said, drawing a reluctant Walter forward, 'this is the author.'

Henry grinned at Walter and raised his eyebrows in mock astonishment.

'So, Master Blunt!' He bowed. 'Will you be leaving the employment of Elyot's bookshop and setting up as a writer of books now?'

Walter grinned sheepishly at being teased. We both knew that Henry was well aware of the progress of Walter's book, which had been in the making for a year now.

'This shall be my first and last,' Walter said firmly. 'I never knew that writing a book could be so hard. Harder by far than copying Master Aristotle without mistakes, or slaving at those wretched *peciae* days together.'

'We are come to choose a fine binding,' I said, 'something suitable for Walter's magnificent work. We shall be keeping it at the shop, not selling it, so that customers may choose their own version, the whole or a selection of the tales.'

I turned to Walter. 'Have you a colour of binding in mind?'

'Nothing in especial,' he said. 'Just a plain brown calf will do very well.'

'Nonsense,' Henry said. 'If this is indeed to be your first and last *opus*, then we must find an appropriate skin.'

He set down the pages and began to lay out various leathers on the far end of the table. Despite Walter's continued insistence that a cheap brown binding would suffice, I saw that his eyes continued to be drawn by a supple skin dyed a delicate sky blue. I picked it up.

'This is very fine,' I said. 'What think you, Henry? Would it suit the text? You are the best judge of such things.'

Walter opened his mouth as if to protest, but there was no mistaking that look of longing. Henry had noticed it too.

He nodded. 'Aye, I believe that would suit very well.'

He took it from me and laid it beside the pages. 'There is enough here, without skimping, and it is the last piece I have in this particular shade. You will have it tooled and gilded, I suppose? Since this volume will be unique.'

'Aye certainly.' I smiled. 'And since it is a very large volume, I think we must have clasps. Nothing gaudy, I think, Walter? What say you?'

'Clasps?' He swallowed and flushed. Usually only the very finest books were fastened with clasps. Lesser books of the bulkier sort might have straps of leather to tie them together, but clasps were reserved for the finest.

'Something like this, perhaps.'

Henry had gone over to a side table where he kept various samples, and came back with three clasps, all elegant without being overly ornate. Still looking slightly dazed, Walter chose one.

'And will you have the edges gilded?' Henry asked.

At that, Walter baulked. 'Nay, surely not!'

'Perhaps not,' I said. 'But I think crimson would not sit well with that delicate blue of the leather.'

'I agree,' Henry said. 'A dark blue would be better. Like this.'

He lifted down a volume from the shelf where books awaiting collection were stored.

'Aye.' Walter looked relieved. 'That will do very well.'

Henry assured us that, although he had a good deal of work in hand, he would give preference to this book. Walter had to endure more teasing from Henry's senior journeyman, Thomas Needham, before we emerged from the workshop.

'It will be very costly,' he said, with some nervousness, as we walked back to the bridge over the Thames, 'such a fine binding, with tooling and clasps.'

'No more than it deserves, after a year's labour on your part,' I said. 'It will be an ornament to our shop.'

'We are gathering a fine collection of books from which the customers may choose,' he said. 'Roger's hero tales, Emma's books of hours, and soon the troubadour song book. Your father-in-law would be proud of you, Nicholas.'

I had never thought in such terms, but it was true that I had taken the business into new ventures of late. Both of my long-serving scriveners had shown great enterprise, while Emma's skills as an illuminator meant that we could now produce books to rival anything I had seen in Oxford. I dared to believe we might come near the finest work even London might produce.

My father-in-law, Humphrey Hadley, had been content with the trade offered by the university – the renting of *peciae* to students, the handling of secondhand books (mostly battered student texts), and the selling of stationery (ink, quills, parchment, and cheap paper). He had been a practical man, and had seen the value of educating his daughter sufficiently that she might help him in the shop, but he was no great scholar, and did not often read for pleasure. I fear he might have regarded both the hero tales and Walter's traditional stories passed down by his mother as something not quite worthy of a licensed university bookseller. Master Hadley was a devout man, and would have approved of such sacred works as the books of hours and lives of saints, but I had not Walter's confidence that he would have been pleased at our less serious secular books. However, if they brought in more business to the shop, that *would* have pleased him.

On our way back we turned aside briefly into Northgate Street, that I might purchase the inks Roger needed. John Barton was a reliable purveyor of inks and paints, used by all the colleges and the monastic establishments in Oxford, stocking his shop with a dazzling array of colours and qualities, which ranged from the everyday to the most precious, like the lapis blue used for the Virgin, angels, and saints. He would have nothing to do with the poorer sort of colours sold by the other paint shop located down an alley off Fish Street. Patchy and unstable, those might do for cheaply produced work, but I never bought there.

My purchases complete, we continued on down the High, where I noticed Edric Crowmer standing outside the deserted cottage which had provided the Queen's intruder access through the back gardens. On our way to the bookbinder I had not even glanced that way, but now I saw that every line of Edric's back expressed outrage. He was standing stiffly erect, clenched fists thrust into the waist of the somewhat grand robe he had taken to wearing of late. Beyond him, a local carpenter was perched atop a short ladder, hammering a wide plank in place across the shutters which had previously been wrenched apart.

'Trouble, Edric?' I asked.

So absorbed was he that he had failed to notice our approach, and gave a start. Several passersby paused and stared at the sound of hammering, before walking on.

'Aye,' he said grimly. 'Trouble.'

'Broken in again, has he?' Walter said, with some sympathy.

The audacity of the intruder cast a certain doubt over Edric's ability to sustain his authority as constable.

'The b'yer lady effrontery of the fellow!' Edric burst out, unable to contain his indignation. 'It was done in the night, although I had warned the Watch to keep a careful eye on this house. Somehow he managed to break open the shutters without them noticing. Probably off drinking in some snug corner of the town, or asleep. I'll have their hides for this! And then he props the broken shutters so cunningly closed when he leaves that my apprentice did but notice the damage an hour ago.'

The carpenter, who had descended his ladder, was now climbing it again with a second plank, which he began to fix in place.

'If 'twas that difficult to see,' I said, 'mayhap it did not happen last night, but a day or two ago.'

I was still wondering whether the tampering with the lime bucket had happened last night, or earlier.

Edric shrugged. 'Probably we would have noticed, though I'd not swear to it. However,' he smiled grimly, 'he'll not remove those planks in a hurry. We have him now.'

Walter and I continued on our way, both absorbed in our thoughts.

'Surely this must be an end to it now,' he said. 'As the vintner says, he cannot break his way through both those planks *and* the shutters without rousing the whole street.'

'Probably not,' I agreed, 'but I wonder whether he has left any other nasty traps behind at the college. That bucket could have collapsed at any time. There may be other unpleasant surprises awaiting Master Hanbury and his men.'

Early the following morning I was just finishing my breakfast when I heard a tentative tap on the street door. I opened it to find Thomas Bokeland, rector of St Peter-in-the-East, standing on the doorstep in the grey light of dawn.

'I apologise for troubling you so early, Master Elyot,' he said, 'but I know you have been concerned in the search for the missing student from Hart Hall.'

I stepped out into the street to join him.

'Indeed I am,' I said, 'Piers Dykman. Have you news of him?'

'News, nay, but I think I may have had a sighting of him.'

'You have *seen* him!'

'Only a glimpse,' he said hesitantly, 'and I am not even sure if it was the boy. I know he attends Mass at St Peter's along with the other students from Hart Hall, but I have never paid him particular mind.'

'Where did you have this glimpse,' I said, 'however brief?'

'You will forgive me, Master Elyot,' he said, turning aside, 'but I must finish preparing for Mass.'

We began to walk toward the church as he explained.

'I was coming from the rectory to the church, across the churchyard, as I do every morning. My mind was not on my surroundings, thinking of the preparations to be made for the Easter services. I stumbled, knocked my toe against a fallen gravestone, and you know how it is. I must have let out a yelp, for it was painful, and that was when I saw him. He was curled up in the space between the old charnel house and the de Howard family monument. The moment he heard me, he sprang up and darted off before I could catch him or even call out to him.'

He ran a hand over his face, and gave me a worried smile.

'I am not as young as I was. I had no hope of overtaking him. The grass was flattened where he had been, and dry, as though he had been there all night, for the rest of the grass in the churchyard was damp with the dew.

There was a heel of stale bread there, as though he had saved it for his breakfast. But you see, I am not sure whether it was Master Brinkylsworth's missing boy, or some other poor lad from the town. So many are orphaned since the pestilence. It might not have been the student at all.'

'Did you notice what he was wearing?' I asked.

He looked vague. 'Not a student gown.'

'Nay, he had parted with that.'

'I am not sure.' He frowned. 'I am afraid I am a poor hand at such things. I noticed nothing colourful, so he must have worn browns or greys.' He shook his head. 'Nay, I am no use to you as to his clothes.'

We had reached the lane and turned up toward the church.

'What age of boy, would you say?' I was growing more disappointed the more he said. It could indeed have been any homeless lad.

'Certainly not full grown,' he said firmly, as though he was on surer ground here. 'No higher than my shoulder. And very slight, so it could have been a pauper lad.'

This cheered me a little.

'Piers is small and slight, even for his age,' I said. 'He comes from a poor family and is not well grown.

The rector led me across the churchyard to the small stone-built charnel house standing against the far wall. Beside it the de Howard family's grand tomb dwarfed its humble size. In the past, the charnel house had probably served its purpose, but when Death cut his great swathe through the parish, there was no time for anything but hasty mass burials. Even the sexton was taken, so it fell to the men of the parish to dig the great pit. Now we were so reduced in numbers within the parish of St Peter's that there was no need to remove the bones of the dead to the charnel house to make room for new burials. Besides, the churchyard had recently been extended. One end of the charnel house roof was falling in. It would probably be left now to rot.

Rector Bokeland pointed out the patch of flattened grass and the heel of a loaf. A field mouse which had been nibbling it whisked away at the sight of us.

'There,' he said. 'I was coming from the rectory.' He pointed. 'And the boy ran off through the gate into the lane, then headed toward the High Street. I fear he will be long gone now.'

He could tell me nothing more, so he hurried round to the church door to begin his preparations for early Mass. There was little to see here. Already the fresh new grass was beginning to spring back, but I could see that the flattened area was about the right size for a boy of twelve or thirteen. But which boy?

Leaving the mouse to his bread and the rector to his church, I walked up Hammer Hall Lane, to Hart Hall.

Jordain's face lit up when I told him what the rector had seen.

'Jesu be praised!' he said. 'The boy is still alive!'

'We cannot be sure,' I cautioned him. 'Master Bokeland caught no more than a glimpse of this boy, and in any case is not certain that he would recognise him. Certainly a boy slept there last night, but it might be some other lad. One of Oxford's many orphans, or even a runaway apprentice.'

He shook his head. 'I am certain it was Piers. St Peter's churchyard. Aye, he would feel safe there, under God's hand, and not very far from us here. Whatever has frightened him, he has not chosen to go far.'

I hoped he had the right of it.

'He lay just beside the wall of the charnel house,' I said. 'Part of the roof has fallen in, but it would have provided some shelter. Although the days are warm now, the nights are still cold. Yet I cannot blame him for avoiding the charnel house. I do not know if it is empty now, but no child would want to sleep alone there, even if it contains naught but the memory of old bones.'

Jordain shuddered. 'Poor lad. I am thankful, at least, that he has not been driven to such a fearful resting place.

The rector said he ran toward the High Street?'

'Aye, but he did not see which way he went after that. Even as early in the day as this he would soon be lost amongst the folk walking to their day's labours.'

It occurred to me that Jordain might not have heard of the latest accident at Queen's chapel, so I told him briefly what had happened. He gasped in horror when he heard of the apprentice Wat's injuries.

'He will be maimed for life?'

'So it seems. I thought to visit St John's today, to ask after him,' I said. 'It is not clear when the bucket was tampered with, for it seems the intruder may have made his way through the gardens again.'

I told him of Edric's discovery of the broken shutters.

'He will not gain entrance by that means now,' I said. 'And I am mighty glad that my own garden cannot be used as a way into the college. It makes me feel as though I am some way at fault, for not having heard and stopped him.'

'Your dog Rowan did not hear him and give the alarm?'

I shook my head. 'She is no watch dog, I fear. And in any case, he seems to keep to the far end of the garden, well away from the house.'

'Well, you may comfort yourself that he will not go that way again to wreak havoc on Master Hanbury's works.'

'Aye.' I shrugged. I could not share his implied optimism. 'For all we know, he may have set further traps. The damage to the lime bucket might have been done some days ago. There may be more trouble to come.'

'Let us hope you are wrong. And at least we know that Piers is still alive.'

I did not want to crush his hopes by pointing out again that the boy seen by the rector might not have been Piers. I was reluctant to place too much faith in it myself. As Jordain was due at the Schools to give a lecture, we walked together back down the lane, but I parted with him at the church. I felt the need of quiet and consolation.

'In any case,' he said finally, 'it certainly could not have been Piers who tampered with the lime bucket. He would never do such a thing, something which could cause injury. And where would he get the saw to cut through the metal hoops? He can no more have done this than he could overthrow the stones of the half built wall. Whatever is amiss with him, it can have nothing to do with the troubles at Queen's College.'

I thought that the saw used on the bucket had probably been taken from amongst the workmen's tools, so anyone might have used it. I wondered whether any of the men had found a saw badly blunted. Robert Hanbury might know. But I was inclined to agree with Jordain. Piers seemed an unlikely culprit.

In Oxford I usually attend church only on Sundays, although back in Leighton-under-Wychwood I will often attend Sire Raymond's services. He observes the full canonical hours at the most holy times of year, and his congregation is sometimes very small, so I go when I may, in gratitude for all he did for me when I was a boy. Now, however, I slipped into the back of St Peter's just before Master Bokeland began to say Mass, first kneeling quietly at the back of the nave to say a brief prayer, then rising to my feet and allowing the familiar words to wrap round me, comforting and reassuring.

Despite its being a weekday, there was a fair congregation, mostly women and the elderly, with a scattering of a few workmen with their bags of tools which clanked faintly. Near the front I saw Robert Hanbury's apprentice who had so determinedly defended the lad Wat against the accusation of carelessness. He still looked white and drawn, his eyes reddened with weeping. I hoped that the news of the injured apprentice was not worse.

The chanted words of the Mass twined about my own prayers, like melody and counterpoint. I prayed, as I always did, for the souls of my wife, my father, and my brother John, and for Margaret's two young boys. And I prayed for two more boys – the apprentice Wat, gravely injured and lost in a deep fever, and for Piers Dykman, the quiet student, who may have slept last night in the grass of the churchyard, curled up between the charnel house and a tomb.

Chapter Six

After Mass, I walked slowly back to the shop in sombre mood. If the rector had indeed seen Piers, where could he have run off to? It would be easy enough to lose himself during the busy daytime crowds of Oxford, but at night he must find somewhere to hide himself away and sleep, or he would be taken up by the Watch. It seemed that he had probably spent at least one night in the deserted cottage, but that was now barred to him. Last night might not have been his first in the churchyard, but having been seen once by Thomas Bokeland, he probably would not wish to risk sleeping there again.

Yet there were many empty cottages in Oxford these days, and most of the college grounds were easily accessible, by climbing over a wall. It would not be difficult for him to find some hidden spot. More difficult would be finding food. Sometimes the stallholders in the market would discard unsold and spoiled vegetables in the street, knowing that the town's beggars would scavenge anything edible once the stallholders had gone home. Piers might even find raw eggs. Most of us kept chickens in our gardens.

But what could have driven the child away from the safety and relative comfort of Hart Hall? Persistent questioning of the other students had merely left Jordain and everyone else as baffled as ever.

As I passed Queen's on my way home, I could hear the normal sounds of sawing and chiselling, so the work was continuing unabated, although there was not the usual whistling and singing which had accompanied the work before Wat's accident. Later today I would go to St John's hospital and enquire how the apprentice fared.

Walter had already lowered the shutter in front of the street window of the shop. I opened the door and pushed my way through the blanket over the door, noticing that one corner had torn away from the nails which secured it to the door frame. I should receive a scolding from Margaret for that. It was dim inside, after the bright morning in the street, and I did not at once notice that we had a customer.

Roger was not seated at his work, but standing beside the long table I used as part desk and part counter, and was poring over a book with the customer, who had his back to me. Then he turned and I realised that it was the young gentleman who had visited us before. De Musgrave, that was his name. He had expressed an interest in a book of hours, but as he had never reappeared, I assumed that he had left Oxford. I saw that Roger was showing him his book of hero tales. We had begun to call it that, for many of the stories concerned such great heroes as King Arthur, Guy of Warwick, and others, but it included several other stories of the sort told in the homes of great nobles – very different fare from Walter's ancient tales told by the simple firesides of villeins and cottagers.

'Good morrow to you, sir,' I said politely. 'Can we be of service to you? You mentioned, I believe, a book of hours?'

I had guessed that he had never intended to commission a book of hours, and watched with interest when he looked somewhat disconcerted.

'Ah, indeed,' he said. 'Certainly, at some time . . . but your man here has been showing me this book, this collection of hero tales. I have offered to buy it, but he tells me it is not for sale.'

'He tells you truly,' I said. 'We keep this original volume in the shop so that our customers may choose to have a copy of the whole made for them, or instead select a portion only. You may have full page illuminations, or simple capitals and borders. We will happily accommodate your wishes.'

I had assumed the pose of the obsequious shopkeeper, eager to oblige, but determined not to part with the original book. I could not make the man out. The first time he came to the shop, he had merely poked about, casting critical looks at the secondhand student texts. The second time he had pretended to be interested in a book of hours. Now, it seemed, he had actually offered to buy Roger's book. As it was not for sale, no price would have been mentioned, but given its size and the many illuminations, it would clearly be expensive. What game was the fellow playing? And what was his business in Oxford?

I took my seat behind my desk and drew toward me the ledger in which I wrote down my customers' commissions. With a quill poised above my ink pot, I smiled blandly at de Musgrave.

'If you will tell me your requirements, sir, I will be able to give you a price.'

He shifted from foot to foot, and turned over the pages. He handled the book carefully, as if he were accustomed to costly volumes, although I noticed a painful looking cut on the base of his left index finger.

'It would be unfortunate to select only a portion,' he said. 'I will have a copy of the whole volume, complete with all the illuminations.'

'And the binding? Our books are bound by Henry Stalbroke, who can offer you a wide choice of leathers.'

'Oh.' Clearly he had not given this any thought. 'We will discuss that when the pages are ready.'

'Very good,' I said, making notes in my ledger. 'Will you have it written in this same script? We can offer you a choice of several. Walter?'

Walter got up from his desk and reached down a rolled up parchment from a shelf which normally held a selection of books for sale, all of which I had stored away when the building work began.

'All of these scripts are possible,' I said, unrolling the parchment and laying it out on my desk, weighing down the corners with an ink pot and three of the brass weights I used for checking that coins paid to me had not been clipped.

The parchment showed short passages written in eight different scripts, any of which my scriveners could write. The idea of this sample parchment to show to customers had come from Peter Winchingham, who told me he had seen such samples hung up on display in the bookshops of Paris. I had felt it would be too ostentatious to have it out permanently on display, but when a customer ordered one of our more expensive books I had begun to offer them a choice of scripts. Walter and Roger both enjoyed exercising their skills from time to time. Some of the scripts were very beautiful, although not always as easy to read as the workaday script we used for the *peciae* and the occasional copies we made of complete student texts, bought by the wealthier students to save them the trouble of copying.

De Musgrave seemed a little taken aback at this abundance of choice and carried the parchment over to the window in order to study it better. Roger grinned at Walter, who bent over his work to hide his smile. As I expected, de Musgrave chose the most flamboyant script. I jotted down the rest of his requirements and named a price – about half as much again as I would have charged one of my regular customers. De Musgrave nodded, as though the cost did not trouble him. Interesting, I thought. He must be wealthier than I had first reckoned.

'How long will you remain in Oxford, sir?' I said. 'There is considerable work in completing such a volume. Several weeks, at the very least.'

'I shall be here until past Easter,' he said. 'Certainly until the end of April. Perhaps even part of May. I have not yet decided.'

I nodded. 'Very well. We will do our best to have the pages complete by the middle of May, shall we say? It might be best to speak to Henry Stalbroke before then, to be certain that he can complete the binding before you leave. Would that be to London?'

It was no affair of mine, where he lived or where he would be going after Oxford, but my curiosity was aroused. Some might give it a ruder name.

'Nay.' He shook his head. 'Nay, I will be returning to my father's manor. I thank you, Master Elyot.'

He laid the parchment back on my desk, where it promptly rolled itself up and knocked the smallest of my brass weights on to the floor. With ceremony we bowed him out of the shop, Roger holding the blanket to one side. I was forced to crawl about on the floor to find the weight, before I lost it altogether. It was smaller than my thumbnail and had rolled away into a dark corner. When I had retrieved it and stood up, I looked at the scriveners.

'Well,' I said, 'what do you make of that?'

'It will be a deal of work,' Roger said. 'I needs must set everything else aside.'

'Walter?' I said.

'I think you should have asked for a deposit,' he said. 'I have an unpleasant feeling that we may not see that gentleman again.'

He echoed my own thoughts, but I shrugged.

'Even if he disappears, I am sure I can find a customer for such a fine volume. Lady Amilia is not our only rich client.'

After I had dined with Margaret and the children, I was occupied for some time with the children's lessons, which had been somewhat skimped of late, with all the distractions of the building works and the accidents there, and then the search for the missing student. Alysoun was making excellent progress with her Latin and had now moved on from Caesar's *Wars* to Tacitus's *Agricola* and some of Vergil's poems. I managed to work in a little of the history of the Romans in Britain when we were reading Tacitus, but she preferred Vergil, finding *Eclogue IV* particularly intriguing.

'Was there really a time when the sheep grew wool in different colours?' she said. 'Think how pretty it must have been, all of them dotted about in a green meadow, like a tapestry! And you would never have the trouble of smelly dyes.'

'I think,' I said cautiously, 'that Master Vergil may simply have been imagining what a golden age might have been like. I do not think we know any such things for certain.'

She was too young, as yet, to understand the poet's implied prophecy that the age of Caesar Augustus would prove to be another such golden age. Or that many scholars believed that, pagan though he was, he had somehow foreseen the birth of Christ. Later, I would discuss the eclogue's deeper meanings. For the present, it was enough that she was beginning to follow the Latin, although it was still difficult for her.

Although her reading was excellent, Alysoun's writing was inclined to be careless, and although she wheedled to be taught more Greek than the simple alphabet, I had told her firmly that she should have no Greek until she could scribe a good clean hand in English and Latin. Surprisingly, Rafe wrote better than his elder sister. He was slow, but careful. He was still but five, yet he had a good hand, although his Latin had not really progressed beyond the simple moral fables I had also used first with Alysoun.

I felt that I was becoming quite the schoolmaster, for Emma's cousin Juliana now came to me once a week for lessons in Greek, and today was her day. When she arrived, Alysoun, who had lingered beside the kitchen table (where I conducted my schoolmastering) demanded of Juliana whether she believed Vergil's stories of rainbow hued sheep.

Juliana answered carefully, clearly not wishing to disparage a famous poet, but having a practical mind.

'That I cannot say, Alysoun. And indeed, how can we

ever know? For this golden age was so very, very long ago that none of those sheep now walk the earth, and the garments woven from their wool would have perished long since.'

She gazed thoughtfully out of the window, where Rafe was romping with Rowan under the fruit trees.

'For myself,' she said, 'I would rather the sheep we have nowadays. For we might not care for those strange fleeces. Our own sheep give us wool in soft shades of white, brown, grey, and even black. They are all good colours of themselves, and the paler fleeces can be dyed to whatever colours we choose. I think that is far better.'

'Perhaps you have the right of it,' Alysoun said, 'but I do think they would look pretty, grazing in the fields.'

She ran off and Juliana and I grinned at each other.

'Very diplomatic,' I said. 'Shall we proceed with Master Herodotus?'

When Juliana and I had finished, she joined Margaret, who was weeding our vegetable patch, where as usual the weeds seemed to be growing faster than the vegetables, as if determined to choke them to death before they had a chance to reach a decent size. After ensuring that my scriveners had all they needed, I set out for St John's hospital.

I had some slight acquaintance with John de Idbury, the warden of the hospital, for he had purchased a *Life of St Frideswide* from me last year, and had a regular order for the stationery needed by St John's. The hospital stood at the top of the sloping bank which led down to the Cherwell, outside the East Gate of the town, but before the bridge. Apart from delivering their order from time to time, when Roger was not available, I had little familiarity with the buildings, although I knew that half the establishment was managed by sisters, and half by brothers, all in holy orders and devoted entirely to the care of the sick. It was also well known in Oxford that the two were not always on the best of terms. The founder of the hospital, more than a hundred years before, had been the king himself, who had given the former Jewish burial ground as the site for the hospital. There were still a few Jews in Oxford then, but now all Jews have been exiled from England.

Warden de Idbury received me courteously in his own house, urging on me a glass of a fine pale French wine, brought up cool from the cellar. Although the hospital was said not to be rich, clearly there were funds enough to supply the warden's table.

'And how may I be of service to you, Master Elyot?' he said.

I explained that I had been present at Queen's College when the injured apprentice had been carried off to St John's and that I had come to enquire after the lad.

'A very serious injury.' He shook his head. 'We will do our best for him, but in places the burns have penetrated the flesh to the very bone. This has so enflamed the whole body that he is consumed with a raging fever. He has been bled twice to ease the fever, but I am told that he has not regained his wits since he was brought in. Do you wish to see him?'

'If I may,' I said. 'For all of us who were there . . . it was very distressing.'

'These young fellows, they should be more careful in their work. Such accidents should not happen.'

'It was no accident,' I said grimly. 'The bucket had been tampered with, so when it was filled, it collapsed, spilling the burning lime over the boy's legs.'

He eyed me sharply. 'Tampered with?'

'Perhaps you have not heard of the troubles which have plagued the building works at the college?' I said.

The hospital was never quite part of Oxford. Neither town nor gown, and lying outside the wall, it was something of a little world all to itself. I gave de Idbury a brief account of all that had been happening, and he frowned.

'It seems it is fortunate that there have been no injuries before this one to the apprentice. Let us hope there will be no more.'

'Amen to that,' I said fervently.

He conducted me himself to the long ward for male patients, where beds were arranged in lines along the walls, leaving a wide space in the centre, where the attendant brothers moved quietly from bed to bed. At the far end of the ward there was a small open chapel, so that the patients could attend services while lying in their beds, since the grace of God is as effective a physician as any mortal man.

The boy Wat lay in the furthest bed on the left hand side, nearest the chapel, having been placed here, perhaps, as the patient most in need of divine aid. He no longer appeared to me to be flushed with fever. Instead his face was greyish pale and gaunt, his eyes sunken, the lids swollen and puffy. His left arm lay flaccid on the blanket, a blood-stained dressing bound around it where the knife had been inserted to bleed him. The injured legs had been left open to the air and were smeared with a brown salve which did not conceal the dreadful, mangled flesh beneath.

I averted my eyes and sat down on the stool beside the bed. De Idbury gave me a nod and turned to go, but spoke in a low voice to a man in a physician's gown, whom I recognised as the one who had come to the college. He walked over and pulled up a second stool.

'You know the young man?' he said.

I shook my head. 'Nay, but I know his master, and I was there shortly after the boy was injured. How bad is it?'

'If he lives, I hope he will not lose his legs, provided gangrene does not set in. We have applied a salve for burns in the first instance, but next we will use honey – it is a sovereign treatment to speed the healing of flesh.'

'You said "If he lives". Do you think his life is in danger?'

'An older person who suffered such burns would certainly risk the failure of the heart after such a shock to the body. But he is young, and – until this happened – strong and healthy. I would say that his chances for life are good.'

'But he will be permanently maimed?'

'Aye. The body is wondrous clever at mending itself, but where so much of the flesh has been burnt away . . ' He shook his head. 'I cannot think the body can heal completely. His legs will be much weakened. How severe the damage to the bones and joints will be, we cannot yet tell. It may be that he will be able to walk with the assistance of a stick.'

We both glanced down at the boy. Without the grievous marks of illness, he would be a fine looking lad. Not particularly handsome, but with a good, honest, open face. I felt a hot surge of anger against whoever had tampered with that bucket.

As if he read my thoughts, the physician said, 'Master Hanbury was here yesterday evening. He tells me it was not an accident.'

'It was not.' I explained how the supporting hoops of the buckets had been sawed through.

'As if there were not enough terrible illness visited on mankind,' he said, looking down the length of the ward, with its many occupants, some silent, some moaning with pain or illness.

'Indeed,' I said.

I was not sure whether our voices had somehow reached Wat's deadened mind, but he groaned and muttered, and licked his dry and cracked lips.

'Should we give him somewhat to drink?' I asked.

'Aye,' he said, getting up. 'I will send one of the brothers.'

A young man, not much older than the apprentice, came with a cup of some drink, and I help him raise Wat from the pillow.

'What is that?' I asked.

'Small ale steeped with febrifuge herbs,' he said. 'I think he is past the worst of the fever now, but they can do no harm.'

Although Wat did not open his eyes, he managed to drink most of the ale, swallowing greedily, as though the fever – and perhaps the bleeding – had left him very thirsty.

'I will sit with him a little while,' I said, when we had eased him back on to the pillow.

The brother nodded and went to attend to other patients. I laid my hand over the strong brown hand lying so limp and helpless on the blanket, and sent up a prayer for the boy's recovery.

That evening we were just sitting down to our supper when Mary Coomber bustled in and heaved herself on to the bench next to Alysoun. She was out of breath, and did not speak for a minute or two.

Margaret smiled. 'Will you take a bite and sup with us, Mary?'

The dairywoman chuckled.

'I do not come a-begging supper from you, Margaret, but I have a plan.'

Margaret continued to ladle out pea soup, and fetched an extra bowl, which she placed before Mary. I sliced bread and handed it round the table.

'Ah, well, I thank e'e, Margaret,' Mary said. 'I have been that busy since I finished the afternoon milking, I have not found the time to make supper.'

'And what is your plan, Mary?' I asked cautiously. Her last plan, concerning St Frideswide's Fair, and involved us all in a great deal of work.

She began to spoon up her soup, and crumbled a little of her bread into it.

'You remember, when little Aelyth went off to bide with that niece of hers? I cannot say I like the woman – the niece I mean. She treats her poor aunt little better than a servant, but she is the only family Aelyth has. I met her in Fish Street only yesterday, Aelyth, I mean, and she admitted she was there only because she felt she was not welcome at her niece's house. "Always in the way," she said.'

'Better than trying to live next door to the building works,' I said. 'That poor cottage must shake every time they hammer a beam or saw a block of stone.'

'Aye, well, that's as may be. But you remember how we said – was it Aldusa said? – that 'twas a pity she had no young girl in her family to train up to the ribbon weaving? Aye, thank you, Margaret. I'd not mind another bowl of that excellent soup. Now I think on't, I never took any dinner today noontide.'

'Aelyth,' Margaret prompted, doling out more soup for all of us. 'Her tiresome niece.'

I silently cut more bread. Mary would reach her point in her own good time.

'After I left her yesterday, Aelyth,' she said, 'and when I was turning my cheeses later, I thought, Why should the poor woman be obliged to live hugger-mugger with her niece's family in Grandpont, where as I think they barely fit in the space even without her?'

'And?' Margaret said.

'Well, there am I with all that space, over and behind the dairy. In my grandfather's time, three generations of us lived there. There must have been ten of us – nay, twelve – at one time. And now I rattle about like the last dried pea in a pod. So why not?'

'Have her to lodge with you?' I suggested, catching her drift.

'I've rooms a-plenty. Seems she cannot even do her weaving at her niece's place, and how is she to live? She would be better biding in one of my empty rooms.'

Margaret gave the children each a slice of gingerbread and told them to run off, for they were beginning to fidget with boredom.

'I think it sounds an excellent plan, Mary,' Margaret said. 'She might even help you in the dairy, as well as Maud Farringdon.'

Mary laughed. 'Nay, she's such a little slip of a thing! Can you see her milking a cow or churning butter? But that is not all of my plan.'

She took a large, appreciative bite of her piece of gingerbread. 'Excellent. You do not stint the ginger,

Margaret.'

'There is more to the plan?' I asked cautiously.

'Aye, it concerns what we said at the time, that Aelyth should train up an apprentice. 'Twas you that thought of it, Nicholas. I remember me very well.'

I did have some recollection of saying it. 'I suggested finding a deserving orphan,' I agreed.

'Prophetic words!' she said triumphantly. 'You would not know the family. They lived down in that maze of lanes between the High Street and Merton Street. You go down past John Brinley's cobbler shop, past what used to be the vintner's, Hamo Belancer's, him that was murdered by that French fellow.'

'I know where you mean,' I said. 'What family?'

'Most of them died in the plague,' she said. 'Tonkin, they were called. The women spun cheap white stuff, and the men took any labouring job that was going. There was one child left, a girl, and she has been living with the grandmother ever since. Only the two of them still living of the family, and now the grandmother is gone, died two or three weeks ago.'

'And the child is on her own?' Margaret said, with compassion. 'With none to care for her?'

'Aye, though lately 'tis she as has cared for the grandmother, not t'other way about. She would be about twelve now, I'm thinking, and a bright little thing, for all that she comes from that family, who barely had the brains of a chicken between them.'

'This would be your deserving orphan?' I said, in the hope of reaching the point.

'Exactly!' She beamed at me. 'It was no more than a hovel they lived in, but I found her sitting in the street this very afternoon, weeping, for she has been turned out. One of the colleges owns the place – Oriel, I think it is – and they want a tenant who can pay the rent, which she can't.'

'Where is she now?' Margaret asked.

'Sitting in my kitchen, wearing an old shift of mine. I scrubbed her down and burned the rags she was wearing. I can't have anything from those alleyways near my dairy.'

I grinned at the thought of Mary, who had muscles to match any of the stonemasons, scrubbing down some terrified waif to rid her of fleas and lice, but she was quite right. You cannot be too meticulous in a dairy.

'Well,' I said carefully, 'it might be a good plan, Mary, and I daresay Aelyth will be grateful for a better roof over her head, but how will she feel about you choosing an apprentice for her?'

'As to that,' Mary said frankly, 'she may not like it. Then I will find somewhere else for the child. But she is a good girl, in spite of all that has befallen her, and neat fingered. I think she might do very well.'

'You say you had made no supper.' Margaret got up. 'Has the child had nothing to eat since your scrubbing?'

'I am going to see to it now, after I've spoken to Nicholas.'

'Me?' I said in alarm, uncertain how I fitted into the plan.

'I will fill a jug with the rest of the soup,' Margaret said. 'You may take that back with you.'

'Me?' I said again.

'Aye, Nicholas.' Mary nodded. 'I thought, could you not ride down to Grandpont in the morning and tell Aelyth that she is welcome to lodge with me? No need for her to pay me any rent, the rooms do but stand empty. Then, if she is happy to come, you could bring her back pillion. You do have a pillion saddle?'

'I can borrow one from the Mitre,' I said faintly.

How is it that Margaret and her friends seem able to organise my life and I cannot say them nay?

'Aye, I could do that,' I said. Best not to argue. 'I shall need directions to the niece's house.'

'No need for directions,' Mary assured me. 'The niece's husband is the only wheelwright in Grandpont. You cannot miss him. That is excellent, then. I give you thanks.'

She surged to her feet and picked up the jug of soup. Margaret tucked a loaf of bread under her arm.

'I must make up beds,' she said happily. 'And that girl looks a sight, drowning in my shift. In one of my coffers I should have some old gowns of mine, from when I was a girl and was half the size I am now.'

She roared with laughter. 'Nay, a *quarter* the size I am now.'

Margaret saw her out and came back to the kitchen. We both looked at each other, and began to laugh helplessly.

'You know, Nicholas,' Margaret said, wiping her eyes, 'it might even prove a good plan. In the end, most of Mary's plans do.'

I did not make an early start in the morning, for I had no desire to come knocking on the wheelwright's door before he was busy about his trade and I could speak to Aelyth quietly, if it was ever quiet in a small cottage overflowing with children. Once Walter and Roger were settled at their work I walked round to the Mitre, where I was able to borrow a pillion saddle without difficulty.

'Still faring well with you, is he?' the head groom said. 'Our Rufus?'

My Rufus, I thought, but I smiled and assured him that Rufus was well.

'But somewhat lacking exercise of late,' I said. 'He will grow fat. I am only going as far as Grandpont today.'

'Heard you had that new stable thatched,' he said.

'I have.'

Sometimes Oxford seems no better than a village for gossip.

Normally I would have walked to Grandpont, not ridden, but if I were to bring Aelyth back with me, together with her modest belongings, it was best to ride Rufus. I remembered that she had taken very little with her when she left. I would strap on one saddle bag – two are awkward if you have a woman sitting sideways on a pillion saddle. Aelyth could probably carry the rest in a bundle.

Rufus showed his delight at the prospect of an outing

by becoming quite skittish as I saddled him up. After a working life as a hired hack, his recent leisure in my stable might have been relaxing, but perhaps tedious. Even a horse may become bored with nothing to do. Now that I owned a horse, I must make more use of him.

Margaret insisted on giving me a basket of honey cakes for Aelyth's niece.

'For,' she said, 'although Mary may have the right of it, that Aelyth is unwelcome there, the niece may take it amiss that you come to spirit her away to another home. No harm in sweetening her a little.'

'I shall be tactful,' I said. 'I shall say that Aelyth will be staying just across the street from her home, where she can keep an eye on it. And I shall mention that there has been some thieving, so we are all being particularly watchful.'

I led Rufus out into the street and mounted. Although I was obeying Mary's orders like any serving man, privately I enjoyed the idea of a brief holiday from minding my nearly empty shop and waiting nervously for some new disaster to strike the neighbouring college.

It is no great distance to Grandpont – up the High to Carfax, then south along Fish Street to the South Gate. Grandpont sprawls south of the town, either side of the road, and I suppose it derives its name from the fact that the road spans a very maze of branches of the Thames, before eventually reaching solid ground. The whole area is, indeed, a kind of long bridge between Oxford and the land to the south.

As Mary had foreseen, I had no difficulty locating the wheelwright's premises – a large yard open to the street and cluttered with all the elements which go to make up a wheel. The man I took to be the niece's husband was hammering a bent iron rim into shape, probably part of a damaged wheel he was repairing, while the woman sitting astride the spoke-shaver's bench must be his wife. Dismounting and tying Rufus to the hitching ring beside the yard gate, I crossed to the woman and bowed.

'I beg your leave,' I said, suddenly aware that I did not know her name, 'but I have come with a message for your aunt Aelyth, who is a neighbour of mine in Oxford High Street. I am Nicholas Elyot, the bookseller.'

I held out Margaret's basket of cakes. 'My sister has sent you these. Honey cakes for the children.'

The woman had frowned at first, but her face lightened at the sight of the cakes and she nearly smiled.

'Come you within,' she said, laying aside the vicious curved, double-handled knife she had been using to shape the spokes.

I followed her into the narrow cottage which occupied a corner of the wheelwright's yard, most of which was taken up with timber, broken wheels, iron hoops, and tools. The house crouched apologetically, as though it had no right to any of the space. There surely must have been barely room for the family, before ever Aelyth came to stay.

We found her washing the face of one child, while another tugged at her skirts, and a third sat on the floor, howling.

'Where is Harry?' the niece demanded.

'Asleep.' Aelyth looked more fragile than ever, with dark shadows beneath her eyes, and strands of grey hair escaping from her wimple, as though one of the children had tugged them loose.

'Master Elyot has some message for you,' the goodwife said, accepting the basket I handed her, and laying out the cakes on the table. The wailing child was silenced, and all three scrambled to grab the cakes. The absent Harry, I feared, would miss his share.

'I come on behalf of Mary Coomber,' I said, deciding that I should have no peace to speak to Aelyth alone. The niece was ignoring us anyway, bent on preventing all the cakes disappearing at once.

'Mary?' Aelyth looked puzzled.

'Aye.'

Having sized up the situation I had found – Aelyth

left to mind the children while their parents absented themselves, treating her as a maidservant – I decided that I should not suggest relieving them of an unwanted visitor. Clearly Aelyth was proving useful to them, though she did not seem to be enjoying it.

'You may not have heard, Aelyth, but there has been a deal of thieving and damage in the neighbourhood since you left.'

I did not mention that it was confined to Queen's.

'Mary thought you might like to come and lodge in one of her rooms,' I said. 'As a friend. So that you may keep a careful eye on your home. There is a big family house as part of her dairy. Mary has room and to spare.'

I noticed that the niece was now listening, and frowning, but Aelyth's eyes suddenly filled with hope.

'Truly? I should not be a trouble to Mary?'

'Not at all. I am sure she would be glad of the company. And it would be wise to keep a watch on your property.'

I emphasised this, for I was sure it was something the niece would understand.

'Why then–' Aelyth looked somewhat helplessly at the other woman. 'I think indeed it might be wise, do not you? I have little, but there is the furniture . . . perhaps I should go?'

'Aye,' the niece said grudgingly. 'You have some fine furniture that belonged to my grandmother. We would not want it damaged.'

Ah, I thought. She hopes to inherit poor little Aelyth's few possessions. I had never been inside the ribbon weaver's cottage, but I doubted whether there was much there of value.

'I have brought my horse, with a pillion saddle,' I said. 'I can take you back with me now, if you can gather up your belongings.'

'Oh, aye.' Aelyth looked flustered. The sudden suggestion had perhaps taken her somewhat aback. 'The pottage for dinner is all but made.'

She nodded toward an iron pot standing beside the hearth, waiting to be set to cook.

'I will just . . .'

She went over to a corner of the room, where there was a thin palliasse rolled up. She must sleep here, on the earth floor of the single room, while the family slept above. It took no more than a few minutes for her to bundle up a few clothes. Her precious loom and weaving materials were already stowed away in a sort of satchel of coarse canvas.

We were able to fit everything except Margaret's basket into the saddle bag, so little had Aelyth to bring home with her. I mounted, then reached down to lift her on to the pillion behind me. The niece handed her the basket. She was grim faced now, all too aware that she was losing an unpaid servant. Aelyth leaned down and laid her hand on the niece's shoulder.

'Thank you, my dear, for all your kindness, and for taking me in when I was in need. But it is best if I go back now.'

The woman gave a curt nod, then with no further word turned her back on us and returned to her work. From inside the house there was a crash, as if a stool had been overturned.

'Oh, dear,' Aelyth said. 'The children should not be left alone.'

'They managed without you before,' I said, turning Rufus and setting off briskly toward Oxford before she could change her mind. 'They can surely manage again. Why do they not employ a maid?'

'I believe they did, but she ran off.'

Little wonder, I thought, with such a hard mistress.

'Now, Aelyth,' I said, 'you must put your free arm about my waist. I do not want you to fall off, though we have not far to go.'

Rather shyly, she did as she was bid. Perhaps she had never embraced a man before. I thought with a smile that this was a very different companion atop Rufus with me than Emma had been. I rode at a slow pace, for I was not certain how safe Aelyth was, perched behind me, and I did not want to cause her to slip. Even so, we soon covered the distance and were riding along the High Street, to the stares of some of our neighbours, who gaped to see the little ribbon weaver arriving in state upon Rufus's tall back.

Mary must have been keeping a watch out for us, since she appeared at her door even before I had lifted Aelyth down from her high perch. She hardly weighed more than Alysoun. If anything, she seemed even thinner than when she had left us. Had the niece not been feeding her? It seemed Mary had noticed this too.

'Welcome, my dear,' she said, enveloping Aelyth in a warm embrace. 'Come you in-by. 'You look in need of a good dinner. The milking is done and I have made all my deliveries for the day. We shall soon have you settled.'

I followed the two women into the dairy, carrying the saddle bag. Behind the working portion of the dairy, where Mary kept her churns and her cheese-making equipment, we passed the storerooms for her big cheeses, and came to the kitchen of the family house. There were more rooms here, which I had never seen, and an upper floor over the whole, where the family had lived. Out at the back there was a pasture where Mary kept her small herd of cows, and a barn extending back from the house.

'This is all that Aelyth had to bring with her,' I said, unloading the saddlebag on the kitchen table, taking particular care with the satchel of weaving materials. 'I'll be off back to the shop now.'

'I thank you for your help, Nicholas,' Mary said, beaming. 'And here is little Sarah Tonkin, that I told you about.'

I had not noticed the child, who was sitting on a stool in a far corner of the kitchen, curled up and looking as though she was not quite sure what was afoot. She was now clad in a faded green gown, which must be one of those left from Mary's girlhood, but I think that even back then the dairy woman must have been a sturdy lass, for it hung loosely about the child, despite being cinched in at the waist with a girdle of braided cords, giving her the appearance of a half empty sack.

'I'll away,' I said again, but Aelyth laid her hand on my arm as she handed me Margaret's basket.

'It was kind of you to fetch me home, Master Elyot,' she said, and there were tears in her eyes. 'Is it true that my home might be set upon by thieves?'

I grinned. 'Unlikely. Do not worry. All the troubles have been confined within the grounds of Queen's College and the works on the new chapel. I thought merely to give a little colour to your departure.'

She gave me a shaky smile.

'Yay or nay, I am glad to be back here amongst friends. And Mary is so kind–'

I feared she might weep in earnest, and clearly Mary thought the same, for she took Aelyth by the elbow.

'Come, I will show you your room, up the stairs, and then we shall make the dinner together.'

Behind Aelyth's back, she gave me a wink.

'That was well thought on,' I said, setting Margaret's basket down on the kitchen table. 'The honey cakes. The wheelwright's woman very nearly smiled. And I do not suppose those children often see fine baking. They fell on your cakes like wolf cubs.'

'So was the niece glad to be rid of her unexpected visitor?' Margaret asked.

'On the contrary. Aelyth has clearly been filling the position of an unpaid maidservant, the previous girl having run off. When I arrived, she was minding the children and cooking the family dinner. She looked worn as thin as a frayed cloth.'

'I suppose she has no experience of children. She never wed. And for years she has had none to cook for but herself. Mary will soon feed her up on butter and cheese and cream. Even if nothing comes of the great plan to apprentice the girl, it will be good for Aelyth to lodge with Mary.'

'I saw the girl,' I said. 'Another thin little scrap of a thing. She looked quite fuddled with all that has happened to her.'

'Aye, well, if you do not know Mary and the warmth of her heart, she can seem—'

Words failed her. I grinned.

'Somewhat like a tidal wave?' I suggested. 'Or a runaway cow?'

'Not quite my words,' she said, 'but she does thrust aside anything that blocks her path.'

'She does. Including a harmless bookseller, who should be about his work.'

'Aye, he should. Although the shop has been very quiet today.'

'And every day,' I said glumly. 'I hope the work at the college will be completed before too many more weeks are past, else I shall not earn enough to pay the men's wages and put food on the table.'

'Walter tells me you have an order for a costly book.'

'Aye, if the fellow ever comes to pay for it. I fear he may simply be playing with us. I do not altogether trust him.'

'Roger will be cast down,' she said, 'if that is the case. He was working very hard when I walked through the shop.'

'I expect I shall be able to find a buyer, but perhaps not at once.'

I cut myself a slice of bread, and found a chunk of cheese on the coffer.

''Twill be dinner time soon,' she protested.

'My ride has made me hungry. All seemed quiet over at the college when I put Rufus back in the stable. Let us hope we are done with all the alarums there.'

'Amen to that,' she said.

Chapter Seven

Not unexpectedly, Mary Coomber appeared next morning, before even my scriveners arrived for the day's work, and not long after the noise had begun at the college. She parked her handcart, with its round cheeses and buckets of fresh milk, beside the door of the shop, having draped a cloth over all, for fear of stone dust in the air.

'Your jug returned, Margaret,' she said, 'and filled with some of my thickest cream by way of thanks. 'Twas just what the child needed, your pea soup. And here is today's milk.'

She set the jug of cream on the table, and our usual bucket of milk on the coffer. We had learned, from experience, that if it was left on the floor, Rowan regarded the contents as rightfully hers. We had a larger daily order of milk than most in the town. Because Margaret and I had grown up on a farm, she believed that children should be given plenty of milk to drink, as well as small ale. Certainly they thrived on it.

'I thank you, Mary,' Margaret said. 'And how do your guests fare? Nicholas says that Aelyth seems glad to leave her niece's house.'

'Aye, she is. And well settled now, in one of my rooms overlooking the High, where she may see her cottage. Once I have finished my deliveries this morning, we are minded to move her few poor sticks of furniture over to my house. We can easily load them on to my cart and trundle them across the street.'

She looked at me expectantly, and I sighed.

'You would like some help, I expect?' I said.

Her feigned surprise was almost convincing.

'Why, Nicholas, that would be a kindness! And perhaps Walter and Roger?'

'*After* they have done their morning's work,' I said, determined to be firm.

'Aye, certainly. The cart will not be free until then.'

As it proved, there was more to move than I had expected, and more than the few 'poor sticks' Mary had mentioned. It seemed that Aelyth had inherited several good pieces of carved oak furniture from her parents, those same items which the niece had referred to, in jealous tones, as belonging to *her* grandmother, as though Aelyth had no right to them. There was a large, throne-like chair with arms, carved with mythical beasts, which must once have been the pride of Aelyth's father, and an enormous coffer which Roger, Walter, and I could barely lift between us. The bed – once probably the marital bed – needed to be dismantled before it could be brought down the narrow steps which led up to the garret. Its curtains, once fine linsey-woolsey, had at some point been attacked by moths, but had been carefully and almost invisibly mended.

As well as these good pieces there was the usual collection of mismatched stools, a scrubbed and dented table, and all the normal kitchen clutter. I had thought Aelyth would not want to move these, but Mary was insistent.

'I have heard a whisper that Queen's College means to turn the tenants out of those two cottages next to you, Nicholas, so Aelyth were better to be sure of all her goods, lest the Fellows take it into their heads to seize the property while she is not living there.'

'But surely she will want to return to her home, once the chapel is built?' I objected. 'I believe her family has lived there for several generations.'

'Aye, that's as may be, but the college is determined

on securing all its property for its own use, except perhaps those filthy hovels up beyond St Peter's. 'Tis as well Humphrey Hadley bought your plots outright, else you would have found yourself and your family turned out some day.'

'They will find it more than they bargained for, to shift Aldusa from her home,' I said.

She laughed. 'Aye, they will. Whether they seize Aelyth's cottage soon or late, she and I will rub along very happily together. She may sit quiet and weave her ribbons while I tend the dairy, with Maud's assistance, then we may take our meals together.'

'And what of the child?' I said. 'Have you unfolded your plan yet to Aelyth?'

'Time enough when we have all shaken down together. For now the child needs feeding up, and she is quite handy helping me in the kitchen.'

'I shall observe you all with interest,' I said. 'Now, where are we to set up this bed? We had best do so before we forget how it all fits together. The curtains we will leave to you and Aelyth.'

Aelyth had decided she would have her familiar bed in the room Mary had given her, so we had to move one bed out before attempting the puzzle of assembling the large bed with its carved posts and elaborate tester. At some time in the past there must have been wealth in Aelyth's family, to have afforded such a bed, but I thought the little ribbon weaver would look no more than a child sleeping in it.

By the time we had finished, the afternoon was nearly past, so I sent Walter and Roger home.

'If you sup tonight at Tackley's,' I said to Walter, 'do you ask Master Hanbury if he has heard aught of the injured apprentice and how he fares.'

Usually Walter was given his supper by his landlady, the fishmonger's wife, but she was away from Oxford at present, visiting an ailing aunt, so he had taken to eating at the inn.

'Last I heard,' he said, 'the boy was conscious, though still in great pain. It will be a long time before he is out of his bed.'

'But no more mischief afoot at the college?'

'Nay, nothing that the master stonemason mentioned.'

While I had been busy with moving Aelyth's goods, it seemed Emma had sent a boy with a message.

'She will come tomorrow,' Margaret said, 'with the first pages of the troubadour book. She would have you approve them before she scribes any more. It appears she has chosen an unusual size for the pages, wider than high, but is not sure whether you will like it.'

I nodded. 'I have seen books of music laid out so. Philip Olney has a few in Merton's collection. Easier for the musicians to use, so he says.'

'I know nothing of the matter, but Emma says the music used by Gaston de Sarlat and the others had pages of this sort.'

'So they did,' I agreed. 'Well, I shall be glad to see what Emma has devised. We have not seen her these many days.'

'We have not.' Margaret gave me an odd look, which I could not quite fathom.

I remembered that look later in the evening, after we had supped and the children were abed. Ever since Emma had started them on the game of inventing a sequel to one of Walter's stories, it had become our bedtime entertainment each night, when they regaled me, rather than t'other way about, although they did not always agree on how the story should progress. For the most part, Alysoun triumphed, but not always.

The evenings were growing lighter as we drew nearer to Easter, so that Margaret could see well enough for her mending after supper, if she sat near the kitchen window, while I would read. This night, however, I was tired after the day's labours, and found myself nodding over the collection of hero tales, which I had decided to approach as a reader might, not as a bookseller.

'Nicholas,' Margaret said, looking up from mending yet another gown Alysoun had torn. 'I wish to speak to you.'

I tried to pull myself back from the brink of sleep, and yawned.

'Aye? You may speak to me whenever you wish, Meg.'

I could not think what could be so important as to lend such a serious weight to her words. As far as I knew, the house was sound, in no need of repair. We were in funds enough for our daily needs, although the recent lack of customers was a little worrying. Perhaps that was my sister's concern. The book commissioned by de Musgrave would make up for our slow business of late, as would Lady Amilia's edition of the troubadour songs, although neither would be ready for some while yet.

Margaret laid her sewing on her lap and thrust her needle into the cloth. What could be of such import that she could not both sew and speak?

'It is about Emma,' she said, and she looked uncomfortable.

'Emma?' I sat up, fully awake now. 'Is something amiss with Emma? Is she ill?'

'Not in the usual sense, I think.' She gave a half smile. 'As far as I know, there is naught amiss with her health. I speak of something more hidden.'

I frowned. 'Has there been word from her grandfather? He has been gravely ill before.'

She paused. 'I went round to see Maud Farringdon when you were visiting the injured boy at St John's hospital. Emma *has* heard from her grandfather, but he is not ill. He is making provision for her future. Maud was worried, for Emma has been very quiet since the letter arrived.'

I felt an instant sinking in the pit of my stomach.

'I suppose he has every right,' I said cautiously. 'She is his only heir, and he is a good age.'

'Aye. And so is she. A good age for marriage. He is looking about for a suitable match.'

I continued to speak with care. 'And what does Emma think of this?'

'Maud says that Emma does not speak of it, but she is troubled.'

I took a deep breath, and swallowed painfully. I knew that some day it would come to this.

'It is his right, nay, it is his duty, to see her well provided for.' I cleared my throat. 'He would fail in his duty, if he did not find a good match for her, a gentleman of her own kind, a landowner like himself, most probably of knightly rank.'

I swallowed again, and felt ashamed at the faltering sound of my own voice.

'Should he die before she weds, would she not, in law, become a ward of the king, to dispose of as he wishes?' I said. 'Kings must build a rampart about themselves of men they can trust, reward those men who serve them well. He could marry her to anyone. Some fellow as old as himself, or to some puking infant, son of a loyal follower.'

'Aye,' Margaret said gravely. 'All that you say is true. And Sir Anthony could marry her off tomorrow, though I think he would choose more kindly than the king. I am sure he would not force her against her will, but he would expect her to bow to his wishes. Have you thought on this, Nicholas?'

I did not answer at once, but got up and walked to the window, leaning my elbows on the sill. A veritable choir of birds was singing Vespers in the garden. Most clearly to be heard were the thrushes and blackbirds, but I could also hear blue tits, and a robin, and the chirping of a pair of sparrows who were nesting in the rosemary bush just below the window. Must it come so soon? Emma would be carried away to her grandfather's manor and wed to some knight of the shire, and I would never see her again.

'Well, Nicholas?' Margaret said again, kindly but

firm.

Still I could not answer, for my head seemed to buzz like a skep full of bees.

'Are you in love with her?'

'I . . . I . . .' It was stupid. I had never allowed myself honestly to confront my true feelings for Emma.

'Elizabeth is long gone,' Margaret said gently. 'She has left you two fine children, and she would not want you to mourn for ever. She was not selfish. She was one of the most generous people I have ever known.'

'She was.' I felt tears come into my eyes. 'She was,' I whispered.

'Everything has changed since the pestilence,' she said. 'The world is turned upside down. We cannot look back at the past. That world is gone. We must step forward into the future. Do you love Emma Thorgold?'

I came back to my chair and sat with bowed head, my clasped hands hanging between my knees.

'What is the use, Margaret? As you have said so truly, Emma's grandfather, who must provide for her, will marry her off to a man of rank. These last months, since she won free of the nunnery, he has indulged her, allowed her the freedom to live with her aunt here in Oxford, to play – as he must think it, if she has told him – at being a scrivener. But it has only been an indulgence, a brief indulgence, to compensate her for the months she spent trapped at the abbey by the actions of her stepfather. She has had almost a year of freedom, after a year spent in what seemed to her a kind of prison. I can see that he would think the time for indulgence is over.'

I looked up then, and fixed Margaret with an unhappy look.

'But what do my feelings matter? I do not know what Emma feels for me, but she must know, as I do, that she would never be allowed to wed a yeoman's son, a mere shopkeeper. Our ranks in life are too widely separated.'

I gave a bitter laugh. 'Aye, we have been playing a game, Emma and I, the bookseller and his scrivener. It could not last.'

Margaret laid aside her sewing and put another log on the fire, then she kindled a spill at the flames and went around the kitchen, lighting candles. I had hardly noticed that it had been growing dark. She brought one of the candles over and set it on the small table between us, then fetched ale and cups.

'Drink this,' she said, pushing a cup toward me as she sat down again.

Barely thinking was I was doing, I drank a deep draught. My mouth and throat felt dry.

'Cast your mind back,' she said, 'to last summer. You will not have forgotten, I am sure, Gilbert Mordon and the Lady Edith, his wife.'

'Hardly.'

'She came from a great landed family, yet she did not marry a man of like rank, but a merchant.'

'A great family which was impoverished,' I said, 'and he a wealthy merchant. You are not, I hope, holding that marriage up to me as a model? The wife murdered the husband.'

She laughed. 'Aye, perhaps it was a poor example. The point I wanted to make was that in this changed world, marriages, too, are changing.'

'Certainly Emma does not come of such a great family as the Lady Edith,' I conceded, 'but hers is a family of substantial means, owning a goodly estate. And I am not a wealthy London merchant.'

'Nevertheless, you are a merchant. Oh, you may shake your head at me and call yourself "shopkeeper", but you are on your way to becoming a merchant, a merchant of books. Think of all your new ventures, far beyond anything Humphrey Hadley ever attempted.'

She smiled. 'You even own a horse! And you are still young. Only six and twenty. I daresay at six and twenty Peter Winchingham could not have called himself a great merchant, yet look at him now.'

'Emma could not wait for me until I am Peter's age.'

I was momentarily distracted, for I had begun to wonder what feelings Margaret and Peter might have for each other, but Margaret brought me firmly back to the point.

'I think you must confront your love for Emma, Nicholas. I have known you since birth, and I can read you as easily as you read that book of tales.' She gestured toward the book which I had laid down, unregarded, on the table.

'Emma makes a great pretence of hiding her own feelings behind a little gentle mockery and teasing,' she said, 'but I have caught her looking at you when she thinks no one will notice. Would you have her married off to some man she barely knows, or knows not at all? Forget yourself. Would you wish that for *her*? That unhappiness?'

'But, Meg, even if you have the right of it – and I cannot be sure – it will be Emma's grandfather who will make the choice for her. I can do nothing.'

'Do not play the coward!' she said sharply. 'Sir Anthony cannot take you into consideration if you do not so much as make yourself known as a suitor for Emma. You have met the gentleman, when you went to seek his help in freeing Emma from her noviciate. You liked him, I remember me well.'

'That was another case entirely.'

'Perhaps, but you made a good beginning by liking each other. Better than hostility!'

'But I do not know that Emma even cares for me, except as a friend, who helped her break free of Godstow, and who has been of some service to her aunt's family. You say you have seen her looking at me, but what does that mean? Hardly a willingness to defy convention and marry out of her rank. Why, her grandfather might disinherit her. I could not wish such a thing on her.'

'From what we know of him, I do not think it likely. Besides, I do not suggest that you try to wed without his goodwill. You must earn his goodwill.'

I ran my fingers through my hair, and clutched my

head between my hands.

'I suppose I have been stumbling along like a blind man, never thinking beyond the present day,' I said. 'Did Maud Farringdon say exactly how Emma had reacted to this letter from her grandfather?'

'Only to say that she had been very quiet and thoughtful ever since. You must remember, Nicholas, that if you do not know how she feels, neither does she know how you feel. You say you have stumbled like a blind man. It seems to me that you have both been behaving like wilful children, blind to the future. Well, I fear the future may overtake you unless you take action to open your eyes to it.'

'I cannot see my way forward, even so.'

Margaret sighed in exasperation. 'Talk to the girl! Not about scripts and illuminations, or fitting words to music. Tell her how you feel, and see how she responds.'

'I have not told *you* how I feel,' I said stubbornly.

'Oh, Nicholas!' She stood up and shook her skirts out. 'You can be very clever at solving other people's mysteries, but at times you can indeed be very blind to your own affairs. Stupid, indeed.'

She leaned over and kissed my forehead.

'I am for bed. Do you cover the fire. Emma will be here tomorrow. You can speak to her then.'

She picked up one of the candles and began to climb the stairs to her bedchamber. I sat on for a long time, till the fire was nearly dead, and the candles were guttering.

Emma would be here tomorrow.

I slept badly that night. Margaret had spoken truly. I had been living these last months from day to day, heedless of the future. Whenever thoughts of what lay ahead ambushed me unexpectedly, I had pushed them away. Matters could not go on for ever unresolved, yet the only resolution I could foresee was separation from Emma. Her grandfather had shown great forbearance in allowing her to stay on in Oxford with her aunt, recovering from a year's unhappiness, after being forced into her noviciate at Godstow Abbey. I suspected she had not told him that she was working for me as a scrivener. Even had she done so, I was certain that he would regard it merely as play, just as I had said to Margaret.

Was that how Emma herself saw it? I could not think so. I knew she found great joy and pride in her work, as much as any man would do. And when I had given her the desk, carefully fitted out with all that a professional scrivener and illuminator could need, she had embraced and kissed me. I could feel her arms about me still.

I threw myself over in bed. The covers were tangled and I kicked them aside impatiently.

Could I declare myself to Emma? Did I even understand my own feelings for her? To admit that I loved her would seem like a betrayal of Elizabeth, but perhaps Meg was right. Elizabeth had been a loving and generous soul. Perhaps she would forgive me. And what of the children? Their lives followed a safe and steady course now, for my sister was all but a mother to them. Could Emma take her place? And then, what of Meg? She seemed to be urging me to press my suit with Sir Anthony, but where would that leave her, were the impossible to happen, and Emma and I were to wed?

Nay, it was surely impossible.

Sometime in the early hours I finally fell asleep.

I skimped breakfast and was somewhat short with my scriveners when they arrived, but I could not at first settle to any work. Finally, as a sort of self punishment, I sat down to the most tedious task ever endured in a bookshop, copying out *peciae*. Although we keep a good supply of these in stock, if one of the scholars orders his students to study a particular text at short notice, we may have a rush in the shop as they all hurry to rent the prescribed passages. And sooner or later the *peciae* wear out from frequent handling and must be replaced. Copying sections from a well known and oft studied text is something I can do without needing to think, following the original with my bone-handled silver *aestel* in my left hand, my quill scribing the words with my right, my mind elsewhere. The meaning scarcely passes through my brain, and I have considerable sympathy with Walter's impatience with the task.

Margaret had not said at what time Emma intended to bring the first pages of the troubadour book for me to see, and the morning dragged past with no sign of her. Roger continued to work, under his makeshift tent, on the book commissioned by Sir Thomas de Musgrave, while Walter had taken over the copying of another collection from the hero tales, leaving space on the pages for Roger to draw and paint the illuminations later.

When midday had arrived without Emma's appearance, I decided that either my sister had been mistaken, or Emma had changed her mind. Like a coward, I was somewhat relieved, for it spared me the necessity of the difficult confrontation that Meg had urged on me.

It was therefore with a mixture of pleasure and apprehension that I saw Emma pass the open window of the shop soon after the dinner hour, then duck in past the hanging blanket.

'Still under siege, I see,' she said, seeming as cheerful as usual. Perhaps Maud and Margaret had been mistaken about her reaction to her grandfather's letter.

Roger poked his head out, like a tortoise from its shell, and grinned at her.

'Be thankful that you live far enough away from this pandemonium to work in peace.'

'Oh indeed, I am grateful.'

She turned to me.

'I have brought the first pages of the troubadour book for you to see, Nicholas. I have only scribed three, until I could be sure that you approved what I have done.'

She unrolled the parchment and laid it down on my desk. She had indeed chosen to set out the words and music so that they ran from left to right along the greater length of the parchment sheet, the vertical height being less than the horizontal measurement.

She sat down on a stool beside me, and if she noticed that I was more conscious of her nearness than usual, she paid it no heed.

'I remembered that Gaston, Azalais, and Falquet had their songs laid out like this, and that reminded me that the troubadour who came to my grandfather's manor when I was a girl also had books of songs which were wider than they were high. I was not quite sure why until I tried writing them out for myself, but I understand it better now. With a narrower page, the usual size we would use, say for a book of tales, it is quite difficult to fit the words and music for one line of a poem all on to one line of writing. If it runs over on to the next line, it looks clumsy. Everything fits much better like this. Also, I have written quite small, so that we may set out both the Occitan words above, then the English underneath, without using too much of the height of the page.'

She smiled at me.

'I have had a few false starts before I solved all the problems, but I think I have it now. That is why you have seen so little of me.'

'We thought you were driven away by our neighbours' activities at the college,' Walter said.

'Nay, even that would not have kept me away from the finest bookshop in Oxford,' she said, 'but I was determined to have a few pages worth showing to you all before I went further. What think you?'

Walter came and leaned over my shoulder, and once Roger had carefully laid aside his brush, he joined us.

'Aye, that is certainly the best way to lay it out,' Walter said.

He spoke from years of experience in the trade, yet he was not so tied to convention that he could not see the advantages for this different way of laying out music.

Roger nodded. 'And you will have room for an illuminated initial here?' He pointed to the first word of the song, which lacked its first letter.

'Now that is a problem I have *not* solved,' she said. 'We cannot have illuminated initials for both the Occitan and the English versions, can we? I suppose sometimes it might be the same letter, but not usually. What think you, Nicholas?'

I had ventured no comment so far, but I was pleased with what she had done.

'This is certainly by far the best way to set out both words and music,' I said, 'so we will indeed make the book wider than it is high. As for the initial, I think it must be the Occitan, since that comes first, but perhaps the initial for the English might be in red, instead of black? And perhaps a little larger that the rest of the letters, if you could fit that in, without spoiling the illumination?'

'I think so.'

She picked up a thin charcoal stick I kept on my desk, which I used for jotting down notes, and which could be rubbed out with a scrap of cloth, although it sometimes left the surface a little grubby. She quickly sketched in a large initial letter for the first Occitan word, but left enough space below it for a slightly enlarged first letter for the English.

'Aye,' Roger said. 'That will serve.'

'Excellently well, do you not think, Nicholas?' Walter said.

I think he was puzzled at my subdued comments. I roused myself to speak normally.

'It is the perfect solution!' I said, smiling warmly at Emma. 'I am sorry it has been such a trouble to you.'

'Oh, I did not mind. I enjoyed devising how best to lay everything out on the page. Once the problems are solved, we shall know how to make books of music in future. After all, Roger must make the copy for his patron, the lovely Lady Amilia.'

'Indeed,' he said glumly. 'I wonder whether she is delivered of her latest child yet, and whether that means she will be returning to Oxford.'

'Courage, Roger!' she said. 'I am sure the lady will not want to risk the babe in town during the heats of summer.'

'Alas,' Walter said, 'the heats of summer are still a long way off. The lady and her husband are usually here from Easter until midsummer.'

If they noticed that I did not join in the usual teasing of Roger, they said nothing, but I was racking my brains, trying to think how I might speak to Emma alone.

'I am afraid that when you rub out your charcoal sketch of the initial, it will leave your parchment marked,' I said.

'That does not matter. These are my rough attempts only, not my finished pages. Now that I have your approval, I can make a true start on the work.'

She rolled up the parchment, and secured it with a knotted tape.

I cleared my throat. Perhaps I could suggest to Emma that she take a walk with me, although it might seem odd, in the middle of the working day? Or better, invite her to admire the spring growth in the garden, and ask how her efforts with Maud in their garden were progressing? That would be better. I could offer her some plants from our herb bed. There was plenty of thyme and sage. And we could take some cuttings from the rosemary bush, without disturbing the nesting sparrows.

My suggestion of the garden met with her approval, and, setting down her rolled pages on my desk, she followed me through the house and into the garden. Fortunately Margaret had gone to the market and the children were across the street at Jonathan Baker's. We would not be disturbed. And I would have no excuse not to speak, although I had not yet framed my thoughts into words.

I fetched a small basket from the kitchen and we dug up several plants from the herb garden, including a large clump of chives and some sweet cicely, which was just showing new growth. Emma cut a handful of soft wood twigs from the rosemary bush with her penknife – which might not bode well for trimming quills later. I had at last screwing up my courage to the point of speaking.

'Emma–' I began hesitantly.

Before I could continue, the air rang with the all too familiar sound of a crash echoing out from Queen's College.

'Oh, Jesu!' I said. 'Not again!'

Emma started and dropped her twigs of rosemary.

'Do you suffer with such noise every day?' she gasped. 'No wonder, then, that you have all grown weary of it.'

'Nay,' I said grimly. 'That is more than the usual. I fear that there may have been another supposed accident.'

I bent down and picked up the rosemary cuttings, adding them to the basket absent-mindedly. After the first crash and the yelling, everything had gone quiet again.

'Perhaps it was nothing,' I said. 'Just some minor mishap. Ever since the terrible injury to the apprentice Wat, the men have been on tenterhooks, waiting for the next disaster. They are liable to cry out of a sudden. There have been mutterings that the whole work is cursed and will never be finished.'

My own laugh was unconvincing.

'Some superstition that the site of the new chapel defiles a pagan holy site,' I said, 'or some other nonsense. Master Hanbury is hard put to keep them at their work. Walter tells me that two of the carpenters and one of the stonemasons have run off, afraid to remain where such accidents happen.'

'But they are not accidents, are they?' she said. 'Have you not established that some intruder has been causing all the mischief.?'

'Aye, that is clear enough, but try telling that to a man of a superstitious turn of mind.'

After the brief silence, there was now a growing noise drifting over from the college. Aldusa peered over the walls between our two properties.

'More trouble, Nicholas,' she said with relish. 'I wonder what is afoot now!'

She seemed to take pleasure in the college's misfortunes, although I did not believe she was so hard-hearted as to be pleased at Wat's injury. No doubt, like Mary, she had heard the rumour that Queen's meant to turn her out of her home and rightly resented it.

'It sounds now like fighting,' Emma said doubtfully. 'Can the villain have been caught? Go you, Nicholas. I know you are wanting to know what is afoot.'

'I shall, then,' I said, handing her the basket. 'Stay here in the garden, or come through to the shop. I shall be back shortly.'

It was not mere curiosity that drove me. If the miscreant had been taken, I wanted to question him about Piers Dykman, for I was sure there must be some thread linking the two.

In the shop, I found only Walter.

'Roger is away to the college,' Walter said. 'You heard it?'

'I heard something, but what, it is difficult to tell.'

'Well, I hope you may keep Roger out of trouble. He is somewhat rash.'

'Aye, he is.'

I hurried past the two cottages and found Roger, together with several other curious onlookers, standing at the opening into the college grounds.

'It seems the men have taken to fighting each other,' he said. ''Tis an almighty brawl in there, though I've no idea what has set it off.'

It was difficult to make out, from the chaos within, exactly what was happening, but it seemed as though the stonemasons were fighting the carpenters. Perhaps it was nothing more than some local quarrel between the men, and had naught to do with the series of earlier mishaps. At first I could see nothing of either Robert Hanbury or John English, the master carpenter, then they burst out of one of the college houses on the far side of the yard, closely followed by Master Brandon, the college Fellow who was overseeing the building of the chapel. It seemed they had been in conference when the fighting broke out, for both Hanbury and the scholar were carrying rolled up parchments, probably plans of the building.

Hanbury's senior journeyman staggered toward me, a gash in his forehead bleeding copiously. Gerard, that was his name. I caught him by the arm to steady him.

'What's amiss?' I said. 'Why are the men fighting?'

Behind him the two master craftsmen and the Fellow were shouting at the workmen, trying to restore order.

The journeyman pressed a rag to his head and swayed slightly. It must have been a heavy blow.

'One of our men climbed up to the new level of scaffolding,' he said. 'The third level, 'tis now. He was carrying a bucket of mortar, so he was mayhap somewhat unsteady on his feet. However it was, when he reached the end of the hurdle, it gave way, and he crashed to the ground. 'Twould not have been so serious, had he not been at the far end. He would have fallen soft down to the next level of scaffolding. As it was, he toppled over the edge and fell to the ground.'

'Is he injured?' We began to move forward together, now that the fighting was coming to an end.

'We hardly had time to see. His mate was left dangling, holding on to one of the beams, and he cried out that the carpenters had not secured the hurdle to the frame. 'Twas held in place by nothing but a bit of twine. As soon as a man stepped on it, the twine snapped and the hurdle collapsed.'

'So your masons blamed the carpenters and started the fight?'

'Aye. And fair enough. My man could have been killed. I must see how badly he is hurt.'

We pushed forward together through the crowd of angry men, looking as though it would need little to set them off again. At the far end of the chapel building a man was lying on the ground, with two others bending over him.

We reached him at the same time as the two masters and Brandon. He was groaning, but did not seem to be seriously hurt.

'Nothing but a bit of thin twine,' one of the other masons was saying, nearly spitting in anger. 'I saw it just moments before Edred fell. Not even bound tight round the timber, just loosely knotted.'

This must be the other man, the one who have been left dangling. I supposed he must have dropped safely down to the next level of scaffolding.

'The whole was secure, I checked it myself.' It was John English, the master carpenter, red in the face and furious. 'None of my men would tie scaffolding together with twine! You lie, churl!'

The mason clenched his fists, then pointed. 'No lie of mine, sirrah! Look for yourself if you doubt me.'

We all looked up where he pointed. The end hurdle on the third level of scaffolding hung down, its inner end still secured to the timber framework with the usual leather thongs, its outer end hanging down and swaying a little. Trailing from it there were, unmistakably, ends of thin twine.

'When was that scaffolding erected?' I asked the journeyman mason quietly.

'Yesterday. Late. We had no need to use it until this afternoon. We were working on the north wall and the pillars for the nave. We only started on the next course for the south wall after dinner. There was one man up there at first, then these two.'

'And with a heavy bucket of mortar,' I said.

'Aye, and this fellow had a hod of stones.'

'So the twine might just hold one man's weight, but not two men and their loads.'

'Aye, you have the right of it.'

'I do not think the carpenters are to blame,' I said.

He shook his head. 'I suppose. Probably not. It would be a dangerous folly. It could have been one of their men who fell. But if it's this b'yer lady devil of an intruder, how could he get in to tamper with it?'

'How indeed? It must have been done in the night.'

It seemed to be gradually dawning on the stonemasons that the carpenters were not to blame for the accident, and a few grudging words of apology began to be muttered.

'We be as angry as you,' I heard one of the carpenters say. ''Tis a marring of our work and a casting of blame where it has no right to be.'

In all the anger and confusion, no one was paying much mind to the man who had fallen. He was not out of his wits, but he seemed disinclined to get up from the ground. I leaned over him.

'Are you hurt?' I said. 'Or merely winded?'

'To tell truth, maister,' he said, 'my legs do pain me middling bad.'

'Best take care getting up, then,' I said.

'Aye.'

He sat up and tried to draw up his legs to rise from the ground, but gave a low cry of pain and lay back again.

'I fear I may have sprained something.' The words came out in a gasp.

'Your back, man,' the journeyman said, crouching down, with his hand on the man's arm. 'Is there pain in your back?'

I caught the alarm in his voice. An injury to the back would be far worse than a sprained ankle.

The man on the ground shook his head. 'Nay, there's naught amiss with my back, Jesu be praised.'

Robert Hanbury, having sent most of the men back to their work on the interior of the chapel, while the carpenters set about repairing the scaffolding, came over at last and crouched down by the injured man.

'Now, Edred,' he said, 'that was an unpleasant fall. You say your back is not hurt?'

'Nay, maister, but my legs are not right.'

Hanbury ran an expert hand over the man's legs. I suppose in the course of a lifetime's work at building, he had come to know a good deal about the common injuries. He shook his head now.

'I fear it may be more than a sprain in you left leg. There's an unevenness there. It could be a break.'

Edred groaned and lay back with his eyes closed. 'Mother Mary and all the Saints! I won't be able to work.'

Hanbury stood up.

'Will St John's treat a man with a broken leg, Nicholas?'

I shook my head. 'Unlikely. They mostly care for the bedridden. There is a barber and bone-setter has a house near St Aldate's church in Fish Street. Send one of your lads for him. He knows his trade. He will soon tell if the bone is broken.'

'Aye, thank e'e,' Hanbury said. 'I'll send one of the boys now.'

He patted Edred on the shoulder. 'We shall soon have you strapped up, never fear, and I'll find work for you. You can do some chiselling sitting down. You wanted to move on from setting to working on the banks. Now is your chance. 'Tis ill the wind, they say, that does no good.'

The man ventured a weak smile. 'I'd be grateful, maister.'

He was looking paler now, as though, after the first numbing shock the pain was beginning to trouble him. The journeyman must have realised the same, for he came now with a cup of ale, and eased Edred into a sitting position so he might drink.

'I'll back to my shop,' I said to Hanbury, who had risen and was frowning at the dangling hurdle, which the carpenters were about to lift back into place.

He turned and looked at me thoughtfully.

'The tampering with the bucket, now,' he said. 'That might have been done the same night as the wall was overthrown, and it only collapsed later. But this?'

We began to walk together toward the High Street.

'Aye, my thoughts have been running that way as well,' I said. 'I am told that this part of the scaffolding was only erected late yesterday. Unless we suppose one of your carpenters is the source of all this trouble, it was built soundly and, as your master carpenter says, checked by him when it was finished. That means that sometime between early evening yesterday and this afternoon, someone removed the leather fixings and substituted some knotted twine.'

'It cannot have been done after we started work today,' Hanbury said decisively. 'Impossible. We have all been everywhere about the building. Although we were mainly working on the north wall and the internal pillars, we have been passing to and fro all day past that end of the building. It could not have been tampered with after we began soon after dawn.'

'So someone got into the site during the night,' I said. 'Again. But how?

He shook his head in bafflement. 'It was clear enough, what we discovered before. His trail could not be mistaken, from the empty cottage, across the gardens behind the houses along the High Street, including yours, then over the fence between the college and the ribbon weaver's house. But the deserted cottage is secure now.'

'It was not always secure,' I said. 'It was broken into a second time.'

'Aye, but there was no sign of anyone coming into the college that way again. We have been watchful, and found no further traces. It might have been some other fellow broke into the cottage. A beggar, perhaps, seeking a place to sleep.'

I nodded. Piers Dykman might have been looking for somewhere to sleep, but I did not think he would have broken open the shutters after they had been first secured.

'There must be some other way into the college that we have not discovered,' I said, 'for certainly I agree that this latest trick must have been carried out during the dark of last night.'

'I must attend to the work,' he said, 'for I had hoped to lay the next course of stones on the south wall this afternoon, but I will bend my mind to how anyone might break into the college.'

'And so shall I.'

I made my way thoughtfully back to the shop, glad to see that Roger had already returned to his work. Were I of a superstitious turn of mind, like some of the workmen, I might suppose that our villain had flown in over the walls by some magical power. However, a thorough grounding in the university curriculum is apt to drive away belief in such idle fancies, although I have known a few scholars who give credit to them.

On the threshold of the shop, I met Emma.

'Are you leaving?' I said, in some dismay.

She smiled. 'I was not sure how long you would be, poking your nose into the latest mystery. Roger has told me what befell. The man is not badly hurt, I hope?'

'One of his legs may be broken.'

'Ah, the poor fellow. Though I suppose it might be worse.'

'Will you not come back in now?'

She shook her head.

'I am eager to make a start, now that we are agreed about the pages of the troubadour book. As soon as I finish the first gathering, I will bring it for you to see.'

With that, she set off, up the High Street. I had been unable to speak of those difficult matters. Perhaps, though I would scarcely admit it to myself, I was somewhat relieved.

Chapter Eight

The mason Edred did indeed have a broken leg. The bone setter came promptly and snapped the bone back into place – we heard the yell of pain from the shop. Once it was strapped to a flat board, the man was given an infusion of willow bark and allowed a day off work, but it seemed he was anxious not to be too long absent, lest he be considered useless and turned away. I doubted that would happen, for Robert Hanbury was a good master and well understood that the injury was not the man's fault.

The following evening Hanbury stopped by the shop as Roger was closing the shutters before going home.

'Fortunately, it seems to be a clean break,' he said. 'The bone setter thinks it will mend without leaving the leg shortened or bent. Otherwise Edred has suffered nothing but a fine crop of bruises, although the leg pains him a good deal.'

'It could have been very much worse,' I said, leading him through the kitchen and out into the garden, where the sun was warm enough for us to sit on the bench under the pear tree, beyond the shadow cast by the house.

'Aye, you speak truly,' he said, accepting a cup of ale and one of the fig sweetmeats Margaret and Alysoun had been making that afternoon. 'Had he landed on one of our blocks of stone, he could have been killed, or broken his back. And the injury will not mar him lifelong, unlike poor Wat.'

'And you are no nearer fathoming who has such a

hatred of you or Queen's College, that they persist in persecuting you?'

He shook his head. I thought he looked exhausted and deeply troubled. Little wonder, when he was so beset with injury to his men and damage to the chapel.

'There seems no reason for it,' he said, a note of despair in his voice. 'I have discussed it also with Master Brandon, who is as baffled as I. Queen's is not a rich college, so it is not likely to attract the envy and enmity of others.'

'The college must have *some* rich benefactors,' I said. 'Like this gentleman, de Luce, who has given the money for the chapel.'

'As to that,' he said frankly, 'it is not so generous a benefaction as I first supposed. It will not be enough for us to build the transepts, which the provost wanted, as I told you, and it will only just cover the cost of one window of coloured glass. If the college wants to enhance the chapel, they will need to find another benefactor. However, I suppose Sir Thomas Luce will have bought himself perpetual fame, as well as masses for his immortal soul hereafter.'

'And have you heard when de Luce will come to Oxford?'

'We have been told it will certainly not be Sir Thomas himself, but his son Anthony, who will come in his stead. The father is still in poor health. The son will be here in time for Easter, when the college hopes to hold the services in the chapel, even though it will be unfinished.'

'Easter? Then you have but another two weeks.'

'Aye,' he said glumly. 'And I wonder how many more accidents we shall have before then.'

It was peaceful in the garden, with the bees busy about the fruit blossom, and the hens scratching hopefully in the loose earth of the vegetable plot, where Margaret had been hoeing earlier. The end of the noisy activity of the day resounding from the college meant that the silence was almost palpable.

'I cannot imagine what is keeping the deputy sheriff away from Oxford so long,' I said. 'He had thought to have returned long before this. Had he been here, I am sure he would have taken matters in hand. He is an able man.'

'Perhaps he has met with more trouble in Banbury than he expected.'

'It must be so. It is unfortunate that he had no better officer than Gurdin to leave in charge during his absence.'

I stretched out my legs and sipped my ale.

'Business is very quiet in the shop. I am half minded to ride to Banbury and warn him of the troubles afoot here. Even if he cannot return himself, he might send his captain, Thomas Beverley. He would deal with matters a deal more effectively than Gurdin.'

'You should not trouble yourself for our sake,' Hanbury said. 'You have already proved a good friend to us.'

'It is little enough I have done, save help you track down the intruder's first means of entering the college grounds. I am as baffled as you now. How did he manage to tamper with the scaffolding?'

I stirred restlessly. Hanbury had the right of it, in some sense. The troubles at Queen's were no affair of mine, yet these supposed accidents were happening almost on my doorstep. Besides, I had the uneasy feeling that somehow Jordain's student, Piers Dykman, was caught up in the events, since he had disappeared, inexplicably, soon after they began, and his gown had been found where we knew the troublemaker had also been. There must be some link between these events, though what, I could not fathom.

'It seems another gentleman from the north country is to come to pass Easter at the college,' Hanbury said. 'So Master Brandon tells me. The Fellows were somewhat surprised, for it is a family which has shown no interest in the college before.'

I was giving no more than half an ear to this, for I was pursuing a thought of my own.

'You know, Robert,' I said, 'there is one other way

into Queen's that we have not considered.'

'There is?' He looked surprised. 'I thought that between us the college and I had every side guarded.'

'You know how Hammer Hall Lane finds its zigzag way through from the High Street to emerge in the north, beside the postern gate, Smith Gate, near the Camditch?'

'Aye.'

'One of the bends runs parallel to the north wall of Queen's. On that side of the college grounds is a cluster of old houses used by the Fellows, and some open ground where the gardeners grow vegetables.'

'But the wall does not run quite along the lane,' he objected. 'There are houses between the lane and the college wall.'

'There are,' I agreed. 'Some houses and some of the smaller student halls. Also one or two of the town lodging houses, where a few students still live, although the university frowns on it. The plan is for students in future to live only in halls managed by a Regent Master.'

He looked doubtful. 'Could the man have come that way? Over the wall from the ribbon weaver's cottage, he would be close by the chapel, and well away from the other college buildings. If he tried to climb in over the north wall, he would need to make his way past that group of Fellows' houses, and the kitchen, and the servants' quarters. Risky.'

'At night, when all were abed? I think we are already sure that this is a bold fellow, who cares nothing for risk. Whatever the reason for his actions, he is determined to plague you. I think he would have no fear of making his way through the Fellows' houses.'

'You may have the right of it.' He was thoughtful, staring into his ale cup. 'Aye, it is possible he might have come that way, this last time, if it is possible to make a way through from the houses in the lane to reach the wall of the college.'

'I am sure there are some derelict houses there,' I said. ''Tis a place not as broken down as the ancient cottages on the other side of the lane, beyond the church, but the properties are mostly old, crowded cheek by jowl, built at many different times. There are paths through between some of them, as well as empty cottages, half ruined. I think there would be no difficulty reaching the college wall. I do not know why I never thought of it before. And as well, in that dark lane at night it would be much easier to come and go than in the High Street.'

'It is well thought on,' he said. 'Tomorrow I will send some of my men to walk along the inside of the north college wall, to see whether there are any signs of someone making his way in there. Indeed, I shall go myself.'

I refrained from offering to go with him, for he was right that it was no affair of mine, though, having thought of this possible way into the college, I would have liked to discover whether I was right.

As I was seeing Hanbury out through the shop, he clapped me on the shoulder and bowed.

'It is a good thought of yours, Nicholas, that there might be some way in from the lane to the north of the college. I will investigate at dinner time tomorrow.'

In the event, dinner time was too late.

I was half hoping, the next morning, that Emma might come with the first gathering of pages for the troubadour song book, but perhaps that was to expect too much. The work was far more demanding than pages of text, for the laying out of the music and the two strands of words would take considerably more time than neat lines of text, proceeding uneventfully one after the other. She would probably want to complete her illuminated initials as well, so that I could admire the finished pages, and that would need several days' work. There was no reason I could not go to St Mildred Street, to her aunt's house, to speak to her as Margaret had urged, but the house was very small for four people, and I was unlikely to be able to talk to her alone.

Perhaps I was merely making excuses for myself.

Of late there had been less noise from the building

works, since Hanbury had previously set the men to completing the shaped stone for the pillars and interior arches before they were assembled, and this was now finished. The work on the outer walls was now mainly the setting and mortaring of the final stones into place. The chapel was starting to look like the building it would eventually become. Even the elaborate tracery for the east window was in place, entirely carved by Hanbury himself, awaiting the arrival of the glaziers in a few days' time.

Some of the carvers were at work, shaping a series of angels' heads, which would adorn the tops of the pillars all along the nave, but the tap of their chisels could hardly be heard from my shop, unlike the sawing of the large stone blocks, a noise which set one's teeth on edge.

Today, Hanbury had told me, they would be working on the interior, erecting the first of the arches which would leap from pillar to pillar along the nave, the pillars dividing the central nave from the side aisles and the stone arches eventually giving support to the main roof timbers.

'We may still be open to the heavens when it is time to hold the Easter services,' he said, 'for I cannot think we will complete the roof by then, so we must pray that there be no rain. A sodden congregation would be a sorry sight for the benefactor's son. We shall do our best to complete the east end of the roof, at least, to provide shelter for the chancel.'

I understood the method of erecting arches now. Where a simple arch was needed over a door or window, the carpenters would make a curved wooden pattern, or 'centring', as they called it, which was then fixed temporarily in place and the shaped stones built around it, culminating in the key stone at the apex. Once the mortar was thoroughly dry and hard, the wooden pattern would be knocked out and – all being well! – the stone arch would stand of itself. Less important doors might have a simple horizontal lintel instead of an arch, a single large and heavy slab of stone, lifted into place by the hoist that I had observed lying on the ground when I had taken the children to watch the erection of the scaffolding. I had not yet seen the hoist working. It appeared that it was powered by one of the larger and heavier apprentices inside the tread wheel, which then hoisted the stone by means of a series of pulleys.

The internal arches for the nave, however, were not to be built up with a series of small angled stones. Instead, each half consisted of a beautifully curved and fluted stone, and these would be held in place by an elaborately carved key stone, to which the angels' heads would later be attached. The curved side stones of the arches were extremely heavy, and so they too would be lifted into place by the hoist which was used for the lintels. Men on ladders would then ease each one into place over the wooden pattern, and secure them, as well the key stone, with mortar. Unlike the building of the simpler kind of arch, this could not be done bit by bit, but must all be secured in one careful operation.

Although Robert Hanbury was a skilled master mason, I could see that the construction of these arches worried him.

'I shall be glad when they are all in place, Nicholas,' he had confessed, with a rueful grin. 'It is the most difficult part of the whole construction. Not only are they awkward to set in place, but if even one angle is somewhat out of true, the roof will not sit aright, and the building will be unstable.'

I thought he worried unnecessarily, for I had seen the sheaves of drawings and calculations he prepared before each stage of the building went ahead. Still, it seemed he was being hurried too much through the work, in a way he was not accustomed to, so it was little to be wondered at that he felt concerned.

This time, when the uproar broke out from the college, I hoped that it was merely the shouts of men engaged in the awkward business of lifting the arch stones into place – shouting advice and instruction to each other. The scriveners and I looked at each other.

'It surely cannot be another accident,' Walter said. 'They must be watching over that chapel as carefully as a cat watches a mouse hole.'

Roger went to the door and cocked his head.

'Myself,' he said. 'I do not like the sound of that.'

I joined him, listening intently. Whereas the crash of Edred falling from the scaffolding had been followed by shouting and the outbreak of a brawl between the men, this was different. I heard a desperate cry, abruptly cut off.

'I shall see what is amiss,' I said. 'Perhaps it is nothing more than concern because a fine carved stone dropped and shattered. They are hastening to complete as much of the work as they may before this Sir Anthony de Luce comes to inspect it. Any damage must set them back.'

I walked off briskly before they could respond, for I did not quite believe my own words. Would a broken stone be greeted by such a sound of desperate lamentation?

No one had gathered in the street this time. The building works and their misfortunes had ceased to be a novelty. Within the college grounds there was no fighting, and hardly anyone to be seen. Remembering that the intention had been to work on the interior of the chapel today, I ducked under the scaffolding and stepped over the threshold of the south door. I was confronted by a crowd of men, silent, white with shock, and standing as if frozen.

The hoist had been set up beside the first two pillars at the south west end of the nave, and the pattern for the arch joining the pillars was in place. At first I could not see what was amiss. The tread wheel, which must have been turning, was gradually slowing down to a stop. Beside it, one of the apprentices lay on the ground, as if he had fallen while driving it. Hanbury had told me that it could be difficult to step from slat to slat, keeping the wheel turning steadily. And if the stone being hoisted was heavy, then, even with the assistance of pulleys, it required someone of weight to work the wheel. If the whole mechanism ran out of control, the man could be thrown headlong out of the wheel. It looked as though this was what had happened. The apprentice lay still, clearly winded, but otherwise seemed not to be seriously injured. If the hoist had merely malfunctioned, this was not a trick of the intruder.

I drew closer and a few of the men turned toward me, their faces stiff with shock. Then, as they drew aside, I saw the real source of their horror.

The journeyman Gerard I had spoken to when Edred had fallen from the scaffolding was also lying on the floor, a few yards further on. Across his chest lay one of the sculpted arch stones, crushing him beneath its great weight. His eyes stared unseeing at the open sky above the unfinished nave, and blood trickled slowly from the corner of his mouth. A length of rope was still knotted like complex cradle about the stone, but where it trailed away across the floor the end lay frayed like a worn brush.

It was not credible. Robert Hanbury would never have permitted an old rope to be used on the hoist, which even under the direction of experienced men was a dangerous machine. Surely, after all that had happened, every part of the hoist must have been checked before the day's work began? The rope was not cut clean through, for that would have be obvious at first glance, and besides, a cut rope would not have lifted the block of stone at all. The arch stone must have been lifted some distance before it fell, or it could not have smashed the life out of a man.

Robert Hanbury was seated on one of the half constructed pillars, slumped over, his head in his hands. I touched him gently on the shoulder.

'How has this come about?' I said.

He lifted to me a face bleak with pain and fear.

'The stone was halfway up, there seemed naught amiss with the hoist. Gerard was reaching up, steadying it so that it would not swing, then it fell, crushing him. He had never a chance.'

'The rope is frayed.'

'Well, 'twas not frayed when I checked it this morning!' His voice was angry. 'Every morning now I check everything. The rope was sound.'

Before I could say more, I caught sight of Provost de Hotham, Master Brandon, and two other Fellows hurrying in through the door in the partially completed north wall. I drew back, stepping round the body, and bent over the frayed rope, which I picked up for a closer look.

There was something odd about this. It was a very thick rope, as one would expect, for lifting heavy stones, perhaps three inches across, plied together with several strands, each twisted separately, then the whole twisted together. It looked fairly new, a strong hemp rope, suited to the task. However, when I am examined it, I saw that it was not all frayed. The inner fibres had been severed, showing the straight cut edge made by a blade, while the outermost fibres were the only ones which were frayed.

I puzzled over how this might happen, hearing behind me the raised and worried voices of the scholars, and Robert Hanbury's voice, quiet and resigned, answering them dully. How could the inner part of the rope be cut, and not the outer? And how could the rope have frayed between the time the master mason checked it before work started, and the disaster so soon afterwards?

Holding a length of the rope a few feet down from the end, I tried twisting it in the opposite direction from the twist in the outermost layer of the rope. It was stiff, but I managed to open it enough to see the inner strands. Aye, it would be possible to insert a thin bladed knife between the outer strands and cut through the inner ones. Released, the rope sprang back on itself. It would, I thought, conceal the damage. That did not account for the frayed outer portion, however. The rope would be weakened, but would it break?

John English, the master carpenter, was watching me. Although the setting of the arch stones was the stonemasons' business, he would have been responsible for the design and construction of the wooden pattern, and he had a close interest in those parts of the masons' work which would support his wooden roof trusses.

'Where are the pulleys?' I said. 'The pulleys the rope

ran through?

He pointed to where parts of the hoist machinery were scattered on the floor beside the pillars.

'All flew everywhere,' he said, 'when the block fell. The rope runs through several pulleys, to make the load easier to lift. Each pulley makes the task a little less heavy.'

I did not understand why this was so, or how it worked, but that was not my interest in the pulleys. I walked over to the first of them and picked it up. It was a solid chunk of oak, as big as my two fists held together, a sort of partially closed wooden cage with a wheel rotating inside it. I tilted it toward the light coming in through the open roof, in order to see it more clearly.

In the better light, I could see several gossamer fine strands caught in the pulley and stirring slightly in the movement of the air caused by several men now struggling to lift the fatal stone off the journeyman's chest. I slipped my finger inside the pulley to pluck out the strands, and felt something prick me. As I drew out the fibres, I saw spots of blood welling up on my finger. I beckoned to John English.

'Strands of hemp, I think,' I said, holding them out to him. 'From the rope.'

He peered at them and nodded. 'You have cut your finger.'

'The pulley must be rough,' I said.

'Never. They are made smooth from the start, and are worn all the smoother, the more they are used. Can I see?'

I peered into the pulley, then handed it to him.

'They are surely not constructed like this,' I said.

Within the casing of the pulley, there was a double row of small pins which did not protrude far enough to stop the movement of the rope over the wheel, but would certainly catch at it, as blackberry thorns will do when a hand reaches to pick the fruit.

Master English raised his eyes from examining the pulley, his face flushed and angry.

'It has been tampered with,' he said flatly.

Without a word, we both began to collect up the other

pulleys. More than half had been fitted with the inner rows of pins, like small malicious teeth, all of them snagged with fragments of hemp. In one there was a matted cluster of the threads, probably the final and fatal pulley.

'As the rope ran through,' I said, 'the outer surface caught on the pins, until the weakened portion broke. Look at this.'

I showed him the broken end of the rope.

'The inner part cut through beforehand,' he said slowly, fingering it, 'then the thin outer shell ripped apart as the rope ran over those pins.'

'Aye.'

'What a devilish trick. And with the weight of the stone on the rope, it would have pressed all the harder on the pins.'

'It seems likely.'

'This is murder.'

'It is murder.'

He let his breath go in a great sigh, as if he had been holding it back.

'We cannot go on,' he said simply. 'How many more men will be injured or killed?'

'I think that is the intention,' I said. 'To put a halt to the building of the chapel. Though why or by whom, seems a mystery.'

He shivered. ''Tis almost like witchcraft, the defiling of a holy work.'

'Nay, I think not. This, and all the other misfortunes, are the work of a man's hands, not the dark arts of some witch.'

I glanced across at Robert Hanbury and the college Fellows. He was standing now, and shaking his head. Did he feel, like John English, that the work could not continue? Master Brandon was gesturing at the master carpenter to join them.

'Listen,' I said, laying a hand on his arm. 'You have the right of it. Small annoyances could be tolerated, but these last incidents have gone too far. I am going now, this very day, to fetch the deputy sheriff, Cedric Walden, back to Oxford. His business in Banbury must surely be done by now, and if not, he can leave his captain to finish it. I will take this pulley with me, to show the sheriff.'

I held up the one most thickly matted.

'And I should like, if I may, to take the end portion of the rope which has been tampered with. Perhaps not the piece attached to the stone.'

Involuntarily we both glanced across at the stone, where it lay by the journeyman's body. Someone had laid a blanket over his face. They were bringing a hurdle, to carry him away.

Master English nodded his understanding.

'I will cut you a length from the other end.'

He drew a long knife from amongst the tools hanging from his belt, and sliced a foot of rope from the other portion, with its end also clearly showing the severed inner strands.

'They are summoning you,' I said, nodded toward the group of Fellows. 'Tell them what I have said, that I am gone to fetch Cedric Walden. It will be night before we can be back in Oxford. Take no risks before that.'

'We shall not work again today,' he said heavily, 'if ever again on this accursed building.'

'I think it is not the building that is accursed,' I said. 'A chapel raised piously as a place of worship. But whoever is behind these deeds is truly accursed.'

He nodded and walked away, telling the men as he went that there would be no further work that day. They began to wander away, still too shocked to talk. I went swiftly home, thankful that now I possessed my own horse. I could start on my way at once.

I could not make an immediate start, however, for I must first tell Walter and Roger what had happened. While I was at the college, a message had come from the bookbinder to say that Walter's book of tales was ready to be collected, so I found the coin to pay for it, and told Walter that he might go and fetch it.

'Do you not want to see that all is as you ordered?' he said.

'Nay, you can see that as well as I,' I said. 'Besides, we may trust Henry Stalbroke to carry out the work to perfection.'

I was busy emptying my book satchel and stowing the pulley and the section of rope in it. In the kitchen I found Margaret preparing the dinner.

'You may surely eat before you go,' she said, when I told her I meant to ride to Banbury at once.

I shook my head. 'I have already lost most of the morning. It is full thirty miles and I cannot be sure how long it will take to find Cedric Walden. Then there is the long ride back.'

She sighed and shrugged. 'Very well. Go you and saddle Rufus while I pack up some food for you to take. At least the days are growing longer now, though it will be near dark by the time you return.'

Rufus was the only one who seemed pleased at the prospect of the ride, stamping and snorting his approval while I hastened to saddle up. As I led him out of the stable, Margaret came from the kitchen, carrying a bag of food, which she stored in my saddle bag, next to my satchel, then wedged in a leather jack of ale.

'I hope it may not spill,' she said, 'if you set Rufus to the gallop.'

I laughed. 'My satchel is sturdy enough to withstand a few splashes of ale, and the food will be none the worse for a light dowsing.'

I mounted and looked down at her.

'You do see why I must go, Meg. The man was killed. This is no idle game, if it ever was. It is murder.'

'They might have sent one of their own men.'

I shook my head. 'Cedric knows me and he knows I would not fetch him back but for something serious. A stranger might have wasted precious time, explaining.'

'Aye, I do see that. Come, I will open the gate for

you, then bolt it when you are gone.'

As I rode up the High toward Carfax, I reflected that it was near enough a year since I had last ridden Rufus to Banbury, on a very different mission. Then it was to bring the welcome coin to Widow Preston and her daughter Sissy from the sale of her husband's books. That was a journey with a pleasurable outcome. This was very different. A mission prompted by murder. I thought I should have little difficulty in persuading Cedric to return to Oxford, once I had explained all that had been happening at Queen's, and showed him the evidence of the rope and pulley. But it might be difficult to find him. It was possible the villains and masterless men he was pursuing had taken to the surrounding countryside, so that I should not find him in Banbury at all, but would need to scour the neighbourhood. It might not even be possible to return today.

At least I could be grateful for the weather. It was not raining, which would have been a great hindrance, but the sky was slightly cloudy, so that there would not be heat enough to trouble Rufus. He had been having an idle time of late, and was already straining to go faster, but I would wait until we were through the North Gate.

As was so often the case, the street was crowded inside the gate, with the usual petitioners creating chaos outside the town prison which was built over the gatehouse, but I pushed my way through with little ceremony, earning a few curses, then I was out on the wide stretch of St Giles, where I could give Rufus his head.

We went the same way as we had gone the previous year, passing through a series of villages, some of which had been deserted since the pestilence. One seemed even more ruined than before, the cottages fallen in and even the ranging stray dogs departed. However, in another, which had been quite abandoned a year ago, there were signs that a few cottages had been patched up. Smoke rose from their chimneys, a man was hoeing a vegetable patch, and a woman with a small child peeping out from behind her skirts, gave me 'Good-day' as she spread out her washing to dry.

I stopped in the same spot as before, not because I needed to pause while I ate the food Margaret had given me – I could do that in the saddle – but because I thought Rufus needed a drink from the stream and a few mouthfuls of grass while he had a brief rest. I did not allow him long, however, for the sun was already past midday.

By mid afternoon we reached Banbury, and I made at once for the castle. This is a formidable structure, pentagonal in shape, largely rebuilt in the last century. Unusually it does not belong to some great local family, but to the bishops of Lincoln, who make use of it as a prison. It seemed likely that Cedric and his men would be lodged here while they set about rounding up the villains who had been plaguing the neighbourhood. I guessed that the bishop would not object to their prisoners being confined in his prison, a building which seemed excessive for his own customary needs.

'Aye,' the porter at the gatehouse said. 'The Oxfordshire sheriff is lodged here, but un don't be here now.'

'Then where is he?' I asked. I had dismounted, for Rufus was beginning to look somewhat weary after the long ride.

'That I don't know, maister,' he said. 'Him'll be somewheres about. They rides out every day after these fellows that have been causing all the trouble. We'm got a deal o'them shut up inside.' He jerked his head toward the interior of the castle.

'Do you know when he will be back?' I said.

He shook his head. 'Likely round about dusk. They usually makes a day of it.'

My heart sank. If Cedric did not return until dusk, we could not set off until tomorrow. Even though all work had now stopped on the chapel, I had an irrational feeling that we must return as quickly as possible.

I was standing irresolute, wondering whether I should set off to hunt for Cedric, which would probably be pointless, when I caught sight of a familiar figure crossing the courtyard.

'Thomas Beverley!' I shouted.

He stopped and turned, a look of astonishment on his face, then he loped over to the gatehouse.

'Nicholas Elyot! What do you here?'

'I have come to fetch Cedric Walden back to Oxford, he's urgently needed. But this man does not know where he might be found, and thinks he will not return until dusk.'

'Ah, but I know where he is.' Thomas grinned. 'I was with him until my horse cast a shoe and we hobbled back to the town. My horse is with the smith now, and I am kicking my heels. It is urgent, you say? I can send a man to bring the sheriff back. We have mainly cleared that area of the miscreants. Come within. I can show you where to see to your horse while I send off my messenger, then you may tell me all that is afoot. We were near done here anyway. We can leave a few men to see to the last of it.'

It seemed that luck was with me after all. Thomas led me to the castle stables, where I removed Rufus's saddle and bridle, gave him water and hay, and rubbed off the sweat from his sides. I had just finished when Thomas reappeared.

'That is my messenger gone,' he said, taking me by the arm and leading me over to the central keep of the castle. 'It should be possible to make a start on the road before dusk, though I fear it will be dark before we reach Oxford.'

I was glad that he also planned to return with me. Between them, he and Cedric should be able to deal with the trouble at Queen's, or at least so I hoped.

'You will find,' he said, 'that these bishops do themselves very well when they visit Banbury. We have luxurious quarters and fine food.'

'You do not fare so poorly at home,' I said, recalling the pike I had been served before they left.

In truth, the private quarters in the castle were richly furnished, and a servant brought us an early supper – or perhaps it was a late dinner – washed down with French wine. As we ate, I told Thomas everything that had been happening at Queen's College since the building of the chapel had begun. Thomas listened intently, frowning and even forgetting to eat when I reached the recent serious injuries, and then this morning's death.

I took out the rope and the pulley and laid them on the table between us. He examined them carefully.

'It must have taken a good while to fix these pins inside the pulleys,' he said, laying my two pieces of evidence back on the table.

'I was thinking on that as I rode here,' I said. 'It need not have been done all at one time. Think! If a sound rope passed through one of these pulleys, it would catch a little, and some of the surface would be snagged, but I do not suppose any great harm would be done. And they have not made much use of the hoist until now, only lifting a couple of the straight lintel stones about a week ago. It is in constructing the arches which are to span the spaces between the pillars inside the chapel that the hoist is mostly needed, to lift the large curved side pieces, like the one which killed the journeyman. So it was only when the damaged rope passed through several of the pulleys that the fatal break occurred. The pulleys could have been tampered with days ago, then the inner part of the rope only severed in the last day or two, well after the hoist was last used.'

'It sounds to me,' he said thoughtfully, 'very like the trick with the mortar bucket that you have described. Contrive damage that will not be noticed, but which will wreak havoc when the perpetrator is far away.'

'That too had struck me,' I said. 'You can sense the same cast of mind at work.'

'And you say no one has any idea who could be so determined to destroy the work on the chapel?'

'So it seems.'

We were both silent. Then Thomas got to his feet.

'I will fetch my few possessions. I have some spare linen with me, and my horse must be done at the blacksmith now.'

He paused, looking out through the window.

'Here is Cedric come back. I will speak to him on my way to the smith. It will save time. Do you saddle up your mount.'

I felt a great sense of relief as I ran down the steps to the castle yard. Master Hanbury and I had been helpless, confronted by this invisible devil with his devilish tricks. To hand all over to the sheriff and his men was to lift a burden I had somehow come to assume. They would not waste time asking idle questions but would seize the crux of the matter at once and act with decision.

Cedric called out to me across the yard.

'Thomas has told me the gist of your story. We shall hear the rest as we ride. This is a borrowed horse. I shall fetch my own lad and we can be on our way in half an hour.'

It seemed optimistic, but it cannot have been much longer than that when we formed up in company to ride out of the castle gate. The sheriff was leaving behind a small group of men, under one of his young officers, to finish the work of listing the miscreants and the accusations against them, so that they might be tried at the next assize. In the meantime they would remain in the bishop's convenient prison. The rest of the company from Oxford castle would ride with us. A couple of scullions from the kitchen came out with parcels of food for all of us. It seemed these soldiers were as concerned as Margaret that none should starve on the road between Banbury and Oxford.

Cedric set us a brisk pace out of the town and on the way south, but once we had ridden a mile or two, he dropped back beside me.

'Now, Nicholas,' he said, 'Thomas has told me there have been attacks on the stonemasons building the new chapel at Queen's College. Trivial matters at first, then serious injuries, and now a death. You are quite sure these have not been accidents?'

'Quite sure,' I said, and went through again the whole

series of incidents. 'I have the evidence of the severed rope which caused the stone to fall and kill a man this morning, but it is in my saddle bag.'

'Thomas has seen it, and I believe you. And you also say there has been no hint as to why anyone should want to do this?'

'None at all. The Provost and Fellows have been urging speed upon the masons and carpenters, because the benefactor who provided the money for the chapel is due to come and assess the work at Easter. Or rather his son, since the father is ill.'

'Who is this man? This benefactor?'

'A knight from Cumberland. Sir Thomas de Luce. Son of the man who was patron to the college's Founder, Robert de Eglesfield.'

'Never heard of him.'

'De Eglesfield?'

'Oh, aye, I know of him, but I'd never heard of de Luce. No other connection with Oxford?'

'Not as far as I know,' I said. 'The college has this link with the north country, especially Cumberland and Westmorland, set down by the Founder.'

'There seems no connection there, then, with these mishaps.'

'As well as this trouble at the college,' I said, 'there is something else which concerns me. Jordain Brinkylsworth's youngest student, a boy of twelve, Piers Dykman, has disappeared.'

'That is surely another matter altogether,' Cedric said.

'Possibly not. He disappeared about the same time as the troubles began. And he is one of the poor boys sponsored by Queen's. He comes from Westmorland.'

'Ah, I see how your mind moves. Yet it may be no more than coincidence. Unless you think the boy is responsible?'

I shook my head. 'Impossible, on two counts. He is a small, slight child, undersized for his age. And he is a good, pious boy. Jordain swears he would never harm another. It would be impossible for him to have carried out these tricks.'

'Well, as you say, it is odd that they should happen at around the same time.'

We rode on through the gathering dusk. The slight cloud cover which had lingered all day meant that the light began to fade early. The soldiers were used to moving at a brisk pace and we covered the distance at a good speed, but I could feel Rufus tiring. Unlike the other horses, who had done no more than ride a little way outside Banbury, he had already made the long trip from Oxford that day, and had but a short rest in the town.

As it began to grow darker, two of the men rode to the front, with candle lanterns fixed to tall poles, and two more took up a position in the rear, to assure no one was left behind. If anything, the lanterns made the surrounding darkness seem even darker, and inevitably we were forced to slow our pace to no more than a trot.

Not only Rufus was exhausted. By the time we rode down St Giles toward the North Gate, I could barely keep my seat, although the soldiers seemed as fresh as when we had set off from Banbury.

Cedric shouted to the gatekeeper to open the gates for us, and he grumblingly complied. The clock of St Michael at the North Gate struck eleven as we rode through into Oxford.

Chapter Nine

I parted with Cedric Walden and his men at Carfax and rode wearily down the High Street, meeting the Watch near Edric Crowmer's vintner's shop. The men, who had worked in pairs since the troubled times after the pestilence, barred my way and lifted their lanterns, scrutinising my horse and my face until they recognised me.

'Late abroad, Maister Elyot,' one of them said, a note of suspicion in his voice.

His dog, a great brindled brute, whose sweet temperament belied his looks, lay down with a sigh at Rufus's feet. The horse lowered his head and blew out his breath thoughtfully.

'Back from fetching Sheriff Walden home from Banbury,' I said. 'Fortunately his business there is done.'

The two men exchanged a glance. Even in the poor light of their lanterns, I could see the relief on their faces. No doubt the Watch had been having a poor time of it under the rule of William Gurdin.

'Aye? He's back then?' the same man said. 'You'd best be away home, Maister Elyot. All's quiet.'

'I'll be glad of my bed,' I said. 'Good night to e'e.'

'And to e'e, maister.'

The man nudged the hound aside, and he moved reluctantly as Rufus stepped round him. Ahead I could see that there was a lantern burning outside my shop, and a candle in Margaret's room above. She would have the door barred by this hour of the night, but I must wake her, else I should be forced to sleep in the street. However, she must have been listening for me. I saw the candle taken up and carried away from the window. A few moments later I heard the bolts being drawn back from the door.

'At last,' Margaret said, shading her eyes from the candle as she held it up. 'I had almost decided that you would not come tonight.'

'We made what speed we could,' I said, sliding stiffly down from Rufus's back. 'I was luckier than I might have been, for I found Thomas Beverley almost at once, but it took time to fetch Cedric Walden, then arrange all and set out from Banbury. Most of the way back it was dark, so we could not ride fast.'

'Aye, 'twould be dangerous. I am glad to see you safe home. I will unbolt the yard gate, so that you may bring Rufus into the stable.'

By the time I had Rufus unsaddled, fed, and watered, I think I must have been rubbing him down with my eyes closed, for I had no recollection of doing so. I could not even eat the food Margaret had kept for me from supper, but stumbled up to lie flat on my bed, shedding nothing but my shoes.

It was full morning by the time I woke. Margaret must have kept the children quiet, so that I might sleep, and by the time I came down, yawning, into the kitchen, they had already taken Rowan and gone to St Mildred Street.

'Juliana came with a book she had borrowed from you,' Margaret said, cutting bread for me. The scent of the fresh loaf was nigh intoxicating. 'So when I said you were over tired from yesterday's ride, she offered to take the children back with her. They are to help her and Maud in the garden, while Emma works at her scribing, though I doubt they will prove much use.'

'Alysoun knows the difference between a weed and a sprouting bean or pea,' I said, 'though Rowan is as apt to dig one up as the other.'

I cut myself some cheese, and tried to bring my mind

to bear on what needed to be done that day.

'Has all been quiet at the college?' I asked.

She nodded. 'They held the inquest on the death of that journeyman. Very quick they were, this time, almost indecently quick. Then his family sent a cart for his body. He came from Marston, it seems.'

'What was the verdict of the inquest?'

'They could not reach a decision. Robert Hanbury called here afterwards and said he thought the coroners – it was the two of them again – were clearly urging the jurors to bring in a verdict of accidental death, but the men were stubborn. They had paid heed to the evidence of the rope and the pulleys, that both Master Hanbury and Master English insisted on placing before the coroner, and most of them wanted to bring in a verdict of murder. In the end, the inquest was adjourned and it will be held again now that the sheriff is returned.'

'Good,' I said. 'Matters have gone too far to be swept aside as accidents. I have told Cedric Walden all that has been happening and he will take charge of everything, now that he is back in Oxford. They have not resumed work on the chapel?'

'They have not,' she said, 'though Master Hanbury told me the provost has been urging them to do so. It appears he cares more for the college's reputation in the eyes of its benefactor than the danger to the stonemasons and carpenters.'

I grunted. Provost de Hotham was somewhat to be pitied. He could never have anticipated the series of disasters which had overtaken the building of the chapel, and a college with few means must needs stay on good terms with its benefactors. They would make a poor showing in the eyes of this benefactor's son when he arrived at Easter, if they had nothing to show for his father's gift but a half built chapel and a group of frightened and injured workmen. If the resumed inquest brought in a verdict of murder on the dead journeyman, this would cast a dark shadow over the whole business of building the chapel. It could be enough for Sir Thomas de Luce to withdraw his patronage of Queen's.

'Cedric Walden has said that he will call for me here, on his way to Queen's this morning,' I said, getting up from the table. 'Walter and Roger are at work?'

'Long since.' She smiled. 'I expect Walter is still stroking the book of his tales. You have had it very finely bound, Nicholas.'

'He deserved no less. He has worked on it for a year, and he has served this family loyally and ungrudgingly since before I married Elizabeth. He should have a book to be proud of.'

When I examined it, I agreed that it was indeed a magnificent volume, one of the most handsome secular books to have graced the shop.

Walter was not exactly stroking it, but he had set in on a shelf close beside his desk, where he could glance aside at it every few minutes. As there was little danger of stone dust today, with the building work halted, I decided he might keep it there for the present.

'In fact,' I said, 'I think I shall take down the blanket from the door. I believe most of the cutting of stone has been finished, There is only the fine carving now, and that is not so troublesome. We have endured this discomfort long enough.'

I carried a stool over to the doorway and began prising out the nails which held the blanket in place, passing them down to Roger. Once the blanket was free, I rolled it up and dropped it down to him.

I was just returning the stool to its place behind my desk when Cedric Walden and Thomas Beverley came in.

'You have little stock to tempt your customers, Nicholas,' the sheriff said, 'but I hear that you have been living under siege these weeks past.'

'Indeed,' I said. 'It has been a trying time, but nothing to what those workmen have suffered. Do you go to Queen's now?'

'Aye, shortly. There were matters to settle at the

castle before I could set out.'

Thomas grimaced, though he said nothing. No doubt some of these 'matters' were connected with the actions of William Gurdin, in command during their absence.

'I thought you would wish to come with us,' Cedric said, 'and I should be glad to have the end of rope and the pulley that you brought to Banbury.'

'I will fetch them,' I said, 'though I am told that Master Hanbury produced the other end of the rope and a damaged pulley as evidence at the inquest yesterday.'

'So they tell me. And the man's body has already been collected by his family. By rights, I should have viewed it.'

'It was a sorry sight,' I said. 'His chest was completely crushed by the stone.'

'It was a vile trick,' Thomas said.

I nodded. 'It was. Yet I wonder . . .' My voice trailed away.

'What is it that you wonder?' Cedric said.

I tried to put into words the ideas which had gradually been taking shape in my mind.

'The first mishaps were very minor,' I said. 'Missing tools – even tools as trivial as wooden mallets, of no real value. Then several chisels blunted. Unnecessary extra work for their blacksmith. They have a smith with them, for tools are for ever needing repair or sharpening. All of this causes brief delay, but nothing serious.'

'You think it was not the same miscreant as the fellow who caused the later damage?'

'Nay, I believe that all along it has been the same person. Someone who – for what reason we cannot fathom – wants to delay or stop the building of the chapel.'

I ran my hand over my face, for I was still feeling the fatigue of the previous day's disaster and my long ride.

'Next, there was the overthrowing of the wall,' I said. 'This was a more serious setback. Some of the dressed stone was broken and needed to be replaced, and that whole section of the wall must be rebuilt. It lost the stonemasons' two days. More delay, you see, more than before, worse damage. But the wall was rebuilt and the work continued. Our unknown miscreant had achieved part of his purpose, and we then discovered how he had gained access to the college at night. The way in was blocked, although he broke into the cottage again.'

I corrected myself. 'He *may* have broken in again. We cannot be sure. It might have been someone else. However it was done, on the same night as the breaking of the wall, or another night, he tampered with the mortar bucket.'

'And that caused a serious injury,' Thomas said.

'Aye, it did, but injury may not have been intended. It happened that the setters were short of mortar and they were shouting at the apprentices to hurry with more. Because of the rush, the boy Wat lifted the bucket when the slaked lime was still fiery hot. In the normal way of things, it would only have been lifted when it had cooled. The accident then would have caused more trouble, more delay – a whole batch of mortar wasted, probably, strewn about the ground. Perhaps a morning's work lost.'

'What you mean,' I think,' Cedric said slowly, 'was that he did not mean harm to the stonemasons even then? Just annoyance and a halt to the work?'

'That is how it seems to me. I think this is a man who is very clever in devising his tricks, but I think he does not trouble to look ahead to the graver consequences. He wants to stop the work and does not consider what may happen to the men.'

'You may be right.' Cedric looked somewhat doubtful.

'But the accident with the scaffolding,' Thomas said. 'That came next, did it not? *After* the boy was burned by the lime?'

I nodded. 'It is possible the intruder did not know how badly the apprentice was hurt. In any case, the accident with the scaffolding might have been quite trivial. If the twine had given way when Edred was part way along the hurdle, as might have been expected, he would have fallen down on to the layer of scaffolding below the one tampered with. He would merely have bounced on the lower hurdle and looked foolish. There would have been another delay. As it was, he was carrying a heavy bucket, and surprisingly the twine held until he reached the far end. Master Hanbury thinks the weight of the bucket caused him to pitch forward and fall off the end of the scaffolding to the ground. A broken leg instead of a red face.'

'I see.' Cedric rubbed his chin. 'So once again embarrassment and delay, but no serious harm intended.'

'I am but guessing,' I said, apologetically. 'But it squares with what went before. An intention to cause trouble. A man who is clever, but not wise, who can foresee only what he plans will happen and cannot see beyond that.'

'But then,' Cedric said, 'a man is killed.'

'A man is killed. Once again, a clever device. Who would have thought a rope could be tampered with so that it looked sound, but would be severed by the pins hammered into the pulleys?' I paused. 'It must have taken a deal of time to doctor those pulleys,' I said thoughtfully.

'Surely!' Thomas protested. 'Surely he must have realised how dangerous it would be to damage a great machine like a hoist? 'Tis little surprise a man was killed.'

'I think Nicholas has the right of it,' Cedric said slowly. 'This is a man bent on some plan of his to make trouble, to delay or stop the building of the chapel. He cannot see further than his own plan. He thinks, "I will make it impossible to use the hoist, so they cannot construct the interior of the chapel." He does *not* think, "If I cause the hoist to fail, a heavy stone will fall and someone will be killed." His thoughts run only along the path he has set for them, and he cannot conceive of anything else.'

All this while we had been standing in the shop, and my two scriveners had been listening. Now Walter ventured to speak, somewhat hesitantly in the presence of the sheriff.

'It seems to me,' he said, then stopped.

'Aye, Master Blunt?' Cedric smiled at him. 'All thoughts are useful here.'

'It seems to me, this is a young man's doing,' Walter said. 'Hardly more than a boy. A clever youth. Old enough and strong enough to overturn that wall, although Master Hanbury says that with a crowbar it would not be too difficult. But young enough to be blind to the outcome of his actions.'

Cedric looked at him thoughtfully.

'That is well thought on, Master Blunt. It does show the marks of an ingenious young mind, heedless of possible outcomes. As Nicholas has said, clever but not wise.'

'But why should some youth have such a bitter hatred against the college or the stonemasons?' Roger said, himself now daring to speak for the first time.

I shook my head. 'Some student turned out of the college for misbehaviour? I have heard of none. Some young man hoping to gain a place as a Fellow, but refused? That is possible, I suppose, but seems unlikely.'

I turned to Cedric. 'Perhaps it would be worth asking Provost de Hotham if he knows of any such. Yet it would surely be a very strong sense of grievance to drive a man to so much cruel mischief.'

I felt that 'mischief' was a poor word for what had ended in murder, but I could think of no other.

'Let us go to the college,' Cedric said, 'and you also, Nicholas.'

'I will fetch the rope and pulley for you,' I said.

As the sheriff making an official visit to Queen's College, Cedric Walden chose not to enter the grounds through the rough opening where the demolished cottage had stood on the High Street, but to walk all the way round to Hammer Hall Lane and seek admittance by the gatehouse, which was manned by a porter. In formal terms, he requested a meeting with Provost de Hotham, and the three of us were quickly shown into the largest and best of the buildings which made up the somewhat haphazard college, this one being designated the provost's lodging. The provost came in, apologising for keeping us waiting – which he had not done.

I had glimpsed him only briefly and in the distance the previous morning, but now that I saw him close to, I was struck by the change in his appearance since the day when he had first come to tell me of the building of the chapel. His face was grey with fatigue, and hollow eyed. I thought he had even lost weight. I had been blaming him, silently, for urging speed on the masons and carpenters, but now I thought that he seemed hag-ridden with worry. Perhaps Sir Thomas de Luce was a grudging or demanding patron, and the provost was sick with anxiety, not only because of the death and injuries amongst the men, but also because he feared dire consequences to the college if the benefactor's son were to take home an unfavourable report to his father.

We all bowed stiffly.

'I have returned early to Oxford,' the sheriff said formally, 'because I have been apprised of the unpleasant occurrences here at your college, Provost. Master Elyot rode out to Banbury yesterday after witnessing the death of one of the stonemasons building your new chapel. He has given me a full account of the mishaps which have occurred throughout the building work, and the fact that no man responsible has yet been apprehended. Quite rightly, he felt that I was needed here. However, before we can discuss these matters further, I would ask that you send for Master Hanbury and Master English to join us.'

'Certainly.' Provost de Hotham was equally formal. 'It is quite proper that they should be here, as they have more closely witnessed these events than I have. I should also like to send for Master Brandon, who is the college Fellow tasked with overseeing the work, both the construction in conformity with the agreed plans, and the expenditure of coin on materials and labour.'

From the strain in his voice as he spoke these last

words, it was clear that the matter of expenditure was no small worry to him.

'That would certainly benefit our discussions,' Cedric said.

While these exchanges took place, I withdrew a little way. I had no real business here. I could hear Margaret's voice in my head, warning me not to interfere, but it was somewhat too late for that. In any case, Cedric had asked me to come.

'You have a nose for puzzles, Nicholas,' he had said, as we walked up to the college gatehouse. 'And you have had an eye on this matter from the start. Moreover, you have just given a very credible description of the kind of miscreant we must look for. I want you to watch and listen. Perhaps you will catch some hint of the truth that I might miss.'

I doubted that I would notice anything that Cedric might miss, but I was glad to be party to the discussion at the college. The two master craftsmen came in together, both looking pale and worried, and were followed by Master Brandon, who seemed hardly better.

After the introductions had been made, the provost invited us to take seats around a long table beside the window which overlooked the central part of the colleges grounds. From here, I could see the east end of the new chapel, with the finely carved stone tracery of the window, awaiting its glass. One might almost suppose the building to be nearly finished.

'Let us first consider the events which Master Elyot has described to me,' Cedric said.

The provost nodded, and Cedric briefly summarised what I had told him.

'Master Elyot has also suggested,' he went on, 'the kind of person who may be behind these events, and I agree that it seems likely. Someone young, intending trouble for you, hoping to delay or stop the building of the chapel, for some reason we cannot guess, but perhaps not intending the serious consequences which have followed upon his tricks and devices. Is it possible that the college has some enemy who might do such a thing? A student barred? An unsuccessful applicant for a Fellow's position?'

'Or perhaps a dismissed servant?' Thomas ventured.

Provost de Hotham shook his head. 'I can think of no one. Can you, Master Brandon?'

The Fellow shook his head. 'It has always been my belief that these were attacks on the stonemasons by some rival in their craft. It is they, after all, who have suffered.'

Robert Hanbury gave him a sharp glance. I had the feeling that matters were somewhat strained between the two men.

'I have no such enemies,' he said crisply. 'Never before has my work been attacked in this way, only here at Queen's College. We must look for the reason here.'

'That is my belief also,' John English said. 'Although it is the masons who have mainly suffered, we have had some minor troubles too, amongst the carpenters. A few of our tools have also gone missing, and two of the more complex centrings for window arches were found smashed this morning. It might have happened at any time after they were made more than a week ago. While there has been a halt in the building work, I decided to make an inventory of which centrings were complete and which still need to be made. That was when I discovered the damage. It is mere chance that none of my men have been killed or injured. One of them might have fallen from the scaffolding or been under the stone when the hoist broke. I cannot think that both Master Hanbury and I have the same implacable enemy.'

It was clear that Provost de Hotham was very reluctant to admit that the cause might lie with the college, but the evidence did seem to point that way.

'You have had no strangers lurking about the college grounds?' Cedric asked. 'Someone who might have perpetrated these deeds?'

'The college has been full of strangers!' The provost almost spat out the words. 'How are we to know who is a workman under one of these two masters, and who is a rogue posing as one?'

It was a good point, which had not occurred to me. A stranger might mingle amongst the men during the working day, the stonemasons thinking he was a carpenter, and the carpenters thinking he was a mason. It would not account for the wall overthrown at night, but the theft of the tools might have been carried out during the day by someone passing himself off as one of the workmen. It might even have been possible to tamper with the bucket and the scaffolding during the day, by choosing a moment when the rest of the men were eating, or busy in some other part of the site. The fixing of the sharp pins in the pulleys would have taken far longer, but the machinery of the hoist had been lying about, unregarded, since the beginning of the work. The pulleys might have been carried off one by one and worked on elsewhere. That suggested a careful plan, devised well ahead of time.

I said nothing for the moment, however, for I saw that the sheriff and both the masters were thinking, as I was, that someone posing as a workman was a possibility.

'We should question the men,' Hanbury said, and English nodded.

'Have there been any visitors to the college?' Cedric asked. 'And what of the poor boys supported by Queen's? Are they ever about the grounds? And might one of them have a grudge?'

'I think not,' said the provost, bristling with annoyance. 'They have every reason to be grateful to us for our support. Besides, a boy could not have broken down the wall.'

'One of the older boys might,' Hanbury said firmly. 'The mortar was not set, and a crowbar was used. It needed no more strength than a well grown youth would have.'

'And where would one of our poor boys have obtained a crowbar?' the provost said, glaring at him.

For myself, I thought it would not be difficult, but I kept my tongue behind my teeth, and so did Hanbury.

'We are merely considering possibilities, Provost,' Cedric said mildly.

'And visitors?' Thomas Beverley asked. 'The sheriff has asked whether you have had any visitors in the college in recent weeks.'

'An official visitor to the college would have had no hand in these affairs,' the provost said coldly. 'Our visitors are either other scholars or gentlemen who take an interest in the college. And sometimes officials from the Court. You will recall that the Founder named the college in honour of Queen Philippa.'

'Indeed,' Cedric said politely. 'Of course your visitors would only be such persons of undoubted honour. However, they may bring servants. Or they may have noticed something afoot.'

'Doubtful.' The provost shook his head. 'There is one guest staying here at present. However, he arrived but four days ago. Long after these disturbances began. I believe he travelled with servants, but they are lodged elsewhere in the town.'

'A fellow scholar?' Cedric said, alert. 'From Cambridge? Or some university in foreign parts?'

I thought he was pursuing the idea of some sort of jealousy of the college, some academic rivalry, but that still seemed to me the least likely reason for the attacks. Who could be jealous of a poor college like Queen's?

'Nay, not a scholar,' Master Brandon said, when it appeared the provost did not deign to answer. 'A gentleman from the north. You know that we have a connection with the northern counties of Cumberland and Westmorland? We hope that he may be considering providing some benefaction for the college. Perhaps enough to enable us to extend the chapel with transepts.'

'From Cumberland,' Cedric said, 'like your Founder?'

'Nay, this gentleman is from neighbouring Westmorland. It is a family which has had no previous dealings with us, and the present guest is a young man. We think that he has probably been sent by his father to look us over.'

Brandon smiled weakly. 'I fear he has not chosen the best of times,' he went on. 'Alas! All the recent misadventures may have cast us in a poor light. It is unlikely they will wish to become patrons.'

Cedric nodded, clearly thinking this gentleman, a recent guest of the college, could be of little interest. For some reason, I was moved to ask, 'What is the gentleman's name?'

'Sir Thomas de Musgrave.' The provost said, frowning slightly at Master Brandon, as though he would have preferred to keep the existence of this potential benefactor out of the discussion.

'It is a wealthy family in Westmorland,' he added. 'His father, also Sir Thomas, is a gentleman of note in those parts. He has been High Sheriff of the county, and he was granted permission by the king to crenellate his castle, Hartley Castle, at Kirkby Stephen, because of the dangers from invading Scotsmen. As you know, not many are granted permission to crenellate.'

He paused, then added, 'It would be a great advantage to Queen's College, should they become patrons, and very much in accordance with the Founder's intentions. Already we have the de Luce family from Cumberland. To gain the patronage of the de Musgraves from Westmorland would be most satisfactory.'

'Indeed.' Cedric inclined his head. As deputy sheriff, he would be familiar with such negotiations for patronage, and he would respect a gentleman who had served as High Sheriff.

I hesitated. Should I speak? In the end, I decided to tell only part of what I knew.

'I have met this gentleman, the younger Sir Thomas de Musgrave,' I said slowly. 'He has been in my shop and commissioned an expensive book.'

I did not say how often the young man had visited my shop, nor that he had told me that he was staying at the

Mitre. Moreover, that had been considerably more than four days ago. He must have stayed first at the inn, then moved to the college. If his intention was to investigate the college for his father, why had he not gone there directly? Perhaps he wished to discover the standing of the college amongst the townsfolk. It seemed that both these northern families were sending their sons to look over Queen's at this most unfortunate time. Little wonder, then, that Provost de Hotham looked so worried. The miscreant could damage the college in the eyes of two potential rich patrons.

The provost nodded at this mention of a book, but did not seem particularly interested in my contribution.

'They are a cultured family,' he said. 'It does not surprise me that he should commission a volume while visiting Oxford. No doubt the young gentleman will be glad to take home a fine book of hours, or a saint's life, perhaps as a gift for his father.'

I forbore to mention that the book in question was a collection of secular tales, though in truth many were of a moral tone, and those in the Arthurian cycle were assuredly devout. Or at least some were. Perhaps not the adultery of Sir Lancelot and Queen Guinevere.

'I fear we are no closer to finding the culprit,' Cedric said, 'but I should be grateful if you would give very careful thought to any man who might hold a grudge against the college, for in my opinion the trouble does seem to arise from the college and not from either the stonemasons or the carpenters.'

'We will do so,' the provost said, without enthusiasm, 'but I can assure you that it is very unlikely that we will be able to think of any such person.'

For most of the time Robert Hanbury and John English had spoken little, but now the master stonemason turned to Cedric.

'Sheriff, what are we to do? Should we resume work on the chapel? My men are fearful of what may happen next. Two men injured, one of them grievously, and now one killed. If we continue, I think I may find more of my men slipping away. I have already lost three.'

'And I have lost two,' John English said. 'One discovered to be gone just this morning. We may have serious trouble on our hands if we try to continue.'

'I think it will be best if I come and speak to all your men,' Cedric said, 'both stonemasons and carpenters. I am minded to post a body of my soldiers here, both to protect you and to deter this villain from making any further attempts. It is clear that he wants to frighten you so much that you will abandon the building of the chapel. Whatever his reason may be, I say that we should not allow him to intimidate us. Do you not agree?'

With some understandable hesitation, the two masters agreed. The provost and Master Brandon, however, looked immensely relieved, the provost even honouring Cedric with a deep bow, far surpassing his initial bow when we arrived.

'Tell the men to gather inside the chapel after their midday dinner,' Cedric said to the two masters, as we left the provost's lodgings together. 'I will come then and tell them exactly what I plan to do, and how we will protect them.'

They nodded their agreement and set off toward the site of the chapel, but as Cedric, Thomas, and I turned toward the gatehouse, I stopped.

'I remember me,' I said. 'I had meant to ask the provost about Piers Dykman, Jordain's young student. I think I will go back and speak to him now, before he attends to other business and while he is still feeling relief that you have ordered the continuation of the building.'

'I do not care to be intimidated by some dangerous fool and his tricks,' Cedric said grimly. 'We will leave you to question the provost. Will you come to my meeting with the men?'

'I shall see you there,' I said.

Let him try to keep me away!

I turned and made my way back the few yards to the provost's lodgings, where I found him still seated with

Master Brandon in the room where we had all met.

'Forgive me for disturbing you again, provost,' I said, 'but I had intended to ask you before . . . Has the college any news of your missing poor boy, Piers Dykman? I have been involved in the search for him, and he is a student of my friend Jordain Brinkylsworth, Warden of Hart Hall.'

'Certainly by yesterday evening he had not been found,' de Hotham said. 'Master Brinkylsworth came to see me then. He had written a letter to the family, to be directed to their parish priest. He hoped that we might know of a carrier travelling to the northern counties, because of our connections with that part of the realm. However, we know of no carrier going that way at present.'

It seemed to me that he was not as concerned over the fate of the boy as by the college's financial worries.

'Sir Thomas de Musgrave might be willing to take the letter with him when he returns,' Master Brandon said, 'but he does not go north again until after Easter. I think Master Brinkylsworth will not wish to wait until then.'

'Indeed, he will not,' I said. 'I know he has no desire to worry the family, but the boy has been missing too long now. They must be told.'

'You think he has come to harm?' the provost said.

'I do not know,' I said grimly. 'There has been no sign of him since he vanished, except that we found his academic gown in an abandoned cottage, and there was a possible glimpse of him by Rector Bokeland, sleeping in St Peter's churchyard. It might have been some other boy.'

They seemed not to have heard of this, which surprised me, but perhaps Rector Bokeland was too unsure of identifying Piers, so that he had not wanted to bring word of it to the provost. I was not certain how matters stood between the rector and the college. By rights, the college lay within the parish of St Peter-in-the-East, but Queen's had been using one of its assorted cottages as a temporary place of worship and was now building its own chapel. I would never accuse the kindly and somewhat unworldly rector of financial greed over losing parishioners, yet all the cottagers who had previously lived in the buildings now owned by Queen's had been part of his flock. However, no man likes to see a sizeable portion of his realm cut away without so much as a by-your-leave.

'Let us hope that it was the Dykman boy,' Master Brandon said. 'At least that would mean he is still alive.'

'You cannot say why he might have run away?' I said. 'He was not in trouble with the college?'

'Not in the least,' Master Brandon said. 'Despite his youth, he was one of the most conscientious of the poor boys, and promised fair to be an accomplished scholar in time. Let us hope we have not lost him for good.'

'Amen to that,' I said, somewhat ironically.

I took a hasty dinner with Margaret, the children still being away at the Farringdons' house. Margaret was occupied with the weekly linen wash, but took her mind from it long enough to ask how we had fared at our meetings in Queen's.

'Little enough accomplished,' I said. 'Cedric Walden pressed them on the matter of enemies to the college, but they would have us believe that they have none.'

'And do you believe it?' she said.

I shrugged. 'They seemed certain enough, but perhaps they would not wish to reveal any college problems to outsiders. I cannot see that all this devilment arises from some jealousy of the stonemasons. As the master carpenter said, they too have suffered, and it is pure chance that in some cases it was not carpenters who were injured or killed. They have also had tools stolen.'

'I did not know that.'

'Nor I. Everything points to an attack on the college, but the reason remains a mystery.'

She stood up and began to clear away the remains of our simple dinner.

'Does the building work continue?' she said.

'Aye.' I got up from my stool to help. 'Cedric has said that it should. He takes it ill that some villain can carry out such tricks and devilry in his town. 'Tis not to be endured! He will send soldiers to guard the work and the men. He holds a meeting for them all now. I shall go to hear what he will tell them.'

'I am glad that you are no longer in the thick of it,' she said, 'trying to hunt out this villain with Master Hanbury. Remember, a man was killed. One day, you may run a risk too far.'

'I am sure there is no potential danger to me in this affair,' I said. 'Now Cedric has the matter in hand, and will guard the work with soldiers, I think we shall have no more trouble. Perhaps the provost's two wealthy visitors may go home satisfied with what they see. What I find of greater concern is the missing boy. There has been no sign of him for days.'

'Aye,' she said, with a sad smile. 'He has been much on my mind. And you say that his family still does not know?'

'Jordain has written them a letter, but so far has not found a means to send it.'

I made my way round to the college and joined the crowd of stonemasons and carpenters gathering in the interior of the chapel. The parts of the hoist had been removed, and the double line of pillars still marched along the unfinished nave, not yet linked by the stone arches, although the wooden pattern for the first of them still stood in place between the two pillars at the southwest end. The curved side stone which had killed the journeyman had also been taken away. I thought Robert Hanbury would not care to use it now, for the men would think it an ill omen, and indeed I felt myself it would have no place in God's house.

Cedric came in through the north doorway, accompanied by Thomas Beverley and Master Barton. The provost, it seemed, felt it beneath his dignity to mix with the workmen.

The sheriff began by expressing his sympathy with all that the men had suffered and his hope that the two injured men were recovering.

'As we do not know who has been perpetrating these attacks on you and your work, nor what reason lies behind them, we find ourselves like blind men in the dark. However, we shall not allow ourselves to be bullied and frightened by him, whoever he is and whatever drives him. We are Englishmen, with hearts of lions! We are not namby-pamby, mincing, frog-eating Frenchmen, to be running away in fear!'

This patriotic hint, reminding everyone present of the English victory at Crécy, had all the men cheering.

'You must be able to go about your work undisturbed,' he said, 'without forever looking over your shoulders. It is not a part of your task to be fighting off villains, that is the work of me and my men. This afternoon I will be bringing a troop of soldiers to act as guards for you and your work, under the command of Captain Beverley here.'

He gestured at Thomas, who bowed.

'They will be keeping a watch over all – your tools and machines, this building, and your persons – one half of the troop by day, the other by night, so that you may also sleep quiet in your beds, without worrying about any mischief this villain may be preparing.'

He grinned down at the group of apprentices, who were sitting cross-legged on the ground at his feet.

'Perhaps some of you have not comfortable beds to sleep in, but must roll yourselves in a blanket on the ground. As soldiers, we are familiar with an earthen bed, but will wish you as sound a sleep as this hard ground permits you.'

This drew an appreciative laugh from the boys.

'Now there is one further thing I want you to think on .' he said. 'It has been suggested that the trouble-maker might have slipped in amongst you unbeknownst – stonemasons thinking him a carpenter, carpenters thinking him a mason. I want you to try to recall whether at any time you saw a man who might have been a stranger amongst you. I have a clerk at a table out in the yard, who will take down your names and trades, so that we have a list of all who are rightfully working here. If you think you have noticed a stranger, you may tell him, and he will pass the word to me.'

He then asked if all was clear, and one or two raised questions about when the work was to start again and whether they would be paid for the last two days, when nothing had been done. Cedric referred them to the two masters, who reassured them, particularly on the question of wages, although I saw that Master Brandon looked as though he might object to this extravagance. Afterwards I heard Robert Hanbury speaking to him.

'Best to pay them, rather than have grumbling and grievance. They will work all the harder and the work will be sooner finished.'

Master Brandon shrugged, but seemed to accept this reasoning.

We dispersed, the men to have their names enrolled, and the two masters to oversee it, along with Thomas Beverley. I walked with Cedric to the gatehouse.

'Let us hope that will put an end to all these troubles,' he said.

'Indeed,' I agreed. ''Tis pity William Gurdin took no heed of the earlier troubles when he was informed of them. We might have been spared injury and death.'

'I regret it. I had not anticipated any trouble he could not deal with. I am lacking in able officers, but another time when I must leave Oxford, I shall leave Thomas in charge. I plan to make a great show of my men taking up their duties in the college, so that the villain is quite sure what awaits him, should he try any more of his tricks.'

'Excellent.' I nodded. 'Although I have a feeling that he never intended a death. He may well be horror-struck by what has happened, and would cease of his own accord.'

'You may have the right of it, Nicholas, but we will take no chances.'

We paused outside the gatehouse.

Cedric stood with arms folded, looking up and down Hammer Hall Lane.

'You do not think he made his way into the college from the lane?' he said.

'Certainly not at first,' I said, 'Robert Hanbury and I found clear traces of where he had broken into the cottage near the vintner's shop in the High, then made his way through the gardens behind the houses and into the college over the fence on the west boundary. I admit that part of my original interest sprang from my anger that he had dared to use my garden as his way into Queen's. I felt implicated.'

'No blame to you.'

I shrugged. 'After that, we were not so sure. The provost's suggestion that he might have mingled with the men is certainly possible. Shortly before the fatal accident with the hoist, Hanbury and I were considering whether he might have made his way through from the part of the lane which turns to run parallel to the north wall of the college grounds.' I gestured up the lane to our left. 'There are houses there, but a man might be able to slip through. Hanbury intended to investigate, but then the man was killed. I am not sure that anyone has looked.'

'We could look now,' Cedric said, 'although I am not sure it will tell us much. I may be able to put a stop to any further trouble, but I will not rest until I have this villain under my hand.'

'I am for Hart Hall,' I said. 'We can walk that way together.'

We turned left and headed up the lane, leaving the church on our right, and the swarming huddle of filthy hovels to the north of it.

'That place is a disgrace to the town,' Cedric said. 'Everything should be pulled down.'

'Perhaps one day it will be,' I said.

The lane now veered left, with a motley collection of buildings on both sides – some small, dark shops, some cottages, one or two student halls and some of the older type of lodging house run by townsfolk, which the university had begun to frown on. Behind the houses on our left, but out of sight, lay the north boundary wall of Queen's.

'To tell truth,' I said, 'I have never seen the wall, never even been to that part of the college property. Until this building work began, my only business with the college has been to supply stationery and an occasional book.'

'Nor have I seen it,' Cedric said thoughtfully. 'As the college is new and not wealthy, it may not even be very high or very strong. Look, there is a way through here, between this tin smith's shop and the next cottage.'

It was an alleyway barely wide enough for a man to squeeze through. You could not have taken a horse along it. Cedric led and I followed, almost scraping my shoulders against the walls on either side.

'Filthy!' Cedric said in disgust.

The alleyway certainly stank. We stumbled over indistinguishable rubbish, and there was a foul odour of both urine and some dead animal. Neither building had land for a garden behind, just a gap, perhaps a couple of yards wide, before the wall, and also filled with ancient rubbish quietly mouldering away.

'Easy enough to climb.' Cedric pointed to the wall as I emerged from the alley.

It was no more than five feet high. Any man could scramble over it.

'There is no sign this is where he broke in,' I said, 'but I expect there are other gaps between the houses, further along.'

'Aye. It might be clearer to see on the inside of the wall. I shall have my men check the whole length tomorrow.'

With some relief we made our way out of the stinking alley and continued along the lane. We found two more gaps which seemed to lead through to the wall, but Cedric had the right of it. It would be easier to judge whether anyone had come over the wall by looking at the other side.

'I have left my horse at the college,' Cedric said. 'I must go back that way. I wish we had been able to gain more understanding of what lies behind these troubles. I did not find our meeting with the provost very enlightening.'

'Nor I. Though I can see that he is worried about the visits of these two sons of benefactors, or possible benefactors. He would like best to keep all very quiet until they have gone.'

'Aye.' Cedric grinned. 'He will not like me stringing up some malefactor by the neck while he is trying to persuade them of the merits of his college. But I shall not rest until I have the fellow, of that you may be sure.'

'And I hope also that we may have your help in trying to find the missing boy. I try to keep hope alive by reminding myself that we have not found his body.'

'Certainly I will do what I can,' he said, 'although if the child is frightened, I fear that a body of soldiers searching for him might cause him to burrow even deeper, like a terrified rabbit.'

'Aye, that is true,' I said. 'We must be discreet. I will discuss it with Jordain Brinkylsworth. I am going there now.'

'Did you not say that he has written a letter to the family?' Cedric said. 'But has not yet found anyone to take it?'

'So Provost de Hotham told me.'

'I would say, let Master Brinkylsworth wait a little,' he said. 'At least until my men have joined you in the search. With more of us, it may be that we shall find him, and there will be no need to cause the family unnecessary worry. Let it wait until after Easter, when the provost said that Sir Thomas de Musgrave might be willing to carry the letter. They are from the same county, though perhaps not nearby. I have never been there, but I believe the county is large, and in parts very wild and bleak, bordering on Scotland.'

'Aye.' I laughed. 'Hence the remarkable

crenellations, authorised by the king! I will do as you suggest, and try to persuade Jordain to retain the letter for the present.'

We parted then, Cedric retracing his steps back along the lane to Queen's College gatehouse, while I continued to the north end of the lane, beside Hart Hall.

Chapter Ten

I found Jordain overseeing his students' work in the only large room at Hart Hall, a room which served in turn for eating, teaching, and studying, and was scarcely adequate for so many purposes. However, as the rest of the hall was a warren of small rooms and passages, apart from the dark and smoky kitchen, Jordain had nowhere else. His reputation as a fine teacher and a kindly warden meant that Hart Hall never lacked students, despite its relative poverty and the jokes known throughout the university about the dreadfulness of its food.

Jordain looked up at me with a hopeful smile. I suppose he thought I might bring news of the missing boy, but my face must have conveyed no such message, so that his look of hope quickly faded. Leaving the students to their books, he joined me by the door, and we stepped outside, walking a short way down Catte Street as we talked.

'I have not seen you for several days,' he said.

'You have heard of the latest accident at Queens's?' I said. 'A man killed when the rope on the hoist snapped?'

'Aye. That was a terrible thing. And it was no accident. I attended the inquest, but I did not see you there.'

'I decided that matters could not continue any longer without the presence of the deputy sheriff,' I said. 'I rode off at once to Banbury, to fetch him home to Oxford. Fortunately his business there was nearly done, the outlaws rounded up. He was able to leave one of his sergeants to deal with the last of it. He rode back with me late last night, with Thomas Beverley and most of his men.'

'That was well done. If anyone can put a stop to this, Sheriff Walden will do so.'

'He will certainly do his best,' I said. 'I went with him this morning to meet Provost de Hotham in the college. We both think that the source of the trouble lies at Queen's, although the provost is very reluctant to admit it. Then Cedric held a gathering of all the workmen – stonemasons and carpenters both – this afternoon. He has authorised the resumption of the work, but will provide a guard of soldiers, to protect both the men and the building.'

'Let us hope that is an end to their troubles, then,' Jordain said.

'Indeed, we may hope so, although Cedric will not rest until he has apprehended the villain who is responsible. Even if injury and death were not intended, this last affair amounted to murder. I had been speaking to the man only the other day. One of Robert Hanbury's journeymen, a skilled carver, and still a young man.'

'May God have mercy on his soul.'

'Amen,' I said, crossing myself.

I could not drive from my mind two sharp images – the journeyman Gerard bending with anxious eyes over his man with the broken leg, and the same eyes staring blindly up at the cloudless sky above the open vault of the unfinished nave.

'I had hoped you might have brought some news of Piers,' Jordain said sadly.

'Since Rector Bokeland told me of the possible sight he had of the boy in the churchyard,' I said, 'I have heard nothing more. Nor you, I suppose?'

He shook his head. 'Whenever we can, the students and I continue the search, but there must be many hidden corners in the town. All the empty houses since the Death. Their unkempt gardens, gone to wilderness. Barns and outbuildings behind shops. The stables of inns and the larger houses and colleges. The building works in other colleges than Queen's. He could be anywhere. I think I must have spoken to every shopkeeper in the town selling food, asking that they watch out for any thefts, but there are always beggars about the stalls in the market. One lad the more would scarcely be noticed.'

'Cedric has promised the help of his men in the hunt, although he says (and rightly, I think) that bands of soldiers searching would probably send the boy even deeper into his bolthole.'

'Very likely, I suppose, although his men can demand entry where I cannot. Most folk are willing enough for us to search, but a few are evasive. I do not know what they are concealing.'

I grinned. 'Best not to ask, perhaps! Illegal goods? Property which would raise their taxes? French wine in ale barrels? Bolts of Italian silk hidden under sturdy English worsted? However, you say truly – Cedric's men can search everywhere.'

'It will not make him popular,' Jordain said.

'Nay, but if he combines it with searching for the Queen's evil doer,' I said, 'folk may not be so reluctant. Word of the attacks has spread about the town and some are muttering that the troubles may pass from Queen's to other colleges, and even to the rest of the town. My scriveners came back from their dinner full of the rumours running through Oxford. Since the killing, a real fear is catching hold.'

'Perhaps with good reason, do you suppose?'

I shook my head. 'All the malice seems directed at Queen's alone, and the provost is sick with worry. He has the sons of two noble families from the north coming to look over the college, perhaps with the intention of their fathers becoming patrons. Or extending their patronage. One is here already, Sir Thomas de Musgrave, and the other is expected at any moment, Sir Anthony de Luce. They could hardly have lit upon a worse time. Or else whoever the miscreant is, he must have known they were coming.'

'Curious,' Jordain said. 'That suggests someone very close to the college, does it not?'

'Cedric and I both believe it is a man seeking vengeance against the college for some wrong, or imagined wrong. Perhaps a student or servant turned away, but the provost will not have it.'

'Mayhap he is wilfully blind,' he said. 'I hope Sheriff Walden arrests his man soon, before anyone else is injured, or worse. And in his searches, perhaps he may find our boy.'

He stopped in front of Catte Hall. 'I must go back to my students. Will you tell me when the sheriff plans to search the town, Nicholas? I will join him, with any of my students who are free.'

'Aye, I will send you word.'

We parted, and I continued down Catte Street, past St Mary's church, to the High. Coming toward me from Carfax, pulling her handcart, was Mary Coomber, accompanied by a young girl I could barely recognise as Sarah Tonkin, the orphaned waif she had taken into her home. The girl was no longer swamped in one of Mary's ample dresses left over from her girlhood, but neatly dressed in a faded green gown made fit for her thin figure. Her hair was clean and smoothly braided, and she no longer looked like a stunned and frightened mouse.

Mary stopped the handcart, which held only empty buckets and one unsold cheese.

'I see you have a new maid to help deliver the milk,' I said, smiling at the girl, who blushed, and smiled tentatively back.

'Sarah is learning my route through the town,' Mary said, 'so that she may deliver the milk when she is strong enough to haul the cart by herself. And Aelyth, who is skilled with the needle, as I am not, has been altering clothes to fit her.'

'Sarah is not to become a ribbon weaver, then?' I asked.

'Aye, she is learning the art. She helps Maud and me

with the dairying in the morning and weaves in the afternoon, but today Aelyth is working hard to finish an order, so Sarah has come with me.'

'So, are you to be apprenticed to Aelyth?' I said to the girl.

She seemed not to know how to answer, and Mary answered for her.

'There is no coin for a formal apprenticeship, you understand, Nicholas, but there is no need for that, when we are all agreed. Aelyth has received notice from the bursar at Queen's College, that they will be taking possession of her cottage next Quarter Day. It seems the rumours we heard are true. 'Tis as well we moved her possessions. We have made an agreement to suit us. Aelyth and I will share my house and the cost of food between us, I shall continue with the dairy and she with her weaving, and Sarah will help us both. It works very well for us all. I rattled about in that big house on my own, and they both needed roofs over their heads.'

'It sounds an excellent arrangement,' I said, 'helpful to all three of you.'

And I thought, although I did not say, that Mary Coomber might enjoy organising the lives of those around her, but she was also one of the kindest creatures on God's earth.

We spoke a little about affairs at Queen's, and Jordain's missing boy.

'Let us hope all is happily solved soon,' she said, and paused, eying me shrewdly. 'I have not seen Emma Thorgold about your shop as often as usual.'

She raised her eyebrows, and her face sharpened inquisitively. I wondered whether she and Margaret had been putting their heads together about my affairs.

'It has not been the most pleasant of places, my shop,' I said, 'while the stone was a-cutting, though it is better for us all now, is it not? Very little dust. Besides, Emma is hard at work making a book of troubadour songs. You have heard us speak of it.'

No use trying to keep from Mary that Emma worked for me as a scrivener, or that the troubadour book had been occupying us for several months now. She nodded.

'Aye. And there is this matter of her grandfather sending for her to go home to his manor. When will she go, do you know?'

I felt my heart give a sickening lurch. He had actually told her to go home? It seemed Mary knew more of these matters than I did. I made some vague answer, which caused her to eye me more thoughtfully still, but she did not probe me further and we parted, Mary and Sarah heading back down the street to the dairy. Without my conscious volition, I found my steps turning in the opposite direction, toward St Mildred Street. I could not hide, cowardly, behind other affairs any longer. I must speak to Emma.

I had forgotten that Juliana had carried the children off to her mother's house in the morning, when Margaret had wanted our home quiet so that I might sleep after yesterday's long ride. The Farringdons' house was a-swarm with people. It was a small cottage, crowded at the best of times, with Maud Farringdon, her daughter Juliana and granddaughter Maysant, and her niece Emma, all living there, for there were but two rooms on the ground floor and two bed chambers above. Now, in addition to these four, there were my two rascals and our dog Rowan. And somehow Jonathan Baker had found his way here as well, bringing Rowan's brother Digger.

Some work was afoot in the garden, with the two young dogs happily joining in, and the children looking as though they had been digging with their bare hands. Gradually the forest of nettles and brambles, which had turned the empty cottage garden into a wilderness, had been cleared, and a vegetable plot laid out, as well as a small herb garden. The present task seemed to be the digging over of more of the garden at the far end, where I knew Maud hoped to plant fruit bushes. An old apple tree still stood there and was now in full bloom, and a gnarled pear tree, from which the blossom had recently fallen. Against the fence which separated this garden from that of the apothecary next door there were two quinces and a somewhat unpromising looking grapevine, of which I knew Maud had little hope. Half a dozen hens were enthusiastically scratching about in the newly dug earth where the fruit bushes were to be planted.

'Papa!' Rafe cried. 'Come and see what I found!'

He grabbed the sleeve of my cotte with a muddy hand and dragged me down the garden, to where a shallow basket stood, containing a few treasures unearthed by the gardeners. Rafe picked up a grubby disk and held it out to me.

Crouching down and rubbing some of the dried earth off the surface, I saw that it was an old coin.

'It's very, very ancient, a'nt it, Master Elyot?' Jonathan said, peering over my arm.

'Indeed it is,' I said. 'I think it is Roman, though very late Roman, probably.'

The coin depicted the head of a man who might be an emperor, though not one of the great ones. Philip had shown me a few Roman coins owned by Merton College, and this was crude by comparison, poorly defined and struck off centre. The crown on the emperor's head – if it could be called that – seemed to consist of a lot of uneven spikes. Still, it was an exciting find for my son.

'And I found this,' Alysoun said, holding up an unsavoury looking object. 'I think it must be the tooth of a dragon.'

It was certainly a tooth, and if I thought it more likely to be the tooth of a horse, I held my peace, and exclaimed in wonderment. I looked up and caught Emma smiling at me.

'What treasures have you found?' I asked.

'A firkin of earthworms,' she said, 'a handful of earwigs, and several spiders large enough to provide steeds for Queen Mab and her court. Oh, and a dozen slugs long enough to rival grass snakes.'

'And I thought you would be seated at your desk, scribing the songs of our friends from Provence.'

She gave a guilty smile. 'It has been a lovely day, too beautiful to sit indoors, and there is a great deal to do in the garden. My aunt wants to grow as much food as she can. There is a fine lot of space, now that we have cleared the weeds, with the help of Jordain's students.'

'I do not suppose you could work, in any case, with the noise these young ones are making.'

Indeed, the four children were running about, chasing each other and the dogs, like wild things. Being out from under Margaret's firm hand had gone to the heads of my two. I had continued sitting on my heels to admire the coin and the tooth, but now I stood up, dusting the earth from my hands.

'If you are not occupied with the troubadour book, and if you can be spared from the digging,' I said, 'will you come with me?'

She cocked her head to the side. 'All the digging we plan to do today is finished. Come with you where?'

I shifted my feet awkwardly. It was clearly impossible to talk to her here, with the children shouting and running about us, and I had said the first thing that came into my head. Where could I suggest we might go?

'The meadows south of the town wall are very fair at this time of year,' I said cunningly. 'Do you remember how we walked there at the time of the fair last autumn? The first of the spring flowers will be out now. It is good to escape from the town sometimes, and these weeks of breathing stone dust have made me long for the clean air down by the river.'

This was certainly true, and I felt that my suggestion, somewhat feeble at first, now carried conviction.

'Very well,' she said. 'Let me first wash the earth from my hands. I do not know how they have become so dirty, for I was digging with a spade, not my fingers.'

'And bring a cloak,' I said. 'The afternoons can still

grow chilly later.'

I followed her into the house and waited while she washed and fetched her cloak from the bed chamber she shared with Juliana. I thought how much the character of this cottage had changed. When I had first seen it, it had been desolate and filthy. Now it was a warm and pretty home, very much a home of women, with brightly embroidered cushions, half finished needlework laid down here and there, a sketch of flowers that someone – probably Emma – was inking in, a tumble of Maysant's toys.

'Here I am,' Emma said.

She had thrown a light summer cloak over her shoulders, but was otherwise in one of the simple gowns she wore for preference every day. A stranger seeing her for the first time would not easily guess that she was a gentlewoman and an heiress. I remembered how Sir Thomas de Musgrave had taken her for a servant – or had pretended to. Perhaps that was where my own difficulty lay. I allowed myself to remain blind to her real rank. Emma might dress like a simple Oxford townswoman, she might dig over the earth in her aunt's garden, but she was playing a game, pretending to a role which was false. Sooner or later we must both face reality. I dreaded the thought that the time might be now.

We set off along the short distance past the Mitre to Carfax, then turned down Fish Street toward the South Gate of the town. Emma slipped her arm through mine.

'We had a fine time of it at St Frideswide's Fair in the autumn,' she said, 'with our stall of preserves and sweetmeats, but I am not sure I should want to do it again. It was very tiring and has made me sympathise with those women who have stalls in the market all year round.'

'Margaret says she does not intend to take a stall at the fair again.' I said. 'Her feet, she thinks, will never be the same.'

Emma laughed. 'We would never have thought of it, had Mary Coomber not planned it all.'

'Have you heard of her latest scheme?' I said.

'And what is that?'

So I regaled her with the tale of Mary opening her house and taking in both Aelyth and Sarah, one of them homeless, the other soon to be.

'It is Mary, of course, who makes a good living from her dairy, selling her milk and cream and butter and cheeses. She works as hard as any man, milking the cows morning and evening, churning the butter, making her cheeses, then trundling her handcart around the town every day but Sunday, delivering her produce. She says that she and Aelyth will share the costs of the household, but I am sure Aelyth earns with her ribbons barely enough to feed a mouse.'

'You have the right of it, Nicholas,' Emma said, 'but Mary has no family, now that her parents and brother are gone, and her sister wed and moved to Abingdon. She will make a new family and they will all live contented. I know that Aelyth and the little orphan will benefit, but so will Mary.'

We had reached the gate and waited for a cart to pass through before following it out of the town proper, although Oxford straggled on outside the walls, flowing out along the continuation of Fish Street down to Grandpont. We turned aside to the left and followed the boundary wall of St Frideswide's Priory east into the meadowland, then turned south across the meadow toward the Thames.

'You guessed rightly about the spring flowers,' Emma said. 'Not quite the middle of April and already the grass is sprinkled over, like jewels on a gown, though far lovelier than any courtly damask.'

'Do not say as much to Peter Winchingham,' I said, laughing. 'He would declare that his finest cloths capture the beauties of nature and enhance it. I saw the flower drawing in the cottage. Was that yours?'

'Aye, it is a design I am making for my aunt. She wants to embroider some curtains for the bed I share with Juliana. We have but plain linsey-woolsey at present. She is a very good needlewoman, my aunt, though at present she is too wrapped up in her garden schemes to think of embroidery. It will wait until the weather turns to rain.'

'In an English summer,' I said, 'she should not have long to wait.'

'Very true,' she said. 'The garden will be the better for it. I should not like to live in a hot, dry land, like the one the troubadours came from.'

We had reached the narrow bridge over one of the streams which run through the meadow to join the river, and she let go of my arm so that we could cross it one after the other. On the far side she did not at once take my arm again, but stooped to gather some of the wild flowers, primroses and red campions and early bluebells. She twisted them into a small posy, bounded with plaited grass stems, and tucked it behind her ear. Then she made another, and thrust it behind mine.

'Come away!' I protested. 'I am no young maiden, to wear flowers in my hair.'

'But these suit you, Nicholas. You look five years younger. You might almost be taken for a heedless student in the spring of life.'

'Ah,' I sighed. 'The heedless days of youth. Long passed for me, I fear.'

She stopped and looked at me, suddenly serious. 'Are they, Nicholas?'

I felt another of those sickening lurches of the heart, and did not answer at once. At times I could not tell for certain whether Emma was serious or teasing. Often, I suspected, she hid seriousness behind a teasing manner. I had urged her to come with me on this walk, that I might speak to her at last of serious matters, but I could not find the words, nor was I sure whether she would respond seriously. She might turn all aside lightly. And I was afraid. If I once raised the question of the future with her, there would be no going back. I would have changed for ever the easy companionship which existed between us, and I longed to hold it fast.

When I still did not answer, Emma again slipped her

arm through mine and we walked on, over the second small bridge and down to the edge of the river.

'Here is the fallen tree where we sat before,' she said, drawing me down to sit beside her.

The river was quite high, filled with the snow melt from faraway hills which was still finding its springtime way along tiny rivulets through boggy ground and small streams, feeding the greater streams, until it joined the Thames to flow down to London and the sea. Just in front of us a mother duck with a procession of six very young ones was darting in and out of the reeds and marshy grasses. On the far side of the river a raven sat quite still on the branch of a willow, watching them thoughtfully.

Emma must have seen it too, for she said, 'I hope that raven may not take the ducklings.'

'At the moment, I think he is merely wondering whether it is worth getting a dowsing in the river. They are probably safer on the water than on land.'

I could feel that Emma was waiting for me to explain my reason for our walk. From the time we first met, our minds often moved together, and I knew she would have guessed that it was no idle suggestion I had made, yet I still felt that a thick mist hid her deepest feelings from me. I cleared my throat, but did not look at her, fixing my gaze on the raven across the river.

'I am told,' I said, 'that your grandfather has written to you.'

'He has. How did you come to know?'

'It seems to be knowledge commonly shared,' I said, perhaps with a touch of bitterness. 'It was Margaret told me first, who learned it from your aunt, but it seems even Mary Coomber is acquainted with the contents.'

She gave a rueful laugh. 'Ah, they are all great gossips, are they not? Try to keep a secret in our household! And those two forever have their heads together with my aunt. I trust it has gone no further.'

'Mary says that Sir Anthony wishes you to return and live at his manor.'

'He has said so.'

'And.' I cleared my throat again. 'And Margaret told me that he is making arrangements for your marriage.'

Still I did not look at her, but I felt her stiffen beside me.

'My grandfather is conscious of what he feels is his duty toward me,' she said.

Which told me nothing.

'Of course,' I said formally, 'it is his duty toward you, as his heir, to ensure that you make a good match. A gentleman of suitable rank. A landowner. A knight, no doubt, in good standing with the king.'

I could hear my voice growing colder as I spoke, but there seemed to be nothing I could do about it.

She sat silent for so long, that in the end I was forced to speak again, from sheer discomfort.

'You will no longer wish to live in a cottage in Oxford and work for me as a scrivener.'

Still she did not speak.

'Will you be able to complete the book of troubadour songs before you leave? When do you leave?' I asked at last, in a kind of desperation.

'I have not said that I am leaving,' she said, so quietly that I could barely hear her.

My heart, which I could swear had stopped beating, gave a faint tremor of life.

'Is it not *your* duty to obey your grandfather? For a lady of your rank . . . it is for him to decide your future.'

'The course of my life,' she said carefully, 'the course of my life so far has been far from that which is usual for what you call "a lady of my rank". For the first few years I lived happily with my mother and father on my grandfather's manor, and had all remained the same, no doubt by now I would have been wed to some gentleman chosen by my father and grandfather. I am a grown woman of nineteen! I should probably have children by now. Were you not a father at nineteen?'

I stole a glance sideways at her. She too was staring

across the river. She had taken her knot of spring flowers from her hair and was twisting it between her fingers. The petals were beginning to shed, dusting her gown as they fell.

'Then my father died, and my mother married Falkes Malaliver. I shall never know why. Perhaps she felt out of place in my grandfather's house, now she was a widow. Perhaps she wanted a home of her own. However it might have been, I think she misjudged what manner of man Malaliver was.'

She began to tremble, and I took one of her hands in mine, putting an end to the slaughter of the innocent spring flowers.

'And then your mother died,' I said gently, 'and your stepfather shut you up in Godstow Abbey.'

'I thought at the time that he wished merely to rid himself of my unwanted presence, but of course you discovered that he was plotting to seize my inheritance.'

'I am not sure he would have succeeded,' I said. 'The law is unclear on the rights of relatives by marriage.'

'I do not greatly care,' she said, 'for I have learned that one can live a happy and fulfilling life without great estates.'

'Nevertheless, you *are* your grandfather's heir, and you have a duty to your inheritance.'

'Perhaps.' She gave a great sigh and slumped a little, turning her eyes down to the ducks, who had now come boldly very close to us.

'I think,' I said slowly, 'that Sir Anthony has been very understanding, according to his own measure. He has given you nearly a year without making any demands, has allowed you to live in Oxford with your aunt. I do not know whether you have told him of your work for me, but it is certain that he has given you a great deal of freedom. Far more freedom than most maids in your position.'

'I know it,' she said. 'And I am grateful for it.'

'I think you must go to see him, if naught else, and discuss what way lies best for your future.'

'He will press me to accept one of these two suitors he has chosen for me,' she said carefully.

This time, I was quite sure that my heart had stopped. I could feel the blood drain from my face.

I managed to speak at last.

'He has named them?'

'Aye, he has. And you predicted very accurately. Both of knightly rank. One holding a goodly manor in Berkshire, the other is from Devonshire, with vast holdings. The first, a solid, dependable man in his late fifties, who has buried two wives, the second, a man widowed but once, and just past sixty. He was a fine soldier in his day, but lost an eye, fighting the French. My grandfather is quite honest about them both.'

I am sure I felt my jaw drop. 'That is monstrous!'

I looked her full in the face at last. Tears were gathering in her eyes, and she gave me a shaky smile.

'I think he wants a man of good age, who will care for me. Replace my lost father.'

'Is that what you want?'

I was shouting now.

'Well, what am I to do? Refuse his careful plans for me?'

'Of course you must refuse! You cannot wed some old man, old enough to be your father, or even your grandfather! Aye, they are nearer to your grandfather's generation than yours.' The blood which had drained from my face had rushed back, so that I felt myself flushing.

'But what else am I to do? It is not uncommon, marriage to a man of much greater years, for a lady of rank. I cannot live forever in my aunt's back bed chamber, scribing books on my beautiful desk.'

'Marry me!' I said, grabbing both of her hands, so that her posy fell to the ground. Two of the ducklings scrambled on to the bank to investigate.

'How can I? My grandfather would never permit it.'

I put my arms around her and drew her close, so that she buried her face against my shoulder. I could feel her tears through the fabric of my cotte.

'I think I have loved you since the moment I saw you,' I mumbled into her hair, 'bundled up in that ugly novice's habit, your fingers stained, like mine, with ink.'

'You have never said.' Her voice came muffled. 'I have never known what you thought of me.'

'It has been difficult,' I said, and even now I could only speak with difficulty. 'You were vowed to the abbey when we met. And as well . . . I too am a widower, like these suitors for your hand. I loved my wife, and she died young, terribly, of the pestilence. We were children when we met. It seemed disloyal . . .'

She pressed my hand, but did not speak.

'You say that you have never known what I thought of you,' I said. 'I think I did not know myself. I suppose the guilt I felt at the memory of Elizabeth . . . and uncertainty about the children . . . and I am so much older that you. Seven years!'

Suddenly I gave a faint laugh. A difference of seven years seemed as nothing compared with these grandfathers she was being offered.

'But above all . . . you say you did not know how I felt, but I could not know what *you* felt, except friendship. There can be friendship, can there not? Between a man and a woman? And then when you saw the desk I had made for you . . .'

The moment came back to me, sharp and clear, when she put her arms around me.

I tightened my arms around her now and she lifted her tear stained face from my shoulder.

'Seven years,' she said, 'is not so *very* vast a gulf. However, I know my duty. I will bring you hot possets of honey and cream and French wine, and tuck a soft blanket about your knees, before I go off a-dancing and merrymaking with all the young lads and lasses. And when you are too blind to see and too feeble minded to understand, I will read you the tales from Walter's book, before you fall to snoring in your dotage.'

This was the Emma I knew, and I was warmed with laughter.

I cupped her face between my hands and kissed her, long and slow.

'Then you will marry me?' I said, when I could breathe again.

'Oh, Nicholas, we are children, playing games, just as we have, these months past. I cannot wed without my grandfather's permission, we both know that.'

The moment of delirious joy passed as swiftly as if cloud had darkened the day at noon. Perversely, the true sun continued to shine, the river murmured softly at our feet.

'I could only wed you if we ran away to some distant place,' she said, 'where we are not known. Which we cannot do. You have your children. There is Margaret.'

'Margaret,' I said firmly, 'has been pushing me toward you, despite my saying that you could never wed a simple Oxford shopkeeper. For all my evasions, she has been clear eyed about my love for you, when I would not dare to admit it to myself. Margaret chooses to call me a merchant, like Peter Winchingham, and points out that in this new world, after mankind has been scourged by the pestilence, it is not unknown for ladies of rank to marry merchants.'

I saw a light of hope kindle in her eyes.

'Perhaps Margaret has the right of it,' she said. 'Could we not present you to my grandfather as a merchant? He is not unreasonable, and I do not think he would force me to marry against my will. At present, he does not believe my heart to be engaged.'

'And is it?' I realised that she had not admitted as much, although she had responded with her lips on mine.

'I find a certain attractiveness in a bookseller with inky hands. Nay, I ask pardon. A *merchant* of books, the finest in Oxford.'

'I could never give you what these other men offer,' I said. 'Lands, wealth, fine gowns and jewels.'

'A scrivener needs none of these. I shall demand only the finest parchment, and inks of the highest quality – no stinting on the lapis blue – and as much gold foil as I can lavish on every initial and saint's halo.'

'If it can ever come about,' I said, 'you shall have them all.'

'It is growing chilly,' she said, rising and brushing the fallen petals from her skirt. The ducklings skittered over and began to peck at them. 'My grandfather wishes me to travel to his manor after Easter, and will send a troop of his retainers to escort me. I think you should accompany me, and we will see what we may achieve together. I know that he liked you when you met before.'

'He did not then look upon me as a possible suitor,' I said unhappily.

'But rather as the man bent on rescuing his granddaughter from the plotting of her stepfather. It was a good beginning.'

'Aye, I think it was,' I said.

I stood and took her hand. A glimmer of hope flickered for a moment in my breast, but I extinguished it firmly. I must not let myself hope, for hope is the most cruel of all the feelings, raising you up, only to dash you down into a slough of the deepest despair.

'If it is your wish,' I said, 'I will ride with you to your grandfather's manor after Easter, but I will not present myself as a suitor. That, I am certain, would have me cast out as soon as my foot was over the threshold. I will come as your friend, and a man already known to him as someone previously caught up in your affairs.'

She nodded. 'Very well. We will proceed by small steps, as cautious as a mouse under the eye of a cat, or a duckling under the eye of a raven.'

'Those ducklings are as incautious as the most foolhardy of children,' I said sternly. 'I do not approve your choice of exemplar.'

'But see!' She pointed across the river. 'The raven is gone.'

'I take that as a good omen.'

It seemed that the mother duck did also, but she had not abandoned caution. We watched her round up her brood as carefully as a shepherd's dog will gather the sheep, and she led them back to a thick clump of reeds, a little further up river, where they disappeared from sight.

'It does grow somewhat colder,' she said, 'but before we turn homeward, let us walk a little more here in the meadow. As you said, it is good to leave the town behind sometimes. The meadows here are not quite the country, but nearly.'

'Aye.' I gestured toward the flock of sheep grazing over toward the priory grange at the top end of the meadow, near where we had watched the players at the fair, who had performed the life of St Frideswide. 'We have sheep here, and cows on the far side of the river, so we are almost in the country.'

She bent down and picked up the tattered remains of her posy.

'Alas,' she said, 'I have destroyed my handiwork.'

'Have mine,' I said, conscious that it was drooping, foolishly, over my ear.

I drew it out of my hair and tucked it very carefully over her ear, smoothing her unbraided locks down over the stems. I had never touched her hair before, and the tips of my fingers tingled. Unable to stop myself, I drew her close and kissed her again. She did not resist, but wound her arms about my neck and thrust her fingers up through my hair, drawing my head down to her. When we drew apart at last, she gave a trembling laugh.

'It is fortunate that the season is too early for the meadows to draw the Oxford folk to stroll here. We might be compromised.'

'Now that,' I said with a grin, 'might be an excellent plan.'

'Perhaps we may come to it, as a final desperate resort.'

'I shall give it serious thought,' I said.

Once again she slipped her arm through mine, but this time she clasped my arm close to her side, so that I could feel the beat of her heart through her gown. Its rhythm was quickened, like my own.

'Let us walk down river,' she said, 'to where the Cherwell flows into the Thames. I expect we shall see other families of young ducks there, for there are more reed beds along the Cherwell, where they may nest.'

The spring grass had grown thick and lush here, drinking up the moisture along the river's edge, and it swished about our feet as we walked, with a sound like the silken skirts of ladies' gowns. My thoughts were in turmoil. In her own gently mocking way, Emma had revealed that she cared for me as much as I dared to admit I cared for her. And her kisses had not been those of a dutiful friend. But the thought of silken skirts was a painful reminder of all I could not offer her, should I try to present myself as suitor when we visited her grandfather.

For all that my sister said, I was no merchant. Had I been the owner of a great international business, like Peter Winchingham, Sir Anthony Thorgold might have been prepared to consider my suit for his granddaughter, but I could not pretend to be what I was not. Indeed, I had no ambition to be such a merchant, forever travelling in foreign lands, bargaining with strangers, evading the attacks of brigands, sleeping at a different inn every night amongst a fresh crop of fleas and bed bugs.

Indeed, Peter himself had tired of such a life, which was what had brought him back to England. For myself, I was happiest where I was. The bookshop I had inherited from my father-in-law had been good enough to serve the simple needs of university students, with a very few sales to the wealthier townsfolk, but I had made my bookshop the finest in Oxford. The books we had been producing in the last year were far beyond anything Humphrey Hadley had ever known. I now had secular customers not only amongst the townspeople of Oxford but amongst the county gentry.

And the habit of reading was spreading. In our grandfathers' time, or our great-grandfathers' time, few except the clergy could read, although some amongst the eccentric gentry took up the habit. Nowadays it was become much more widespread. Ladies with hours of leisure on their hands had discovered the pleasures of reading the tales of heroes like King Arthur, as well as following the prayers and devotions in their own small books of hours. As England's business became more complex – and the king's taxes more demanding – small shopkeepers and farmers needed some simple understanding of the written word to avoid being cheated. I had even supplied very simple, unadorned books of hours to two servants, one from Lady Amelia's household, and one from Exeter College. This was a world transformed, when servants were learning to read.

Indeed, the king's reforms to the whole government of England meant that the ability to read was becoming more and more widespread. Bookshops like mine must take their place in this changing world. The popularity of Roger's collection of hero tales bore witness to a hunger for reading beyond books of prayers and the lives of saints.

'You are grown very quiet, Nicholas,' Emma said, interrupting my thoughts.

'I have been considering how best to present myself to your grandfather,' I said. 'Not as a great merchant, I could not pretend to that, but as a man with ambitions for a fine business dealing in books, in the most learned town in England.'

'You know that he is himself a lover of books,' she said. 'That was why I was educated with my cousin William.'

'I remember me,' I said, for now that she brought it to my mind, I recalled sitting with Sir Anthony, discussing books, when I had visited him, hoping to persuade him to help Emma escape from her unwilling noviciate.

'Aye, a mutual love for books may help my suit, though it is little enough to set against a knight's rank and great estates.'

'We shall make our attempt,' she said, 'after Easter.'

'Aye, after Easter.' The thought of Easter prompted other thoughts. 'I hope that once Queen's College has bid farewell to its wealthy visitors from the north, that may be an end to their troubles.'

She looked puzzled, and I realised I had not told her of the visits of Sir Thomas de Musgrave and Sir Anthony de Luce, which were causing Provost de Hotham such worries.

'And you think the attacks on the chapel are somehow connected to these visits?' she said.

'Impossible to tell, but they may be intended to harm the college in the eyes of these two wealthy families, so that they withdraw any promised hope of patronage.'

'It is a foul way to go about it,' she said with a shudder. 'That boy maimed for life, another injured so that he cannot work for weeks, and now a man most wickedly killed. Who would do such things?'

'We are no nearer to discovering,' I said.

By now we had reached the grassy spit of land around which the river Cherwell curled before mingling with the Thames. Like the larger river, it too was running high, and Emma had guessed rightly – there were several families of ducks feeding amongst the reeds and sedges along the bank. As we watched, a water vole plopped from its burrow beneath our feet and swam across to the further bank.

Because people often walked this way on fine summer days, there was usually a well trodden path following the nearside bank of the Cherwell, which led from here all the way up to the East Bridge, but this early in the year the fresh spring growth had not yet been trodden down. We cannot have been the first to walk this way since the beginning of spring, but there seemed not to have been many before us.

A few hundred yards or so ahead of us there was a clump of several willow trees, decked out in the pale silvery green of their new leaves, and trailing long fingers in the water, like idle maidens boating on the river.

'The trees have grown a good deal since last year,' I said. 'We must either duck beneath them, or circle round behind.'

''Tis not too difficult to duck,' she said, suiting her actions to her words.

She slipped her hand out of mine, which I had continued to hold, hoping she would not mind, and stepped ahead of me, for the path was narrow and overgrown here. She ducked her head, but not far enough, for her hair snagged on one of the branches and she was held fast.

'Stay still,' I said. 'I will free you.'

It is extraordinary how quickly and thoroughly nature can entrap you. I have been caught thus by blackberry thorns and taken minutes on end to release myself. I began to untangle her hair, strand by strand, thankful that the clutching fingers were but small twigs and not vicious thorns.

'I am free!' she said, pulling away, and entangling herself again.

'Nay, wait!' I said.

The twigs had caught her again, but at last I had the last lock of hair parted from the tree.

'Keep your head well down, now,' I said. 'Or shall we go round?'

'Nay, we are halfway through,' she said, stooping low and making her way past the rest of the copse.

I was about to follow her when something caught the corner of my eye. The willows were rooted in a rough circle, and at the centre, a few yards away on my left, there was a clear space between their trunks, although the branches reached across and tangled together in a canopy, so that the whole space formed a sort of tent. Lying on the ground, curled up like some small animal in hiding, was a boy in torn and dirty rags.

'Emma,' I called softly but urgently. 'Wait. I have found Piers Dykman.'

Chapter Eleven

Emma came slowly back to join me, dipping her head to avoid being caught up again in the branches. She looked where I pointed to the small bundle, a fearfully small bundle, and unmoving. Was the child sleeping? Or had he died here, alone, one of these cold nights, without even his academic gown for warmth?

Emma raised a stricken face to me.

'You are sure? It is Piers? Is he . . . oh, Mother Mary, prevent! . . . Is he dead?'

'I am not sure.'

So low were the branches that I needs must bend nearly double to make my way through the encircling trees into the bare centre of the copse. I knelt down beside the small body and saw that a spider had spun a web between the tall grasses and the toe of his right shoe. He must have been lying unmoving a long while.

With a kind of horror, I brushed the cobweb away. There was no sign of any other creature molesting him, no worms, no bites.

I sensed, rather than saw, Emma kneel down beside me, and heard her catch her breath in a suppressed sob. Hesitantly I reached out and touched the boy's cheek. His head was turned away from me, pillowed on his hand, his knees drawn up almost to his chest. His skin was very cold. But . . . was it the cold of death? We had all come to know the touch of that cold during the years of the pestilence.

Cautiously, I slid my fingers down below his ear. At

first I could feel nothing, then I thought there was the very faintest of tremors, no stronger than the quiver of a leaf stirred by the lightest breeze. Was I imagining it? Were my finger tips sensing what my mind hoped for?

'I believe,' I whispered, 'I believe I can feel a pulse, but it is barely there. Tell me what you think.'

She slipped her hand in where mine had rested, and closed her eyes, as though that made it easier to feel for the beat of blood.

She opened her eyes. 'He lives, I am sure, but only just.'

'I must carry him back to Hart Hall,' I said, starting to slide one arm under the small body.

'Wait!' She stood up and unclasped her cloak. 'Wrap this around him. It is not very warm, but 'twill be better than naught.'

I did not argue. Emma might feel the cold, now the day was drawing to an end, but the child's need was far greater. He might already be dying, have passed that point from which one cannot summon back the fleeing soul, but we would do our best to stop its flight. I wrapped Piers in the cloak, which went twice round him, then lifted him in my arms. He seemed to weigh almost nothing at all. He had always been slight and undernourished, but now his young face was pinched and gaunt with hunger.

As I lifted him, a few crushed leaves fell from his slack fingers. Emma picked them up and examined them.

'He has been eating dandelion leaves,' she said.

'Well, at least those would not poison him,' I said, 'but they would offer very little nourishment. Do the French not call the *dent-de-lion* the *pis-en-lit*?'

'Very vivid,' she said wryly. 'Let me go first. I will hold the branches out of the way, so that they do not whip you both in the face.'

Even so, I had to stoop very low to make my way out to the faint trace of the river path, and below the rest of the willows. It meant a maddeningly slow progress, but at last we were free of the trees, and the remainder of the path up along this edge of the meadow was relatively clear.

'This is probably our best way to go,' I said, once we were able to walk side by side again. 'We come out near the town end of the East Bridge, then it is not far to the East Gate and Hammer Hall Lane, with Hart Hall at the end of it.'

'We would reach Beatrice's house first,' Emma said. 'Before even we come to the gate. Would it not be better to stop there? She would take us in, and we could warm the child all the sooner. Perhaps he will wake enough to take a little food.'

From the lifeless feel of the small body in my arms, I thought it unlikely Piers would wake soon, if ever, but the suggestion showed good sense. Since Piers had chosen to run away from Hart Hall, perhaps it would be better not to return him there until we had fathomed the reason for his flight. No one would expect to find him at Beatrice Metford's cottage, and we could send for Jordain to come there. It was also growing late and it would be as well for Emma to return to St Mildred Street, else her aunt would begin to worry.

'Aye,' I said, 'that is well thought on. We will seek Beatrice's help. Not only will we come there more quickly, but she has a young boy of her own.'

Beatrice's son Stephen was a little older that Alysoun, some five years younger than Piers, yet despite his lame leg he was not much smaller than the older boy. Beatrice might have clothes which would fit Piers, in place of his torn and damp rags.

As we drew near the end of the path, where the ground rose in a slight slope to the road, I realised that this was the very spot where I had pulled the body of Emma's cousin William out of the Cherwell a year ago. I hoped she was unaware that this was the place, but she grew very quiet and pale as we neared the bridge.

The grass here was slippery, and I needed to go carefully as we made our way up to the road, where it emerged from the bridge to our right, but once our feet were on the road, which was the continuation of the High Street beyond the East Gate, the walking was easier past St John's Hospital. Just ahead of us on the right was Beatrice's cottage, with its neat herb beds laid out in front, and the lavender hedge on either side of the path leading up to the door.

'I will go ahead to warn her,' Emma said, and before I could answer had broken into a run.

I saw the door open almost as soon as she knocked, and then both women came out to greet me.

'Bring the child in here, Nicholas,' Beatrice said, wasting no words on greetings or trivial matters. 'Emma says he is cold, and I have a cookfire going. I am just making supper.'

I stepped with relief into the familiar small room, Philip Olney's secret home away from Merton College. There was a heartening smell of supper rising from the three legged pot hanging over the fire, and Philip himself was here, slicing bread. Stephen was setting out plates and knives on the table, moving skilfully and using just one crutch now, his leg stronger than it had been when I first knew him.

'Philip,' Beatrice said, 'fetch down the spare palliasse. We will put it close to the fire.'

She laid her hand on the child's cheek.

'Jesu! He is cold as ice,.' She raised worried eyes to me.

I nodded. ''Tis not so cold outside, but I fear he is suffering a cold from within.'

None of us said, *the cold of death*, though it hung unspoken in the air.

Once Philip had fetched the straw palliasse and placed it as close to the fire as was safe, the two women unwound Emma's cloak and stripped off the damp rags from the small body, then began chafing his arms and legs, trying to bring some warmth back into them.

Beatrice looked up at Stephen, who was hovering uncertainly. 'Fetch your new winter night shift, Stephen.

We will put that on the lad. It should be large enough. And bring a blanket. There are some in the coffer in my bed chamber.'

As Stephen made his dot-and-carry way up the stairs, I sank down on a stool beside the table and ran my hand over my face. My relief at finding Piers was marred by the fear that I had come too late, and must carry word of his death to Jordain.

Philip sat down opposite me. 'Where did you find him?'

I told him of the willow copse, and the dandelion leaves Piers had been clutching in his hand.

'It must have been some desperate fear that drove him to such ends,' Philip said. 'He has said nothing?'

I shook my head. 'He was quite unconscious.' I glanced over to the group near the fire. Beatrice was easing a warm woollen night shift over Piers's head. He still showed no sign of waking, but lay as flaccid as a child's doll made of cloth. 'I fear he may never wake.'

Emma looked up from where she was kneeling opposite Beatrice. 'He feels a little warmer now, I think. And his face is not quite so grey.'

It seemed more the eye of hope than reality, but we could do no more than cherish that hope. At least the child was now warm and dry. Beatrice got to her feet and began heating something in a small potlet on a brandreth at the edge of the fire. She had moved aside the large cook pot. The family's supper must wait.

Seeing my eyes on her, Beatrice said, 'I have a little broth here. It will be the easiest thing for him to take, if we can persuade him to swallow.'

Without being told, Stephen fetched a spoon from the table and handed it to his mother. While Emma lifted Piers and braced him against her knees, Beatrice pressed a spoonful of the broth to the boy's lips. At first there was no reaction, then he moaned and turned his head away. It was the first sound he had made, surely a hopeful sign?

Patiently Beatrice tried again and again, and at last

Piers's lips parted slightly and reluctantly, as if against his will. Quickly Beatrice tipped a little of the broth into his mouth before he moaned and turned aside again. Some of the broth had dribbled down his chin, and Emma wiped it away, but some must have been swallowed.

The minutes stretched out, but gradually Piers's reluctance subsided and he began to open his mouth readily. More and more of the broth was safely swallowed. I was growing anxious about seeing Emma home, but we were all concentrating on the child, and I knew she would not leave until she felt Piers had begun to show some signs of recovery.

Then, without warning, he eyes fluttered open and he looked about himself, first in confusion, then in panic. He began to struggle in Emma's arms, and kicked out, nearly knocking over the broth.

'Nay!' he cried weakly. 'Nay, I will not!'

'Hush,' Emma said. 'There are none but friends here. You are quite safe.'

He ignored her and began to struggle again. The women were both strangers to him, and I suppose that, emerging from whatever fearful dream had held him in darkness, he could not trust anyone. Of all of us, I was the only one he knew. I got up and walked quietly over to the group by the fire, then knelt down so that Piers could see me.'

'Piers,' I said softly, 'you know me, Nicholas Elyot, of the bookshop. I am a friend of Master Brinkylsworth. You are in the home of Mistress Metford, and this is her son Stephen. His father is sitting over there, beside the table. The lady who is holding you is the Lady Emma Thorgold. She and I found you amongst the willows by the Cherwell and brought you here, to our friends' house, where you could be warmed and fed. I think you have not eaten for a long time, have you?'

I made my voice very slow and clear, and as I spoke, he began to relax. What was almost a smile came to his lips.

'I know you, Master Elyot, and I thank you,' he whispered. He twisted his head to look about him, seeing all the signs of simple family life. 'And I thank all you good people.' He sank back, as if these few words had exhausted him.

There were tears in Emma's eyes. 'The poor mite,' she said, 'near dead, alone and afraid, and yet his good manners assert themselves.'

'I think you had best stay here for now, Piers,' I said. 'Mistress Metford will look after you, but I will take word to Master Brinkylsworth that you have been found safe. You can go back to Hart Hall when you are stronger.'

I glanced across at Beatrice, for I had not asked her agreement to this, but she nodded and smiled.

Piers began to struggle again, as if he would stand, had he but strength enough.

'I cannot go back!' he cried weakly. 'He would find me.'

Silent tears began to pour down his cheeks, though he made no sound of sobbing. It was unnerving to watch a child weep so silently.

'Who?' I said. 'Who would find you, Piers?'

He merely shook his head and continued to weep. I laid my hand over his, and was glad to feel that the skin was no longer that deathly cold.

'Do not distress yourself, child,' I said. 'You may stay safely here, and we shall tell no one, except Master Brinkylsworth. He has been mighty worried, searching Oxford from end to end.'

'I am sorry,' he whispered. 'But I did not know what else to do. I told him I would not, and then he threatened–'

'Hush,' Emma said. 'No one will threaten you here.' She eased him down on to the palliasse again, and tucked around him the blanket Stephen had brought. 'All you must do is to sleep and eat, until you are strong again.'

She got to her feet and looked down at him. 'Master Elyot and I will come and see you tomorrow, but now you must sleep.'

He gave a slight nod and closed his eyes. I think he was already nearly asleep. Beatrice gathered up the potlet of broth and moved the family supper to heat again on the fire.

'And what do you make of that?' Philip asked.

I shook my head. 'It seems we were right, that something – or someone – had frightened him, but I cannot make it out.'

'When he said "he threatened",' Emma said, 'surely he did not mean Jordain?'

'Nay, I am sure he did not,' I said, 'but he is afraid that this man, whoever he is, will find him if he goes back to Hart Hall.' I turned to Beatrice. 'I am sorry, I should have asked you first. May he stay here?'

'Of course,' she said, smiling. 'I will sit up with him tonight. I should not like to find that he has rolled into the fire in his sleep! Do not worry, Nicholas. I think he has begun to mend. Warmth, quiet, sleep, and food. Come tomorrow about midday, and I am sure you will find him much better.'

Philip saw us to the gate.

'Never fret, Nicholas. Beatrice could not be happier. I remember me – when she was a young girl she once nursed a young blackbird, fallen from its nest, feeding it worms and caterpillars. She had just that same look on her face.'

Emma and I both laughed.

'I knew we were right to bring him to Beatrice,' she said.

'I thank you both,' I said, 'and Stephen, too. Now we must walk quickly, or Maud Farringdon will be beside herself with worry.'

Emma and I hurried through the East Gate, which would be closed soon, as the night drew in, and continued up the High Street.

'What do you make of it all, Nicholas?' she said.

I shook my head. 'Little enough, I fear. The boy was hardly coherent. Some man, some "he", has frightened him, forced him to do something, or tried to force him to do something, made threats. But what kind of threats? To hurt him? It seemed more than that, somehow, to me. The fear seemed to go deeper. Or perhaps that is nothing more than my imagination.'

'This man knows that he lodges at Hart Hall. That is why Piers is afraid to return there, and why he has been hiding, I suppose.'

'Aye, so it seems.'

'Did you notice the bruises on the child's arms?'

I stopped and looked at her. 'Bruises? Nay, I did not.'

'Beatrice and I saw them when we undressed him. Large bruises, circling both arms, just above the elbow, as though someone had gripped him hard.'

'Jesu!' I began to walk again. 'This same man, do you think? Or some stallholder in the market, who caught him stealing food?'

'There is little enough sign that he has stolen much food. Besides, they were not recent bruises. They had begun to turn yellowish. At least a week or more old, so I would say.'

'Probably this man who threatened him, then.'

'Aye.'

'I wonder whether it could be the same man that Giles saw talking to Piers outside the Schools,' I said. 'Although he did not notice any threatening.'

'That was in view of anyone passing in the High Street, was it not? He might have taken care not to draw notice to himself.'

'Hmm.'

We had reached St Mildred Street, and turned up it toward the Farringdons' house.

'You think it is connected to the troubles at Queen's, do you not?' she said.

'It may be. Could the villain who has carried out all the attacks on the chapel have tried to use Piers in his villainy? But why a slight young boy like Piers?'

'He is one of the college's poor boys. He would be able to come and go about the college, without drawing notice.'

'Aye, that is true.' I shook my head. 'From all we have learned, it seems that whoever is behind these attacks wishes to make trouble for Queen's just when they have two important visitors from the north: Sir Thomas de Musgrave and Sir Anthony de Luce, two young men whose fathers may bestow patronage on the college. Cedric and I believe that it is someone who seeks revenge on the college, though for what reason, we know not. The provost clings to the belief that all is aimed against the stonemasons.'

We were nearly at her door now, but she laid her hand on my arm to stay me.

'If you and Cedric Walden have the right of it, it must be someone well acquainted with the college's affairs. Someone who would know that these two important visitors were about to arrive.'

'Aye, so we reason also.'

'I suppose,' she said slowly, 'word of these visits would be known not only to the Fellows, but to the college servants, who must prepare rooms, arrange for food and wine . . . Indeed, word might have spread amongst some of the townsfolk.'

I sighed. 'Aye, that is probably true. And it widens the field of those who might know the two young men were coming. We seem to wander round in ever wider circles.'

'Perhaps tomorrow, when Piers is stronger and Jordain visits him, he will be able to make all clear.'

'Let us hope so.'

She raised herself on her toes, her hands on my shoulders, and brushed her lips lightly against my cheek.'

'God give you goodnight, Nicholas.'

I took her hand and kissed the palm.

'God hold you safe.'

She opened the door and slipped inside.

It was nigh on curfew when I knocked at the door of Hart Hall, and Jordain opened it cautiously, not being accustomed to callers at this hour of the night. He looked tense and strained, as if he thought a visit so late in the day must surely herald bad news. I drew him outside, away from the hearing of his students.

'Good news, Jordain, Piers is found.'

He let out a hesitant breath,

'Alive?'

'Aye, alive and well. Nay, to speak truth, not altogether well. Cold, wet, near starving. And when I found him, out of his wits, but he is well enough now.'

'You found him? Yourself?'

'I did. Emma and I had been walking in the meadows, down by the Thames, and by some good saint's intervention, she suggested that we should walk back up the Cherwell to the East Bridge.'

'He was *there!*'

'He was,' I said. 'Curled up in a nest he had made for himself in a clump of willows, on the bank of the Cherwell. But he was very cold, and his clothes were torn and wet through. I think he had not eaten for some time. We carried him to Beatrice Metford's house, since it was nearest.'

'I must go there at once,' he said, thrusting past me.

'Nay, you must not,' I said, grabbing his arm. 'The gate will be shut. Besides, the lad will be sleeping now, and that is what he most needs. Beatrice and Emma stripped him of his wet clothes and dressed him in a warm night shift of Stephen's, then Beatrice was able to spoon some broth into him. What he needs now is warmth, food, and sleep.'

'Aye,' he said reluctantly. 'I suppose you have the right of it. Has he spoken? Told you anything of why he ran away?'

'Only a few confused words. Some man threatened him, but we could get little sense out of him. Best to let him sleep well tonight. Beatrice will sit up with him. Tomorrow we will go together to see how he fares. Beatrice bids us come at midday.'

'I must bring him back here,' Jordain said, 'where he

belongs. He should not be a burden to Beatrice Metford.'

'I do not think she sees it as a burden. And he is still a young boy, Jordain. Do you not think a woman's care is what he needs?'

I did not mention the poor diet Piers would receive at Hart Hall, compared with Beatrice's excellent cooking.

'There is something else that you are not telling me, Nicholas. I can see it in your eyes.'

'Aye, there is something else.' I hesitated. 'He said very little, but one thing he did say was that if he came back to Hart Hall, "he" – that is, the man who threatened him – would find him. He is very frightened lest he should be found. I think it best that you should say nothing of this to your students, for the present, lest they let something slip and word flies about.'

'What devil can this man be, who would so terrify a young boy?' Jordain clenched his teeth. I had never seen him so angry. 'Could he have died there, where you found him?'

Once again I hesitated, but I owed Jordain the truth. 'Aye, he might have done. He had nothing to eat but a few dandelion leaves.'

Jordain gave a grim smile. 'Poor fare indeed.'

'You may set your mind at rest now. Beatrice will know how to care for the lad, better than you or I. Go to your bed. In the morning – do you have any lectures?'

'Aye. I finish at ten o'the clock.'

'That will do very well. Time enough for the lad to sleep the night through and eat a good breakfast, before we try to discover his story. Come to my shop when you have finished at the Schools. Then we will go to Beatrice at midday.'

'Aye,' he said, 'I will so.' He laid his hand on the latch of the door.

'And, Jordain.'

'Aye?'

'No word to the other students,' I reminded him.

He smiled. 'I shall do my best, but my countenance

may speak louder than words.'

I hurried away down Catte Street. I had no wish to encounter the Watch, and even less to confront one of the dark figures who slipped through the lanes of Oxford at night, intent on some secret and nefarious business.

When I reached home, the children were already abed, while Margaret's face wore a mixture of worry and annoyance.

'You cannot, I hope, have been walking in the meadows with Emma until this hour,' she said, stirring the remains of a cold pottage fiercely, with her back to me.

I stared at her blankly. Then I remembered that the children had been at the Farringdons' house when I had set out with Emma. Though it was but a few hours ago, it felt like a week.

'Nay, I have not.' I sank down on a stool beside the table, suddenly weary. 'We found Piers Dykman.'

Her head came up sharply and she turned around.

'Alive? Or dead?'

'Alive, Mother Mary be praised. Though only just. I carried him to Beatrice's house, where we managed to revive him, though he is very frail, and may still grow sick, I fear. Then I saw Emma to St Mildred Street, and went to tell Jordain what had happened.'

'I see.' Relenting, she returned the pot to the fire and began to reheat my supper, while I told her in more detail what had passed at Beatrice's house.

'You did right to take him there,' she said. 'Beatrice will know better how to care for him than Jordain. He would mean well, yet he is but a man.'

'Indeed,' I said with a smile. 'We are poor creatures.'

She sniffed, then gave a reluctant smile. 'There is some of today's bread in the hanging cupboard, fetch it to table. I do not suppose that you have supped.'

'Nay, I have not,' I said, realising suddenly that I was very hungry.

She joined me at the table while I ate, and demanded that I tell her exactly what had happened.

When I had finished, she sighed, and rested her chin on her fist. 'It is terrible, what has been done to that child. He may well be a student of the university, but he is not so very much older than our Alysoun.'

Five years, I thought, but as I carried the slight figure in my arms, it had seemed less.

'So you and Jordain will speak to him tomorrow?'

'Aye, Beatrice bade us come at midday. Let us pray that his mind is clearer and he may tell us what has truly been happening.'

'You believe it has to do with the troubles at Queen's,' she said.

'I do. It must. Surely? He is one of Queen's poor boys. The man who frightened him, who caused him to run away, must be the villain behind all that has happened there. But who he may be, and why he is so intent upon damaging the college, is still as much a mystery to me as ever it was. The only explanation that Cedric and I have been able to think of is some connection with the visits of these two young gentlemen from the north.'

'Certainly it would do the college no favours in their eyes, when they learn what has been happening there.'

'Sir Thomas de Musgrave must know already,' I said, 'for he has been lodging in Queen's for a few days now. It has not driven him away. Although, to be sure, he told me he planned to remain in Oxford until past Easter. Indeed, when I told him that the book we are making for him could not be ready until the middle of May, he seemed unconcerned.'

'And you think he will pay for it?' she said. 'Walter is doubtful.'

'Aye, I have my doubts also,' I said, 'for he talked first of a book of hours, then changed his mind. But Provost de Hotham assured me that they are a cultured family and it would not be surprising for the son to take home a book from Oxford as a gift for his father.'

I did not add that a collection of hero tales was perhaps a surprising gift. A book of hours, or a life of St

Frideswide, would have seemed a more appropriate gift from a devoted son to his father. However, as the provost had taken care to inform us, the father had crenellated his castle against the Scots with the king's good favour, so perhaps a secular book of hero tales would be more to his liking.

When I had finished eating and rose wearily to head up the stairs to my bed chamber, Margaret laid her hand on my arm.

'This walk with Emma in the meadow – did you speak to her of those matters we discussed?'

Part of me rebelled at saying anything to Margaret, for those moments beside the river belonged only to Emma and to me, but whatever my future held, it must also affect my sister's future.

'She told me honestly what her grandfather has proposed for her,' I said, 'and I said I feared my suit was certain to fail before ever I uttered a word.'

'Emma would not, I think, accept that,' Margaret said shrewdly.

I gave a weak smile. 'She might not wish to, but she is no idle dreamer. She knows that her grandfather must approve her marriage.' I paused. 'She was much taken with your idea that I am a merchant and no shopkeeper, but I too am not blind to the truth.'

Margaret made an impatient noise. 'But you have both admitted your feelings?'

I smiled inwardly. Much of what occurred I would keep to myself.

'Her grandfather is to send a group of his retainers to escort her to his manor after Easter. We have agreed that I will go with her. Then we shall see what we shall see.'

I would not say more, but Margaret did not press me. It seemed I had said enough to satisfy her. And what of you and Peter Winchingham? I would have liked to ask her, but it was late, and besides I had no more than a suspicion.

'I am for bed,' I said, kissing her lightly on the forehead. Then I relented a little. 'You had the right of it. It was best to speak out to Emma, though whether aught will come of it, who can foretell?'

Lying in bed that night, I could not easily sleep. The finding of Piers Dykman relieved us all of a great burden of worry, although much still remained unanswered. As for Emma . . . I smiled into the darkness. I knew her mind now, as well as lifting the concealing veil from my own. The way ahead was as dark as my midnight chamber, but at least now we might venture into it together. Though how to persuade Sir Anthony Thorgold of my worth as a suitor was beyond my ability to conceive.

Jordain arrived soon after ten o'the clock the next morning, full of impatience to be off at once to Beatrice's house, but I forbade it.

'Beatrice has bidden us come at midday,' I said, 'and so I agreed. Remember, she has nursed your lad and sat up all night caring for him. We must abide by what she has said.'

Jordain agreed, reluctantly, but he was so restless, pacing about the shop, that I took him through into the garden to stop him interfering with my scriveners' work.

'Here,' I said, 'you may walk back and forth as much as you will, and disturb no one but the hens.'

He grinned in rueful apology. 'I have been worried so long about the boy . . . I know you say that he is alive and recovering, but I need to see him for myself. The saints be praised that I never sent that letter to his family. His father would have been in great distress, and needlessly. I have torn it up and tossed it on the fire this morning, to my relief.'

'And your students still know nothing?'

'Well,' he admitted apologetically, 'I have *said* nothing, but I am no travelling player, Nicholas. I have no skill in playing a part and concealing my thoughts. I expect my countenance is an open book to them.'

I shrugged. 'As long as they merely suspect, but know nothing for certain, we are probably safe from rumours spreading. I am but mindful of how afraid Piers is, lest word of his reappearance reaches this man who has frightened him.'

Jordain took another turn about the garden, examined the health of the fruit trees, had a word with my bees, and detached a curious hen from the laces of his shoes.

'Is it time yet, do you think, Nicholas?'

'You have heard the bells of St Peter's as well as I have. That is eleven o'the clock.'

'We might start on our way, then.'

''Twill not take an hour to walk to Beatrice's house. However,' I rose from the bench where I had been watching his meanderings, 'we might visit Queen's on our way, and see how the work is faring under the protection of Cedric Walden's men.'

He agreed eagerly and we went out through the shop. I am sure Walter and Roger were glad to see him leave, after suffering his agitation. I had said nothing to them of finding Piers, but I suspected they had guessed what was afoot.

Across the road I saw that Aelyth was seated at the window of her room in the dairy house, bent intently over her loom. Mary would be out and about on her deliveries now, with the assistance of the girl Sarah. I must ask how Sarah was faring in learning to weave. Margaret had told me that Mary had purchased a second ribbon loom, so that Aelyth's own loom should not be tangled up with her new apprentice's stumbling efforts.

There were no idlers hanging about the opening into the college grounds today. Perhaps the presence of two soldiers, one on either side of it, was proving a discouragement. The men knew me, so that we passed inside without hindrance.

Jordain gave a small gasp at the sight of the chapel.

'I had not realised that the building had gone so far,' he said.

Even since my recent visit, I could see the change. Both stonemasons and carpenters were going about their work with greater determination and speed than ever before. Perhaps an audience of soldiers spurred them on, or perhaps the thought that they should now be safe from further attacks.

Robert Hanbury approached us, a roll of plans under his arm.

He bowed to Jordain and took me by the arm.

'It was a good deed, indeed a blessing, what you did for us, Nicholas, fetching the deputy sheriff back to Oxford. The men are determined to complete as much of the work as possible before Sir Anthony de Luce arrives. Tomorrow he comes, so we believe. We have repaired the hoist and have several of the nave arches already in place. As you can see, Master English and his men have begun to set the roof beams. Come within.'

We entered the chapel by the south door.

'Changed indeed since I was last here,' I said.

'I decided it was best to construct the arches starting from the east end,' Hanbury said, 'after the accident. Best to leave that one in the south west till last, once any remaining fears amongst the men are overcome. There have been a few superstitious whispers amongst them. That way also the carpenters may roof the choir at least in part, before the Easter service is held here.'

'It is remarkable, how much you have achieved,' I said. Indeed, I was struck with admiration.

'The stones for the arches were already cut,' he explained. 'So once the hoist was working again, setting them in place has taken no great time, especially when the men are eager to have the task over and done with.'

'It is all very fine,' Jordain said, looking about him with interest. 'I have never seen a holy building under construction before. And these angels, where are they to be put?'

He indicated a row of carved angel heads, each with a pair of wings behind, which had been laid out on the floor of the north aisle.

'You see the keystone at the top of each arch?'

Hanbury pointed. 'Each will have an angel. We shall set the first of them this afternoon. By then there will be eight arches complete, four on each side.'

I noticed for the first time that the wooden patterns, which held the stones for the arches in place until the mortar dried, had a small shelf just below the keystone. This must secure the angel in place.

Through the open roof space we could see the carpenters standing on the highest level of scaffolding and lifting the first of the roof beams, ready to secure above the stone arches.

'Is the mortar dry enough to take the weight?' I asked.

'Aye, on the first two pairs of arches. We set those yesterday.'

We made our way out through the south door again, where I saw the mason Edred, with his broken leg strapped to a board, sitting and working at a carving with chisel and mallet. He grinned at me, and Hanbury nodded to him.

'Seems his accident was not all disaster,' he said. 'Edred is proving not unhandy as a carver. I have given him some simple work to do and he is making a better showing of it than I expected.'

He saw us to the edge of the college grounds.

'No more trouble, then?' I said.

'None. As you can see, the soldiers are keeping a careful watch all about us. And the men are so thankful, they are working harder than ever.'

'So your intruder has been out-foxed,' Jordain said.

'The saints be praised,' Hanbury said, then added cautiously, 'although I shall not rest easy until every stone, every timber, and every roof slate is in place.'

'And now,' Jordain said, as we stepped through into the High Street, 'we may make our way to Mistress Beatrice's house with a good conscience.'

'We may,' I said, as we turned toward the East Gate. 'Curious, is it not, that all the cruel tricks played on the builders have finally spurred them on to work all the faster?

I wonder how the miscreant will feel about that, if he discovers what is afoot.'

'From what little we know of him,' Jordain said, 'I would judge that he will be angered.'

'I think you have the right of it,' I said. 'And if he is angered, will he attempt one last dangerous trick?'

'Let us pray he will not,' Jordain said, but I could tell that his mind was not on the chapel a-building at Queen's, but on the lost lamb from his own flock. It occurred to me for the first time how much Jordain resembled old Godfrid, my cousin's shepherd. One might be an unlettered man, born of villein blood, though since freed, and the other a learned academic, Regent Master of the university, yet Godfrid with his sheep and Jordain with his students had much in common.

As we neared the East Gate, Jordain quickened his pace, although when we reached Beatrice's house he suddenly hesitated. I could not remember whether he had ever entered here before. He was, after all, a man in holy orders, while she was the mistress of a Fellow of Merton College. Their union had been as loyal as any marriage, and since it had lasted eight years or more, Beatrice would be regarded by many as Philip's common law wife. That might put his Fellowship in the university in jeopardy even if it gave her protection, but nevertheless it did place Jordain in an awkward position, something to which I suppose neither of us had given a thought, being too caught up in the rescue of Piers.

'Will Mistress Beatrice be offended at my coming here, uninvited?' Jordain asked humbly, and I realised that I had misread his hesitation.

'In no way,' I assured him. 'She will be expecting us both.'

I saw that Stephen was watching from the window and he opened the door before we could knock.

'Come you in-by, Master Elyot, Master Brinkylsworth,' he said. 'Piers is already much better.'

Beatrice greeted us both with her usual grave

serenity, not at all disturbed, so it seemed, by a tonsured Regent Master entering her home. After all, she knew Jordain, even if he had never come here. Perhaps she saw him as merely another of Philip's calling, although a little younger. Looking about, I saw no sign of Philip.

As though she read my thoughts, Beatrice said, 'Philip was lecturing in the Schools this morning, then he had a meeting with the Warden of Merton. I am not sure that he will be back today. However, he asked me to tell you that he will say nothing about finding Piers until you wish it, and if you need further help, you are to send to him at Merton.'

'I thank you, Beatrice,' I said. 'And how does Piers fare?'

We all looked across the room. The palliasse had now been moved away from such close proximity to the fire, for the spring day was warm and the windows open. It was now placed against the wall, so that Piers might sit up, propped against cushions. Although he was still fearfully gaunt, his face had regained a more normal colour, and his hair had been neatly combed, perhaps even trimmed judiciously.

'How do you find yourself today, Piers?' I said, cheerfully, as if I were speaking to one of my own children. 'See, here is Master Brinkylsworth come to see you.'

'Much better, I thank you, Master Elyot,' he said, but he looked at Jordain his eyes wide with anxiety. 'I am sorry, Master Brinkylsworth. I never meant to cause you trouble, but I did not know how to send word to you.'

He looked ready to weep again, and Jordain was not much better, looking down at the boy's wasted frame, so I became brisk.

'Here, Jordain,' I said, 'bring up a stool and Piers shall tell us all that has happened, from the start of this affair.'

We carried over stools and placed them beside the palliasse, while Beatrice and Stephen withdrew politely to the other side of the room, although it was clear that both were listening keenly.

'Take us back,' I said, 'to the day you attended your lectures, but then never went home to Hart Hall for your dinner. You were seen talking to a stranger.'

'I was seen?'

He glanced nervously at Jordain, who smiled reassuringly.

'Aye, Giles saw you talking to a man, then the man walked away. He did not notice where you went, and not a sight of you or your shadow have we seen since.'

'Unless,' I said, 'you slept one night in St Peter's churchyard, where Rector Bokeland saw you.'

'I did. I am sorry. I should not have done so . . . in that sacred place. I hope the rector is not angry.'

'Not at all,' I reassured him. 'He was only sorry he could not help, but you ran off.'

Piers hung his head. 'I did not know what to do.'

'So after you were seen with this stranger outside the Schools,' Jordain said, 'where did you go? And who was he?'

'Oh, but it started before that,' Piers said. 'It started when he caught me in the street beside Hart Hall and told me I must steal the stonemasons' tools.'

I let out my breath in an audible sigh. Our suspicions were justified. Piers's disappearance and the events at Queen's *were* linked.

'You stole the tools?' Jordain said, unable to keep the note of reproof out of his voice. 'Did you also wilfully blunt others?'

Piers nodded, and silent tears again began to roll down his cheeks. Accustomed to Alysoun's noisy weeping – a sudden squall, as suddenly over – I found this silence sadly disturbing.

'I did,' he whispered.

'But why? And had you a hand in any of the other dreadful accidents which have befallen the stonemasons? Two men badly injured. One man killed.'

'Nay!' The cry broke from him wildly, and his tears

flowed more freely.

I thought he looked as terrified as he had done the previous night when he first regained his wits and found himself surrounded by strangers.

'I heard,' he gabbled. 'I heard about the men. That was why . . . I never wanted any part of it.'

'Piers,' I said, laying my hand on his, in the hope of calming him, 'no one can blame a child forced into misdeeds by a man much bigger, older, and stronger than he. This was the same man you were seen with outside the Schools? And he wanted you to carry out more wicked tricks? That was when you decided to run away?'

'Aye,' he said, relieved I had found the words for him. 'There were going to be worse things. I would never have stolen the tools, but he threatened me.'

'But why did he want to do these things?' Jordain asked, still as baffled as we all were.

'It was because Sir Anthony de Luce is to come to the college,' Piers said. 'I do not understand it, but he hates the de Luce family. He did not explain, but he said he wanted to destroy the chapel, to teach the de Luces a lesson. That is all I know. I do not know why.'

He looked from Jordain to me, his eyes pleading.

'We believe you, Piers,' I said gently, 'but you have not told us who this man is, or how he knew who you are, or in what way he threatened you.'

'But he is my father's lord.' Piers gazed at me in astonishment, as if he had already explained this. 'And he said that if I did not do as he ordered, he would turn my father and all my family off their land. My mother is dead. My father is ill. What will become of them? I thought, if I ran away and hid, he might think I was dead and could not do his bidding, and then he would not harm them.'

So that was the cruel threat held over the head of this boy. I found my anger, which had been steadily growing throughout Piers's story, near to bursting out, but I swallowed it down and steadied my voice.

'Piers,' I said quietly, 'you have not told us the name

of your father's lord.'

    His glance darted back and forth between us.

    'His name is Sir Thomas de Musgrave.'

Chapter Twelve

I stared at him. This made no sense at all. The damage to the building of the chapel, the halting of the work, even the injuries to the stonemasons – all of these, surely, were intended to cast Queen's College in the worst possible light before the visits of the two young noblemen from the north country. Cedric Walden and I were both certain of that. Whether they had achieved their purpose was yet to be revealed. Besides, Sir Thomas de Musgrave was a very elegant young gentleman. I could not picture him breaking into a derelict cottage, climbing over walls, breaking down stonework, tampering with the stonemasons' bucket and hoist . . . Yet somehow I had no difficulty in imagining him frightening a young lad with the threat to destroy his family.

Then, oddly, I remembered that deep cut at the base of one of de Musgrave's fingers, something he would hardly have come by in the ordinary course of his pampered life, unless he had been hunting or jousting, neither of which was likely while living in Oxford. Nonetheless, could Piers's explanation possibly be right? Some vengeance against the de Luce family? The long-standing feuds between noble families could last for generations of hatred and even armed skirmishes. I knew nothing about such feuds in the wild north country of England, but they were not altogether unknown in the quieter shires like my own. But were such underhand actions as those at Queen's College likely in such a feud?

Jordain, however, was more concerned with the full story of what had happened to Piers than the reasons for de Musgrave's actions.

'Once this villain tried to force you to help him further,' he said, 'you ran away into hiding. We understand that. We found your academic gown in an abandoned cottage on the High. Was that where you had gone? Did you force open the shutters?'

Piers shivered and shook his head.

'Nay. That I did not do, I swear you my oath, Master Brinkylsworth. That was not how it happened.'

He began to look distressed again, drawing great gulping breaths. Beatrice rose from her stool and brought him a cup of cool raspberry cordial.

'Drink this first, Piers,' she said, 'and take all the time you need. Master Brinkylsworth and Master Elyot will not rush you. They are in no haste. They want only to solve the mysteries which have been puzzling us these many days past.'

Piers nodded, and drank the cordial obediently. Beatrice's words seemed to have calmed him.

'I thank you, Mistress Metford,' he said, handing the cup back to her. 'I will do my best to make all clear.'

He turned to Jordain. 'I thought I could simply mingle amongst the crowds in town. No one takes note of one student amongst so many. Sir Thomas had found me first by waiting outside Hart Hall. It was known, back at home, where I lodged. It would not have been difficult for him to learn. Perhaps he asked our priest, saying he was coming to Oxford. It would have seemed honest enough. No need to hide it.'

Jordain nodded. 'Aye, so it must have been.'

'I wandered about for the rest of that day, thinking that I might be able to creep back at dusk and ask you if I might lie low until Sir Thomas left Oxford, but when most people began to go home for supper, the crowds thinned, and suddenly, there he was, next to me, and I had no time to run. He caught me fast and swore that if I cried out, he would soon silence me.'

He drew a deep breath and shuddered.

'He showed me his dagger.'

'Villain!' Jordain muttered.

I heard Beatrice give a convulsive movement, although she was behind me.

'Then, when it was dusk, he prised open the shutters on that cottage. He had a crowbar. And he picked me up and carried me inside. He is very strong.'

'The footprints in the dust,' I reminded Jordain. 'The smaller ones only began halfway across the floor.'

He nodded. Piers looked surprised, but carried on with his account.

'He tried to make me go with him into the college, but I swore I would not, so he shut me into a chamber on the upper floor. He did give me a little water. There was no lock, but he wedged something against the door so that I could not open it. The saints be praised, he did not tie me up, but I do not think he had any rope. He would not have expected to have found me.'

'So you managed to escape?' I said.

'It took me a long time, and all the while I was afraid he would come back, but in the end I managed to force the door open enough to squeeze through. He had jammed some broken furniture against it, but I suppose he had not time to make it secure. Besides, it was quite dark up there. It was night, and the only window was shuttered. He might not have seen how well he had succeeded.'

'You left your gown behind,' Jordain said.

'I thought, without a gown I could pass for a boy of the town, and it would not be so easy for him to find me. Downstairs there was a little light coming through the open window, from the lanterns outside some of the shops.' He gave a grin. 'I stepped carefully, for I could see the way through the dust, where he had walked. I thought if I stepped only where he had stepped, he would think I was still held safely above.'

'And since then?' Jordain prompted.

'Since then, I have hidden where I could. In an empty barn. Twice in St Peter's churchyard. But I heard the gossip that I was searched for, and several times I saw Giles and the others hunting, so I thought I had best take myself out of the town. The last few days I have been in the meadows. It only rained one night.'

Jordain shook his head. 'Then you were lucky. Luckier still that Master Elyot and Lady Emma found you when they did, else I think you would not have lived to tell us your tale.'

'I know,' Piers said, and those tears welled up again.

I could see how courageous he had been, to stand up against the threats and cruelties of a strong and violent man, but now he could let himself give way to a normal child's fears.

'You could have come back to me,' Jordain said. 'At any time. We would have kept you safe until this man was caught.'

'I'm sorry.' Piers was beginning to look very tired, now that he had heaved his story on to other shoulders. 'I am sorry, Master Brinkylsworth. I did not want to bring trouble on you.'

'Well, never mind now.' Jordain patted him on the shoulder and rose from his stool. 'Beatrice, may we leave him in your care this while?'

'Certainly you may.' She smiled at him. 'He will be company for Stephen, who pines to become a student himself, some day. And we will feed him up.'

Repeating our thanks to her, we left the cottage, closing the door softly behind us. I glanced about, hoping that de Musgrave was nowhere in sight, lest he connect Jordain with the missing boy. It was unlikely the man would be here, amongst these humble houses beyond the East Gate, but he seemed to possess a talent for appearing unexpectedly.

We were silent at first as we walked back up the High Street.

'And now what is to do?' Jordain said at last.

'As for Piers,' I said, 'I think best to leave him peacefully in Beatrice's care. She has said she will feed him up, and that is what he needs. That and sleep, and some peace to recover from the fears of these last days. He will do well enough, and come back to Hart Hall all the better when these affairs are settled.'

'Indeed,' Jordain said, 'and how are they to be settled? Surely Sheriff Walden must be told.'

'Aye, he must. The difficulty, however, is to bring any proof against de Musgrave as the villain behind all the troubles at Queen's. We have no evidence but the word of a twelve-year-old boy, a boy we would do well to keep away from all this. I fear if we brought him forward, de Musgrave would laugh him to scorn. Who would believe the word of a poor tenant's son against the son of his father's overlord, Sir Thomas de Musgrave the elder, favoured by the king? Nay, I cannot think of a way forward.'

'But we should tell Cedric Walden what we know.'

'We must,' I said. 'Do you go back to Hart Hall and go about your business in the ordinary way, as if Piers had not been found. Try not to set your other students guessing. I will seek out Cedric. He may be at the castle, or he may be visiting Queen's to see how his men are faring there. Wherever he is, I will find him and tell him all we have learned. Then let him decide how best to go on. He may think he knows enough to arrest de Musgrave, but it will be difficult for him, since the father seems to be a man of influence.'

'Did not Master Hanbury say that the other young man, Sir Anthony de Luce, is expected at the college tomorrow?'

'Aye, so he did.' I thought for a moment. 'I wonder what manner of confrontation that will be, when the two young men come face to face. All this while I have been thinking of them as possible benefactors of the college, perhaps even as friends. I could not have been more wrong.'

'We can hardly expect to know the state of family rivalries in those faraway parts,' Jordain said reasonably.

'Hmm. It sounds something more than mere rivalry, from what Piers said. I think he used the word "hate".'

'He did.'

We had reached the end of the lane.

'Are you sure you do not wish me to come with you to Cedric Walden? Two witnesses of what Piers has told us?'

'Nay,' I said. 'Time enough for that later. Or mayhap Cedric may wish to have a quiet word with Piers himself. Do not fret!' For Jordain had opened his mouth, frowning. 'It would be done only with the greatest care. Go back, and when I have anything to tell, I will come to you. It may be that Cedric will want to wait, to see how the encounter goes between de Musgrave and de Luce tomorrow.'

He nodded, and set off somewhat reluctantly up the lane. As the college was much nearer than the castle, I decided to call in there first to look for Cedric, and so save myself the long walk across Oxford to the castle.

Even in the time since we had called in on our way to Beatrice's house, the builders had made progress on the chapel. The first of the roof beams were now in place, and the carpenters were carrying further timbers up to the highest part of the scaffolding. I found Robert Hanbury inside the chapel, supervising the setting of the stones for another arch on the south side of the nave. The first of the angel heads had been fixed in place, and one of the stonemasons was up a ladder setting the next one to the keystone of the opposite arch.

'The deputy sheriff?' Hanbury said. 'Aye, he's here. Just gone to see Master Brandon, but he will be back here shortly. Captain Beverley is here. Will he serve your turn?'

I hesitated. I had hoped to speak to Cedric himself, but Thomas Beverley could take my message.

'Aye, let me speak to Captain Beverley.'

Hanbury sent one of the apprentices off to fetch Beverley, and returned with him in a few minutes. I drew him aside.

'I have the name of our villain,' I said, speaking low, for the stonemasons were working all around us. Later, I realised I should have taken him well away from the chapel.

'You have?' He seemed astonished. 'How can that be?'

'We have found the missing student,' I said. 'Piers Dykman. It appears that he was briefly involved in these affairs, though not of his own will. Your criminal is his father's overlord, or rather the son of his father's overlord, and he threatened to drive the boy's family from their land. It seems all this was aimed not to discredit the college, but the benefactor's family, the de Luces, with whom his own family has a long-standing feud.'

Thomas frowned. 'I do not understand. Sir Anthony de Luce arrives tomorrow, I believe. This villain – you say he is the boy's overlord? A man of rank? Surely you do not mean Sir Thomas de Musgrave?'

He did not lower his voice when he spoke, and then his eyes went up, over my shoulder, and I thought he flinched. Turning half about, I saw that Cedric Walden was approaching, accompanied by the Queen's Fellow, Master Brandon, and by Sir Thomas Musgrave himself. But surely they were too far away to have heard?

'I will leave you to tell Cedric yourself,' I said, 'but privately. If he comes to my shop, I can give him all the details that Piers Dykman has told me.'

Thomas nodded, and then the others reached us.

'Nicholas,' Cedric said, 'you have seen how well the stonemasons' work flies ahead? And the carpenters', too?'

'I am sure the presence of your soldiers was all that was needed to protect them from further trouble,' I said, trying to avoid de Musgrave's eye, though he seemed not to wish to avoid mine.

'And how is my book of hero tales progressing, Master Elyot?' he said, smiling with what would have seemed innocent pleasure, had I not known what I knew.

'My scrivener Roger Pigot has completed the first two tales,' I said, hoping that he would not notice the constraint in my voice. Could he have overheard Thomas?

'He is working at your book most diligently, but as I have said, it is a large work.'

'Indeed, indeed!' He looked positively benign now. I felt my stomach sicken. 'I might call round to your shop, if I may.'

'At your pleasure, sir.'

'It will indeed be my pleasure.'

'And we have good news also,' Master Brandon said.

I think he did not like to be brushed to the side of any discussion.

'Good news?' Any good news at this awkward moment was to be welcomed.

'Our other guest from the north country, Sir Anthony de Luce, has made better time on his journey than he expected. He sends a message that he will be with us before the day's end.'

'Good news indeed,' I said. If my voice croaked, I hope de Musgrave was unaware. And if de Luce arrived before I was able to explain everything to Cedric, there might, for all I knew, be bloodshed.

I gave Thomas Beverley what I hoped was a meaning look. 'I must away and attend to business, but you have my message, Thomas.'

'I have.'

I bowed all round, and made my escape. Would Thomas be able to speak to Cedric privately before de Musgrave visited my shop? He might have heard nothing, and his visit to me might signify no more than a chance to look at Roger's work, as he claimed.

I hurried back to the shop and found it curiously quiet. Only Walter was at work and there were no sounds from the house beyond. Rowan lay asleep under my desk.

'Where is everyone?' I asked.

'Margaret has gone with the children to the market,' Walter said. 'She needed help to carry her purchases home, she said. Seems she has had a letter from Master Winchingham to say that he and his daughter are coming to Oxford for Easter.' He grinned. 'Reckon Margaret will be cooking up a feast against their coming.'

I grinned back. 'Reckon she will. That is good to hear. The lad is not coming? Hans?'

'Seems Master Winchingham has left him in charge of the manor for a week, so that he might try his hand at managing it. There will not be much to do, save overseeing the spring planting, and the reeve will have that in hand.'

'Still, 'twill be good practice for young Hans,' I said, sitting down at my desk with relief. It was good to be away from Queen's and the troubles washing up there from the north, and to think instead about spring farming back at Leighton-under-Wychwood.

'But where is Roger?'

'Ran short of forest green ink,' Walter said. 'He needs a deal of it for all the woodland illuminations in that book for de Musgrave. He has gone off to the paint shop in Northgate Street. I gave him the coin.'

He nodded toward the small locked box we kept behind the stack of paper on one of the shelves. It contained a small amount of coin and Walter held the key, in case either of them needed to make a purchase when I was not here. They would write down the item and the cost on a scrap of parchment or paper and leave it in the box.

'Good,' I said, 'as long as he does not linger.'

'He may make a stop at the sweet pastry shop next door,' Walter said.

We both laughed, for Roger's sweet tooth was well known to us all.

I had barely settled at my desk and Rowan had shifted out of the way of my feet, back against the wall, when the door burst violently open and Sir Thomas de Musgrave strode in. Walter stood up courteously, though he looked a little puzzled at the man's manner.

'Have you come to view the pages of your book, Sir Thomas?' he said.

He picked up the small pile of parchment from Roger's desk and stepped forward to hand it to de Musgrave.

'Out of my way, old man!' de Musgrave shouted, and punched Walter hard in the chest.

The pages went flying, all across the floor, and Walter collapsed backwards, striking his head on the corner of Roger's desk as he fell. I sprang to my feet.

'How dare you strike out like that! Let me see to him. He may be gravely hurt!'

I tried to step round the edge of the desk, but de Musgrave thrust it at me, pinning me against the wall.

'You,' he said, his face drawn up in a rictus of hatred. 'You puny churl, poking your nose in where you have no business to be! I'll not have you interfering in my affairs. Time to put an end to your meddling, you worthless little shopkeeper. Thought yourself man enough to interfere between gentlemen, did you? We shall soon settle that.'

To my alarm, he drew his sword.

This could not be happening. The man spoke like a tuppence-ha'penny strolling player, performing a trite story upon a makeshift platform. Or else I was caught up in some foolish dream.

Except the sword looked real enough. And I was pinned helpless behind the desk.

Then de Musgrave gave a yell and looked down.

'Get off me, you damnable cur!'

His raised his sword to bring it down on Rowan, who had him by the ankle. I thrust the desk away from me, catching de Musgrave on the hip and causing his sword arm to falter. The sword swept down and missed Rowan by no more than an inch. She yelped in terror and threw herself back against the wall.

'You villain!' I shouted, clawing my way out from behind the desk. 'A fine nobleman you are, a chivalrous gentleman! You are ready enough to terrify children, strike down old men, and draw your sword on a dog. And to set traps for men who have done you no harm. That boy Wat is maimed for life, and the young journeyman Gerard robbed of his. He had a wife and a babe on the way, but what care you? They stood between you and your murderous games.'

I was deliberately provoking him, yelling at the top of my voice, in the hope that the noise might bring someone to my aid. Cedric should be coming to learn what I knew, but he might not make haste. If only Roger were here! I was usually ready to lay a restraining hand on his eagerness to join in a brawl, but I would have been glad of him now. I had no sword, and did not usually carry a dagger, unless I went out at night. I grabbed the only thing I could see of any use – the sharp but small knife I used for trimming pages. Little enough against a sword and a man who knew how to wield it.

De Musgrave was examining his ankle, where Rowan had bitten him. I was glad to see blood seeping out through his torn hose.

'Well?' I said, trying to draw his attention lest he turn his sword on the dog again. She would stand no chance against him. I might have a little more, though not much.

'Why have you been playing your devilish games? Oh, we know all that you have done. The boy is safely hidden away, and four of us heard him bear witness, so even if you silence me, you shall not escape justice. Thomas Beverley also knows, and will have told Sheriff Walden by this.'

'I heard,' he said, through gritted teeth, 'and aye, I admit it readily. It is no affair of yours. It is between me and de Luce.'

'And never a care who might get in your way?'

This time I had provoked him too far and he came for me, his sword raised. I dodged, but there was little enough room to move in the shop, especially with Walter sprawled on the floor. I dared not look at him, for fear of what I might see.

De Musgrave missed me with his first thrust, but as I twisted away the sword came down again and sliced through my left sleeve. I felt a sharp pain, and blood began to well out and run warm down my arm. I saw him smirk with satisfaction, and it so angered me that I lunged at him heedlessly with my knife, scoring it across the angle between his left shoulder and his neck. The blade was sharp, and I too drew blood.

He was so astonished at my temerity that for a moment he simply stared at me, then he lifted his sword and came for me, though I backed away until I came up short again the shelf of secondhand books which stood just inside the window. I hit it so hard that most of them fell to the floor, hampering me even more. The man was afire with such unreasoning rage that I could read my death in his eyes. So this was how it was all to end, ignominiously amongst a pile of battered student textbooks. I found myself seized by an urge to hysterical mirth at the irony of it all, or perhaps its fittingness, for an Oxford bookseller.

Just as he raised his sword again, the door was flung open and crashed back against the wall. Cedric! I thought. But when I dared to turn my head, a total stranger stood there.

'So this is your latest victim, is it, Musgrave?'

The man was a little older than my assailant, perhaps two or three and twenty. Dressed like a gentleman, solidly built, and also wearing a sword. He laid his hand on the hilt.

'You are Sir Anthony de Luce?' I said, managing to find enough breath to speak. 'Have a care! He means your harm.'

'He always means me harm,' the man said. 'Like all his tribe. We are a festering sore in their side.'

'Aye, you speak truly!' de Musgrave shouted, his face reddened with fury.

Suddenly he whirled toward me and I took a step back, until I came up short against the bookshelf again, but it seemed he was no longer bent on attacking me, now that he had other prey. Instead, he seemed to want to justify himself.

'Aye, they are a thorn in our side, these traitors, these

de Luces! They have stolen our lands and our titles, and all through treachery.'

'And who was the traitor first?' de Luce said. 'Your father's uncle, Andrew de Harclay. It was he who betrayed us to the Scots!'

'Never!' De Musgrave turned back to face him. 'He secured peace along the border and saved lives, more than a weak king could do, the weakling son of the first Edward.'

'And made a treasonous treaty with the Bruce back in '23, without the king's permission.'

'It was no treason, as well you know. He was Earl of Carlisle, and made governor of Cockermouth castle by the king after defeating the Earl of Lancaster at Boroughbridge. Aye, Lancaster! He was in truth a rebel traitor. Andrew de Harclay was no such traitor. He never raised a hand against the king. It was never the king who cried treason.'

De Luce shrugged. 'Making a treaty with the Scots without the king's consent, that was treason.'

'It was no treason!' de Musgrave shrieked. 'And what of that sneaking traitor your grandfather? A lesser man, nothing but poor gentry. No man to compare with Andrew de Harclay, Earl of Carlisle. Oh, aye, de Luce saw his chance to steal our birthright!'

He whirled around to me again.

'Do you know how it fell out? Nay, I suppose you do not, living snug here in your soft southern counties, without the chance every night of a Scottish raiding party seizing your cattle, killing your men, and defiling your women. This man's grandfather,' he gestured at de Luce with his sword, 'another Anthony de Luce, he who was served by the Queen's Founder when he was a man-at-arms . . . this Anthony de Luce went to pay a *friendly* visit on Andrew de Harclay at his castle of Cockermouth. He took with him a troop of men hiding arms under their cloaks, and at every point where there were guards, he left a few, chatting merrily with de Harclay's men, until he came with a few retainers to the solar, where de Harclay poured him a cup of wine in good fellowship.'

He paused, and added thoughtfully, 'For all I know, the Queen's Founder was one of those men-at-arms who aided him in his treachery.'

I began to see where this was leading, and some reasons for de Musgrave's hatred became clearer.

De Musgrave drew a shuddering breath. 'Then at a signal, de Luce seized Andrew de Harclay, and his men overpowered the castle guards. My father's uncle was dragged away to be hung, drawn, and quartered treacherously by de Luce, the parts of his body displayed like some murderous felon at Newcastle, York, Carlisle, and Shrewsbury. My grandmother, Andrew's sister, petitioned the king and in the end his body was returned for Christian burial. The king had no part in it, but was too feeble to make a stand against a ruthless villain like de Luce.'

'My grandfather,' de Luce said, 'captured and punished a traitor. De Harclay had signed a treaty with the Scots.'

De Musgrave glared at him. '*Your grandfather* cared nothing for the Scots or for the weak king who could not stop them destroying our north country. He knew what reward to ask for from the king, and he got it. All our lands and privileges in Cumberland. I can even quote you the words of the charter, for they were drummed into me by my grandmother from the time I could speak:

King to Anthony de Luce: castle and honour of Cockermouthe, and manor of Papcaster in Allerdale said to be appurtenant thereto, with knight's fees, advowsons of churches, fairs, markets, free chases, warrens and all other royal liberties in castle, honour and manor, and return of royal writs in the honour; for service of one knight's fees.'

He spoke with a kind of wild-eyed bitterness.

'Then the following year, the king made a marriage between Anthony de Luce's son Thomas, your father, with his royal kinswoman, his cousin Agnes Beaumont. Oh, aye, the de Luces, petty gentry, did very well out of their treachery against my father's uncle, the Earl of Carlisle!

Those are not *your* lands, titles, and privileges. They belong to *my* family, to *my* father, and some day to *me*.'

Throughout this bitter speech, de Luce had stood quite still, fingering the hilt of his sword. He had flushed when his grandfather's treachery was described, and I could see he did not like it, but he made no attempt either to defend it any further, or to deny it.

'And now,' de Musgrave said, 'you shall answer to me for your family's treachery.'

I think they had both forgotten by then that I was there. De Musgrave still held his sword, and as he rushed forward de Luce drew his in the single swift movement of an experienced swordsman. They began to circle each other warily, like two hostile dogs awaiting the moment to leap forward, then they came together with a clash of steel.

There was so little room to move that neither could make use of any clever tactics. They shoved and grunted, hardly able to swing their swords, half wrestling, half fighting with steel. They crashed together against Roger's desk, tipping it over, so that pots of ink smashed on the ground, their contents flowing in wide arcs across the floor and the scattered parchment. I could not even force my way past them to get help.

I do not know how long it lasted. It seemed for ever, although it cannot have been many minutes. Both had received slashes and were bleeding freely, when at last through the window I saw Cedric Walden and Thomas Beverley approaching from the direction of Queen's, followed by three or four of their men.

'Hurry!' I shouted, 'before murder is done!.'

Suddenly the shop was full of people. The two combatants had been separated, their swords seized, and they were held, sweating and panting, glaring at each other.

'He attacked me!' de Luce shouted.

'Filthy de Luce traitor!' De Musgrave had gone red at first, then white, and began to sway.

'Have a care,' I said. 'He may be playing you false, or else he is about to lose his wits. He is half crazed. I beg of you, let me come to my man Walter. When de Musgrave hit him, he fell and struck his head.'

They parted so that I might reach Walter. He lay very still and I knelt down beside him, fearful of what I might find. I thought that there was a pool of blood beside his head, until I realised that it was Roger's smashed bottle of crimson ink.

'Walter!' I said urgently. 'Walter, can you hear me?'

There was no response. I was barely aware that the room was less crowded, but when I looked over my shoulder, I saw that the two northerners had been taken away and only Cedric Walden remained.

'Your scrivener,' Cedric said, 'how bad is he?'

'Can you lift his head and shoulders?' I said. 'I will fetch water to bathe his head. The skin is broken, but I cannot tell if the skull is damaged.'

'But that . . .' Cedric pointed to the spreading pool of red.

'Ink.'

He laughed. 'The saints be praised! You stay with him. I will fetch the water.'

Between us we eased Walter until he was propped half sitting, and we had bathed his injury, wiping the blood and ink from his hair. At last he moaned and his eyes fluttered open.

'Nicholas, that man, de Musgrave?'

'Gone,' I said.

'Safe in hold in the castle by this,' Cedric said. 'Do not fret.'

'How do you find yourself?' I said, relieved that at least he could speak.

'My head feels as though a herd of cows had trampled on it, and I must have struck my elbow, for my left hand is numb.'

'Your left hand? That's as well,' I said. 'You can get back to work, then. We have an hour or two before we close the shop.'

He gave me a weak grin. 'One day such foolery will

land you in trouble, my boy.'

'I think I have had enough trouble for one day.' I grinned back at him. 'What say you, shall we close early, and share a cup of ale with Sheriff Walden?'

'Your best thought yet,' he said. 'Though I fear Margaret would ban ale after a blow to the head.'

'Not so troublesome as wine,' I said. 'Besides, we will not tell her.'

Between us, Cedric and I managed to get Walter to his feet, although he did not quite have control of his legs. When he saw the scattered and trampled pages of Roger's book, the broken ink pots, and the tumbled books, he groaned again.

'Jesu, Nicholas!'

'Nay, as Cedric says, do not fret. It is nothing. We are both alive, and that it all that matters.'

'Amen to that,' Cedric said.

After an hour or so, Cedric returned to the castle to deal with his prisoners, and Walter remained, at my insistence, sitting in the cushioned chair in the kitchen. He protested that there was no harm done, but he was still pale and clearly shaken. I went through to the shop and looked about in despair. To my relief, I saw that the book of Walter's tales still lay safely on its shelf.

When I lifted Roger's desk up, I saw that there was no great damage, apart from a dent in one corner – I would accuse Walter of denting the desk, rather than the desk denting his skull. There were some smears of ink on the writing surface, which I managed to rub away with a cloth, but the broken pots and spreading pools across the floor would need more drastic treatment. I set the tumbled stools upright and was picking up the fallen books, pressing them into shape, and returning them to the bookshelf when Margaret opened the door. Right behind her were the children, each carrying a market basket, and Roger.

My hopes of having restored most of the shop to rights before they returned were dashed as Margaret shrieked and Roger, peering over her shoulder, gave a yell of outrage. Everyone began talking and crying out at once.

When I was able to make myself heard, I tried to explain.

'Jordain and I went to see Piers Dykman, and he told us who has been playing these foul tricks at Queen's.' I paused, unsure whether they would believe me. 'Sir Thomas de Musgrave.'

'What!' Roger said. 'The nobleman who ordered my book?'

'The same.'

He slid past Margaret and stared at his empty desk, then caught sight of his beautifully scribed and illuminated pages scattered across the floor, trampled on by de Musgrave and de Luce, and smeared with five or six different shades of ink.

'Oh, Jesu!' he cried in despair, sinking down on one of the stools and putting his head in his hands.

'But why . . . why *this*?' Margaret gestured around at the chaos of the room.

'I went to tell Cedric at the college, but had to leave a message with Thomas Beverley. I fear de Musgrave overheard us. He followed me here, and threatened me. Then Sir Anthony de Luce arrived.'

They looked at me blankly.

'The other young nobleman from the north,' I said. 'It seems there is a deadly feud between the two families.'

I looked around at my shattered shop.

'They fought.'

'Nicholas!' Margaret said sharply, 'your left arm is bleeding.'

'Ah,' I admitted, 'de Musgrave slashed me before de Luce arrived and called his attention away from me. At least I managed draw blood myself, though I barely scratched him.'

I picked up my small knife from the floor, which I must have dropped in all the confusion. There was blood on it. I wiped it clean with the rag I had used on Roger's desk.

'It might have gone far worse for me,' I said, 'had Rowan not bitten him. Where is the dog?'

I went down on my hands and knees and peered under my desk. A small fur ball was shivering, crouched back against the wall, with two eyes staring anxiously out at me.

'Come out, Rowan,' I said, 'brave dog! The villain is gone now.'

She came crawling out on her belly, still uncertain, but when she saw none but family and friends, she bounced up in excitement and began licking my face with enthusiasm. I got hastily to my feet.

'She bit him?' Alysoun said, awed. 'A man with a sword?'

'Indeed she did, and in a moment you may go and buy her a string of sausages to have all to herself, as a reward for her courage.'

'Me too!' Rafe said.

'Aye, you too.' I reached in my scrip and gave Alysoun the coin for the sausages. 'Leave your baskets here.'

They ran off, taking Rowan with them.

'Nicholas,' Margaret said dangerously, 'your arm.'

''Tis nothing,' I protested. 'There is all to set to rights here in the shop first.'

'Roger can scrub the floor,' she said, 'though I fear the stones may be stained for ever. Where is Walter? He should be helping you.'

'He's hurt, and resting in the kitchen.'

She surged through into the house, like an avenging angel.

'Badly?' Roger asked.

'Pushed over by de Musgrave,' I said, 'and cracked his head on the corner of your desk.'

'And ruined my pages and broke my ink pots?'

'Nay, that was the others, fighting and crashing about the room.'

He picked up the pages and shook his head over them

sorrowfully. 'Ruined. All of them, I fear me. Still, I suppose they are no longer wanted.'

'Not for de Musgrave. You may begin afresh. I am sure I can find a buyer. Canon Aubery of St Frideswide's Priory has started to replenish their library.'

'With a collection of secular tales?' He looked at me doubtfully.

'Not all their books are pious.' I smiled. 'Francis Aubery appreciates a good story, and most of these depict the triumph of good over evil. Besides, he will appreciate a fine book far more than that particular young gentleman.'

'I wish I might have been here,' he said, with a certain longing in his voice.

'I would have been glad of you.'

Margaret swept in, carrying a bucket, a brush, and cloths.

'Haste to it, Roger, before the ink soaks any further into the stones. There is verjus in the water which may help, though I doubt me we shall be rid of it.'

She turned to me. 'Will you come to have that gash dressed, Nicholas, or must I drag you by force? Walter is asleep.'

'I am coming, Meg,' I said meekly.

It was while she was dressing my arm that Emma arrived, rushing into the kitchen with almost as much fury as Margaret.

'What is this I hear from the children?' she cried. 'You have been in a sword fight, but with no sword? And Rowan has savaged a nobleman?'

'Nothing quite like that.' I was becoming ever more embarrassed with the two women standing over me, glowering. Had I really deserved this?

I gave Emma a much simplified account of what had happened, and she sank down on a stool beside the table.

'What are we to do with him, Margaret?' she said.

'I have warned him before.' My sister was aligning herself decidedly with Emma. They were united in their disapproval of me. 'He should keep to his trade and not be for ever sniffing out mysteries. As well poke your finger into a wasps' nest.'

'Come!' I said, thinking this had gone far enough. 'If two young gentlemen with swords decide to fight each other in my shop, am I to blame?'

They exchanged a glance, then Emma shrugged. 'I suppose you could not prevent. What is amiss with Walter?'

'Blow to the head,' came a voice from the chair. 'Do not blame Nicholas. That young brute came storming in like a wild beast.'

'I do believe he suffers from some kind of madness,' I said. 'You could not hear, Walter, for you were out of your senses by then, but it seems his family has suffered grievously for many years, owing to a treacherous act by Sir Anthony de Luce's grandfather, he who was the overlord of Queen's Founder.'

'Then let them keep their quarrels in the north,' Walter said, 'and not bring them to trouble decent folk in Oxford.'

'I wonder how it will end,' I said. 'There is little to hold against de Luce, apart from affray, and he could hardly help but defend himself. As for de Musgrave, he is responsible for death and injury, but it may be difficult to prove, on the word of a young boy. I suspect he will deny everything.'

I was not to hear the outcome until Holy Week. Peter Winchingham and his daughter Birgit reached Oxford on the Monday. Although they lodged at the Mitre, they spent much of their time with us and Margaret was indeed put on her mettle, creating fine meals within the restrictions of the final days of Lent. I saw little of Emma, for Birgit had persuaded her to accompany her to the best tailor in Oxford, for the bespeaking and fitting of new summer gowns cut from some of her father's finest cloth. She had brought more lengths for gifts to Emma and Juliana, and there remained enough even to make a gown for Alysoun.

Margaret issued dire warnings that she was never to wear it when climbing trees or playing in the mud with Rafe and Jonathan.

The apprentice Wat was slowly recovering in St John's Hospital. Thanks to swift action by Robert Hanbury, and early care by the physician who had taken him in charge, the burns did not damage his bones and Wat would be able to walk again, with the aid of a stick. Once he could bear the touch of hose on his skin, the maimed flesh would be hidden from sight.

'I may be able to train him up to work simply as a carver,' Hanbury told me. 'He will never be able to do the heavy work, but he has a good eye and a steady hand. If Edred can carve with his leg bound fast to a board, I do not see why Wat should not sit and carve fine work.'

'You are a good man, Robert,' I said.

'I feel in some measure to blame,' he said. 'It happened at my works. Had I been near, I would never have let him lift the slaked lime until it cooled, however much the setters yelled for mortar. At least I shall try him out for the carving work.'

Now that de Musgrave was imprisoned in the castle, Piers returned to Hart Hall, although he may have regretted the loss of Beatrice's cooking. Most of the students had gone home to their families for the Easter season, but Piers was anxious to recover the lost ground in his studies. Besides, his home was so far away, he would scarcely have arrived before it was time to set off back to Oxford.

Whenever I had the chance, I observed Margaret and Peter carefully, but I was still unsure how matters stood with them. They were easy in each other's company, and took long walks together when the girls were away at the tailor's and I was busy in the shop. I supposed in good time, Meg would tell me her mind. After her terrible marriage to Elias Makepeace, she deserved a better life for herself than caring for a brother and his children, yet we had been a contented family.

As for Emma herself, she had little chance to be with

me, so we must bide our time in patience. Once, when we were set about with so many people – Mary Coomber was there at the time, with Aelyth and Sarah – she whispered to me, 'After Easter.' With that I must be content.

It was on Good Friday that Cedric came at last to see me, his face gloomy but resigned. The shop was closed for the holy day, and I took him through to the garden, where we walked under the trees of my small orchard. The petals from the pear trees floated down about us as we brushed the branches, but the apples were still in full blossom.

'It looks to be a good harvest,' Cedric said. 'I am half minded to resign my position and go back to my manor. There, at least, I would contend only with blight, pests, and the weather, not with men.'

'I heard that Sheriff de Alveton has come to Oxford,' I said.

He laughed. 'Aye, I know you are a shrewd one, Nicholas. You put your finger squarely on the sore.' He kicked at a tussock of grass and a bee flew up and away in annoyance.

'And so why has the High Sheriff of Oxfordshire and Buckinghamshire deigned to visit us?' I said. 'I thought he left all matters here to you.'

'Not when they touch the honour of great houses, and even the king himself.'

'The king?' I was astonished.

'Well, not directly. It seems that the older Sir Thomas Musgrave, lord of Hartley Castle, Kirby Stephen, and lands round about, formerly High Sheriff of Westmorland – replacing the Cliffords, mark you – and granted licence by the king himself to crenellate . . .'

'I have not forgotten the king's favour,' I said solemnly.

'This senior Sir Thomas is not only in favour with the king, but a close friend of our Sheriff de Alveton.'

'Ah,' I said.

'Indeed. It seems that the father knew nothing of the activities of the son, a son who is a troubled soul. No villain, you understand, but a young man who is not quite right in his wits, a young man to be pitied.'

'And?'

'And at the urgent request of Sir Anthony, father, Sheriff de Alveton rode in haste and gained the king's pardon for the young man's deeds. He was sent home yesterday.'

I grimaced, but what could simple men like Cedric and me do in the face of alliances between great men?

'What of de Luce?' I said.

'I reprimanded him for affray, but on your evidence that he acted in self defence, no charge will be brought. He stays at Queen's to attend the service in his father's chapel on Easter Sunday.'

'That is probably just,' I said. 'The fight was not of his making, although I think he smashed as many bottles of ink and trod on as many finished pages.'

'As for that,' Cedric said, 'he has asked me to tell you that he will call in at your shop before he leaves for home, and pay you the cost of your losses.'

'Then he will need to be quick about it, for I leave Oxford shortly after Easter.'

He raised an eyebrow in query.

'A family matter,' I said. 'I go only a short way into Buckinghamshire. Come, let us fetch a jug of ale and bring it out here. Margaret has been baking, and we need not leave everything for Peter Winchingham.'

We began to walk back to the house.

'In the end, Queen's has not lost by de Musgrave's actions,' I said, 'and Piers is a resilient lad, now that he is back amongst his books, but the injured apprentice has suffered a great deal and the young journeyman's widow has lost her husband. They are the true victims of de Musgrave's villainy.'

'I am mindful of it,' Cedric said. 'I have dropped a hint or two in de Alveton's ear, that it would be unfortunate, should the de Musgrave family name be tarnished by word getting about, that the actions of Sir

Thomas had left his victims so damaged. I think we may expect some compensation from the father.'

'It can hardly make up for the death of that good man,' I said, 'but it may help the wife in her distress.'

On Easter Sunday, we made our way to St Peter-in-the-East for the most solemn service of the year – my family, my scriveners, the Winchinghams, the Farringdons, and Mary's household. We met Jordain coming down the lane with his few students who had remained in Oxford for Holy Week. Within the church the mourning draperies and vestments had been replaced by white and gold. It was full of flowers, and great white candles burned on the altar, held in golden candlesticks, brought forth only for the greatest occasions of the Christian year. We stood, and knelt, and murmured 'Amen' as Rector Bokeland celebrated Mass. The dark days of Lent, with all their troubles, were past, and it was time to begin afresh.

'Christ is risen!' we cried, all with one voice, as the rector raised the host. 'Christ is risen!'

We came forth into the beauty of the spring day, where the birds courting and nesting amongst the trees and bushes of the churchyard gave voice to their own joyous Mass. Under the eaves of the crumbling charnel house, I saw that a pair of swifts had built a nest. They swooped past us as we walked to the gate. Even from death comes life.

The children ran ahead to release Rowan from the house, and Margaret and Peter were walking slowly behind. Emma slipped her arm through mine.

As if she had been reading my thoughts, she said, 'Time for a new beginning.'

'Aye,' I said, smiling down at her. 'Time for a new beginning.

Historical Note

Sadly, none of the medieval buildings of Queen's College survive today. In a fit of modernisation, the college was rebuilt in the classical style, mostly in the early eighteenth century, so that the oldest building now standing dates from the last decade of the seventeenth. It has resulted in a very handsome college, all in the same architectural style, unlike most Oxford colleges, but it has meant considerable difficulty for me in trying to track down the very limited information about the earlier college buildings. I have used whatever I have been able to find, including the earlier gatehouse, the approximate position of the original chapel, and the miscellaneous collection of small houses bought up on the site just before and after the years of the Great Pestilence.

Thomas de Musgrave and Anthony de Luce are historical figures. At this point in their lives they might not have been knighted, but could be given 'Sir' as a courtesy title. The feud between the two families dates back to the betrayal of Thomas's great-uncle, Andrew de Harclay, Earl of Carlisle, by Anthony's grandfather, another Anthony de Luce, in 1323, during the reign of Edward II. Andrew de Harclay was Sheriff of Cumberland as well as Earl of Carlisle, and therefore confronted by continuous attacks from Scottish raiders and more organised Scottish armies. Although Edward I had been able to hold back the Scots, his son Edward II was a feeble king and useless warrior. In the interests of peace and to put an end to bloodshed, Andrew de Harclay signed a peace treaty with Robert the Bruce. Unfortunately, he did so without getting the king's permission first. These powerful northern lords were almost kings in their own lands, but from the point of view of the English king, this could be regarded as an act of treason.

The account of Anthony de Luce's treacherous seizure and execution of Andrew de Harclay is taken from contemporary records.

De Luce was hardly acting in a purely selfless and disinterested manner. As a result of his actions, he was rewarded with Andrew de Harclay's lands and titles (apart from his earldom), as detailed in the charter quoted by Thomas de Musgrave. Andrew's sister Sarah (Thomas's grandmother) successfully petitioned the king in 1328 for the return of her brother's body for decent Christian burial, but his nephew's attempts to gain a posthumous pardon were rejected. However, Sarah's son, the elder Thomas de Musgrave referred to in *The Stonemason's Tale*, was able to repurchase the de Harclay estate of Hartley Castle in Kirby Stephen, which had been forfeited under the terms of the charter.

Sarah de Harclay married into the de Musgrave family of Great Musgrave, in the neighbouring county of Westmorland, and the younger Thomas de Musgrave in *The Stonemason's Tale* was her grandson. The younger Anthony de Luce was the grandson of the betrayer, and his family had continued to enjoy the lands and titles which had originally belonged to Andrew de Harclay and his family.

We do know what happened later to the two younger men. Thomas de Musgrave returned to an apparently respectable lordship in Westmorland, following his father's death. However, after serving as sheriff of Yorkshire in 1362-1367, he was removed for malpractice.

Anthony de Luce was something of a loose cannon, making raids on Annandale, and stirring up continuous trouble with the Scots. Annandale lies in southwest Scotland, just over the border from Cumberland, not to be confused with Allerdale, mentioned in the charter, which is part of Cumberland. In 1367, Anthony de Luce joined the "crusade" of the Teutonic Knights against Lithuania, possibly under pressure from his overlord, the Earl of Warwick, who was attempting to keep the peace along the Scottish Marches. Under the guise of a crusade again a pagan country, this was really a raiding and plundering expedition. Anthony de Luce was killed at the battle of New Kaunas, and his body was brought home.

In 1981, an archaeological dig at St Bees Priory (today in the modern county of Cumbria) unearthed a body wrapped in lead and buried in a coffin, which was found to be in remarkable condition despite being about 600 years old. Later forensic tests have established that this is almost certainly the body of the Anthony de Luce who appears in *The Stonemason's Tale*. Next to him was buried his sister, Maud de Luce, clearly identified. As Anthony was the last de Luce male heir, Maud inherited the estates and married into the powerful Percy family (of later Hotspur fame). Maud had strong connections with St Bees Priory.

The feud between these two families ended with Anthony de Luce's death, but the northern counties of England continued to be a breeding ground for uprisings and rebellions for centuries afterwards.

The Author

Ann Swinfen spent her childhood partly in England and partly on the east coast of America. She was educated at Somerville College, Oxford, where she read Classics and Mathematics and married a fellow undergraduate, the historian David Swinfen. While bringing up their five children and studying for a postgraduate MSc in Mathematics and a BA and PhD in English Literature, she had a variety of jobs, including university lecturer, translator, freelance journalist and software designer. She served for nine years on the governing council of the Open University and for five years worked as a manager and editor in the technical author division of an international computer company, but gave up her full-time job to concentrate on her writing, while continuing part-time university teaching in English Literature. In 1995 she founded Dundee Book Events, a voluntary organisation promoting books and authors to the general public, which ran for fifteen years.

She is the author of the highly acclaimed series, *The Chronicles of Christoval Alvarez*. Set in the late sixteenth century, it features a young Marrano physician recruited as a code-breaker and spy in Walsingham's secret service. In order, the books are: ***The Secret World of Christoval Alvarez, The Enterprise of England, The Portuguese Affair, Bartholomew Fair, Suffer the Little Children, Voyage to Muscovy, The Play's the Thing, That Time May Cease*** and ***The Lopez Affair***.

Her *Fenland Series* takes place in East Anglia during the seventeenth century. In the first book, ***Flood***, both men and women fight desperately to save their land from greedy and unscrupulous speculators. The second, ***Betrayal***, continues the story of the dangerous search for legal redress and security for the embattled villagers, at a time when few could be trusted.

Her latest series, the bestselling *Oxford Medieval Mysteries*, is set in the fourteenth century and features bookseller Nicholas Elyot, a young widower with two small children, and his university friend Jordain Brinkylsworth, who are faced with crime in the troubled world following the Black Death. In order, the books are: *The Bookseller's Tale, The Novice's Tale, The Huntsman's Tale, The Merchant's Tale, The Troubadour's Tale* and *The Stonemason's Tale.* Both this series and the Christoval Alvarez series are being recorded as unabridged audiobooks.

She has also written two standalone historical novels. *The Testament of Mariam*, set in the first century, recounts, from an unusual perspective, one of the most famous and yet ambiguous stories in human history, while exploring life under a foreign occupying force, in lands still torn by conflict to this day. *This Rough Ocean* is based on the real-life experiences of the Swinfen family during the 1640s, at the time of the English Civil War, when John Swynfen was imprisoned for opposing the killing of the king, and his wife Anne had to fight for the survival of her children and dependents. Both are also available as unabridged audiobooks

Ann Swinfen now lives on the northeast coast of Scotland, with her husband, formerly vice-principal of the University of Dundee, a rescue cat called Maxi, and a cocker spaniel called Suki.

You can receive notifications of new books and audios by signing up to the mailing list at www.annswinfen.com/sign-up/ and follow her monthly blog by subscribing at www. http://annswinfen.com/blog/

Learn more at her website www.annswinfen.com

Made in the USA
San Bernardino, CA
03 September 2018